PRAISE FOR PATRI

"This is the story I wish
ship. Detective story. Tomlinson takes such discordant elements and weaves them into a fascinating story: a Manet painting, advanced probes, exoplanet imaging, and more. There are echoes of Robert Sawyer's *Red Planet Blues* here and I'm hoping that this is the start of a new subgenre: detectives in space!"

J Daniel Batt, author of Young Gods, Book I: A Door Into Darkness

"The writing is excellent, the pace superb and it's one of those books that feels like a quick read until you look out the window and see the sun rise, realising you've been reading for several hours."

The British Fantasy Society

"There is so much good stuff wrapped inside *The Ark*: a locked-room murder mystery, bare-knuckle action, and the kind of hard-boiled science fiction that will make your brain pop. Climb aboard."

Adam Rakunas, author of Windswept

"The stakes are high in this thrilling debut."

Kirkus Reviews

"Is it worth the read? If you're looking for a fusion of excellent hard science fiction and action thriller, with a soupcon of mystery, then yes, absolutely. I'm already looking forward to seeing what the next book in the series has in store."

SF & F Reviews

BY THE SAME AUTHOR

CHILDREN OF A DEAD EARTH

The Ark

Trident's Forge

PATRICK S TOMLINSON

CHILDREN OF THE DIVIDE

CHILDREN OF A DEAD EARTH III

ANGRY ROBOT

ANGRY ROBOT
An imprint of Watkins Media Ltd

20 Fletcher Gate,
Nottingham,
NG1 2FZ
UK

angryrobotbooks.com
twitter.com/angryrobotbooks
Divide and rule

An Angry Robot paperback original 2017

Cover by Lee Gibbons
Map by Stephanie McAlea
Set in Meridien and Amraam by Epub Services

Distributed in the United States by Penguin Random House, Inc., New York.

ISBN 978 0 85766 682 6
Ebook ISBN 978 0 85766 683 3

Printed in the United States of America

9 8 7 6 5 4 3 2 1

This book is dedicated to the rebel living inside all of us.
The naive dreamer who risks all
for a chance to build a better world.
Find yours. Let them run.
Long fight ahead.
I've got your six.
And I'm really fucking cranky.

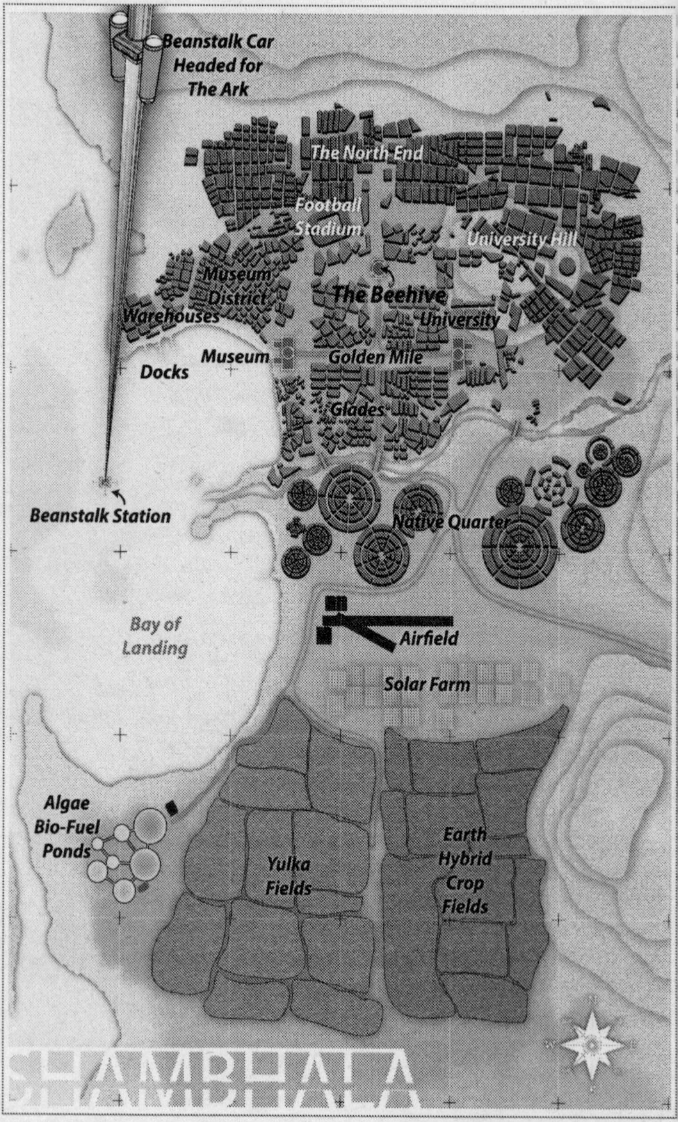

Beanstalk Car
Headed for
The Ark
The North End
Football
Stadium
University Hill
Museum
District
The Beehive
Warehouses
University
Museum
Golden Mile
Docks
Glades
Beanstalk Station
Native Quarter
Bay of
Landing
Airfield
Solar Farm
Algae
Bio-Fuel
Ponds
Yulka
Fields
Earth
Hybrid
Crop
Fields
SHAMBHALA

CHAPTER ONE

"That's not supposed to be there," Jian Feng remarked as a small handheld fire extinguisher tumbled past his face and gently bounced off one of the shuttle's cockpit windows.

"Goddammit." Jian checked the countdown timer. Eighty seconds to undock. He unlatched his restraints and grabbed the bright red cylinder out of the air. "I said secure the cabin!"

"Sorry, commander," one of the harvester techs said from the back of the split-level flight deck. "I think I bumped the latch with my foot."

Jian shook his head. He pushed off from his chair hard enough to float to the rear bulkhead, then reoriented and kicked off to where the offending tech sat strapped into her seat. He waved the bottle at her face.

"Technician Madeja. Do you really want this banging around in here while we're burning under six gees?"

She shook her head. "No, sir."

"Do you want the top to snap off and send it flying around the cabin like a missile, striking control panels, breaking windows?"

"No. Of course not."

Jian put it in her hand. "Then you're going to hold onto it."

"Sir? Shouldn't I secure it in its cradle?"

"You *should* have. But you didn't, so now you're going to hold it."

The tech swallowed. "Yes, sir."

"Good. Both hands, don't let go until after we're coasting again." Under their six gee burn, the little red can of inert gas would go from three kilos to eighteen pushing down on the tech's chest. Certainly not enough to keep her from breathing or crack any ribs, but heavy enough to make the next few minutes an uncomfortable and embarrassing lesson.

Jian returned to his chair just as the thirty-second burn warning sounded.

"A little hard on the tech, weren't you?" his copilot, Kirkland, asked.

"Not as hard as that canister would've hit me in the head if I hadn't spotted it. Maybe next time she'll remember to secure the bloody cabin."

Kirkland shrugged. "Your ship." They'd gone through flight school together. He'd come in a few points behind her on the final tests, but he'd drawn the first command billet. Jian knew her well enough to know she was a little salty about it, but she was professional enough not to let it show.

Jian was still fumbling with his straps when Flight Control's voice burst through the cockpit speakers. "Fifteen seconds to burn, *Atlantis*. Board is green. You are cleared for departure."

"Roger that," Jian said. He glanced at the red command stripe on his skinsuit's shoulder. It was the first time he'd worn it. If this milk run of a mission went to plan, it wouldn't be the last. "We're buckled up and ready to transfer local control. Switching over… Now." Jian pressed the button that flipped navigational control over to the shuttle from his console to the Ark's traffic control computers, a necessity while they were still so close to the ship and its elevator ribbon. Any mistake this close had the potential to do tremendous damage and set back the Trident's development plan by months, even years.

"We have the ball. T-Minus five seconds to undock.

Four. Three. Two. One. Zero."

On the count of zero, the mechanical latches that held the shuttle *Atlantis* in place among the small forest of other shuttles released. Maneuvering thrusters gently pushed the shuttle away from its nest in the aviary on the outside of the Ark's engineering module. They drifted away at less than a meter per second, slowly revealing the immense bulk of the first and only interstellar generation ship mankind had ever built. It was thirteen kilometers of aluminum, steel, and carbon composites, down from sixteen kilometers after its stardust shield had been ejected in preparation for insertion into Gaia orbit eighteen years ago. Behind them was the reactor bulb, which held a pair of fusion reactors whose size was matched only by their thirst.

Which was why the harvester techs were hitching a ride on his boat. One of the Helium-3 harvesters had gotten stuck trolling through the regolith of Gaia's small moon, Varr, and bent an axle. Which was a hard thing to do in three percent gravity, but that had just been their run of luck as of late.

"*Atlantis*," Flight Control said, "I have Ark Actual on the line."

Jian held back a sigh. He knew the pep-talk call from the captain was inevitable, he just wished it wasn't also coming from his father.

"Put him through," Jian said.

"Mission Commander Feng," Captain Chao Feng said in a booming voice. "This is Ark Actual. On behalf of the crew, and everyone on both ends of the tether, I wish you good luck, and Godspeed."

"Thank you, captain. We won't let you down."

"I know you won't, son."

Oh lord, here it comes.

Chao's voice took on a softer, more nurturing tone. "Your mother would have been very proud of you, Jian."

I sure wish I could've heard it from her directly, Dad, is what

Jian managed not to say, either aloud or into his plant. "Roger that, Actual. *Atlantis* out," he said instead, in a curt, professional voice only a few degrees warmer than the empty space on the other side of the shuttle's hull.

By then, they'd drifted past the invisible line that marked the minimum safe maneuvering zone, where their thrusters and main rocket motors could operate at full power without worry about damage to the Ark's hull. Thrusters at the shuttle's nose and wingtips fired, spinning it around and away from the Ark, bringing the white, blue, and lavender jewel of Gaia herself into view. Sitting as they were in geosynchronous orbit, the planet could be viewed in its entirety. As consolation prizes went, it was pretty spectacular.

In the eighteen years since mankind had put down stakes, they'd mapped the entire surface, from its low, rolling mountains and endless windblown plains, to its deep valleys and canyons, extending all the way down to the craggy sea beds of its oceans. Over sixty thousand species of plants and animals had already been described. And although the old biome wasn't nearly as diverse as Earth at her end, it was expected that number would continue to grow for generations.

Reaching out from the Ark, the gleaming carbon ribbon of the space elevator streaked all the way down to the planet's surface like an impossibly long cat whisker. At its base, the bustling hub of human civilization, Shambhala, went about another day, the majority of its fifty thousand plus inhabitants blissfully unaware of all of the work happening in orbit to keep them alive and in comfort, or the risks being endured on their behalf.

Jian had been a young boy when the Ark made planetfall, just after his mother had been killed onboard the grand old ship. Jian still remembered how her hair smelled of apple blossoms. He'd been only five when she'd died. Asphyxiated, along with twenty thousand other people when a lunatic blew a hole in Shangri-La module's hull and let all the air out. A terrorist attack that might have been discovered in time to save her had it not been for his father trying to save face. He'd spent a few years living on the surface in Shambhala until in a most unlikely turn of events, his disgraced dad had somehow weaseled his way into the captain's chair of the Ark, a precarious position that he'd managed to hold onto for fifteen years and counting.

But it was that moment as a boy, when he'd seen his mother and many of his childhood friends swept away by a single act of unfathomable malice that he'd decided to do whatever he could to protect people. Which had led him to be sitting in this chair today. Most people mistook his ambition as an attempt to follow in his father's footsteps. It was an insulting thought. Nothing could be further from the truth. But, it was a useful illusion to maintain. Being the son of the captain had afforded him certain opportunities over the years, and in the end, pride had taken the copilot seat next to pragmatism.

The slight vibration of the thrusters spiked as they froze the shuttle in space, then ceased entirely as the *Atlantis* lined up with its destination. Or, more precisely, with where its destination would be in thirty-one hours.

The moon, Varr, hung in the sky to Jian's left, just beyond the thin blue haze of Gaia's atmosphere. The tiny satellite was nothing like Luna, Earth's companion to the last. Varr was scarcely large enough for its meager gravity to collapse it into a rough spheroid. At only three and a half percent Earth standard gravity, escape velocity was only a kilometer per second, which made lifting huge loads of the precious Helium-3 fuel trapped in its surface dust a ridiculously easy prospect. There were plans to install a solar-powered railgun system on the surface to take pressure off the cargo drone fleet, but it kept getting pushed down the manufacturing priority queue.

Varr's orbit was wildly elliptical. At its perigee, Varr was scarcely further from Gaia as the Ark was, while at apogee, it was almost a million kilometers away and growing by a few centimeters with each passing year. The huge swing meant shuttle operations had to take place inside a relatively narrow, eleven-day window before the moon traveled too far away from Gaia and the Ark for the shuttle to make the return trip. Anyone caught out after this curfew would just have to settle in and wait for Varr to swing back around again on the return leg of its orbit.

The shuttle *Atlantis,* named after an old NASA shuttle which had itself been named after a fictional continent, was now ironically the namesake of a very real continent some tens of thousands of kilometers below. The Atlantians were the native sapient species of Gaia. It was from their language and legends that their destination of Varr had been named. Varr was one of their triumvirate of Gods, their own version of the Holy Trinity. It was said that Varr was a cosmic protector, clashing every month with Cuut and zer explosive tantrums and harsh, asteroid-based justice.

It was fitting, then, that the second half of their mission was meant to protect everyone in the system, whether they lived on the ground, in the sky above, or in the caves beneath.

"*Atlantis,* we're ready to transfer local control," said Flight's cool, practiced voice.

"Copy, Flight. *Atlantis* is ready for the handoff."

"Transferring now."

A small red light flashed on his console as Jian took control of his boat for the first time. "Thank you, Flight. I have the ball. Main engine start." The shuttle shuddered as the half-dozen shockwave spike engines at its tail rumbled to life. The shuttle lurched forward in response to the trickle of thrust coming from the motors. But they were merely pilot lights compared to the torrent that was about to hit.

"Five seconds to throttle up. Everyone tighten your

straps and hold onto your asses," Jian announced to the crew. His crew. "Three. Two. One. Go!"

On "Go," Jian slid the holographic controls to one hundred percent. At the back of the shuttle, butterfly valves and turbo pumps opened wide, dumping thousands of liters of liquid hydrogen and oxygen per second into the hellish maws of the rockets, converting the energy of the reaction into fire, steam, and punishing acceleration.

The skin on Jian's face pulled back and tried to settle into a new home somewhere behind his ears. He couldn't help but smile.

"The injectors on the number four motor are redlining," Kirkland shouted, not out of fear, but merely to be heard over the roar of the engines. Jian tore his gaze away from the window and brought the diagnostic displays up on the augmented reality interface in his plant. Kirkland was right, the number four rocket motor was faltering. It had already dropped to eighty-seven percent thrust and falling. The turbo pump feeding it fuel was bad, probably the "frictionless" magnetic bearings throwing in the towel. At this point, they could probably still be rebuilt, but push them much further and they might not only burn out permanently, but disintegrate with enough force to crack the engine bell and maybe even damage one or both of the adjoining motors. The monkeys back in the maintenance hangar wouldn't thank him for that.

Jian cut the number four motor entirely to prevent catastrophic failure, then adjusted the flow to engines one through three to compensate for the uneven thrust and keep them from drifting off course. The weight pressing down on Jian's chest eased fractionally as the shuttle lost one-sixth of its acceleration. Some quick calculations from the navigational computer determined that they'd need another thirty-seven seconds of burn at their reduced five gees to stay inside their flight profile, but they'd be well inside their fuel reserves on both the outbound and return legs of the trip.

Just another one of the charms of commanding a two-hundred-and-fifty year-old boat through space.

Jian keyed on his com back to the Ark. "Flight Control, *Atlantis*. Be advised. We've had to cut number four motor," he paused to take a strained breath, "but we've adjusted our burn and are still well within our safety envelope. Mission remains a go."

"Roger that, *Atlantis*. Keep us apprised."

"Acknowledged."

Jian relaxed and let the gees push him back into the contours of his chair. Now that he wasn't trying to move his arms, the pressure wasn't as exhausting, even though it was still a task to breathe. A few of the older members of the team weren't having as easy a time of it, he knew. Three of them were original Ark crew members and had spent the majority of their lives in the micro grav of either the Command module, labs, or Engineering. Even with anti-atrophy drugs artificially bulking up their bone and muscle density, nothing beat the pull of gravity on body development, whether that gravity was real or spin. They wouldn't be happy campers for the next few minutes.

Jian let his breathing settle into the same rhythm he used to meditate, not that he was at any risk of slipping into that fuzzy, dreamlike state while his body was being pressed like a panini.

The great weight pressing down on his chest vanished as quickly as it had appeared. Jian's attentions snapped back to the present and checked the shuttle's flight profile.

"Flight, *Atlantis*. We've completed our burn. Profile is five-by-five. We're on our way to Varr."

"Good work, *Atlantis*. Smooth sailing."

"Thank you, Flight. *Atlantis* out."

Kirkland let out a long breath, then allowed a small smirk to curl up her cheek. "Well, that was exciting."

Jian couldn't help but agree. "Hell yeah it was." Jian unbuckled from his seat and faced the rest of the team. "Spread your limbs and get comfortable, folks. We've got almost a day and a half to kill in this can."

They soon filtered out to fill not only the flight deck, but the enormous passenger/cargo compartment beyond. The harvester techs passed their time going through and checking their inventory of tools in preparation to fix their wayward unit. Meanwhile, the rest of the team focused on set up for their half of the mission.

On the "dark" side of Varr, final construction was underway on an enormous radio telescope. The telescope's dish was built directly into an ancient impact crater on the moon's surface. There had been plenty of craters to choose from. The Tau Ceti system had ten times the proto-planetary material of the Sol system, and therefore ten times the asteroid strikes. Finding one of the right diameter and depth facing away from interference from Gaia was easy. Finding one that wasn't marred by secondary craters had actually been the hardest part.

The telescope was anything but an idle pursuit. Instead, it was to be the crown jewel in an orbital Early Warning array of space-based telescopes scanning the entire EM spectrum, from IR, to visible light, all the way up to a gamma ray observatory set to launch from the Ark in two months.

It was to be the Trident's eyes, tirelessly scanning the skies for any trace of another attack from whomever had killed Earth.

Because two hundred and fifty years later, they still didn't know. Didn't have the first clue. All anyone knew about the beings who'd murdered an entire solar system was they could control black holes, and a vague direction from which the killer singularity they'd named Nibiru had been thrown. Whoever had killed Earth were like the monsters drawn into the margins of ancient maps. Nothing more than placeholders, humanity's abject ignorance given form to make it easier to digest.

Jian tried not to think about it too hard. The attack that had killed his mother was bad enough, but those villains had faces, they had names. And most importantly, they were very, very, dead. That closure made coping a little easier. Besides – he'd never known Earth. The last person to have ever set foot on it died a century and a half before. His home was the Ark. He had many friends who lived on the surface in Shambhala, both human and even a few Atlantians. Chief among them was Benexx, an Atlantian adopted by humans as a larva. Jian couldn't get angry over the death of a planet he'd never seen, but he would fight tooth and nail to protect his friends and everything they'd built together.

All their new radio telescope needed now was a receiver array. Which just happened to be packed into crates in *Atlantis's* cargo bay.

Kirkland came floating up to Jian as he took inventory of the equipment. Again.

"How many more times are you going to double-check those crates? We're in a sealed, pressurized tube. If they suddenly go missing, it'll be the least of our problems."

"I know. It's just, I..."

"Want to make sure it's done right," Kirkland finished for him. He nodded. "You always obsessively checked your answers on the orbital mechanics tests, too. You wanted the rest of the class to think you were being thorough. But I knew you were scared of getting the answer wrong."

"And you weren't?" Jian let a little more bitterness slip into his tone than he meant to.

Kirkland shrugged, ignoring it. "I knew there was no point second-guessing myself. I always take my best shot on the first pass."

"Guess you never made a pass at me, then."

"Damn right I didn't. Spoiled son of the captain? Sorry, Jian. You're cute, but I'm not going to be someone's ornament."

"Obviously not. Ornaments are pretty." Jian flinched as the punch landed solidly on his shoulder and sent them both drifting away from each other. "Ow! You just struck a superior officer!"

"So go tell daddy, and I'll tell him what you said to earn it."

Jian put up his hands in surrender. "Anything but that. He's still trying to set us up."

"Since when?"

"C'mon. Do you think the captain invites all pilot potentials over for Chinese New Year? In his penthouse?"

"Point. What year is it on that calendar anyway?"

"Hell if I know. Iguana?"

Kirkland's face switched from playful to pensive. She nodded toward the crates. "You really think this is necessary? It's been hundreds of years. We're twelve lightyears away from the scene of the crime. What makes you think they're even looking for us?"

"I hope they aren't. I hope they haven't given us ants a second thought in centuries. Doesn't mean we shouldn't be looking for them. Even if it's just to stay out from under their boot."

"That's reasonable, I suppose. Still, it's a lot of resources and man hours to spend."

Jian shrugged. "Let's hope it's all a big waste."

"I'll drink to that when we get back."

"It's a date," Jian teased.

"That's one thing it isn't." She pushed away, deeper into the cargo bay.

Jian returned to the flight deck and to his private sleeping alcove. It was barely larger than he was, but in micro grav it felt larger, and he didn't have to share it with anyone. Once settled in, he turned on the screen and flipped through his messages. There were well-wishes from his friends and flight classmates, a personal message from his father that he left unopened, and...

Ah, what's this? A vid message from Benexx. Jian opened the file and hit "Play."

"Hey stud," said the Atlantian in flawless, unaccented

English. It was zer first language, after all. "Sorry this is just a recording. We're going to be down by the lake when you launch and there's no com tower there yet." Jian glanced down at the time/date stamp in the corner. Four days ago. Ze must've set up a time delay on the delivery.

"Anyway," ze continued. "Summer is wrapping up. I've got less than a week left before I have to go back to Shambhala and everything that comes with it. You know the score."

He did. Ze'd been nothing but a star-struck kid when Jian was already an adolescent. Kind of a pest, really. His father was friends with zer parents, and he'd insisted Jian humor zer during their frequent contacts. But ze'd grown into a symbol of unity for both of their people, and something of a celebrity in zer own right. It wasn't a role ze was particularly comfortable with. He could relate.

"I just wanted to say good luck on your big first mission, hot shot. I'm sure you'll do great. And don't be mad at your dad if he tries to get mushy. He's proud of you, you know. This was a good summer, like the ones we used to have. Lazy days and late nights. Sakiko says hello, by the way. Get home safe, and it wouldn't kill you to come down the beanstalk for a visit." Benexx backed zer face away from the camera so zer whole head and torso became visible. Then ze raised an arm in a mocking salute. "Cadet Benexx, signing off."

The video ended. Jian watched it again, then closed the screen and quickly dozed off.

The rest of the outbound leg passed uneventfully. With nothing to do but coast along their ballistic trajectory, Jian and Kirkland took turns monitoring things on the flight deck while the other exercised, slept, or otherwise occupied themselves until it was time for their final approach.

The mottled, pockmarked surface of Varr loomed large in the cockpit windows, each crater and valley jumping out in stark relief under the bright glare of Tau Ceti's sun. Without an atmosphere, there was no air to blur the details, which were sharper than any holo. It looked almost *too* real, and it kept growing. It was small for a moon. But even a small moon was a gargantuan object on the scale of human beings.

Jian swallowed. "Looks a lot bigger from here."

"Nervous, Ace?" Kirkland teased.

"Yeah, a little. I've never flown this close to a planetary body before."

"You've been up and down the beanstalk dozens of times."

"That's different. The tether means nothing can go wrong. Well, almost nothing."

Kirkland nodded. "It's fine. We've been through this a hundred times in simulation. Even a few with a mangy engine."

"Yeah..." Jian keyed up the comlink back to the Ark. "Flight, *Atlantis*. We're about to begin terminal maneuvers for our approach to Varr. Priming main engines for burn." There was a slight pause as the message covered the distance between them.

"*Atlantis*, Flight. Acknowledge terminal approach. Good luck."

Jian lit the mains on minimum power just to get them warmed up. He left the number four motor in standby. Satisfied that the other five would burn when he opened the taps, Jian triggered maneuvering thrusters on the nose to flip the shuttle and get the mains pointed opposite their direction of travel. They had a lot of velocity to bleed off before they could insert into orbit around the low-mass moon.

Jian made a final adjustment to their trim, then put hands on the throttles. "Here we go, kids. Hold on tight."

A few bruising minutes later, they'd slowed to just over a kilometer per second at an altitude of fifteen kilometers above Varr.

"We're in. Everybody relax, but stay buckled up."

Kirkland pointed to a discolored patch near the horizon. "There's the Helium-3 field."

Jian nodded and enlarged the image using the feed from the shuttle's forward camera. Parallel rows of turned regolith hugged the uneven terrain, marking where the autonomous harvesters had already done their work. Two of the machines were still busy churning through the silt. The third, not so much. Jian reoriented the camera and zoomed in on the stricken machine, which was sitting at an odd angle, as though it had fallen halfway into a sinkhole.

Kirkland whistled and looked over her shoulder at the techs. "Looks like you've got your work cut out for you, fellas." A chorus of groans revealed their feelings of the prospect.

"Think we have time to land this boat?" Kirkland asked.

Jian shook his head. "Nah. Let's do a flyby and survey the scene for the best LZ. We'll catch it on the next orbit. That'll give us a chance to check out the telescope site on the far side as well."

"Sounds like a plan."

Their orbit carried the *Atlantis* closer to the field until it was directly underneath. Looking straight down on the immobilized harvester, Jian could see the hole it had fallen into. It was irregularly shaped, and about half the size of the harvester. Its front two drive wheels dangled over open space. Lidar put the hole's depth at more than twenty meters.

"What do you think?" Kirkland asked. "Roof collapse? We know there are some lava tubes leftover here and there."

"Well it's definitely not a crater." Just then, something in the lidar return caught his eye. It was sharp-edged and hexagonal, sitting on the floor of the cave, or whatever. And it wasn't alone. Something reflective with an edge that was a perfect ninety-degree angle jutted out from the dark next to the hexagon. Jian swiped the image from the small lidar monitor to the main screen.

"Are you seeing this?" he asked.

Kirkland traced the shapes with her fingertip. "What the hell are those?"

"Hey, Madeja," Jian called to the back of the cabin. "Unbuckle and come up here a minute."

The nervous tech floated into view to his left. "Yes, commander?"

Jian pointed at the mystery objects. "Any ideas? Could they be parts of the harvester that broke off in the accident?"

"Not anything that I can think of."

"Well then what is it?"

"I'm sorry, commander, but I have no idea."

"Survey equipment, maybe? Probe? A crashed satellite?" Jian asked even as he opened a data query to search probe landing sites or equipment lost on the surface, but there were no landing or crash sites within a hundred and fifty kilometers. "Nope. Nothing."

"Well if we didn't put it there," Kirkland said. The implication of the question floated in the air between them.

Despite the zero gee, Jian's stomach sank.

"That's not supposed to be there."

CHAPTER TWO

Varr rose above the horizon as night crept over the village of G'tel. Alone in the long-abandoned signal tower, Benexx watched the small moon slowly gain altitude against the dark ocean of stars. Few came up here anymore. Not since the road network had been supplied with human-built radios. Once their proudest technological achievement, the signal tower was now little more than a tree fort for village kids.

In truth, calling G'tel a "village" was a misnomer. In the fifteen years since the humans' appearance on the continent, the population had exploded. For the first time, houses were being built well outside of the village's ring of protective halo trees. Where once crops had grown in the sun, rings of streets had been laid down. New three-, four-, and now even five-level buildings were being erected as fast as the mudstone could set.

As the village grew, human advisors helped plan for new issues that cropped up, such as infrastructure, aqueducts, and sanitation. All this development was necessary to keep up with the growth fueled by the twin booms in both fertility and immigration. G'tel was now *the* place on the road network for trade, sitting as it did next to the largest landing strip, and only sea port, on the entire continent. And with the explosive increases in crop yields owed to the humans' desalinization plant and irrigation channels, there was finally enough food to feed all those hungry mouths. The days of culling new clutches were fading into memory.

Which was just fine with Benexx. Ze'd narrowly escaped being decapitated only moments after zer birth, along with every other member of zer clutch, save four. It was a barbaric practice, one ze'd only been spared from by the intervention of zer father, Bryan Benson. Benexx had never bothered to search out zer biological parents. Ze didn't feel the need.

"Ah, there you are, Benexx," a familiar voice called from below. It was Uncle Kexx, G'tel's long-serving truth-digger. Ze was shadowed as always by zer human apprentice, Sakiko, who was in turn shadowed by Gamera, an orphaned ulik she'd adopted as a pup.

"We wondered where you'd run off to before the evening cleansing," Kexx said.

"Just wanted to watch one more sunset over the plains," Benexx called down.

"Well, don't be too late. The evening cleansing is starting soon and you have an early flight tomorrow."

"Yes, uncle."

"Goodnight." Kexx said something to Sakiko in Atlantian, a little too quiet and fast for Benexx to pick up, then headed back down the trail to the old village inside the ring of trees. Zer house was there, near the outskirts, as it had been since before Benexx was born. Sakiko remained behind and started up the ladder to join zer at the top, while Gamera whined softly at the base of the tower before stomping down a bed in the underbrush and lying down to wait for her return.

Sakiko sat down. "Varr's bright tonight."

Benexx nodded. "The *Atlantis* should be landing just about now."

"How do you know that?"

"Because it's Jian Feng's first mission. He's kept me updated."

"You mean he's been sending you love letters," Sakiko

said, then made a kissing face. She was three years older than Benexx, but because of how long it took humans to develop she still acted less mature.

"We're just friends!" Benexx punched Sakiko in the shoulder to emphasize the point.

"Ow!" she protested. "That hurt!"

"Whatever, wuss." Benexx wiggled zer four tentacle-like fingers. "I don't even have hand bones."

"Could've fooled me."

They made an odd pair, Benexx and Sakiko. The Atlantian raised among humans and the human raised among Atlantians. In many ways, Sakiko was more accepted among the people of G'tel than Benexx was. She knew their language because it was hers too, while Benexx still struggled with the different dialects. She'd grown up in their clothes, (with some small additions for the sake of modesty), their food, and their rituals. She was Kexx's chosen protégée for village truth-digger, and her mother, Mei, was the respected and beloved ambassador from the human colony.

Benexx was... none of those things. Back home in Shambhala, ze was an unwilling celebrity. The adopted Atlantian child of humankind's greatest living hero. A symbol of the Trident between all the peoples of the planet. But here, surrounded by zer people, Benexx was a curiosity. The bearer who wouldn't bear, talked funny, and could never get zer skinglow right. The villagers weren't openly hostile to zer, but they could be aloof, never quite sure what to do with zer.

Benexx loved it. The Varr cycle ze spent every summer in G'tel were some of the quietest, most relaxing days ze had all year. But now, break was coming to an end.

"What is he doing?" Sakiko asked.

"Hmm? Who?"

"Jian," she pointed at Varr. "Up there."

"Oh, right. Sorry. They're fixing a busted helium harvester or something."

Sakiko nodded. "Dangerous?"

"Everything in space is dangerous. But I don't think this is particularly so."

"Still, it's kinda hot, right? Commanding a shuttle mission."

"I'm sure I wouldn't know," Benexx said.

"Oh come on," Sakiko prodded. "That's sexy."

"Now whose boyfriend is he?" Benexx teased. "I don't have any of those parts, remember? And even if I did, they wouldn't line up with anything your people have."

Sakiko smirked. "That's no obstacle to the curious."

Benexx put zer fingers over zer earholes. "Lalalalala…"

"There are even some adaptors…"

"LALALALA!"

Sakiko laughed at her friend's discomfort. "You look ridiculous."

Benexx sighed. "I'm going to miss this."

"What?"

"The peace and quiet, mostly."

"What quiet?" Sakiko asked incredulously. "It's a madhouse around here. G'tel has quintupled in size in the last ten years."

"Yeah, to fifteen-thousand. Shambhala is fifty thousand and counting, with transit cars and quadcopters and drones and the spaceport. Humans and Atlantians running about at all hours. The noise never stops. At least G'tel still sleeps at night."

"So stay here," Sakiko said. "Mom loves you. We already keep your room open when you're not here."

"I can't. My parents would never allow it."

"You can. You'll be fifteen in a few days and can make your own choices."

"It's not that simple, Kiko. I'm… important there."

"Yeah, as a symbol of yadda, yadda, yadda. You hate that shit."

"Doesn't mean it's not important. Besides, I've started teaching the immigrants in the native quarter. Who else can do that as well as I can?"

"And you enjoy it?"

Benexx shrugged. "I'm starting to, yeah."

They sat in amicable silence for a long moment. "So, your great bird leaves in the morning?" Sakiko asked, using the Atlantian phrase for "airplane".

"Yes."

"Last night in G'tel until next summer?"

"Yeess?"

"Want to go prank Chief Kuul's house?"

Benexx smiled broadly. "Absolutely."

Benexx was already on the plane ride home by the time Chief Kuul saw what they'd done to the statue commemorating the Battle of the Black Bridge in zer courtyard. Ze'd had it commissioned not long after ascending to Chief after Tuko died... er, returned. At six meters tall, it depicted the famous moment when Kuul, run through the hip by a Dweller spear, fired a borrowed rifle back into the encroaching horde while Bryan Benson carried zer across his shoulders to safety.

The sculptors had, out of deference to their new Chief, taken some generous liberties with the proportions of the statue's figures, especially where Kuul's muscle definition was concerned. Benexx and Sakiko had added their own artistic flourishes in the form of garishly colored flowers and ink paste strategically placed to be as unflattering to Kuul's Chiefly sensibilities as possible. Benexx didn't really understand the Atlantian social taboos their display was crossing, but Sakiko assured zer they were not only dead on the mark, but would be quite a chore to clean up once the ink paste set.

Benexx didn't mind. In a few weeks, it would be Sakiko's turn to travel to Shambhala and stay with zer family, where she would be just as awkward and out-of-place as Benexx felt in G'tel. It was why they'd become such fast friends years ago, each foreigners to their own people, each helping the other fill in the cultural blanks.

It was a uniquely codependent relationship.

Ze leaned back in zer chair and settled in for the long flight home. Longer now than it had been the first few summers ze'd spent abroad. In the early days, shuttles were still being used for the transoceanic voyage. But their enormously thirsty hypersonic engines, and the increasingly demanding schedule doing the work of building the space-based infrastructure the development plan demanded, meant they were pulled from airliner service as soon as alternatives became available.

The airplane Benexx sat in now was one of six that had been manufactured in the Ark's factories, then shipped piece by piece down the beanstalk for final assembly on the surface. It was a high, swept-wing design with high-bypass turbofan engines mounted on top of the wings. It sat just over a hundred people, making it much smaller than the shuttles it replaced, but also drastically more fuel efficient.

But it was also subsonic, which meant a trip that used to take three hours now took closer to nine. Benexx shut off the artificial window display and its endless blue ocean. Ze reached into zer bag to retrieve zer specially grown headset, scrolled through zer music files, selected a soothing synth-jazz playlist from the turn of twenty-second century old Earth, and let the kilometers slip by at almost eight hundred an hour.

Ze loved flying. The acceleration at takeoff, the fleeting sensations of weightlessness. It reminded Benexx of swimming, only so much faster. Ze envied Jian Feng, floating thousands of kilometers above the planet in zero gee. Commanding his own shuttle with its immense power. Ze'd skipped a summer in G'tel two years ago and spent the time aboard the Ark with both Jian and Sakiko. It was part of their "enrichment," and everyone's parents had insisted on it.

Sakiko had been miserable in null gee, utterly useless. She flapped around like a wounded bird until she gave up and spent the rest of the trip either clinging to handrails or hiding in the centripetal gravity at the bottom of the habitats. Benexx, by contrast, was a natural. Ze'd picked up on how to fly through null gee like a fish took to a pond, which considering ze race's relatively recent aquatic lineage, was probably as accurate a metaphor as any.

The Ark's longtime captain, Chao Feng, even remarked that Benexx, "Must have gotten zer flying genes from zer father." Which kind of ignored the fact ze was not only adopted, not only a separate species, but indeed traced zer origins to an entirely separate genesis of life from Bryan. Still, considering his hallowed career as a Zero player, it was a flattering thing to say.

For a moment, Benexx felt a pang of guilt over defacing zer father's image, but the feeling quickly passed. They'd been increasingly butting heads lately, and even if they hadn't been, Benexx knew he hated the "Bronze monstrosity" that had been erected in Mahama Park not three years before. For a former sports star, zer father was strangely averse to hero worship, or at least of being the target of it.

The airliner's descent announcement interrupted zer music, letting the passengers know they'd be landing in a half hour. Benexx shifted uncomfortably in zer chair. The designers had gone to great lengths to make them ergonomically compatible with either human or Atlantian physiques, but instead simply ensured they were equally inappropriate for both.

The seat wasn't zer only source of discomfort, however. The fifteenth anniversary of the Trident approached in only two days. There would be a parade. Zer parents expected zer to participate, solidly against zer expressed wishes. Benexx hated zer role as icon, and with zer critical fifteenth birthday fast approaching, ze felt like it was time ze should be able to make these sorts of calls for zerself.

Ze was leaving vacation and flying straight into a confrontation ze didn't want to have but wasn't willing to back down from just for the sake of expediency. Benexx put away zer headset, buckled zer lap belt, and steeled zerself for a fight ze knew ze was probably going to lose.

CHAPTER THREE

Third down and long. Down by two. Fourth quarter with no timeouts and under three minutes to play. Standing on the sidelines, Benson read blitz. Two of the Flying Injri's linebackers shifted forward subtly. It was a small movement, but enough to tip Coach Makhlouf's hand on the play.

<Blitz. Blitz. Blitz,> Benson said into the open plant link he shared with the rest of the Mustangs. <Scratch the run, we're throwing hot. Shift left. Leave Hillman uncovered. Cha'ku.> Benson paused long enough for the Atlantian to make eye contact. Ze didn't have a plant. Great strides were being made mapping the Atlantian brain, but not enough was known as yet to make the technology compatible for their new allies. So Benson's voice was being routed into a small com inside zer helmet. Benson couldn't afford to be misunderstood on the play.

<Cha'ku, forget your route. Run to the empty spot Hillman leaves open. Can you do that?>

<OK coach,> the Atlantian receiver said. Which was less reassuring than it would have been if "OK coach" didn't comprise ninety percent of Cha'ku's conversations with Benson.

The offensive line shifted left. Under center, Boswell called for the snap before the defense could make any adjustments. The millisecond the ball left the center's hand, the blitz of defensive linemen came. Bodies far,

far bigger than anything that had been *allowed* to exist in two hundred years onboard the Ark slammed into each other. Irresistible forces meet immovable objects with a thunderclap. Hillman, intentionally left uncovered to Boswell's right where the Mustang's star quarterback would have a clear line of sight on the charging linebacker, came streaking through the gap like a charging Dux'ah and leveled a shoulder in an all-out effort to sack the QB, kill the drive, and force a punt to essentially end the game.

Just as Benson had hoped.

Miraculously, Cha'ku had actually understood Benson's instructions and ran to the patch of turf Hillman's charge had left undefended. Ze didn't manage to shake zer man-on-man coverage, but with the Atlantian's two-and-a-half-meter tall frame, it hardly mattered. Boswell zeroed in on his open receiver and let loose a rifle shot of a pass well over the head of the human Flying Injri player struggling desperately to match up with Cha'ku.

The oblong football streaked through the air in a tight spiral. Cha'ku reached up with a single hand and stretched as far as ze could. With a *slap,* the synthetic pigskin smacked into zer palm as the Atlantian's four tentacle-like fingers curled around it and hauled it in for a seven meter reception. Ze was hit immediately from two sides by zer own man coverage and a free safety, but the nice thing about having receivers with thousands of tiny suction cups on their fingers was no matter how hard defenders hit them, they *never* coughed up fumbles.

They also never got much in the way of meters after the catch. As hard as they could be to tackle because of the extreme flexibility their omni-directional joints offered them, Atlantians were absolute shit in straight line running. With two defenders wrapping zer up like a Christmas present, Cha'ku toppled over like a felled tree. With one last desperate grab for centimeters, Cha'ku threw out zer arm and stretched the ball as far as ze could before zer knee touched turf and the play was whistled dead.

Benson didn't have a great angle on the far side of the field and couldn't tell where exactly Cha'ku had been brought down in relation to the first down marker. The ref made her way over to the pile of tangled limbs, recovered the ball, and placed it on the far side of the marker.

"Yeah!" Benson's arms rose into the air along with the hoots and hollers of some three thousand Mustang fans, drowning out the boos of the Flying Injri fans that also filled the stands. Football had come a long way in the fifteen years since Benson had pioneered his little rec league, hoping to fill the hole left in his heart from the death of Zero.

Since those early days, their borrowed field had grown into a proper stadium, with seating for eight thousand people, nearly as large as the old Zero Stadium back on the Ark. The original four teams had swelled to a proper semi-pro league of six, one for each of Shambhala's five boroughs, plus one representing the outlying settlements. Atlantian immigrants had started playing almost as soon as they'd touched down, bringing their unique blend of skills and physical characteristics to a game that was already evolving at breakneck speeds.

But some things never changed. A sudden pall settled over the crowd, squelching their celebration. Benson sensed the trouble and looked back to the field to see what the crowd had spotted. Lying there, not ten meters behind him, was a yellow penalty flag, burning in his vision as if it were the sun itself. It had been thrown far behind the line of scrimmage, close to where Boswell lay sprawled out on the turf underneath Hillman's impressive frame.

Benson's attention had been so focused on the pass that he hadn't been watching the backfield. He hadn't even seen the flag come out, but based on which ref had thrown it, the odds were good it was a holding call against someone on his offensive line. Ten-meter penalty, repeat third down, and give Coach Makhlouf another chance to put the game away for good.

Boswell was slow to get up. He stumbled over to the sidelines holding a limp left arm. "I think it's dislocated, coach," the QB said apologetically.

"That's OK." Benson nodded towards the trio of officials conferring about the penalty in the middle of the field. "Looks like we're just about done anyway."

Boswell saw the flag and was crestfallen. "It was a pretty good throw though, right?"

"Brilliant throw, Mohammed. Right in the suckers where nobody else could touch it."

The lead ref broke away from their huddle and faced the crowd. "Personal foul. Defense. Number forty-three. Roughing the passer."

"What?" Hillman threw his arms out in disbelief and started walking towards the lead ref, but the other two moved to block his way.

"Fifteen-meter penalty. Automatic first down."

The Mustang fans in the stands went wild as the chains moved up. Boswell was out, but with the penalty they were at the outer edge of their kicker's field goal range. A quick QB substitution, three run plays to pick up a few extra meters, a tense moment as the ball sailed through the air before hooking right and splitting the uprights, then his invigorated defense forced a three-and-out. A failed onside kick attempt later and the Mustangs had the ball back, up by one, and with enough time taken off the clock that all the offense needed to do was go into victory formation, take a knee, and let the clock run out to win the game.

Benson ran out into center field to shake Coach Makhlouf's hand as tradition demanded. He leaned in and slapped the younger man on the shoulder. "Good game."

"Lucky call," Makhlouf said. "Holcomb was holding, I know you saw it."

"You wouldn't have complained if it went the other way."

"Nope, not one bit."

"Didn't think so. See you in three weeks. Hope you're ready."

"Count on it."

They parted ways and Benson returned to the Mustang's locker room among a sea of attaboys and ass slaps. He took the opportunity to congratulate all of his players on a hard-fought victory and praise their grit, then critiqued their individual performances. The game ball went to Cha'ku for zer spectacular crunch-time catch. Ze was absolutely thrilled by the honor and cradled the ball like a newborn.

As the players changed out of their sweaty uniforms and stripped off their pads, Benson noticed his wife standing in the doorway, taking in the sights. Benson quickly shuffled her out of view. "Honey, you can't just come in the locker room."

"Why not?"

"It makes people uncomfortable."

"I'm not uncomfortable," she grinned devilishly.

"They're kids, dear."

"Awful big for kids," Theresa said. "But speaking of kids, we have to pick ours up from the airfield, remember?"

"Right!" Benson said.

"You forgot?"

"Absolutely not."

Theresa sighed. "Honestly, Bryan, what's the point of even setting a plant alert for you?"

"It must have glitched again."

"Your head must have glitched again." Theresa started moving towards the door. "C'mon, the pod's waiting for us."

Benson said a quick goodbye to his team, then followed

Theresa to the light rail station in the lobby. A small, four-seat electric transport pod waited for them with its scissor doors open high. Benson settled into the opposing bench seats as Theresa selected the airstrip from the small control terminal. There were no seatbelts. There was no need for them. The doors slid shut and the pod silently rolled down the thin electrified tracks.

The silence extended to the cab as Benson looked out the window, avoiding his wife's gaze. The stadium was on the far northern side of Shambhala, opposite the airstrip. The city's neighborhoods whizzed past as the pod picked up speed. First the Museum district with its exclusive townhouses, cafes, pubs, boulevard of shops, and naturally the Museum itself. In what was considered a minor miracle by most outside observers, Devorah Feynman had, after fifty years and change, let her job as curator pass to her assistant. At eighty-five years old, Devorah was now content to keep herself busy as a tour guide. A slow, methodical, tortuously thorough guide who more than one visitor had faked a medical emergency in order to escape before the tour had reached its conclusion.

Benson was convinced she'd outlive them all.

Next came the Glades, which they called home. Five years after Landing, they'd learned the hard way that this area was prone to semi-annual flooding. A hastily-prepped series of earthen levies had seen to that little hiccup, but for a few months that summer they'd enjoyed the quaint entertainments of living in a wetland. Theresa had wanted a new couch anyway.

Beyond the Glades and across the river was the Native Quarter, but that was just the polite title everyone used to avoid calling it the ghetto. It was a labyrinth for humans to navigate, the Atlantians who built it eschewing the grid of streets in the rest of Shambhala for their more familiar village layout of concentric rings connected by spokes. From the air, the two halves of the city stood in stark geometric contrast. The Native Quarter grew into the unused land between the spaceport and the rest of Shambhala, where the humans hadn't wanted to build due to the noise pollution and potential for crashing shuttles.

Of the fifty thousand plus residents that called Shambhala home, just over thirty thousand of them were humans. The balance were Atlantians who had emigrated from the villages of the road network and Dweller caves in the fifteen years since First Contact and the forging of the Trident.

At least their parents had. The thing about Atlantians was, once you had three of them in one place, it wasn't long before you had thirty *more* of them. This wasn't a problem before the Ark turned up. Life on Gaia had been harsh, forcing harsh choices. Choices Benson had been horrified by when he first saw them in action. Now, he knew enough to understand them in context.

It all started with a bearer with no name. Malnourished and heavily pregnant with a brood, ze'd wandered down the road network in Atlantis until ze found G'tel and the Shambhala Embassy. The bearer wove a tale of abuse at the hands of zer village elders, who demanded that ze adhere to tradition and zer judgment over which among zer brood lived or died. But ze'd heard fantastic rumors about G'tel, where beings from the sky had taught the village to grow two fullhand times as many crops on the same amount of land. Where there was more food than could be eaten, and broods weren't culled anymore.

So ze escaped, and found zer way to this mystical place.

Tuko, still Chief at the time, wished to return the bearer to zer village, as was proper under their traditions. But Ambassador Mei was adamant, which was *her* tradition. Mei taught the bearer a brand new word. A human word that, until then, had never existed on Gaia, not even as a concept.

Asylum.

The political and diplomatic shitstorm that followed took months to settle back down again, but in the end, ze was granted asylum and safe passage to Shambhala, where ze gave birth to zer brood, all thirty-four of them. Ze was not the last. Within a year, over five hundred bearers, most of them pregnant, had requested asylum and moved to Shambhala. Nor were they alone. Many of the parents of the bearer's broods also made the move, just as concerned about the fate of their children as the bearers were.

In short order, Shambhala was dealing with a massive refugee housing crisis. The urban planning council had to throw everything out the window, lift zoning restrictions, loosen building codes, and turn a blind eye to a lot of graft just to attempt to keep up with the unexpected population explosion.

Then, to make matters worse, the bearer with no name disappeared, leaving a hole in the expat community and a leadership fight that had yet to fully resolve itself. That had been ten years ago.

"Your secondary still needs work on their one-on-ones," Theresa said, suddenly breaking the silence and causing Benson's train of thought to derail in a spectacular fashion.

"Sorry, what?"

"Your secondary. They're missing a step on their match-ups. They should be in position to disrupt more passes, even get a few interceptions, but they're too slow out of the gate. Maybe a few more shuttle runs and interval drills."

"Yeah, you're right," Benson said. "Wait a minute. You said you weren't watching the games anymore. You said they were, what was the word, 'Barbaric'?"

"They are," Theresa confirmed. "Totally savage. But you're only one game out of first place, and well, you know how I am about men in tights."

"They're not tights," Benson objected. "They're pads."

"Well they certainly pad all the right places."

"Hello? Your husband is sitting right here!"

"And he's dead sexy," Theresa cooed. "For a fifty-two year-old."

"Oh God, I've hit 'qualified' age."

"Sweetie, you hit qualified age about seven years ago. Which is a lot longer than most men manage, so be proud of yourself."

"I do try," Benson said, then fell quiet again.

"Hey," Theresa pressed, "you're tuning me out again. What's the matter?"

"It's nothing."

"It's something. It's not like you to forget appointments, especially not when Benexx is involved… well, usually."

"Sorry. I've just been distracted."

Theresa reached across the pod and lightly rested her hand on his knee. "You're not just distracted. You've been distant. I hoped that zer summer with Kexx and Sakiko would give you enough time to look forward to seeing zer again, but–"

"No, it's not that at all. I miss zer terribly. You know that."

She leaned in and took his hand in hers. Her hands had lost a lot of their youthful softness, hardened and creased by a law enforcement career now entering its third decade. But to him, they'd always be velvet.

"Then what is it, Bryan? Because I still can't read your mind, even with the plants."

"Benexx and I have…" Benson paused, afraid of what he was going to say. Afraid that putting it into words would somehow cement it into reality. "…have been growing apart. I've tried to fight it, but she, excuse me, ze keeps pushing me further away. We can't agree on *anything* lately. It feels like I'm losing zer to something."

Theresa squeezed his hand. "God, Bryan, I love you so much, but you're an idiot."

"Thanks."

"No, I'm serious. Ze's a teenager, Bryan. How well did you get along with your father when you were a teenager?"

"That's different," Benson said. "Fathers and sons always have a hard time dealing with each other through adolescence."

"And you think mothers and daughters don't?" Theresa said, barely suppressing a laugh. "My mother and I nearly killed each other."

"But ze's not fighting with *you*."

She squeezed his forearm. "Bryan, I know you've tried really, really hard to treat zer like an Atlantian child, but I know you think of Benexx as your daughter. I do too, even if I hide it better. But ze's not a girl, and the expectations you have for what your relationship with zer *should* be are screwing up your ability to process what it *is*."

"That's not it."

"No?"

"No, well, maybe some of it, but not all. I just miss…"

"Being zer hero." Theresa smiled warmly. "Sorry sweetie, but that happens to everyone eventually. Recognizing that your parents aren't infallible or indestructible is part of growing up for every kid. So is rebelling against stuffy old mom and dad, otherwise they'd never leave the damned house. I have a feeling it's just as true with Atlantians and us. But I don't know. Talk to Kexx, ask zer if Atlantian kids are supposed to become insufferable little pricks around fifteen."

"Let's hope not." Benson nodded out the window at the last of the makeshift housing units, lean-tos, and even traditionally-built Atlantian mudstone buildings made by those immigrants with the skills who didn't feel like waiting around for the construction robots to catch up. "Otherwise, we're going to have *real* problems."

Theresa shivered. "Don't remind me. I already have nightmares about what this place is going to look like in another couple years."

Among those living in the Native Quarter, almost eighty percent were younger than twenty, most of those having been born right here after the first wave of bearer immigration fifteen years ago. And thanks to the Atlantians' unusual lifecycle, it would be another eight to ten years before the first of them started transitioning to the elder gender.

An entire generation of adolescents coming of age in an alien city with no one around to mate with. It was a demographic time-bomb no one was talking about, but Benson knew it was already ticking.

But, it wasn't his problem anymore. He'd been out of the law enforcement game for a very long time. This was Theresa's wheelhouse. Benson only had to worry about one unruly Atlantian teenager.

The pod rolled gently to a stop at the small terminal building at the edge of the airstrip. To the north, a large, utilitarian hangar had been erected to service the growing fleet of passenger jets and to shield them from the occasional severe weather that the long summers tended to whip up.

The doors rotated open and Benson held Theresa's hand as she stepped out. The pod reversed out of the terminal and accelerated back towards the city just as the airliner's wheels touched down on the tarmac, throwing out little swirls of blue smoke.

The pudgy blended-wing craft slowed rapidly and coasted to the end of the runway, then rolled down the smaller taxiway to one of the three waiting terminals. A small crowd of people assembled near the door, either waiting to pick up returning friends or waiting to get on the plane before it turned around for the return trip. A security guard waiting by the jetway recognized Benson and Theresa and waved them through. Strictly speaking, he shouldn't have done that, but Theresa was unlikely to complain.

Benson psyched himself up for the reunion. He put on a smile that was at least seventy percent genuine and tried to ignore the other thirty.

"There ze is," Theresa said, pointing down the jetway. Benexx, a large wheeled bag rolling along behind zer, saw them and walked over. Zer skin seemed a little darker from the sun, although with Atlantians' constantly shifting chromatophores, it was hard to tell a sun tan from a foul mood. The finely braided bracelets and choker, however, were new. Tiny volcanic glass beads and the iridescent shells of as-yet unnamed sea creatures adorned zer wrists and neck. New acquisitions from G'tel's constantly expanding bazars.

Ze embraced zer mother in a tight hug.

"Welcome home, sweetie," Theresa said.

"Hi mom." Benexx looked over Theresa's shoulder at Benson's smiling face. "Dad," ze said, cool and non-commital.

"Hello pumpkin." Benson held his arms open to offer a hug, working hard to keep the thin veneer of his smile from cracking under the weight of his child's chilly indifference.

"I'm tired," Benexx said, suddenly bored. "Let's go home." Ze let go of Theresa, then stalked away towards the light rail station and hailed a pod.

"Well," Theresa said, "That could have gone worse."

"How? If ze'd shot me?" Benson asked.

"Yeah." Theresa bobbed her head. "That's one way."

CHAPTER FOUR

"Ah. Flight, repeat your last, please," Jian said anxiously.

"*Atlantis,* your mission objectives have changed. You are to touch down and aid the harvester techs in conducting an initial survey of the anomaly before reporting back."

"Flight, we're not really trained for that kind of assignment," Jian said.

"The order comes from Ark Actual directly."

"Well then put Ark Actual on the line," Jian said, hoping his annoyance masked his apprehension.

The line clicked over a moment later. "This is Ark Actual, go ahead *Atlantis.*"

"Ark Actual," Jian said, sticking to radio titles and protocol. "I'd like clarification on the new mission parameters."

"What do you need clarified? We need you to survey the anomaly."

"But we don't have any trained surveyors aboard. And we certainly don't have the equipment."

"You've got cameras, don't you?"

"Well, yeah…"

"It's not that complicated, Jian. This is just a preliminary survey. You're the only ones there right now. We're prepping another mission with the proper specialists and equipment, but it will be really helpful if they have some idea what they're walking into. Just step outside, poke your head around, and take some pictures."

"Actual," Jian said. "Dad, I'm not qualified to survey some weird, probably alien artifact buried on a moon. I don't have any experience with this."

"Who the hell does?"

Kirkland snorted from the copilot's seat. "He's got a point, you know."

"Not helping." Jian keyed the com again. "Copy that, Actual. Starting our deorbital burn in five. *Atlantis* out."

The shuttle had been orbiting Varr for the better part of a day now, first from its initial fifteen-kilometer orbit, then dropping down to less than five klicks to try and get higher resolution images of whatever was lying inside the cave underneath the crippled helium harvester. They had to wait several hours and many orbits until the system's primary was directly overhead and poured light into the hole the harvester had punched through the cave's ceiling.

It didn't help much. Even bathed in light, the anomaly, as they'd taken to calling it, was covered with too much debris from the cave-in to reveal much information beyond its outline. Which was why they'd been ordered to land. That had been the plan all along, of course. The harvester techs needed a ride down to the surface to fix their broken Hoover. But the stakes had since been drastically raised.

Jian warmed up the mains for a fourth time, worrying about the additional stress he was putting on the five that were still working, but unable to do anything about it. It would be a quick, hard burn. They already orbited so close to the surface that they needed to bleed off almost all of their velocity in less than two minutes to hit their insertion window.

Complicating matters further, Varr was completely airless, so the shuttle's airfoils and control surfaces were just dead weight. They'd be landing ass-first on a column of rocket exhaust, using only their thruster packs for terminal maneuvers.

It was like trying to balance an angry cat on top of a broom handle; a feat far beyond the capabilities of even the most experienced pilot, much less one commanding his first mission. Fortunately, that duty had been turned over to software centuries ago. All Jian had to do was punch in the coordinates of the landing site and a couple of other variables into the computer, take his hands off the stick, and relax.

He absolutely hated it.

"OK, kids, this one is going to be fast and rough. Deorbit burn in. Five. Four. Three. Two–" With the suddenness of a car accident, Jian was slammed back into his seat under seven gees, damned near the limit of the five engines they had left.

"One?" Kirkland asked through clenched teeth.

Jian tried to lift his head to see the readout, but his skull remained glued to the headrest. Not that it would've mattered as his vision was blurring on account of the high gee pressing his eyeballs into the backs of their sockets hard enough to deform their shape. Instead, he routed the flight computer data into his plant's augmented reality display, which was unaffected. He spotted the problem immediately. <The damned computer moved our LZ thirteen hundred meters west, away from the Hoover,> he sent to Kirkland.

<I thought we overrode that?>

<It overrode our override. Looks like we're in for a stroll.>

<You mean a skip?>

<True.>

Jian grumbled. The LZ might be marginally safer for the shuttle, but the longer walk would leave his team exposed to the shooting gallery that was Varr's surface. The Tau Ceti system was a notoriously dirty place to begin with, and without an atmosphere or the Ark's nav lasers to burn them up, micrometeorites were an ever-present risk.

As suddenly as they had come on, the gees disappeared as the mains cut out. Jian felt a moment's sensation of pure freefall before the shuttle's flight computer fired the forward thrusters to reorient itself for a vertical landing.

With all its forward momentum bled away, the shuttle started falling straight and true towards Varr's surface. The only indication of movement Jian could see as he looked out the cockpit windows was their altimeter readout dropping, glacially at first as the moon's paltry three and a half percent standard gravity clawed meekly at the craft. But without any atmosphere to drag against the hull, their velocity built up until at a hundred meters the engines fired again, although less exuberantly. At only five meters above the regolith, the flight computer pitched the shuttle over again until it was level with the ground, then settled down into the billowing dust on thrusters alone.

The shuttle nestled into the ground on its belly. They didn't dare open the landing gear doors; the statically-charged dust played merry hell on any moving parts it clung to and shorted out electronics like a bucket of salt water. Everyone unbelted and silently, solemnly started prepping their vacuum suits. Jian picked up on their dour moods.

"Hey, everyone." He clapped to get their attention. "What's with the faces? Is this a funeral?"

"Potentially," technician Madeja muttered.

"Look." Feng ignored her. "I know this isn't what any of us were expecting to find out here. I certainly wasn't. And I'd be lying if I said it wasn't scaring the living fertilizer out of me..." A round of polite, if awkward laughter passed around the cabin. "But whatever it is has been buried here for God only knows how long. If it was going to hurt anybody, it probably would've done it a long time ago.

"So, instead of a boring maintenance assignment, we're out here right on the knife's edge of exploration and discovery. C'mon, that's exciting, right? Let's get buttoned up and get started. Last one into the hole is a reclamation chute."

Kirkland hopped over and whispered in his ear. "Great speech, commander. Are you going to call them doody-heads next?"

"If it gets the job done," Jian said. "Speaking of jobs, don't bother getting dressed."

Kirkland cocked her head. "Why not?"

"Because if I'm wrong and things do go sour down there, we'll need a fast evac. So you're going to stay here and keep *Atlantis*'s engines warm and ready to dust off on a tripwire."

"And if things go *really* wrong down there?"

"Then you may have to bug out and make the return trip alone." Jian noticed Kirkland wasn't exactly broken up by the prospect. "Which would be terrible. Right?"

"Hmm? Oh, yeah, just awful. Me, alone, commanding my own shuttle? A real tragedy. C'mon, let me help you get in your suit."

"Only if someone else checks my seals."

"So suspicious," she said teasingly. "We're a team, remember? Our trust is our foundation."

"I'm doomed."

Kirkland laughed. "Get in those jammies, commander. You've got work to do."

Twenty minutes later, six of them walked across the dirt. Actually, "walked" was entirely the wrong verb. With the incredibly low gravity, they hopped across the surface in great, bounding leaps, like the ancient footage of the original Apollo astronauts bouncing across Luna's terrain, only exaggerated.

But unlike Luna's rocky, bone-dry surface, Varr was a dirty snowball. Layers of rock and water ice laid buried under meters of cosmic dust that had fallen over eons. Outcrops of ice protruded from the surface here and there, while deep fissures crisscrossed the surface, pulled and stretched by the tidal forces Gaia exerted on the moon with each orbit.

Instead of Luna, Varr was more like Ceres, or even Pluto from back in the Sol system. Between the wildly elliptical orbit and the moon's composition, the consensus among the Ark's astronomy department was that it had been captured by Gaia several billion years earlier as it plunged towards the system primary, likely disturbed from its orbit by the outward migration of the ice giant Tau Ceti F, before it too found a stable orbit to call home.

With each hop, Jian sailed effortlessly several meters above the surface. Indeed, it was almost impossible not to. In such a shallow gravity well, he weighed scarcely four kilos, vac suit included. Each footfall sent out a little plume of dust, pulverized into a fine powder from billions of years of micro, and not so micro, meteorite impacts. But he didn't take long to adapt to it. Considering the amount of time he'd spent in zero gee aboard the Ark over his lifetime, it felt almost natural.

<Ravine ahead,> Madeja said into the plant link. <Looks like about ten meters across. It's really deep.>

The rest of the expedition stopped at the edge of the cliff and leaned over to inspect it. Jian rolled his eyes. Instead of slowing down to stop, he took two long hops to build up momentum, then hurdled over the crevasse. He arced through the sky in a perfect parabola, easily clearing the icy canyon and landing on the far side with meters to spare.

<It doesn't matter how deep it is, guys. Just jump over it, we're burning O2.>

Tentatively, the first of them backed up and charged at the divide, jumped, and landed with room in reserve. Three more made the leap without incident. Then, it was Madeja's turn.

She stood at the edge, wringing her hands nervously. <I'm not sure I can do this,> she said into the group link.

<Oh for God's sake, Madeja,> Jian said. <Rakunas

made it, and he's got a shitty knee.>

<Hey!> Rakunas objected.

<Your left knee is crap, Adam. I've played enough handball with you to notice.>

<Easy for the twenty-six year-old to say,> Rakunas answered. <Let's see how your joints hold up in twenty years.>

<Whatever, old man.> Jian returned his attention to Madeja. <C'mon, you can do it. We'll catch you.>

<I'm scared.>

<It's either jump or go back and wait on the *Atlantis,*> Jian said, losing patience. <Make your choice, technician, because the rest of us have to keep moving.>

<OK, OK,> Madeja said. She took quite a few long hops back, then paused.

<While we've still got air!> someone said into the comlink.

Madeja winced, then started to run, building up speed and height with each bounding leap. But she misjudged her final jump, landing and pushing off almost five meters from the edge of the cliff. At first, it looked like her parabola would be high enough to clear the icy schism, but as she reached her apex and started to drift down, the augmented reality display projecting her trajectory into his vision said she was going to come up almost a meter short.

"Shit," he said aloud inside his helmet. Jian took three small hops and got right up to the edge, then kicked his legs out from under him and floated down into the dust flat on his stomach.

<Oh my God, I'm going to fall!> Madeja shouted through the plant.

<No you're not.> Jian stretched out his left arm as far as the range of motion in his suit's shoulder joint would let him and scrambled for grip with his free hand.

<Grab my arm.>

With barely a meter left to fall, Madeja reached out

in a panic. But in freefall, the wild flailing of her arms caused her entire body to rotate around her center of mass, quickly spinning her outstretched hand out of his reach. With her back now facing him, Jian made one last, desperate lunge for the grab handle on the top of her suit's life support backpack before she slipped into the inky black of the yawning chasm.

Jian managed only to get two fingers on it, but in the weak gravity two was more than enough.

<Gotcha,> Jian said. <Now stop struggling so I can pull you up.>

Madeja went obediently limp as Jian firmed up his grip on her backpack handle. With almost no effort, he flexed his arm and tossed her entire body up and out of the ravine.

For just a moment, he felt like a superhero.

He was not a strong man by any measure of the word, but with Madeja effectively weighing in at less than four kilos, it was easier than throwing a baby. Not that Jian would ever throw a baby. But his ego, not caring about the details, swelled up a notch anyway.

<Did you see that!?> Rakunas shouted into the com as the rest of the team bounced up to help both Jian and Madeja to their feet. <That was amazing, commander.>

<It was nothing,> Jian lied and turned to Madeja. <Technician, are you all right?>

Madeja took a moment to regain her composure before answering. <Yes, I think so.>

<How's your suit integrity?>

<Pressure's green. No leaks detected. Pack isn't throwing any error codes.>

Jian nodded. <Good, but keep an eye on it. Any trouble, anything at all, tell me immediately.>

<Yes, sir.>

<OK, let's get moving.>

The rest of the jaunt to the stricken harvester was, mercifully, uneventful. The machine itself was enormous, nearly the length of the shuttle from which they'd arrived. Each one had taken a dozen shuttle flights to deliver the components to Varr's surface for reassembly. With six wheels and an articulated body, it looked like a strange, gargantuan insect. Its "head" rested on two of its wheels and mounted a broad, shallow scoop to shovel up the first several centimeters of regolith for processing further back in the beast's body. Only a thin layer of dust needed to be collected, because the lion's share of the fusible Helium-3 that rained down from the system primary in the form of solar wind was trapped there.

Once inside, a series of sifters and vaporizers separated the individual helium atoms for capture, along with a handful of other useful elements and compounds, and were routed into storage containers for later collection. The remaining dust was then spread out the back of the harvester and combed to cover any trace of the machine's passing.

That feature had been retrofitted to the harvesters out of respect to the Atlantians, who had insisted that any disturbances to Varr's surface be mended before they would grant permission for the endeavor. It was the face of one of their Gods, after all. Such considerations had not been important when the harvesters had been built to stripmine Earth's moon, which was just as doomed by Nibiru as mankind's homeworld had been.

The resurfacer wasn't the only field modification the harvesters had gone through. Despite their size, their weight was a problem, or more accurately, their lack of it. They'd been designed to operate in one-sixth standard gravity, and while that didn't seem like much, it was still nearly five times greater than Varr's environment. Huge concrete slabs made of thermally fused regolith had been strapped to their backs to give their wheels enough purchase to push through the dust. Likewise, metal paddles had been fixed to the wheels themselves for extra grip on the silty surface.

It was probably a combination of the extra weight and the sharp wheels that had caused the roof of the hidden cave to collapse as the harvester rolled over it. Jian came near the edge and prodded at the ground with his foot to make sure it wasn't about to give way. It held. Still, to be safe, he hooked a line to the harvester's hull with a carabiner and instructed the rest of his team to do the same.

Their lidar scans from orbit had pegged the cavern's depth at around thirty meters. Peering in through the hole, it looked more like sixty.

Well, nothing for it, Jian thought as he let his line play out all the way to the bottom. The distance was safe to jump in only three percent gravity, but he clipped a repelling arrestor to the line anyway. No such thing as too careful. With a flourish befitting his new superhero status, Jian stepped off the ledge, rotated to face his teammates, and saluted as he plunged out of sight.

Slowly.

Very, slowly.

He didn't so much plunge as... sink. By the time he was halfway down the shaft, Jian was already bored. He hoped for some vivid hallucinations a la Alice's visions as she tumbled down the rabbit hole, but none were forthcoming. He finally touched down many seconds after stepping off, his boots sending out little clouds of dust which flew off in perfect little parabolas before settling down again. His helmet's floodlights bounced around the chamber, illuminating it with a dim glow and giving him a sense of its proportions. It wasn't much bigger across than it was deep, but if it had a back wall his suit's lights couldn't find it. Debris from the roof collapse littered the floor like discarded building blocks.

Then, he looked right, and his heartrate jumped twenty BPM.

<Commander,> Kirkland's voice broke through from the shuttle. <Your vitals just spiked. Is everything all right?>

<Standby, *Atlantis*,> Jian said. As he spoke, his eyes swept over the anomaly. Until that very moment, Jian had been holding out hope that it had been some strangely improbable arrangement of ice slabs, or a trick of light and shadow, like the face on Mars that had captivated so many fools back on Earth centuries before.

But staring at it, he knew it was neither. Covered in rocks and ice, it was unmistakably manufactured. And unmistakably alien.

Jian pulled a light beacon from one of the pockets of his pants, switched the little globe on, and let it tumble to the ground. <I guess the rest of you had better get down here. We have work to do after all.>

It took almost an hour to clear away most of the debris from the top and front of the anomaly, which was surprisingly light work in the low gravity. Still, even with their relative super-strength, some pieces were too large or too wedged in to move by hand.

They were going to need some help.

<Hey, commander,> Rakunas said as he surveyed one of the largest slabs pressing against the side of the anomaly. <Check this out.>

Jian maneuvered over the block and crawled up its surface to take position beside Rakunas. <What do we have here?>

Rakunas wiped away a handful of dust from one corner of a small ledge built into the anomaly's face. Below it was a circular depression, maybe three meters across. Jian's helmet banged off the wall, so he used one of his wrist lights to get a better look. Running diagonally across the circle was a line separating it in two.

<Shit,> he said a moment later. <Looks an awful lot like an airlock, don't it?>

<That's what I thought too, commander.>

<Can we get around this damned thing?> Jian pointed at the slab.

<I've walked all the way around it. There are some small cracks here and there, and a little bit of shimmy space underneath, but I certainly wouldn't fit. I don't think anyone else here would either.>

<Right. We have a doorway here, people,> Jian announced to the rest of the team. <How do we get this honking block of rock and ice out of the way? Suggestions?>

<What about electric winches?> Rakunas asked. <I thought I saw one on the front of the harvester.>

<Could work,> Jian said. <Although I don't know if they've got enough cable to reach all the way down here and wrap up these blocks.>

<Are you crazy?> Madeja said. They both turned to face her.

<You have something to add?> Jian said testily.

<Yeah, what do you think is anchoring the winch? If you try to pull those blocks out with it, you could bring the rest of the roof down on top of us, and the harvester with it.>

<OK, that's a fair point,> Jian said. <What are our alternatives?>

<Go home?>

<*Useful* alternatives.>

Madeja took a deep breath obvious even through her vac suit. <Well, there's one possibility.>

<Let's have it, then.>

<We brought a couple of inflatables with us, in case we needed to lift the harvester to make repairs. They're just giant air bags made out of Kevlar and synthetic spider silk. You wedge them under something heavy, or in this case, stuck, turn the valve, and let the magic of air pressure and surface area do the rest.>

<And you think they're strong enough to pop this monster loose?> Jian wrapped his gloved knuckles on the slab.

<They can individually lift a couple metric tons in

standard gravity. Here? They could lift dozens.>

<But that's just weight. What if it's wedged in too tight?>

<Then nothing else we have with us will be strong enough either. Unless you want to blow it up with seismic survey charges.>

<That's not high on my list, no. What about torches?>

<Cut it up?> Madeja considered the question. <They would certainly be hot enough, but I think they'd run out of fuel before making enough of a dent to matter.>

Jian nodded. <Airbags it is. You'll be in charge of placing them and monitoring their inflation, Madeja.>

<Me? But, I've never done anything like this before.>

<Who the hell has?> Jian winced as his father's words tumbled so easily out of his own mouth. <What I mean is, you'll be fine. If it works, it works. If it doesn't, we'll just have to think of something else, OK?>

Madeja nodded and signaled for LaSalle to come over with his pack. Together, they fished out the inflatables and argued over their optimum placement. After a gentle reminder of how much O2 their deliberations were burning up, consensus was quickly reached. Madeja popped the valves and backed away almost to the far wall. With no atmospheric pressure opposing them, the airbags expanded and quickly filled nearly all of the void-space between the floor, slab, and the front face of the anomaly, unfolding in total silence in the airless chamber.

The expansion stopped abruptly as the airbags met real resistance. At first, nothing happened. Jian was preparing to call it a day as the sides of the bags bulged helplessly against the stubborn monolith. But then, he felt a rumble of something shift through the soles of his feet.

<Everybody get back against the walls,> Jian warned.

As the team took cover, the slab cracked in half with a shudder. The airbags, already pressurized to their full capacity, launched the two pieces with tremendous force, one towards the opposite wall, and the other up towards the–

<Oh, shit,> Madeja said as they all stood by and helplessly watched the chunk of rocky ice pinwheel through the cavern, drawing slowly but inexorably closer to the harvester wheel dangling over the open ceiling, backlit by the stars.

<Everybody to the far side!> Jian shouted.

With the sort of bad luck usually reserved for compulsive gamblers, the spinning block struck the wheel dead on before rebounding back towards the floor.

<It's coming back down,> Rakunas yelled as the chunk returned to the floor, bounced off one of the other blocks at an angle, then came to rest with a *thunk* everyone could feel through their boots.

But no one was paying it any attention. Instead, all eyes remained fixed on the wheel of the harvester as it shifted and ground its way further over the hole. Little flakes and pebbles of debris floated down through the cavern like gray snow. Jian sucked air through his teeth. Sphincters clenched down on colostomy tubes as everyone watched in horror, expecting the rest of the roof to collapse and send the harvester tumbling down, dragging their anchored lines along with it.

Another section of ceiling ice almost a meter across broke free where the wheel's axle had sat and followed the dust down to the floor in a fresh pile. But then, movement stopped. The harvester settled into its new position and rested.

The sighs of relief were audible even through the plant comlinks.

<Maybe we should move the harvester before we continue the survey,> Jian said.

<You think?!> Madeja shouted.

<At least he didn't hit it with a rock,> Rakunas said.

<Says the man who wanted to tie it to the rock with a damned winch.>

<That's enough, you two. We're still on the clock.> Jian bounded over to the anchor lines hanging from the

harvester far above. With more than a little trepidation, he gave one line a cursory tug. It held, and nothing came crashing down on his head. He gave the line a harder jerk. It felt solid enough, so he grabbed it with both hands and put his full weight on it. No change.

<OK, the lines are intact. Madeja, can you and LaSalle go back up to the surface and recall one of the other harvesters for a tow?>

<Should work. The winch may not be powerful enough, but the cable will be plenty strong for the other harvester to go in reverse and pull it out.>

<How long?>

<Hour, tops.>

Jian checked his suit's air supply. The CO2 scrubbers were still at sixty-seven percent and they had another four hours of battery charge on this trip. Hour to secure the harvester, hour to walk back to the *Atlantis*, hour for safety margin, still gave them an hour to play with. It was worth it.

<OK, shimmy on up and get that thing out of the way.>

Madeja nodded and started working her way up the line back to the surface with LaSalle close behind on another rope.

<What are we going to do?> Rakunas asked.

Jian looked at the anomaly and its freshly revealed airlock.

<Knock.>

CHAPTER FIVE

The "Welcome Home" dinner Benexx's father had prepared for them was a textbook example of trying too hard.

In what had surely been intended as a grand gesture, Bryan had spent the better part of three hours in their home's kitchenette preparing an entire buffet line of Atlantian dishes to the very best of his somewhat limited ability.

He'd apparently spent the morning before football wandering around the small, but growing bazar in the Native Quarter, spending lavishly on imported yulka beans, fenta root, smoked kujin fillets, even freshly slaughtered dux'ah meat, and a bag of exotic spices not even Benexx could properly identify. Of course, Shambhala's fields and plains grew nearly all of them as well, save the kujin fish which were native to the reefs around Atlantis.

But they were grown in strange soils, using strange methods, in a strange climate, by strange tools and inexperienced hands. They were grown packed together to increase yields, and in half the usual time to double the number of harvests each season. These tradeoffs did what was necessary to feed the city's swelling masses, but they left locally grown food tasting strange and weak to the discriminating palate. Genuine Atlantian imports grown in the traditional way commanded quite a premium as a result.

The smell of it all filled the house as he worked, thoroughly putting Benexx off zer appetite. Ze'd been eating authentic Atlantian food from all over the damned continent all summer. *Fresh* Atlantian food, not stuff that had been processed, frozen, and stuck on a drone cargo ship for the nine-day voyage across the Sukal Ocean. Food prepared by indigenous people who knew all the little tricks to cooking it, had the same sense of taste in their hands and mouths as ze, and knew from long personal experience what it was supposed to taste like.

And ze was *still* sick to death of it.

Ze'd been craving genuine Shambhala junk food for weeks. It was the taste of home, zer version of comfort food. Ze wanted falafel rolled inside a genuine wheat flour pancake. Ze wanted breaded, deep-friend chicken and mushroom kabobs dunked in creamy cucumber sauce. Ze wanted to eat an entire thirty-six count bag of Little Smokies. Ze wanted a perch and wild rice sushi roll as long as zer arm and to suck up the soy sauce through a straw until zer tongue shriveled up like a raisin.

Raisins! Ze wanted raisins. There had to be some in the pantry.

"What are you doing in here, Squish?" Zer father looked up from the induction range.

"Don't call me that. I'm just grabbing some raisins."

"Now? You'll spoil your dinner. Have a cup of tea instead. There's a fresh pot on the counter."

Benexx scoffed. "It's a couple of raisins, dad. I'm not a larva anymore."

"Well, OK, but just a handful. Dinner's almost ready."

"Yes, dad."

Bryan grimaced, but ze ignored him and found the raisin container on the third shelf next to the ever-present bunch of bananas that were, as always, turning brown and destined for bread. No one in the house ever seemed to remember they were in there until they'd ripened almost to the point of spoilage. Ze poured a glass of the green tea sitting on the counter. It was a little tepid by human standards, but just right for the more temperature-sensitive skin of zer Atlantian mouth. Benexx was constantly waiting for things to cool off while zer human family, friends, and coworkers were busy pouring boiling hot liquid and food down their throats.

Ze sat down on the couch next to zer mother and popped a few of the tiny brown bits into zer mouth. Raisins were a guilty pleasure for zer. One amino acid or another didn't agree with the later stages of zer digestive system. They weren't poisonous to Atlantians, just difficult. But they were so sweet and chewy. Ze could get away with a handful without too much discomfort later on.

"How's dinner coming along?" Theresa asked.

"The kujin is going to be dry and he's overcooking the yulka bean pudding again."

"Yes, well, it's tricky to hit yulka's sweet spot for everyone. Your father's first experience with it was... memorable."

"He threw up on Chief Tuko."

"*Near* Chief Tuko," zer mother corrected.

"That's not how the people in G'tel tell it," Benexx said.

"Stories tend to grow in the telling," Theresa said gently. "Be nice, Benexx. Your father is working very hard on this. It means a lot to him."

Benexx rolled zer eyes. It seemed to come naturally to zer, even if ze had discovered just how human a gesture it was during zer first summer in G'tel. Theresa saw, but studiously ignored it in favor of pushing the conversation forward. "So, how's Sakiko? Did you two have a chance to catch up?"

"I guess. She's sounding more and more like Uncle Kexx every day."

"Well, she *is* taking over zer job in a few years."

"I know, I just miss the way it used to be."

"We all do, sweetie. That's part of growing up. What would she say?"

"What do you mean?"

"Who would Sakiko say you're sounding more like?"

Benexx paused, unexpectedly thrown out of zer train of thought. "Um, I don't know."

"I'm sure you could think of something," Theresa pressed. "Just try to see things from her point of view."

"Food's on! Come and get it!" zer father announced, saving zer from answering the question. Ze and Theresa stood from the couch and moved to the table at the back of the family room that served as the dining area. The table was more accustomed to bearing clutter than food, but again, zer father was making a show of them eating tonight's meal together, as a family.

He brought out the first course; mashed fenta root served on Cuut's tentacle vine leaves. The silverware remained in the drawer. Traditional Atlantian dishes were eaten with bare fingers, as they were the first part of the body to experience the food, checking it for toxins, impurities, ripeness, or proper cooking before the more sensitive taste buds in their mouth explored the full bouquet.

What Benexx's fingers tasted made zer rather wish for a fork. Ze reached across the table for the salt and applied it liberally. Atlantians descended from an aquatic, invertebrate ancestor that had been the first to leave the ocean behind. They could still drink seawater straight, having never lost the use of the small filtering organs in their ears. Benexx could afford to drown out the bitter fenta until the salt overwhelmed everything else.

"How's the root?" Bryan asked.

"It's fine, dad. Just a little bland," ze said.

"Never ceases to amaze me how much salt you can put on everything. If I took in that much sodium, I'd stroke out in a week."

Benexx sat and quietly chewed on tough fenta. The

trick was to soak it for a day in a brine of kuka juice before mashing the roots, although here in Shambhala many chefs had taken to using lime juice, which was just as effective at breaking down the tough cellular walls of the husks, but imparted a unique flavor humans found more agreeable.

But Bryan apparently didn't know this and tried to overcome the problem by simply beating the roots into submission with a potato masher, and eventually a meat tenderizer. Zer father was not a subtle man.

"So, how was your summer vacation?" Bryan asked, testing the waters between them.

"It was fine," Benexx said between mouthfuls of fenta. "We tracked the dux'ah migration for almost a week, most of the way to Xekallum. Then we spent a few days on Lake Tumlac. I caught a xezer fish. Well, actually," Benexx laughed at the memory, "it caught my foot, thinking my toes were bait worms. I just squealed and pulled it out of the water. Sakiko caught it as it flopped around on the beach. We laughed and laughed until Uncle Kexx told us to let the poor creature go back to its home."

"That sounds hilarious," zer mother said. "Did you get any of that recorded?"

Benexx shook zer head. "Sorry, mama, but I was too caught up in the moment. Besides, it's not like Lake Tumlac has a repeater tower."

"Not yet," Bryan conceded. "But it's in the queue."

Benexx sighed without even trying to hide it. "Everything is 'in the queue,' especially on Atlantis."

"What is *that* supposed to mean?"

"It means Shambhala gets first priority in the manufacturing queue and everyone knows it, dad. And only *certain* parts of Shambhala, at that."

"That's not fair, Benexx," zer mother said. "The Ark's factories are running at full capacity and have been for fifteen years."

"Sure, on vanity projects like the Alcubierre drive prototype and the telescope network," Benexx said, zer mouth full of bitter junma flowers. "Meanwhile, the road network is still using dux'ah drawn carts for the majority of their trade."

"The Early Warning network is not a 'vanity project,'" Bryan replied. "How are we supposed to know if another attack is coming without it?"

"So what if one is?" Benexx said. "It's not like we can all hop back aboard the Ark and hike on out to the next solar system. Even if you believe the stories."

"Stories?" Bryan said more quietly.

"Well, yeah. Not everybody believes the Nibiru legend, you know."

"It's not a *legend,* Benexx. It's our history. Somebody threw a black hole at us, and there's no telling if or when they're going to do it again."

"You know how crazy that sounds, right? Most Atlantians don't even understand the concept of a black hole, much less how anyone could throw them around space. Hell, you don't have a proper explanation for how that's even possible."

"Don't tell me you're buying into some wild conspiracy theory about Nibiru never existing."

"No," Benexx insisted. "But it doesn't matter what I believe, does it? These are the questions being asked over there. And here, for that matter."

"You mean in the Native Quarter?" zer mother asked. "Is this what your students are asking?"

"Some of them. They don't know what to believe. But they see how long it takes to get anything done on their street, and keep getting told about all these amazing things we're building up in orbit that they'll never use. It's easy for resentment to build up when your house has been waiting for running water for two years and keeps getting pushed down the priority list so that the humans can build telescopes to look for something that you say can't be seen in the first place."

"It's a lot more complicated than that."

"*I* know that, dad, but *they* don't. Not having to carry a couple of buckets of water back to their houses every morning before they go work all day in the fields is an immediate benefit that they can understand. What am I supposed to say to them?"

"The truth," zer father said. "That we're working as fast as we can, and that there's good reasons why we're prioritizing the projects we are."

"Daddy knows best," Benexx said, then pushed back from the table. "I'm going for a walk."

"But we haven't even gotten to the dux'ah tenderloins yet," Bryan protested. "Is there something wrong with the food?"

"No, dad, your food is fine. I'm still a little airsick from the flight home."

Theresa gave zer a look that said she recognized the lie for the polite fiction that it was, but zer father continued on, oblivious. Really, it was hard to believe that he'd ever been a detective.

"Oh, well OK then. I can whip up something quick to settle your stomach."

"It's fine, dad," ze called over zer shoulder. "I just need some fresh air."

"Be home before ten," zer mother said as ze reached the door.

Dammit, Benexx thought, zer hopes of a curfew-free night dashed at the last possible moment. "Of course, mom," ze said instead as ze closed the door. Benexx stood under the awning covering the home's front door and sighed.

Feeling adrift, ze picked a direction and started walking. Where wasn't important, just so long as it put literal distance between zer and the house that ze felt increasingly distant from. Ze chose left, towards the Museum district. The Native quarter was to zer right, and ze would be spending plenty enough time there in the coming months as ze returned to tutoring the kids there. Besides, ze craved *human* junk food.

Zer feet carried zer down the street as the sun faded and the solar lamps warmed up to take over the important work of illuminating the way home for the evening's drunks in a few hours, human and Atlantian alike. Inebriation knew no bounds in Shambhala, or stigma. Only the chemicals necessary to induce the high varied between the species. Alcohol had little effect on Atlantians beyond a slight dulling of their natural bioluminescence, while the drinks made from fermented bak'ri mushrooms were a lethal poison to humans. Of course, so was alcohol, but bak'ri lacked any of the more desirable side effects prior to killing the victim, either in hours or decades.

Bak'ri was a mild aphrodisiac back on Atlantis where users would simply chew the dried fungus tips. But here in Shambhala, human chemistry and Atlantian vice had conspired to concentrate and distill it into a potent drug that was causing all kinds of problems for the population of the native quarter, which is why Benexx avoided it entirely.

With the summer sun fading, ze only had a couple of free hours to spend before ten o'clock rolled around. Ze thought about calling a pod, but decided to just let zer feet carry zer deeper into the city. Soon, the Beehive was off to zer right, still buzzing with activity despite the late hour. The gears of government ground inexorably onward, even if no one outside its walls could tell the difference.

Ze turned left when ze reached the museum, closed for the night so the interns could wipe away all the snotty nose and fingerprint smudges school kids had left on the display glass and clean and restock the bathrooms for the following day's visitors.

At least that had been Benexx's experience. What

the curator and her handful of employees did while the interns toiled, ze couldn't say. Ze'd been under the not-so-tender loving care of Devorah Feynman in her last year as curator. Benexx had rather liked the cantankerous old woman, but the other interns were absolutely terrified of her, as were a healthy percentage of her actual employees. Still, in her last few years, Devorah had worked hard to negotiate and trade for ethically collected items from Atlantis to showcase in a new wing of the museum. She'd even successfully negotiated with Chief Kuul to open a satellite museum in G'tel to showcase humanity's past to curious Atlantians.

When pressed by the budget committee chairman to justify the costs of her pet project, she'd famously said, "Well how the hell are we supposed to move forward together if we don't know where we're starting from?"

She'd also instituted a policy of recruiting half of the museum's interns from the city's Atlantian population. For someone always looking back, Devorah could be surprisingly forward-thinking.

Benexx turned away from the museum and headed down the Golden Mile, as the boulevard of shops, cafés, and pubs was called. In truth, it was scarcely a quarter mile long and held very little gold. What it held instead was hundreds of humans and Atlantians scurrying about the dozens of storefronts, vendor stalls, and even food carts, either to shop, sit down for a relaxing dinner with friends or partners, or just to grab a quick kabob on their way back home from a long day of work.

Soon, the Atlantians would thin out as the sun set and the day's heat began to leech from their bodies, although even that was beginning to change. Atlantians traditionally wore very little in the way of clothing, both because their homeland was subtropical and the cold was seldom an issue, and because their skinglow was such an integral part of their language.

Among the younger adults in Shambhala however, it

had become trendy to wear human clothes tailored for their svelte shape. The jumpsuits helped them retain the heat of the day deeper into the night so they could stay out eating, socializing, and yes, drinking with their human friends, even if none of them were old enough to do so legally.

Their language had changed as a result. They learned Atlantian at home, English in the classroom, and Mandarin curses in the streets. Like Benexx zerself, few of them even bothered learning the skinglow part of their language, a trend the wearing of clothes had only accelerated. The Atlantians of Shambhala were fast becoming their own distinct society, as different from their people living in G'tel or Pukal as they were from the humans living across the street.

But it was a rudderless society, trying to navigate the transition without guidance or direction, partly because no one had traveled their path before, but even more distressingly because the city had a severe shortage of elders to watch over the flock.

And while this shortage was perhaps less of a problem than it could have been because of the Atlantian tradition of a more community approach to child-rearing than practiced by humans, it still left a lot of young adults without enough direct supervision, which meant delinquency, vandalism, fights, and–

"Hey baby, you got a curvy back. Want me to fill it up?"

–street harassment.

"You'll need to find an elder desperate enough to rub wrists with, dux'ah shit," Benexx shouted back reflexively without even looking over zer shoulder to see which infantile jackass had said it.

Zer retort was met with a chorus of *oohs, daayms,* and *frosteds* from the offender's little posse of friends. Benexx glanced back just long enough to see them mocking zer by rubbing their wrists together in zer direction, the

Atlantian gesture for masturbation. Everyone loitering around the café table laughed freely. Everyone, that is, except the harasser who Benexx had burned up like a meteorite.

Zer harasser, unable to handle or contain zer embarrassment, jumped up out of zer chair and stalked off towards Benexx as ze calmly walked down the boulevard. Ze reached out a four-fingered hand, slapped it down on Benexx's shoulder, and let the thousands of tiny suckers coating it adhere to Benexx's skin like glue.

Ze spun Benexx around to face zer straight on. Benexx recognized zer then. Jolk. Ze was one of the oldest of Shambhala's Atlantians, besides Benexx zerself who had been the very first. But Benexx was a bearer. Zer body had developed fast, but tapered off while the other children kept growing right on through their first transition. Jolk was almost a full head taller than zer, and stronger.

Benexx laughed anyway.

"What's so funny, changfu?"

"Oh, so not wanting your larvae wriggling around in my back makes me a changfu? I think you've got that backwards, loser."

The skin on Jolk's face flickered and darkened in anger. "The only thing I'm going to have backwards is you bent over that table," ze said, dripping with a repulsive mix of false machismo and bruised ego.

Benexx kept smiling. "You'll need to be fast, then."

"What the fuck is that supposed to–"

A hand came down on Jolk's shoulder, a human hand. Unlike the modified tentacles gripping Benexx's shoulder, this hand drew its strength from sinuous tendons leading to muscles in a bulging forearm. Humans made up for their lack of suckers through sheer, crushing grip strength. Strength that clamped down on Jolk's shoulder like a vice. Atlantian bodies lacked the calcified bones of humans, and therefore lacked their "pressure points". But what Atlantians did have was a decentralized nervous system that extended out from the brain and main spinal trunks to each of their four limbs. These limbs operated under a great deal of local control, to the point that, if severed in combat, an arm would continue to choke its enemy until the oxygen in its muscles burned up.

However, while this system held distinct advantages for the practiced and educated few, it also held a severe disadvantage. Namely, if you knew exactly where to press, the neurons trying to coordinate between the brain and the peripheral nervous system would fall into a paralyzing, and exceedingly uncomfortable, feedback loop.

Which is how, despite being almost twenty centimeters shorter than the Atlantian, Korolev brought Jolk to zer knees with no apparent effort.

"Is there a problem here, Benexx?" Korolev asked his best friend's adoptive child.

Benexx looked down at zer harasser. "No problem, uncle. Jolk here was just making me laugh." Ze didn't bother trying to hide zer distain. But, the lesson had been taught. Letting it linger served no purpose. "Let zer up."

Korolev nodded and released his hand.

Jolk shot up, rubbing zer shoulder. "Not fair shorting someone out from behind like that. No honor in it, ruleman."

"Ruleman" was a contraction of "rule" and "human," an insult the Atlantians threw at Shambhala's constables and soldiers, the ones they didn't think earned the respect of the title "truth-digger." All were equal under the law in Shambhala, which made no distinctions between human and Atlantian. But the constable force was primarily human, which had led to tensions and accusations of racial bias more than once.

Korolev shrugged. "Like how you threatened to take my friend from behind, big guy?"

"We were just playing around, ruleman. You wouldn't understand."

"Oh, I think I understand just fine, Jolk, was it?" He leaned in until his chest was almost touching Jolk's. "And anytime you feel like 'just playing around,' you come find me."

Despite his smaller size, the implied threat carried real weight. Humans were solidly built, stocky, and simply full of rigid bones. Their hands didn't have the grip of an Atlantian, but they made up for it by curling into bone-filled clubs set into spear shafts for arms. Not to mention their sharp elbows, feet, and punishing kneecaps.

A skilled Atlantian fighter could grapple a human opponent into a pretzel. A skilled human fighter could beat an Atlantian opponent to a bloody pulp. Pick your poison.

The trouble with policing the Atlantians in Shambhala from zer Uncle Korolev's point of view was simple; they didn't have plants, and therefore didn't fall down when he pulled out his stun stick. Which meant he, and the rest of the force, had to get very good at hand-to-hand combat. Which, being serious about his job, Korolev had. Between patrol and the football field, he'd probably been in more scraps with Atlantians than any other human alive. He'd come out ahead in those fights more often than not, and made sure *everyone* knew it.

Jolk backed away, suddenly smiling. "Maybe someday soon, ruleman. Maybe *real* soon."

"Don't wait too long, kiddo. I'm not getting any younger." Korolev looked over at Benexx, who was almost exactly at his eye level, and held out his arm. "Walk with me?"

Benexx put zer arm through his. "Of course, uncle." They walked, Korolev holding zer up so no one would notice zer knees shaking.

"Walk straight, keep your feet under you," Uncle Korolev said so only ze could hear. "Don't let them see you shaking."

Benexx nodded. Ze'd been lucky in the people who

had insisted ze call them "uncle."

"Are they still watching us?"

"Of course they are. They're like an ulik pack, looking for weakness. Show them strength and they scatter."

"How can you be so sure? You're not even the same species."

Korolev hung his head. "I was young and full of testosterone once too, or whatever you guys use instead. Some things are universal, I think."

"What happened to that headstrong boy, uncle?"

"I grew up."

Benexx giggled. "Have you, now?"

"Mostly. You hungry?"

"Starving!"

"Sushi kabob?"

"No. Hot dog. I want a damned half-meter Chicago dog buried in so many onions and tomatoes and peppers and mustard that I can't taste the soy meat."

"Redd's Hots it is."

CHAPTER SIX

"Is ze mad at me?" Benson asked.

"Of course ze's mad at you," his wife said. "Ze's a teenager. We *just* talked about this, Bryan."

"But why?" he said, trying to hide the hurt and disappointment he felt. "I spent half the month's food allotment on this meal."

"It's not about the meal, Bryan," Theresa said as she picked through the tastier bits of her salad. "Which *was* a little overcooked, by the way."

"Then what is it about?"

Theresa shrugged. "Fuck if I know. I'm still amazed we kept zer alive this long."

"That's not funny."

"I wasn't joking," Theresa said as she poured herself a fresh glass of red wine. "We've been raising an alien, Bryan. Forget ear infections and colic, remember when ze almost died when ze was three because zer salt gland wasn't purging properly? Who the hell knows to look for that?"

"Well, we do, now."

"And we're never, ever, doing it again." Theresa shook her glass at him. "Do you hear me?"

"I wouldn't dream of it, even if my boys suddenly remembered which way to swim again."

Theresa drained the contents of her glass in an impressive gulp. "Do we have any ice cream?"

Benson shook his head. "Sorry, I finished it last night."

"Wine for dessert it is." Theresa poured the remainder of the bottle into her glass, nearly to the top.

Benson raised an eyebrow, then slid down onto the couch beside her. "You should've told Benexx to be back at midnight."

"Oh yeah, big boy?" Theresa rested a hand on his thigh and started stroking it. She was almost fifty, but damn if she hadn't aged with the same grace and subtlety as the wine she was drinking. Benson was pushing fifty-three, but he too had been fighting a gallant battle against old age, a battle he was still winning, even if it seemed to get exponentially harder with each passing decade.

He ran a gentle hand through his wife's raven black hair, only recently tinged with silver, tickling the back of her ear with each pass. "How long has it been since we really enjoyed the living room?"

"Hmm, good question. I think it was Benexx's first summer in G'tel, so, four years?"

"Far too long." Benson leaned in and kissed Theresa's pouting lips with the same sort of passion and hunger she'd elicited for twenty years. She kissed him back, hard, grabbing a handful of his hair as she drew his body closer to hers. Within moments, his manhood strained at the confines of his trousers, eager for escape… and release.

Theresa, only too happy to oblige, shifted herself underneath his body and threw a leg around his waist and started to giggle as her blouse came undone.

Benson lifted off her to take a moment to enjoy the view. "We have to stop meeting like this," he said, quoting some dumb movie she'd made him watch in the little classics theater back in Avalon module when they'd first started dating. He couldn't remember the title, but he did remember the end of the date.

Theresa smiled, grabbed him by the lapels, and pulled him into her waiting skin.

<Ring, ring,> someone said through his plant com.

Not the tonal *ring* of an incoming call, someone actually spoke the words. And Benson recognized the voice.

<Jesus Christ, Feng. Did you just 'ring' at me?>

<I did.>

<Why?>

<Because I know how much you hate it when I don't ring first.>

"What's wrong?" Theresa asked.

Benson pointed at his head. "Chao."

Theresa's nose wrinkled. "Seriously? Tell him to call back and hang up."

"What a wonderful idea."

<You'll want to hear this, Bryan. Or actually, probably not, but you do *need* to hear it.>

<Why didn't you actually ring and let me decide?>

<Because if I actually rang, it would have been logged through the central switchboard software and recorded.>

That gave Benson pause. <This isn't being recorded?>

<No.>

<Why?>

<Because we're not having this conversation.>

<We're not?>

<Absolutely not, and it's ridiculous that you would even suggest such a thing.>

Benson sighed. <Shambhala's Chief Constable is lying under me with her tits out. Want to *not* talk with her too?>

<The two of you are alone?>

Benson snorted. <Obviously.>

<Then yes, that would be lovely.>

Benson looked at his wife. "Cover up, dear. We have to take this."

"We do?"

"Yep."

Theresa buttoned up her shirt and growled like a dog who'd just had her bone stolen. Which, Benson realized, she had.

"To be continued, dear." Benson transferred the call to the living room's far wall and scaled the picture down so Feng's head wasn't two meters tall.

"This better be good, captain," Benson said, putting just a hint of strain on the last word.

"It won't be boring, I promise you that," the head floating on the wall said.

Theresa sipped her wine, simmering.

Feng cleared his throat. "As you know, two days ago we launched the shuttle *Atlantis* on a mission to the radio telescope project on the dark side of Varr as part of the Early Warning network."

"Yeah," Benson said. "Benexx told us all about it. Jian is leading his first mission, right?"

"Indeed."

"You must be very proud of him," Theresa said genuinely, her annoyance at the coitus interruptus set aside for the moment.

"I am, thank you. But there's more you probably haven't heard. Along with the telescope service mission, *Atlantis* was also tasked with repairing one of our Helium-3 harvesters on the other side of Varr."

"You're right, we didn't hear about that," Benson said.

Feng shrugged. "I'm not surprised. One of the harvesters got stuck in a hole a couple days before launch. We threw a small crew of techs together that would be dropped off to deal with it while the *Atlantis* delivered the receiver to the telescope crater. We put out a press release, but I doubt it got much traction on the net. Pulling a harvester out of a pothole just isn't very sexy compared to the Early Warning network coming online or progress on the Alcubierre prototype."

"But..." Benson said, "something changed."

"Yeah, you could say that." Feng's head shrank to a corner of the display, replaced by what looked like orbital photos of the surface of Varr. "When *Atlantis* inserted into Varr's orbit earlier today, they found the harvester all right." The image zoomed in to a speck in the center to show one of the now-familiar six-wheeled vehicles working overtime to keep the Ark's fusion reactors burning along and Shambhala's lights on. Its front starboard side wheel hung out over a black, roughly circular chasm.

"That's a heck of a pothole," Theresa said.

"Indeed," Feng agreed. "It turned out to be a ceiling collapse. The hole goes down some thirty meters."

"An old lava tube?" Benson asked.

"That was our first thought, but it's not the right geology for it," Feng answered. "Too much ice in the top layers of Varr's crust. So we ordered *Atlantis* to a lower orbit for a closer look and..." A new, larger image appeared. The hole was no longer black, nor was it empty.

"Are those... Are those structures?" Theresa said.

"Yes indeed," Feng replied. "One of them seems to be a small outbuilding, but the other is considerably larger, and extends quite a way into the ice. The hole only represents a small percentage of the total cavern."

"What the hell are buildings doing buried on Varr?" Benson asked. "Who built them?"

"That's the billion-dollar question, isn't it?" Feng said.

The image switched again, this time to a video feed, probably coming from a helmet-mounted camera. The structure was centered in the frame at ground-level, bleached out in the harsh light of LED lamps. But, right in the middle of the video, two suited crewmembers stood on either side of a circular indentation in the wall, a line running diagonally through the middle of it that looked suspiciously like a door.

"You sent them *into* the hole?" Theresa said, barely containing her disbelief.

"We needed to survey it," Feng answered.

"Send a damned drone!"

"There weren't any packed onto the shuttle. Nobody anticipated needing one."

"Is this a live feed?" Benson asked.

"Yes, well, a couple seconds delayed because of distance and buffering, but it's effectively real-time."

"Where's the audio?" Benson said.

"There isn't any right now. Some software glitch. We can talk to the shuttle, and the shuttle can talk to them, but something's gone wrong in the relays between their suits and the shuttle and the shuttle to here. Techs are working on it."

"What are they doing?" Theresa asked.

"Trying to get inside," Feng said.

"Are you crazy?" Theresa snapped. "That's your son down there."

"It was his idea," Feng answered. "He's commanding the mission, and he's more than a day away by shuttle. He's making the calls right now."

"And that doesn't bother you?"

"Are you kidding? I'm scared shitless. But our people here have already analyzed the images for freeze/thaw cycles, dust accumulation rates, et cetera, and come to a tentative determination that these structures are between a few hundred thousand and a few million years old."

"That's a pretty broad estimate," Benson observed.

"Yes it is, but there are a lot of variables to account for, some of which we don't have great data sets on yet. Still, a few hundred thousand years is the low end estimate. It's pretty doubtful any monsters are going to come charging out at them."

"But why is it there at all?" Theresa said.

"We have three working hypotheses." Feng held up a finger. "One: At some point in the distant past, the Atlantians were far more advanced than we've ever suspected and had an active space program."

"Which they just misplaced?" Benson said. "Along with anything more technologically advanced than the wheel?"

"We know they have gone through several mass

die-offs due to asteroid impacts. It's conceivable they had achieved a much higher level of technological development, but a sufficiently-sized rock literally knocked them back to the stone age."

"OK, number two?"

Feng counted off another finger. "Two: That a technologically advanced civilization developed independently on either Tau Ceti E or F at some time in the past, set up an outpost on Varr, then disappeared for whatever reason, maybe their own asteroid catastrophe, leaving this installation behind."

"And how likely is it that we've seen absolutely no evidence of an extinct space-faring species on the two closest planets to us in almost twenty years of surveys?" Benson asked.

"More likely than you might think," Feng said. "We've been pretty focused on exploring Gaia. There have only been cursory probes sent out to the rest of the system. F is coming out of a glaciation cycle, and its ice would've scraped clean any signs of cities. We know it has a relatively simple biome of algae and other single-cell scale plants around its tropical latitude coastal areas, so life has a history there. Meanwhile, E is still really volcanically and tectonically active, either of which could wipe out any obvious signs of civilization from orbit given a few million years."

"And the third hypothesis?" Theresa asked.

"Do I really need to say it?"

"No," Theresa said, confirming what they were all thinking. "I suppose not."

"But," Benson injected, "if it was built by the same race that torched Earth, why set up an observation post if they're just going to throw a black hole at the planet anyway?"

Feng shrugged. "Without knowing *why* they chose to destroy Earth, there's no way to guess. Maybe we had grown to a level of technological sophistication that they deemed too advanced and nipped us in the bud before we could pose a direct threat. Maybe they didn't like how badly we were treating Earth in those last few centuries and were afraid we would expand that kind of exploitative recklessness to other systems. Or maybe they didn't like our taste in music, who the hell knows?"

"And you think maybe they had one of these installations in our solar system and we never found it?" Theresa asked.

"Maybe so. It was pure dumb luck we found this one as soon as we did. Even while we were stripmining it for resources, we never directly explored more than a few percent of the surface of the moon, and most of that was at the polls and the Earth-facing side. We never got beyond three medium-sized cities on Mars, and only a few dozen asteroids. If there was one of these places hiding in the Sol system, there were a thousand places to put it that we never got around to searching."

"So you think this is a sort of observation post, keeping track of the Atlantians to make sure they don't get too smart or greedy?" Benson said.

"It's certainly possible. Varr would be a natural place to put it. We're building our own listening post on it, after all. Depending on how good its instruments are, it could potentially keep tabs on all three planets in Tau Ceti's habitable zone. But as I said, that's only one hypothesis."

"What do you think the odds of each one are?"

Feng shook his head. "I haven't the slightest idea how to start weighing all the variables and probabilities to even take a crack at guessing. Which is why we need to get inside it and look around."

"Okaaay," Benson said slowly. "But, aside from ruining any chance at a restful night's sleep for my wife and I–"

"I wasn't trying to *sleep* just now," Theresa said angrily.

"Yes, dear. But as I was saying, Chao, why call off the record and tell us about this? You're deliberately keeping it out of the media or we would've heard already."

"That we are, for the time being. No, I called because Shambhala's chief constable would need to be prepared for civil unrest when we do make the news public."

"Thanks for that," Theresa said.

"You're welcome, but also because you, Bryan, have a rather annoying habit of getting mixed up in these sorts of things whether anyone invites you or not and I thought I would get ahead of it this time."

"Thanks?"

"What are we going to do next?" Theresa asked.

"I'm open to suggestions," Feng answered.

"You should pull your son and his team out of there and get them burning back for the Ark as soon as possible."

"And then grab one of the leftover nukes in the bomb vault and drop it in the hole from orbit for good measure," Benson added.

Feng was about to respond when something on the live feed caught all of their attentions. The circle in the installation's wall glowed amber for a moment. The cameraman, Jian Feng according to the suit's data readout in the bottom corner of the image, took a step forward and put a gloved hand on the doorway.

To everyone's surprise, the surface gave way like quicksand as Jian's hand sunk into it. He tried to pull back, but it held him fast. He instinctually stuck out his other hand to try to push away, only to have it too become lodged in the amorphous material. His heartrate spiked as the suddenly gooey material began to lurch up his forearms, pulling him into itself.

"Jian!" his father shouted. Hands flashed in front of the camera as other members of the team grabbed his suit and tried to pull him free. But it was useless. The undulating surface of the wall inched closer and closer to the camera even as Jian's convulsions to free himself reached fever pitch. With a pulse, the liquid rushed out and enveloped Jian and the camera in blackness.

Then, there was only static.

CHAPTER SEVEN

<Whoa,> Rakunas said into the team's plant link. <Ah, commander?>

Jian looked up from the small rubble pile he was still clearing to where Rakunas stood near the door. The circular depression they all assumed was an airlock glowed a faint amber color, pulsing gently.

<What did you do, Rakunas?>

<Nothing! I moved a damned rock, just like you're doing.>

Jian hopped over to stand next to Rakunas as they both watched the doorway. After a moment, the amber glow faded away. Jian cranked up his suit's floodlight and leaned in for a closer inspection.

<Careful, sir.>

Jian stole a glance at Rakunas even as the rest of the team clustered around them. He took a deep breath, then reached out a hand and placed it on the door. It was hard to tell through his thick, heavily-insulated glove, but the surface felt a little less solid than he'd expected, almost putty-like. He pressed down a little harder and the surface gave way entirely, almost as if he'd broken its surface tension. In an instant, his hand sank into the door all the way up to his wrist.

<Oh fuck,> he blurted out. Reflexively, Jian put his other hand on the door and tried to push away, only to watch in horror as that hand sank into the muddy surface as well.

<Help!> Jian shouted as the sticky goop started to creep up his forearms. Rakunas got behind him, grabbed his suit, and pulled for all he was worth. But the material fought back, actively pulling him towards it instead of just immobilizing him.

<For God's sake, help me!> Jian repeated as the surface drew relentlessly closer to his helmet.

<I can't hold on,> Rakunas said, his voice straining with panic even through the plant to match Jian's own.

<Forget it! Get back!> Jian ordered even as a black spot appeared on his helmet's face shield where the amorphous material reached out and touched it. Tendrils snaked out from the spot, expanding its grip, connecting, interlinking, growing, until he could see nothing at all. Pressure built on his suit from all directions. The "Loss of Signal" alert flashed red in the corner of his vision as his plant link to the outside was severed. He struggled against the viscus mass pressing in on him from all sides, but it held him fast.

Jian's heart pounded so hard he thought it might break his sternum. "Shit! Shit, shit, shit…" he said over and over. Was this a booby trap? Was he to be frozen in here forever? Digested like an unwary insect caught in a Venus flytrap? He checked his O2 and battery levels.

Three more hours of each. Well, at least he'd be long dead before any digesting occurred.

But then, the pressure on his fingers eased, then disappeared entirely. The relief traveled up his palms, wrists, and arms. Freed from the muck, his helmet's floodlights bathed a new scene with their white light. One of Jian's feet came loose from the wall, then the other. Off balance, he managed to catch himself before toppling over to the floor.

His plant link was still offline, but he was free. The space around him was little more than a tunnel with a small swelling in the middle. Circular supports built into the walls reminded Jian of a human windpipe. On a hunch, he cut off his helmet's floodlights for a few seconds. Sure enough, as soon as his eyes were able to adjust, he saw the same dim amber glow coming from the ringed segments of the walls.

The tunnel was a good thirty or forty meters long, and angled further down into the crust before reaching what looked like a Y-junction. The inside surface of the tunnel itself looked like it had seen better days. Everywhere, flakes of paint or some other protective coating peeled free of the surface. Here and there, the ice outside had pressed in hard enough to dent the inner walls. Daggers of rock hard, razor-sharp ice pierced the walls themselves in several places.

Jian turned around to inspect the doorway that had just spit him out. His first guess had been right; it was an airlock after all, just not at all like those he was used to. It was better, in fact. For centuries, humans had used two pressure doors with a chamber in between to access space. The trouble was, you could never really pump *all* of the air out of the chamber between cycles, and even the very best pressure doors and seals, built to the very highest tolerances, still leaked air, even if incredibly slowly.

No solution to this had even been found. During its two-plus-century exodus from Earth, the Ark had lost nearly the equivalent of an entire habitat's worth of atmosphere to these invisible thieves. This had been planned for ahead of time with air kept in storage tanks in the engineering module to replace the losses.

But with this... goo, the seal was perfect. Hardly a molecule or atom of atmosphere would be lost during the transition. Jian guessed the entire facility might be coated in a layer of it to preserve integrity against micrometeorite impacts or other unexpected visitors. He made a note to grab a sample of it before they left.

Much to Jian's surprise, his suit's pressure and atmospheric sensors beeped an alert and spit out a reading. There was an oxygen/nitrogen atmosphere in here. It was only seventeen percent Earth sea level pressure and more than seventy degrees below zero, but both values slowly rose as he watched.

The facility was active. It had recognized his presence and prepared itself for use. The realization froze Jian in his tracks. There were really only two possibilities: either the facility was automated and still functional after hundreds of thousands or even millions of years, or someone else was already in here, perhaps still in *here*. He couldn't decide which scenario was more unsettling, but at least whatever was in charge was working to make the environment more hospitable to their visitors, not less.

Still, Jian realized just how acutely alone he was. Well, if the airlock let him in, it stood to reason it would let him back out. He took a deep breath and put his palms flat against the doorway. As before, the surface responded, slowly at first, but then the wormlike tendrils laced their way up his arms more quickly. It probably needed to loosen up after sitting idle for so long. Jian could relate. Even a week away from the gym and he was stiff as a board.

The process felt faster the second time, although frankly the difference in perception could probably be chalked up to the fact his first trip through had been spent in paralyzing terror. It did feel slightly warmer this time, however. The pressure on his hands eased again and soon he stepped back out into the cavern. The "Loss of Signal" alert disappeared as his plant rejoined the local link.

<Stay where you are!> Rakunas shouted from behind one of the small piles of debris, holding a pretty sizable rock over his head in a threatening manner.

Jian put his hands up. <Whoa now, what the hell are you doing Rakunas?>

<Who are you?>

<Don't be stupid.>

<I mean, how can we be sure you're really the commander?>

<Of course it's me, Rakunas. Who the hell else would it be?>

<I don't know, a clone or something.>

<You think somebody grew a clone of me in two minutes?>

<OK, fine, but what about an android?>

Jian went to pinch the bridge of his nose, only to have his glove bounce off his helmet glass. <This isn't some space horror movie, Rakunas.> He pointed back at the doorway. <It's an airlock, just like we thought. It's just a really clever one. There's a tunnel on the other side that leads deeper into the crust. There's a lot more beyond it, too.>

<What the hell is going on over there?> Kirkland said from her seat back on the shuttle.

<We're good,> Rakunas said. <The commander has reappeared and he assures me he's not a pod person or something.>

<And you're just going to take his word?> Kirkland said.

<Seriously, what the fuck is wrong with you two?> Jian asked.

<OK, that's him,> Kirkland said. <Ark Actual is on the line. He's freaking out.>

<No time for that now,> Jian said. <Tell Ark Actual I'm fine and that Rakunas and I are reentering the structure.>

<We are?> Rakunas said.

<Yes. We are. We've got enough charge and O2 to burn an hour down there, and I'm going to use it.>

<Let me know how that turns out,> Rakunas said as he turned towards the ropes leading back to the surface.

<Oh no you don't.> Jian grabbed the recovery handle on the back of Rakunas's life support pack and casually tossed him at the airlock.

<I'm quite certain this wasn't taught in Officer

Candidate School,> Rakunas said as he floated through the airless cavern before landing a meter away from the airlock.

<Commander,> Kirkland said. <Flight Control has issued a recall order. The mission is aborted, return to *Atlantis*.>

<Sorry, XO, but you lost your plant uplink with Rakunas and I before you were able to deliver the abort order.> Jian hurried over and pushed a still-reluctant Rakunas into the airlock.

<But I just delivered it!>

<What was that?> Jian said. <You're breaking up.>

<I said you're an asshole who's only doing this to give your father a heart attack, and be careful, idiot.>

Jian smirked, then stretched out his arms and fell backwards into the gooey embrace of the alien airlock. <Roger that,> he said just before the "Loss of Signal" alert reappeared.

His third trip through was *definitely* faster than the first two, and warmer. Once on the other side, Jian found Rakunas staring down the tunnel. Their plants linked up automatically.

<Well, what do you think?> he asked.

<It looks like a colonoscopy,> Rakunas answered.

<Ugh. Thanks for putting that image in my head.>

Rakunas shrugged. <You asked. There's air in here?>

Jian checked his suit sensors. Pressure was up to twenty-one percent Earth sea level and the temperature had climbed another six degrees. <Yeah, even more of it than when I was in here a minute ago. I think this place is getting itself ready for us.>

<Fuck that, I've seen enough sci-fi movies. I'm not taking this helmet off for anything.>

<Fair enough.> Jian started hopping down the tunnel.

<Where are you going?> Rakunas called out.

<Deeper. Where does it look like I'm going?>

<Deeper into an alien ass.> Rakunas sighed. <This was

supposed to be a milk run.>

<We're nowhere near where the milk comes from.> Jian started hopping down the ramp. Skipping, really. The truth was, now that the abject horror had passed, he found himself feeling excited, ecstatic, verging on euphoria. He hadn't felt this alive since his first solo flight down and back the entire length of the Ark in an EVA pod.

They reached the junction at the bottom of the tunnel, where it split into two smaller tunnels, each heading off at forty-five degree angles, like a windpipe heading to a pair of lungs, just reinforcing Jian's original impression, which he vastly preferred over Rakunas's.

He pointed a finger down each passageway. <Two tunnels, two of us. Which one do you like?>

Rakunas's shoulders slacked. <Have you seriously never seen a horror movie?>

<Not really my thing.>

<You *never* split up.>

<OK.> Jian paused. <Any other rules?>

<Don't be the blonde girl or the black guy.>

Jian looked himself and Rakunas over. <I think we pass that test. So, which way?>

<Rock-paper-scissors?>

<Really?>

<Left I win, right you win.>

<Are you kidding me right now? We're inside a hidden alien base hundreds of thousands of years old and we're making decisions with an RPS game?>

Rakunas gestured towards the branching tunnels. <You favor one over the other?>

Jian regarded each tunnel with a critical eye, but it was no use. They were indistinguishable. <I suppose not.>

Rakunas held out a fist. <Then shoot.>

Jian was fairly certain that, based on his extensive officer candidate training, Rakunas was being an insubordinate little shit right now. But, everyone processes stress differently. So, he balled up a fist and started to shoot.

<One, two–>

<Wait!>

<Wait what!?>

<Shoot *on* three?>

<Yes, Goddammit. One, two, three!>

<Because some people do one, two, three, shoot!>

<On three, stop stalling. One. Two. Three!>

Jian's paper suffocated Rakunas's rock. <Ha! Right it is,> he said in triumph.

<Best two out of three!>

<Go to hell.> Jian started skipping down the right tunnel without looking back to see if Rakunas followed. The tunnel was level, as far as Jian could tell. It was also quite a bit shorter than the ramp leading down to it. Another round door with a diagonal slash across its face just like the airlock that had brought them here. But when he pressed a glove to it, instead of pulling him in, the door split down the diagonal and spread open with a hiss. Not an airlock, then, just a standard door. And why not? Beyond the open door, Jian's floodlights shined into a spherical chamber.

An alert dinged in Jian's suit. The local atmosphere had stabilized at ninety-three percent Earth sea-level and twenty-two degrees. A perfect spring day on Gaia below. The nitrogen/oxygen ratio had also normalized to Gaia standards.

<This place thinks we're Atlantians,> Jian said.

<Well, it's the safest bet,> Rakunas added while reviewing his own suit's data.

Jian smiled. <It just happens to be wrong this time.>

That was when the bugs swarmed out of the door like a Biblical plague.

<What the shit!> Rakunas shouted as the flood of fist-sized, segmented, multi-limbed creatures came rushing towards them. For a brief, horrible moment,

Jian remembered one of the few scary movies he *had* seen as a child, about an Egyptian mummy come back to life and the cataclysms that followed. An unfortunate background character had been eaten alive by a swarm of beetles, stripped to the bone in seconds. But Jian wasn't a background character, was he?

That image was firmly burrowed in Jian's mind as the swarm approached. For the second time in an hour, fear froze him solid. But as the revolting mass of creatures reached his feet, they ignored him and Rakunas entirely, flowing around them like water flowing around river rocks.

Instead, they busied themselves with the facility itself. Some tended to the peeling layers of paint, snipping them loose with pincers, then consuming the peel before regurgitating a fresh layer to replace what was lost. Jian looked back up the tunnel they'd come down. Other creatures lined up with tiny fissures, then liquefied themselves before hardening again, permanently sealing the breach. Still others concentrated over the largest dents and ice intrusions. They burned through the icy daggers with tiny lasers and let them fall to the floor, then assembled into a mass like a hammer and started pounding out the dent. Before long, the intrusion was driven back as the tunnel segment returned to its proper shape.

<They're maintenance drones,> Jian said, hardly believing what he was watching even as he said it.

<Looks like they might be made of the same goop as the airlock,> Rakunas added.

<Programmable goop.> Jian marveled at the implications and potential. Humans had nanites, of course. They were used extensively in medicine and in the repair of nano-scale systems like computer components. But this sort of macro-scale application of microscopic machines had eluded them thus far. The bandwidth needed to keep trillions of individual machines connected,

not to mention the noise and interference trillions of tiny wireless transmitters produced in such a small volume were huge problems that had yet to be cracked.

<This whole place is automated,> Jian said, <even the repairs.>

<Well then why are they only doing repairs now?> Rakunas asked, still on the verge of running back up the tunnel to the surface had it not been crawling with bugs. <This place has been beaten up for a long time.>

<It only just restarted,> Jian answered as a line of bug drones carried one of the chunks of ice they'd cut free away to... wherever they took such things. <It was in standby mode or whatever until just now when we showed up. It was waiting for us.>

<It was waiting for the Atlantians, you mean. To develop a space program.>

<Maybe, I don't know.>

<The ceilings are awfully tall in here,> Rakunas said. He had a point. Jian hadn't thought about it until just then, but an average Atlantian would fit perfectly in these tunnels, which were just a bit oversized for him. Curiosity getting the better of him, Jian reached down into the stream of bug drones and grabbed one by the thorax.

<Commander! Touching creepy-ass bug things is *definitely* against the rules,> Rakunas shouted, but Jian held up a hand.

<It's OK,> he said even as the little bug's legs thrashed about, trying to regain its footing. Jian held his other hand beneath it, gently settling down into his palm.

<When that thing burrows into your skull and turns you into a space zombie, I'm giving my I-told-you-so to your father.>

<Shhh,> Jian scolded. The tiny drone reared up on its back legs and waved its pincer appendages. Jian held his hand further away from his face and readied to shake it loose from his glove, but it quickly settled down once

more. Its... head, for lack of a better term... cocked to one side, and carefully regarded Jian with three green-glowing eyes.

Jian smiled at it. "Hello," he said aloud into his helmet, despite the fact it couldn't hear him through the glass, and didn't speak English even if it could. "You're a cute little creepy-ass bug thing." Jian blinked.

It blinked back. Or, more specifically, turned its three little green eyes off, then back on again.

Jian blinked again.

It blinked again.

Jian winked his left eye.

It winked its left eye.

Jian winked his right eye.

It winked its right eye.

Then, it winked its center eye.

"Ah..." Jian said.

The little drone turned off all its eyes and waved its pincers around in the air.

<What's going on, commander?>

Jian turned to face Rakunas and pointed at the bug drone sitting on his palm. <I think this thing is laughing at me.>

<Want me to smoosh it?>

<No!> Jian pulled his hand back protectively. The small drone took advantage of the proximity and jumped onto his shoulder, where it spun around in a circle before settling down. Jian's helmet prevented him from seeing where it had ended up. <Ah, what's it doing?> he asked.

<Just nesting on your shoulder, from the looks of it.>

<Not getting ready to stick a needle in my neck or something?>

<Not that I can see.>

<Cool. Always wanted a pet. I'm naming him Polly.>

<Why Polly?>

<Oh, Mr Movie Expert has never seen a pirate film?>

<Yes, but that's a really messed-up looking parrot.>

<C'mon, let's follow.>

<Follow what?> Rakunas said.

Jian pointed at the retreating drones. <Follow them.>

With Polly watching him intently from its perch on his shoulder, Jian and Rakunas crossed the threshold into the large, spherical chamber at the end of the hallway. There was a small walkway that led straight across the room to a door on the far side. At the exact center of the walkway was a round platform, with what looked like six slightly oversized chairs arranged in a circle facing outward to the inner surface of the spherical wall.

Jian walked across to the platform, then sat down in one of the too-big chairs.

<Is that a good idea?> Rakunas said.

<Doubt it, but my feet hurt from standing all day.>

<In three and a half percent gee?>

<I have very sensitive feet.> Jian wasn't particularly tall to begin with, which made his feet dangle from the tall chair all the more. But where it was tall, it was also narrow. With the added bulk of his vacuum suit around his legs and hips, it was a very snug fit indeed.

The chair seemingly noticed his predicament. Much to Jian's surprise, it morphed itself beneath him, lowering its stance and giving his hips more room.

<Now, that's better. Grab a seat, Rakunas.>

<Thanks, but I think I'll stand.>

Jian shrugged and stroked the armrests. <Suit yourself.> Just then, Polly stirred on his shoulder and skittered down Jian's arm. It came to a stop on the right side armrest, then stuck its abdomen into the chair like it was jacking into a computer outlet. Which, frankly, was probably exactly what it was doing. Small lines of green and amber light traced pulsing trails at odd angles through the surface of the chair.

<What's Polly doing?> Rakunas said.

<Taking a piss. How the hell should I know?>

They didn't have to wait long for the answer. All

around the two of them, the inside of the sphere lit up like a Chinese New Year's parade. Within seconds, they were sitting dead center inside an achingly-lifelike holographic projection of Gaia. But it didn't have the slight haze and translucence of their own holographic projectors. This was crystal clear and completely opaque. As the world spun slowly around them, Jian felt like he could reach out and touch it. But, something was... off. He couldn't quite put his finger on it until–

<It's backwards,> Rakunas said. <I mean, it's a mirror image. Look...> He pointed to the now-familiar coastline of Shambhala sitting on the delta of the New Amazon river, then traced his finger east across the Sukal ocean to where the village of G'tel sat next to its seaport.

Something in Jian's perception flipped, like looking at an optical illusion. <No, it's right. We're wrong.>

<What do you mean? That's obviously Atlantis, but the wrong way round.>

<Yeah, but look at that mountain ridge to the north. That's not supposed to be there, that's the Dwellers' canyon. Look where we are, Rakunas. This is how a topographical map of Gaia would appear if you were looking up from the planet's core. Which is where we are in this representation.>

<Who looks out at a planet from its core?>

<Somebody who looks at things quite a bit differently.>

Then, bright icons flashed to life next to Shambhala, its small wildcat settlements, G'tel, the Dweller caverns, and every one of the several dozen villages on the Atlantians' road network. Characters appeared next to them, in a wavy form of calligraphy Jian had never seen before in any Atlantian scrolls or texts. The strings of symbols spooled out, then curled in on themselves as new ones entered, spiraling inward before disappearing once they reached the center. Soon, dozens of whirlpools of indecipherable text spun dizzily all across the immense room, trying to convey information or raw data that Jian couldn't even begin to guess at.

Indeed, the format was giving him vertigo. The damned spirals weren't even all spinning in the same direction. It was like trying to read the inside of a kaleidoscope. Jian had to look away. <Damn, that's going to give me a migraine.>

<You sure weren't wrong about seeing things differently,> Rakunas commented.

Polly removed its abdomen from the armrest and turned back around to gaze up into Jian's visor.

<We don't know what any of those symbols mean,> he said, both aloud in his helmet and into his plant link out of habit, not that there was any chance the little drone could hear, or understand either. And yet, Polly looked back at the three-dimensional map of Gaia, then back at him. Jian shrugged and held his hands out, palm up, uncomprehendingly.

The swirling patterns quit abruptly, although the icons and the rest of the simulation continued unabated.

<Did he...> Rakunas pointed at Polly. <Did he just turn those psychedelic swirls off? Because you asked him to?>

<I think he may have,> Jian replied, edging up against the limits of how weirded out even he was comfortable being.

<But he's a bug.>

<A bug made out of nanites networked into a million year-old, self-repairing alien base.> Jian held out his hand, which Polly happily climbed back onto. <I think he's meant to be an avatar, or a guide, or something.>

The inverted image of Gaia abruptly stopped spinning before them. Instead, it zoomed in on Shambhala, passing through it entirely before flipping the image back to normal and displaying the city from some height. The space elevator ribbon reached out past them to the other side of the room where it disappeared into infinity. Even at the miniaturized scale of the image, the Ark would rest several kilometers outside the room. The Pathfinder counterweight station, further still.

Smaller icons appeared over important buildings and areas, such as the Beehive, museum, stadium, airstrip, solar farms, seaport, and the beanstalk anchor barge sitting squarely in the Sea of Landing. Next to these simple icons, complex characters appeared, except much larger and more slowly this time. No more than six or seven at once hovered over each landmark. The lines of characters would glow in place for several seconds before disappearing, only to be replaced with identical sets a moment later.

<It's trying to teach us,> Jian said after a moment's thought.

<Teach us what?>

<Its language. Look.> Jian pointed at the recreation of Shambhala. <It's showing us something familiar, landmarks we'll recognize as important and understand the use for.> He pointed at the symbols playing out slowly next to the icons. <That gives us context for the characters.> Jian's discomfort switched over to excitement in the blink of an eye and threatened to boil over at the discovery. <Think back, way back to when you were a little kid on the Ark. How did the educational software modules and games teach us letters and words? With big bright associations to things we already understood. 'A' is for Apple trees with fruit so sweet. 'B' is for Ball so we can play Zero.>

<'C' is for Chlamydia, which was supposed to be eradicated after Earth, but I still somehow got, twice,> Rakunas said. <Yeah, I remember the damned modules. But even if you're right, you're not going to learn a whole new alphabet in the next…> he paused to consult his suit's levels, <…thirty-seven minutes.>

<But–>

Rakunas shook his head. <No buts, sir. We're just here to do an initial survey, and we *were* ordered to abort, if

you'll recall. They'll send over engineers and linguists to study all this stuff. It's not our job. We still have to go deliver the EWN receiver.>

Jian slumped in the chair. Rakunas was, annoyingly, right. He'd gotten caught up in the moment. The initial terror of the first airlock transition had given way to the rush of discovery and the thrill of being the first person to lay eyes on this amazing place. It was intoxicating, which was exactly the problem.

<Five more minutes,> he said, trying very hard not to sound like a kid begging their parents to delay bedtime. <And we're bringing back a sample.>

<What kind of 'sample'?>

Jian pointed at Polly, who obligingly crawled up his finger and sat down on his forearm.

<Him.>

CHAPTER EIGHT

With zer belly full of thirty centimeters of hot dog, chili fries, a hot-tub full of sweet tea, and a single just-a-little-too-hot habanero pepper, Benexx's ravenous craving for crap was finally satiated.

"OK," zer said. "I'm tapping out. Put me in a wheelbarrow and roll me home."

"I'm shocked and a little disturbed that much fit inside you in the first place," Korolev said. "Didn't they feed you in G'tel?"

"Of course they did. All the yulka flatbread and dux'ah jerky I could eat. Which, turns out, isn't very much after the first couple weeks."

"I could see that. Come on kiddo, you're getting close to curfew. I'll call you a pod."

Benexx blanched. "How did you know about my curfew? I didn't say anything about it."

Zer uncle pointed at his temple. "No, but your mother did."

Benexx smirked. "Of course. Sometimes, I forget you've got those things in your heads."

"Won't be too much longer before you'll have one," Korolev said. "Yours was the very first Atlantian brain mapped, after all. You're the natural choice for the first trials."

"And if I don't want one?" Benexx asked gently, but the question still hung in the air for a long moment.

"You've been talking to Mei, I think."

"No, I haven't. Not about the plants, at least. I've just seen how much more... present she is, and Sakiko, and all the other Unbound. When they stare off into space, it's not because they're reading email."

Korolev laughed at this.

"What's funny?"

"You sound like your dad. Did you know in the early days he actually printed out playbooks for the Mustangs players? Like, on paper? He spent a month's 3D printer credits to build the printer from scratch. And another week's worth of pay to have somebody code the software for it."

"Well yeah, his replacement plant never worked right after the Battle of the Black Bridge. It glitches all the time."

Korolev waved it away. "Naw, that's just his excuse. He read everything on tablets long before they had to replace his plant. He'd do everything he could to take calls on viewscreens."

Benexx fell silent, uncomfortable with the comparison to zer father, even if it was meant to be complimentary.

"Jolk isn't going to forget you shorting zer out like that, you know," ze finally said, breaking the quiet. "Didn't anyone tell you that when you were playing against them in football?"

"It never really came up in football. The shoulder pads make it impossible."

Benexx bobbed zer head. "OK, I can see that. Still, it's considered very bad form."

"How bad?" Korolev asked.

"Like, kicking a human male in the balls bad. Even warriors in the heat of battle won't do it."

Korolev winced involuntarily, but held his ground. "Yeah, well I think laying hands on my friend's kid and threatening them with sexual assault is 'bad form.' He's lucky I wasn't on duty or he'd be up on charges."

"Ze," Benexx corrected.

"Hmm?"

"You referred to Jolk as 'he' just now."

"Did I," Korolev said. "Maybe I did. It's just ze was acting so much like a…"

"Man?"

Korolev shrugged. "A teenage boy, really. But yes, zer behavior was really stereotypical of young men."

"Did you act like a stereotypical 'young man' at zer age?"

Korolev put up his right hand. "I invoke my right not to answer under Section Seven of the Ark Treaty."

"Wuss."

Korolev dropped his hand. "Guilty. But we really need to get you home now."

Benexx crossed the threshold back into zer family home with seconds to spare before the clock struck ten. But instead of the expected parental unit tapping a toe in the dining room the lights only came on in the living room once their motion sensors registered her presence. The house was quiet.

"Mom?" ze called into the stillness. The lights activated as Benexx moved through the house. Remnants of dinner lay scattered about the dining room table, cold and forgotten. Ze glanced in the kitchenette, which was in a similar state of disorder. It wasn't like zer parents to waste food, or to leave dishes unwashed. Thrift and cleanliness were lifelong habits that had been beaten into them living for decades onboard the ark, ze expected.

"Dad?" Ze walked down the short hallway to the bedrooms, glancing in ze own messy cave before trying the door to the Master bedroom, expecting it to be locked while zer parents slept; but to zer surprise, it opened with a gentle push. The sheets of their bed were still tucked neatly from being made that morning.

"What the hell?" Benexx said. Ze mother had gone so far as to pester Uncle K about seeing ze stuck to zer curfew, the last thing ze'd expected to find upon returning home was a house that looked like it had been abandoned without so much as a moment's warning.

"House," ze called to the microphones built into the ceiling and connected to the home's interface.

"Yes, Benex?" replied the smooth, synthetic voice, which even after fifteen years had never gotten the drawn-out double x of zer name quite right. Ze'd learned to ignore it.

"Where are my parents?"

"Your parents are not home, currently."

Ugh, stupid VIs, ze thought. "Yes, I can see that. Where are they now?"

"I do not know their present locations."

"What?" ze said, exasperated. Their plants could be tracked anywhere inside Shambhala, the surrounding farms, in the passenger jets, on a lift car, or in the Ark. Either they had run out into the wilderness beyond the network, or they'd turned their locators off from casual inquiries. But why the hell would they do that?

"Call my mother," ze said.

"I'm sorry, but your mother's link is unavailable for calls at this time."

"Call my father, then!"

"I'm sorry, but your father's link is unavailable fo–"

"When did they leave?"

"They left at 7:57pm."

Less than an hour after ze'd ducked out for zer walk. A pit of worry grew and settled in next to the hotdog in zer stomach. Benexx considered zer next step. What would zer mother or Uncle Kexx do when faced with an unexpected disappearance? Or, Xis forbid, zer father?

"Show me the security footage from the time just before they left."

House took a moment to compile the necessary data for zer request. Zer parents, being not only paranoid current or former law-enforcement officers but not-so-minor celebrities, had built certain security features into their home from the ground up, including an interior/exterior surveillance system that recorded everything to be seen or heard in or immediately around their property, save for the bathroom and bedrooms. Another carryover from their prior lives aboard the Ark, where everything was recorded, measured, weighed, logged, and analyzed to death.

Zer parents had left in a hurry, just as the state of the house would suggest. They were surprisingly quiet, saying few words to each other, and then only in clipped sentences and hushed tones. Once out the door, they exchanged a small hug, then set off in different directions, which felt even more ominous. They were obviously upset, but ze'd thought maybe they'd been fighting, not that they did that as much in the last few years.

Benexx rolled back the recording further to try and pinpoint what had gotten them upset enough to go running off in opposite directions late at night. They'd had a conversation in the living room for quite a while, then a call. They were on the call all the way back to 7:13, only a few minutes after ze'd left.

"House, play back the file of the call my parents took, starting at 7:13."

"I'm sorry, Benex, but there was no call beginning at that time."

"The hell there wasn't, I'm watching them talk to the wall on your security footage right now!"

"I'm sorry, Benex, but there was no call beginning at that time."

Benexx realized ze'd balled zer fists. Ze forced zer hands open and flexed zer fingers a few times. Ze'd half-expected the call file to be marked as private and firewalled. But never logged at all? Ze walked over to the wall-mounted interface screen and dug through the various menu prompts until ze found the raw call logs. House was right, there was no trace of any call. Ze went to the deleted file queue, expecting to find it there awaiting permanent erasure, but found nothing. Nor had the queue been purged for the day as other files from the morning and afternoon still sat awaiting erasure.

"What the...?" ze said.

"I'm sorry, Benex, but I did not recognize that request," House said.

"Fuck off." Ze tried to run through the possibilities. The angle of the security camera in the living room only captured zer parents in frame, not the video itself. But it was obvious they were talking and reacting to someone or something, not passively watching a movie or something. Zer father wasn't even that animated watching "film" from the day's football game.

It was definitely a conversation, and seven minutes in, something happened that sent them both into a near-panic. Ze really wanted to know what. Most of the rooms were covered by cameras with overlapping coverage. Maybe ze could catch a look at the wall display off one of them, provided no one had thought to scrub that footage as well.

"House, play all of today's interior security camera feeds on the living room wall display in separate windows simultaneously, starting at 7:13pm."

Twelve feeds arranged themselves in four rows of three on the wall display. Not even Benexx realized there were so many. Most, ze immediately discarded as useless angles and closed, but one view from the kitchenette held some promise, as did a partial shot from the hallway looking out from the bedrooms into the living area. These two images ze maximized and arranged their positions on the display so that they very nearly provided zer with a complete picture of the call, even if its two halves sat at slightly disorienting angles relative to each other and had different resolutions.

The audio wasn't great, especially from the person on the other end of the call, but Benexx didn't really need it anyway. Even with the bifurcated picture and tinny sound, ze recognized Captain Feng easily enough. Jian talked about him often, well, complained about him often. Which was fair enough; ze'd been doing more than zer fair share of complaining about zer clueless parents lately.

After a brief introduction, the screen split to include a new video feed. Two men in vacuum suits, one of which mounted the camera recording the scene. They were inside a cave of some kind, grey rocks mixed with brownish and white marbling, probably various kinds of ices. It wasn't anything like a cave on Gaia, and their gently bouncing movements meant low gravity. So they were somewhere on Varr, which probably meant Jian's mission. But his expedition was taking place in a crater on the moon's dark side, not a cavern.

Then, a building came into focus sticking out from the wall of the cave. Benexx shuddered. Its construction was angular and sloped, but didn't look anything like buildings in either Shambhala or Atlantis. The humans in the video were clearing debris away from what appeared to be a doorway while Chao Feng and zer parents argued about the implications of the discovery with significantly more calm than Benexx felt at that moment.

There wasn't any audio coming from the two men on Varr, but by expanding the ID stamp down in the corner of the image, ze confirmed the camera suit's wearer was Jian and the knot in zer stomach tightened again. Where was he, and what the hell was he doing digging around in a cave? He was a pilot, not an archeologist.

Then, the unthinkable happened. Like, literally unthinkable. The outwardly solid-looking wall turned to goo at Jian's touch and started sucking him towards it.

"No!" Benexx shouted, but the image paid zer no mind. The wall crawled up Jian's forearms, totally ignoring his struggles. Benexx felt suddenly unmoored from reality, as if ze were watching some cheesy found-footage horror movie. Which, ze was, except this one was real, and the first sacrificial victim was one of zer oldest friends.

"No, no, no, no…" Ze pawed at the wall display as if zer hands could latch onto Jian and help pull him back out again, but to no avail. In moments, he was swallowed entirely as the wall reverted to its flat, impassive state.

"What happened?!" Benexx grabbed the sides of zer head. Zer people didn't cry as humans did. They displayed their grief through involuntary flashes of bioluminescence. Benexx's skinglow was blinking like a Christmas tree. "Where did he go? Is he all right?" ze shouted at the uncaring wall. The image froze.

"He's fine," came a voice behind zer. Benexx shrieked and nearly jumped clear out of zer skin. Ze spun around and came face to face with zer father, who ze slapped on the shoulder.

"Dad! You scared the shit out of me! I didn't even hear you come in."

"You were busy." Zer father pointed at the display. "How the hell did you find that? There was no log for that call."

"Ze patched it together from House's security footage," zer mother said. "Didn't you?"

"Well what the fuck was I supposed to do?"

"Language, Squish," zer father said.

"I came home and you were both gone. Your locators were blocked, you weren't taking calls, and when I tried to figure out where you went there's you two having some mystery conversation on the recording that sent you off to who-knows where."

"It was important to keep this secret, Benexx," zer father said.

"So I wasn't supposed to tug at the thread?"

"No."

"Because *you* wouldn't?"

Zer mother giggled at that. "Ze's got you there, my dear."

"Ze takes after you," zer father said.

"How can ze take after either of us?"

"Hey!" Benexx shouted. "Still *gan* standing here!"

"Language in that language too, little one," zer father said.

"I. AM. NOT. A. LITTLE. ONE."

Zer outburst brought silence back to the house. Benexx spoke first. "What happened to Jian?" ze pleaded.

Theresa sighed and nodded her head. Zer father turned to face zer and held out his right hand, pinky extended. "I'll tell you, but you have to pinky swear not to tell anyone."

"I'm not a child anymore, dad. Pretty sure I just yelled about it, in fact."

"Pinky swear."

"Since when do you keep secrets for the crew on the Ark?"

"You've seen enough to know how big a deal this is. We're not going to keep it forever, but we *do* need to know more and have a plan before we go public. Otherwise, we'll be facing riots on two continents. Pinky swear."

"For Xis's sake, I don't even have pinkies."

Unwavering, zer father flexed his pinky in zer face, just like he used to do when ze would act up as a child. "Ugh…" Benexx reached up and curled one of zer four identical tentacle finger-analogues around zer father's bony little digit. "I pinky swear not to tell anyone about whatever the hell happened on Varr."

"How did you know it's on Varr?" zer father asked. Benexx regarded him with a pained expression. "Right, sorry. But you can't tell anyone until your mother or I give you the green light, OK? Not even Sakiko."

"Not even Sakiko," ze agreed after an annoyed sigh. "But I want concessions."

"*Concessions*?" zer mother said. "We're negotiating now?"

"No, ze must mean hotdogs and soda at the next football game," zer father said. "Right?"

Benexx crossed zer arms. "Not exactly. I don't want to be in the First Contact Day Parade. It's exploitative and I'm not going to participate."

Zer father just laughed. "If I have to put up with passing that goddamned statue of me in Pioneers Park on the way to work every day, you can stand on a parade float for an hour."

"But it's not *me* standing up there. It's some stupid symbol."

"And?" zer father said, an edge creeping into his normally warm voice. "Do you really think that's me standing erect in the park–"

"Phrasing, dear," zer mother interrupted.

"–standing *tall* in the park?" he asked without missing a beat. "Or that nonsense they put on the displays in the museum? Think that's how it really went down? No. They're symbols. Propaganda. A bit of polite civic fluff. Something to give the rest of the city something to look up and aspire to. Not the real deal. It's the same for you. I'm sorry, child of mine, I really am, but you're just as much a symbol as I am. Neither of us asked for it, but it isn't about what *we* want." He swept an arm wide to encompass the entire city, maybe the entire planet. "It's about what *they* need to hear. And right now, they need to hear that the first Atlantian child of Shambhala is a well-adjusted young adult who's happy and thriving in our little experiment of a society."

"Even if that's a bald-faced lie?" ze snapped.

"*Especially* if it's a bald-faced lie," zer mother snapped back. Benexx shrunk, suddenly keenly aware of how outnumbered and overpowered ze was. Sometimes, ze'd been able to play zer parents off against one another. More often than not, that involved zer mother and zer ganging up on zer dad until he broke. But, when they presented a united front, well, forget it. They were two of the most intractable, stubborn, and unmoving people ze'd ever met. Of *either* species.

"I'm sorry, Benexx," zer father said, with the usual compassion and warmth pooling back into his voice. "I really am, but the parade appearance has to be off the table. It's bigger than the three of us. Now, do you want to know what happened to Jian or not?"

Ze did.

CHAPTER NINE

The rest of Jian's mission on Varr was far more conventional, much less dangerous, and not nearly as interesting. By some minor miracle, everyone had gotten out of the cavern intact. Jian had his sample from the mystery facility, Polly, locked away in a hermetically-sealed crate tied down snuggly in the cargo bay. Madeja and her techs managed to winch out the stuck harvester and make the necessary repairs to send it back on its way, with a new twenty-kilometer exclusion zone around the facility of course.

They successfully delivered the receiver array to the Early Warning telescope site on the moon's far side and swapped out the shift of techs and construction workers that had spent the last month on site for the fresh ones that came over on the *Atlantis*. They would spend the next month's rotation on the far side of Varr installing and testing the receiver array, out of sight of the Ark or Gaia, with only the constellations and each other for companionship.

If past rotations were any predictor, they would also pass the time fermenting booze out of freeze-dried apple cobbler rations and filming amateur porn in their bunks, because there were certain things about human beings that never changed.

A quick stop at the telescope site's automated fuel factory topped off the shuttle's tanks. The solar-powered rig mined water ice from the moon's surface, melted it, then cracked it into hydrogen and O2. Just the thing to quench a thirsty rocket ship.

"Flight Control," Jian said into the link back to the Ark, "*Atlantis*. We're beginning our final approach. Ten minutes to flip and deceleration burn."

"*Atlantis*, Flight Control. Message acknowledged. Welcome home."

Jian smiled. "Good to be home, Flight."

And it would be, Jian reflected. Instead of the thirty-two hour flight to intercept the approaching moon, the return trip from the retreating Varr had taken almost two full days. As much as he liked his crew, after sharing the tight confines for eight days, the *Atlantis* had begun to smell like the inside of a laundry bag full of week-old gym socks.

"I'm really looking forward to a full gee and fresh water," Kirkland said from the copilot's station.

"You know all the water on the Ark isn't any fresher," Jian said.

"True, but the filtration is way better, it doesn't taste like batteries, and I'm pretty sure that whatever I drink isn't something I just pissed out in the last twenty-four hours."

"No, but somebody else probably did."

Kirkland shrugged. "That's somehow easier to take when I'm not staring at them."

"True enough. I'm looking forward to a shower. A real hot water shower, with soap and a luffa, no more of these moist hand-towel baths."

"Ugh, I hate that word."

"What, bath?"

"No, 'moist.' Ack, you made me say it! Now my mouth feels–"

"Moist?"

"Aaaah!" Kirkland put her hands over her ears. "Lalala."

"You are so weird."

"What? It's not like I'm alone in hating 'moist.'"

"You're the first I've heard."

"We have a support group that meets every third Tuesday."

"I hate moist too, commander," Rakunas called out from his seat on the flight deck.

"That's enough from the peanut gallery," Jian called back over his shoulder. "Stop sucking up to the copilot."

Everyone had a good chuckle right up until the fire alarm started blaring. Jian's head snapped down to his console to pinpoint the location.

"Shit, it's in here," Kirkland said, just fractionally faster out of the gate. Jian's eyes darted frantically around the cabin, trying to pinpoint the fire from sparks, or a telltale puff of smoke. Fire inside a spaceship was every crewmember's worst nightmare. In moments, a fire could crawl through conduits and circuitry, drawn along by a process like capillary action. Fires burned slow because their exhaust gasses didn't rise away from them. Little spheres of flame floated freely and kept burning at oxygen levels much lower than fires in gravity. And they would spontaneously reignite even after being snuffed out.

"I don't see anything," Jian said, trying to keep his voice even. "Are we sure it's not a sensor fault?"

"Second sensor is registering it now," Kirkland said.

"Shit." Jian hit the release on his chair's restraints. "Abandon the flight deck," he shouted. "Everybody out!"

"Flight Control, *Atlantis,*" Kirkland yelled into her headset while Jian shepherded the rest of the crew and techs out of the deck and into the cargo cabin. "Mayday. Mayday. Mayday. We are declaring an emergency. There is a fire on the flight deck. We are evacuating to let the fire suppression systems take over."

"Now, Kirkland!" Jian shouted to his copilot as he waited by the hatch. "We can't wait."

She loosed herself from the chair and kicked off hard against the instrument panels, sending herself flying for the door like a torpedo. As she passed through the hatch,

Jian hit the emergency button and yanked his arm out just in time for the hatch to snap shut.

With the compartment sealed, it would be a simple matter to vent the atmosphere from the flight deck and kill whatever fire had taken hold. But even as Jian brought up the menus that would do exactly that, something nagged at the corner of his mind.

"Head count," he said. "Everybody sound off." Everyone did so in rapid succession. Everyone, that is, except...

"Madeja," Kirkland said, "where's Madeja?"

"She's still on the flight deck," Jian said, looking through the portal in the door and spotting the tech's back.

"Well, let her out!"

"I can't. The emergency lockdown is in place. The hatch won't open until the fire's out. There's no way to override it."

"Shit..."

"Madeja." Jian pounded on the portal, trying to get her attention. The tech turned and glanced back at the door. Jian thumbed on the intercom. "Madeja, we can't open the door until the fire's out. The air's going to be purged."

"What's she doing in there?" Rakunas said from behind them.

"Good, she's going for her helmet," Jian said. "Once she's sealed in, we can vent the air before the fire gets out of control." As Jian watched, Madeja fitted her skinsuit's helmet and connected it to her emergency air supply. The skinsuits they wore aboard ship weren't proper spacesuits. They used tension instead of internal air pressure to keep one's blood from boiling off, and they lacked the insulation and life support packs necessary to keep someone alive in the cold and radiation of open space for long. But aboard ship, they were more than sufficient to keep you going in a depressurized compartment for an hour and a half, if you conserved air. Which, frankly, most people were simply awful at doing when faced with a space catastrophe.

But Madeja's movements seemed calm and measured. Not at all like the nervous, even panicking tech Jian had been putting up with for the entire mission. Maybe she was finally growing a spine. Maybe the time spent working around the mystery installation had... Why was she sitting in Kirkland's chair?

"Whoa," Kirkland said from Jian's right. "My screen just went dead. I can't trigger the purge."

"Shit." Jian thumbed the intercom again, unsure if Madeja could hear him through her helmet. "Madeja, we've just lost our panels out here. The fire must have reached the electrical cables. You'll need to purge the air in there manually to put it out."

At that, Madeja turned slowly about from the copilot's seat and looked back at him with a wry, unnerving grin twisting up the left side of her face. She held up a hand. In it, she gripped a small candle lighter, a perfect little sphere of blue and white flame glowing from its tip. With a flick of her finger, the fuel to the fire was cut out. It flickered, then a moment later, its fuel expended, and it died.

At first, Jian's mind recoiled at the sight, but then Madeja's wicked grin brought it snapping back into place.

"Oh my God," he said. "She started the fire on purpose. She's not trapped in there. She's trapped us out here."

"What?" Kirkland pushed over to look in the portal. "Holy shit! What is she doing?"

"Did you lock down your station?" Jian asked.

"Huh?"

"Your station, did you lock it down before we evacuated?"

"I was a little busy at that exact moment, Jian!"

With open access to one of the command stations, Madeja had complete control over the entire shuttle. The screen in the cargo cabin hadn't gotten its leads burned out, she'd cut it off deliberately. They were locked out of the system.

"What is she going to do?" Rakunas said as the other techs and crew members began to bunch around them.

"How the hell should I know?" Jian snapped. "But whatever she's got planned, there's not much we can do to stop her from this side of the hatch."

"How much time do we have?" Kirkland asked.

"Before we have to flip and burn? Six, seven minutes, tops."

Kirkland nodded and started disassembling the panel opposite the hatch, probably hoping to get to its physical mechanism.

"Give me a hand with this, I'll need an eight-millimeter socket."

"There's one in the tool kit we brought for the receiver," Rakunas said, and pushed off from the bulkhead, heading back deeper in the cargo bay.

The lights overhead switched from soft white to the flashing red of the decompression alarm.

"Whoa!" Kirkland shouted.

"I wouldn't do that if I were you." Madeja's voice piped into the cargo compartment through the public-address speakers. She sounded steady, confident, and frigid as the space waiting just a few thin centimeters away on the other side of *Atlantis*'s hull.

"Why not?" Jian shouted at the ceiling.

"Because my right hand is hovering over the cargo bay door controls. And if I see any of you trying to jerry-rig the flight hatch, I'll push that button, the doors will open, and you'll all be sucked out into space without helmets. Which, incidentally, are all in here with me. So just sit tight, kiddies. This will all be over in a few minutes."

"What are you doing with my ship?" Jian asked, but the ceiling went silent again. "Madeja?" he demanded.

Nothing.

Jian pounded the bulkhead with his fist until he was

afraid his hand would break, then took several deep, furious breaths. He felt Kirkland's hand on his shoulder, even through the thick compressive mesh of his skin-suit.

"What are we going to do, boss?"

Jian looked around at the rest of his team's anxious, confused, expectant faces. They were looking at him. Looking *to* him. He held his arms out and motioned for everyone to huddle up. Everyone except Rakunas, who'd come to rest at the rear of the cargo hold. Jian motioned to him to stay in place.

Once they were all in a floating circle, Jian opened an encrypted plant link between them, bypassing the shuttle's systems entirely by setting up a temporary dedicated network. It wasn't inconceivable that Madeja could hack into it and eavesdrop on the conversation, but breaking the encryption would take time and attention that he strongly suspected she didn't have to spare at the moment.

<OK,> Jian started. <We need to get through this door without her seeing us and opening those doors.> He glanced up at the folding cargo doors than made up the shuttle's ceiling. <Suggestions?>

<Why is she doing this?> one of the techs pleaded.

<Who is she?> shouted another.

<Well it's safe to assume she's not just a harvester tech,> Kirkland said.

<Stow that shit,> Jian barked. <The *who* and the *why* doesn't matter right now, only the *how*, as in *How the fuck do we get through that door*?>

<Without her seeing us?> Kirkland shook her head. <I don't see how.>

<Think!> Jian snapped. <There must be something we can do.>

<Why should we do anything?> the fretting tech said.

<Because I believe she's going to ram the Ark,> Jian said.

<What! Why?>

<What did I just say about *why*?>

"That better be a prayer circle, children," Madeja said through the PA system.

Jian held his hands together in a rather half-hearted display of piety. <Why else would she hijack a shuttle? Where's she going to go with it? Its only purpose is as a weapon.>

<You really think we've been hijacked by some goddamned terrorist sleeper agent? You've been watching too many early twenty-first century Hollywood movies.>

<This isn't a debate. We have to assume that's her purpose, because if we don't, and we're *wrong*...> Jian let a few seconds slip away while the full implications of his words settled.

<He's right,> Kirkland said.

<Yeah,> Rakunas followed. <I agree. She's flipped her shit. None of us are getting out of here alive unless we stop her.>

<Can't Flight Control just take over the helm? We're getting really close to the exclusion zone,> one of the techs said.

<Not if she's disabled the radio they can't,> Kirkland pointed out.

<Won't they use the Ark's nav lasers to burn us up before impact?> Rakunas asked.

Jian shook his head. <They're mounted at the bow and only have a thirty-degree firing arc. There's no way to maneuver the ship into position to get a firing solution in time.>

<Which explains why she waited until now to spring the trap,> Kirkland said. <But what I don't understand is if she's just going to kill us all anyway, why not just open the doors now and get it over with.>

<Because there's an important psychological difference between passive responsibility for death and actively causing it through direct action,> Rakunas said.

Everyone turned to quizzically look at him floating at

the far end of the cargo bay.

<What? Am I the only one who paid attention in sociology class?>

<Yes,> Kirkland said.

<OK,> Jian said. <I have an idea.>

<Oh crap.>

Jian ignored this. <Rakunas, get Polly.>

<Polly,> Rakunas said. <The artificially-intelligent alien spider made out of technogoo we stole from a mystery installation that may have been built by whoever hoovered-up the Earth? That Polly?>

<Time is money!> Jian said.

<You're a lunatic.>

<Takes one to beat one,> Jian said.

<Are you sure about this?> Kirkland said. <What if it was built by the people who threw Nibiru at us?>

<It's been down here for hundreds of thousands of years, at least,> Jian said. <We were throwing rocks at each other back then. Besides, what's it going to do, destroy the Ark? How is that any worse?>

<Point.>

Smartly, Rakunas floated behind a row of containers that had been lashed down tightly to holdfasts built into the floor for the return journey. It kept him mostly out of sight of the compartments' cameras while he worked his way towards the container where Polly had been stored.

But not entirely concealed. He risked being spotted, to be sure. Jian just hoped that whatever fraction of Madeja's focus was being spent on the cargo compartment, the majority of it rested on the circle of crewmembers and not Rakunas sulking alone among the shadows.

He reached the sealed crate and broke the negative pressure inside with a small *hiss*, then let the lid float gently to the side. With more than a little hesitation, Rakunas stuck a hand inside the container.

<Oh, God, it's wiggling.>

<Just grab the damned bug, Rakunas,> Jian said.

<I'm trying. It keeps changing shape,> he protested.

<It's in a sample jar!>

<No, it isn't. It took the lid off.>

Jian swallowed hard. Clever little bug. His confidence in this crazy idea started to waver.

<Got you!> Rakunas held up the sample jar which, once again, contained Polly. The little bug seemed quite agitated.

<OK, throw him to me.>

<Wait!> Rakunas said. <There's a helmet back here.>

<Yeah, it's broken,> Jian said.

<No,> one of the others said. <Just its electrics are fried. It's still airtight.>

Rakunas shoved the sample jar into the helmet and braced himself with the fixed container.

<Ready?>

Jian put a toe through an anchor loop in the floor and nodded. <Ready.>

Rakunas hauled back his arm, then sent the helmet hurling through the air.

<Catch!>

Jian's eyes locked onto it as it tumbled towards him. He hadn't been old enough to play Zero before they'd arrived at Gaia, but his hand-eye coordination was certainly adequate to catch a helmet moving in a perfectly straight line.

Which was when it took a hard turn to the left and bounced off the wall.

"Shit!" Jian said aloud before cursing himself.

<We're maneuvering,> Kirkland said. She kicked off from the bulkhead and angled towards the ricocheting helmet, expertly compensating for the curvature of her path caused by the changing direction of the shuttle. With her arm stretched out to its absolute limits, she managed to get a single finger looped inside one of the helmet's equipment anchors, but it was enough. Without a second glance, she swung it back towards Jian. At first, his eyes

told him it was going to go wide, but then it curved sharply towards him as the shuttle's course correction took hold of its path.

It plowed into Jian's chest like a guided missile. He slapped both hands around it and cradled it like an infant.

<Nice throw,> he said.

<Thanks.>

"Commander," Madeja's voice boomed from the ceiling once more. "I don't know what you think you're up to, but if you move to put on that helmet, I push the button."

"Go ahead," Jian said.

"I'm serious, Feng!"

"So am I. I don't think you've got the stones. Otherwise you would've done it already."

"Do it, and their deaths will be on your head, Feng."

"I'm not going to let you use my ship to hurt people, Madeja. And it's not my finger on the button."

Silence.

Jian pulled the sample jar out of the helmet, careful to keep his back to the cargo compartment's security camera. Much to his surprise, it was empty. He glanced down into the helmet to find Polly had already worked the cap off again.

Polly looked at Jian with its spikey forelimbs held up threateningly, just as it had done when they'd first met. But then, recognition dawned across its three-eyed face. Jian held out a finger and the tiny alien AI scrambled up his arm and took its place on his shoulder, despite the null-gee.

"OK, little buddy," Jian whispered to the AI, reasonably sure it couldn't understand a word he was saying. "I need your help. I need you to open this door." He pointed at the hatch and made a sliding motion with his free hand. Polly imitated the gesture, but didn't break eye contact.

"No, look at me–"

<What the fuck is that?> one of the techs they'd picked

up at the telescope site said.

<Long story. Just go with it,> Jian said. “The door.” He pointed directly at the hatch. “I need you,” he pointed at Polly, “to open,” he made a sliding motion, “the door,” he pointed once more at the hatch.

This time, Polly followed his finger. Its tiny head shot to the four corners of the hatch, then to the small control panel to its right. After a moment of careful study, it turned back to face Jian with its slick, inky black skin and green glowing eyes, and blinked the middle one.

Jian smiled.

<Did that creepy oil-spider just *wink* at you?> Kirkland demanded.

<It's an inside joke.>

<You have inside jokes with a creepy oil spider? Actually, never mind. I believe it.>

Without warning, Polly shot off Jian's shoulder like a dart. Its eight clawed legs bit into the bulkhead and stalked towards the control panel. Jian moved his body to block the camera angle on what Polly was up to. The gooey construct probed at one of the panel's fastening screws with a claw. As Jian watched, four of Polly's claws morphed into screwdrivers a mirror image of the screw's face. Then, he unscrewed all four fasteners simultaneously, cast the panel aside, then just… melted. His liquefied body poured into the opening.

<Holy shit, it understood,> Kirkland said.

<He's a clever little bug.>

<You'd better put your helmet on in case Madeja really does decompress the compartment when that hatch opens, commander,> Rakunas said.

<She won't,> Jian said, with far more confidence than he felt. He needed to believe it, for their sakes as much as his own.

<Still, better safe than sorry.>

Jian looked around at his crew, looked deep into their faces. He saw the same fear he felt reflected back half a dozen times, magnifying it like feedback. But he saw more in their eyes. Pride. Resolve. Anger.

Their faces magnified those feelings inside him as well. Jian took a deep breath and slipped the helmet over his head. Kirkland's hands were there to secure the seals and attach the hoses.

Through the muffling of the helmet, Jian heard what he assumed was Madeja making another announcement, although he couldn't make out the individual words with the helmet's mics and internal speakers fried. But then, he didn't need to.

Kirkland looked up at the ceiling and her eyes went wide.

<What? What did she say?> Jian said.

<Nothing. Don't worry about it.> Kirkland tried to smirk and hide her fear, but her eyes told him everything. <Stay focused. Don't look back.>

As if on cue, Polly popped open the hatch from wherever it had gotten to inside the bulkhead. Jian pushed through even before it had finished opening. But as soon as he crossed the threshold, he felt a sudden change in air pressure. He looked back, and his stomach clenched at the site of a black line running down the length of the cargo bay doors, growing wider by the moment. She'd done it, she'd actually pushed the button.

<Well, there goes that theory,> Rakunas said, somehow able to crack a joke in the face of his impending death.

<Everybody take a deep breath!> Jian shouted and pushed off from the doorframe towards where the helmets were strapped down.

<Forget about us,> Kirkland said even as the rest of the crew started swearing, screaming, and crying into the plant link. <Just stop that bitch!> But Jian ignored her. On a single breath of air and with the tension of their skinsuits keeping their lungs from bursting, they had maybe a minute of consciousness to get lids on before they passed out. Jian reached the rack of helmets and

started frantically unlatching them, then threw them at the hatch, banking them off the doorframe and into the cargo module.

<Heads up!> he shouted into the link.

<Get her!> Kirkland yelled.

Jian turned back to the flight deck and to Madeja strapped into the copilot's seat. But it was the image floating in the viewscreen that filled him with both dread and terrible purpose. Hanging there in the backlight of stars was the Ark, barely as big as his thumbnail held at arm's length. But it grew, and would grow more quickly with each passing second at their velocity of almost thirty thousand kilometers per hour.

Madeja saw him come, but made no move to leave the controls. Instead, she just hit the throttle. Jian watched in horror as his relative motion inside the flight deck slowed, then stopped, then reversed entirely. As he started to "fall" backwards, he got a hand onto the frame of one of the passenger seats. He pulled himself into it even as his effective weight started to grow.

The gees grew. Everyone else was surely being pressed flat against the rear of the cargo bay. Anyone who hadn't already gotten their helmet on was having the air squeezed out of their lungs by now. Jian tried desperately to fight against the weight pressing down on his chest, but he could scarcely lift his arms.

They were piling on even more velocity, all of which he would need to bleed off again in the increasingly shrinking window between now and impact, but stuck in the passenger chair, with no way to peel himself out of it and regain control, Jian–

A violent shudder rocked the *Atlantis*. A moment later, the elephant sitting on Jian's chest lifted. He knew instantly what had happened. In her haste to deal with him, Madeja had firewalled the throttles as a single unit instead of individually. The number four motor's damaged turbo pump had succumbed, blowing the motor out completely and sending the entire array into an automatic safety shutdown.

It was the first real mistake she'd made since hijacking the shuttle. Jian kicked hard out of his seat towards her station to make sure it was also her last. Rocked by the explosive deconstruction of the turbo pump, *Atlantis* lurched as its nose pitched down. The Ark drifted out of view, but not out of danger. The shuttle was tumbling around its center of mass, but the immutable laws of momentum meant it was still traveling straight and true for its target.

Jian hit the ceiling, reoriented himself, then kicked off and finally reached the back of Madeja's chair. She took a half-hearted swing at him, but her attention was split between him and desperately trying to counteract the shuttle's tumble. But whatever else she was, Madeja was no pilot. Without thrust vectoring from the main engines, bringing the hundred-and-fifty-meter-long bird to a heel was going to be a real challenge.

But first, Jian needed to be sitting where she was.

He tried to open a direct link to Madeja's plant to try and talk her down, but the connection was blocked at the source. *OK, the hard way,* Jian thought. He spun up and over the seat's headrest, lunged at Madeja's wrists, and tried to pry her hands away from the controls. She twisted her left wrist free of his fingers and threw a vicious elbow into Jian's head, but his helmet absorbed most of the blow. Still, he couldn't maintain a grip on her. Madeja was strong, owing to her youth spent deep in Gaia's gravity well. Despite appearances, she was an even match for Jian, and effectively fought him to a draw, even while maintaining her death grip on the shuttle's joysticks.

"Stop!" Jian saw her mouth through the clear polymer of her helmet. More words followed, but Jian couldn't read them fast enough.

Jian needed to complicate things for her. He blocked

a randomly thrown forearm, then stretched down and jabbed two fingers into the release on her harness. Like startled snakes, the five belts of the crash harness retracted into the seat. No longer strapped into the chair, Madeja suddenly found herself weightless. And that, Jian was plenty strong enough for.

With both hands, he pulled Madeja out of her seat even as she was grabbing for the retreating harness belts and threw her against the ceiling. In the vacuum, Jian couldn't hear the *thud* of her body crashing into the overhead panels, but he imagined it made a satisfying sound all the same.

Wasting no time, Jian shifted himself into the copilot's seat. He hit the icon that would close the cargo bay doors, and then the one to begin repressurizing the compartment. Then, he grabbed the shuttle's dual joysticks. With the main engines in shut-down, he only had maneuvering thrusters to work with. It would have to be enough. He focused on the artificial horizon display directly in front of him, which was completely arbitrary in space but was still critical to help pilots orient themselves in three dimensions.

He should have worried about what was above him.

Madeja came crashing back down onto him from the ceiling and smashed his head into the instrumentation display. Again, the helmet absorbed most of the blow, but his forehead hit the inside of the face shield and sent little stars shooting through his vision. He shook it off, but by the time his eyes straightened out again, Madeja was trying to tear out his air hose.

Jian grabbed her thumb and tried to wrench it free, but she was locked in like a vice. Jian shot two quick, desperate jabs into her side, hoping to pop a rib, but the material of her skinsuit blunted most of their force. He switched tracks and grabbed Madeja's air hose, but the angle was wrong for his fingers to get enough grip on the hose's collar to unscrew it, and he didn't have the pure strength to rip it loose.

The grating sound of his air hose being slowly, methodically unscrewed ground into Jian's consciousness. His eyes, rapidly filling with terror at the growing chance that he was drawing his final breath, locked with Madeja's. They were cold, hard, like staring into pearls. There was no mercy to be found there.

Jian's focus on her face was so absolute, that his nerves didn't even register the pinpricks crawling up his arm into a familiar place on his shoulder. But Madeja noticed. The grinding of his air hose unscrewing stopped. Her eyes darted over and went wide with surprise and fear of her own. Jian glanced over to see Polly sitting in its usual spot, its three green eyes half-hooded as it inspected Madeja.

Then, it held its forelimbs up in the same aggressive display it'd made at Jian when he'd first encountered the little AI. Jian's shoulders slumped at the little bug's impotent bluster, but then Polly's right claws twisted together into a wicked-looking spear point.

Before either Jian or Madeja could react, Polly's forearm shot out in a flash, stretching all the way to, then through, Madeja's face shield, pierced her left eye, then erupted out the back of her helmet.

Madeja's body jerked once, then fell into spasms. Her hand clutching his air hose went limp. Without withdrawing his tiny spear, Polly turned its small head to face a horrified Jian. Its left eye blinked. Jian swallowed hard. Their inside joke lost some of its charm.

There wasn't time to waste. Jian shoved the lifeless body aside, momentarily taking a startled Polly with it. <If anyone's still alive back there, brace yourselves.> He grabbed the joysticks once more and fought for control. Reactant mass be damned, he cranked the Reaction Control Thrusters to one hundred and fifteen percent emergency blow and threw them wide open. Superheated jets of steam screamed into empty space like gargantuan tea kettles.

Jian's health monitor inside his plant started flashing heartrate and stress-level warnings, but he ignored them. Slowly, ponderously, the enormous beast slowed its tumble as Jian made the complex series of short, precise inputs necessary to counter its chaotic movements.

Laboriously, he strong-armed the *Atlantis* back into line. Sweat beading up on his forehead, the artificial horizon finally stabilized and the shuttle was flying straight and true once more. Which was when the collision avoidance radar started screaming at him. Jian looked up from the instrumentation and nearly screamed himself. The Ark had grown from a thumbnail to encompass the shuttle's entire windshield. They were less than forty thousand meters out, and closing at eight thousand meters per second. Four seconds to alter course by more than a kilometer. Thrusters alone weren't going to cut it; he needed the mains.

With a flurry of icons, Jian brought up the safety overrides for the main engine shutdown sequence, then hit the button to light them. Engines One, Two, Five and Six reported hot and ready. Three had been too badly damaged by Four to restart even with the override. It would have to do.

Jian pitched the *Atlantis*'s nose down and away from the Ark and firewalled the throttles. The gees threw him back into his chair painfully, but his burning muscles pinned the joysticks forward to maintain the dive as the Ark expanded exponentially in the window.

Just as it looked like he might scrape by without swapping paint, a sliver of light gleamed in the space ahead. The elevator ribbon. In his panic, Jian hadn't even notice its carbon black surface against the background of dark space beyond. With only tenths of a second remaining, he jammed the joysticks to the right in a desperate bid to avoid it, but he knew it wouldn't be enough.

"Oh fu–"

CHAPTER TEN

Benson used to love being the center of attention. He wasn't sure exactly when that had changed, but, as he waved mechanically and smiled at the First Contact Day crowds from his "Place of Honor" on this stupid float, he was pretty sure his perennial position as the ceremonial Parade Marshal had something to do with it.

They stood on a platform built on top of two linked transit pods with a colorful fabric skirt concealing them as they crawled slowly down the electrified track. Surrounding them were all manner of garish decorations made of wire frames, local flowers, and papier-mâché. Every minute or so, the fake dux'ah behind him would "breathe" on Benson's back with a cloud of freezing dry-ice evaporate. Towering over both of them, an eight-meter tall trident loomed over the entire parade.

Benexx leaned in to whisper in zer father's ear. "Happy now?"

"Ecstatic."

"We could've both been sitting on the couch back home right now."

"Just keep smiling and waving, Squish."

"My arm's tired."

"Oh my God, shut up."

The crowds on either side of the route were noticeably thicker than in years past. Part of this was doubtlessly due to the extra effort that had gone into planning and promoting the fifteenth anniversary celebrations. But even more of it owed simply to how much Shambhala's population was growing year over year, both from immigration and natural growth. Shambhala was becoming a very young city. The oldest of the first wave of human natives to the planet were about to turn eighteen. Because of the freeze on new births in the last five years before the Ark's arrival, there were no humans between eighteen and twenty-three. It made for an odd break in the society.

The oldest Atlantian children born of Shambhala were just shy of fifteen, a few months short of Benexx. Looking around at the crowds that had gathered for the parade, Benson spotted quite a few blended groups of these teenagers mingling freely between the species, and generally doing a far better job of integrating and tolerating one another than their parents were doing.

And why shouldn't they? They had more in common with each other's life experiences growing up in the city than their parents living either on the Ark or Atlantis. There was nothing quite like the clean slate of a child's mind to see the ridiculousness of the older generation's prejudices.

Benson, Kexx, Kuul, Tuko, and a few others had forged the Trident, but the children watching the parade with the sort of conspicuous indifference only teenagers could master would be the ones to sharpen and wield it.

Somehow, Benson found the thought oddly reassuring.

Ahead of their little float, Atlantian dancers performed an elaborate and traditional routine celebrating fellowship between people of different villages. It was familiar to Benson; he'd seen it at the inaugural First Contact Day in G'tel, before they called it that, and right before all the screaming, stabbing, and shooting started. Fortunately, they had gotten significantly more civilized in the years since.

In front of the dancers was a special treat for the

crowds; full-sized parade balloons. Since the Helium-3 mining effort had gotten underway on Varr, boring old Helium-4 had been cropping up as a byproduct of both the refining process and of the Ark's fusion reactors. Between the two, there was so much of the inert gas that all of its manufacturing requirements, from welding shield gas, to superconductor coolant, was met with capacity to spare.

So in the tradition of the Macy's Day Parade in old New York, the city council had elected to have their primary school students band together to build a half dozen balloons as a class project for the year.

The results of their herculean efforts over the last few Varrs were... mixed. Benson had spent a few months back in Avalon binging on twentieth-century cartoons in his youth in between bouts of nature documentaries, but he didn't remember Snoopy or Garfield looking quite so lumpy.

Other balloons showed more advanced craftsmanship, probably from Devorah's crop of advanced placement art students. The galloping representation of the Mustangs' mascot particularly warmed his heart. Benson made a plant note to give all of the kids who built it tickets to next week's game.

Benson waved. The crowd waved back. Some lifted their drinks in salute. Some raised a glass from a lawn chair. Some threw confetti down from second and third floor balconies. At one point, he would've been obligated to give them a very big fine for wasting precious resources, but with the conservation codes long buried, Benson tried to ignore it and appreciate the sentiment instead.

A string of polymer beads hit him in the head. When he looked up to see who had thrown them, he was rewarded with an exceptionally firm pair of breasts supplied by a young woman peering over at him from a balcony.

"Hey coach! Make First Contact with these!" she shouted as she shook her shoulders. Benson instinctively put his hand over Benexx's eyes, while just as instinctively kept his own glued to the scenery.

"Oh for shit's sake," Benexx cursed. "Atlantians don't care about tits, dad, remember?"

"No, but I care about you seeing me ogling girls."

Benexx scoffed. "Xis below, you're so *lame*!"

Benson laughed just as the transit pods lurched once, then rolled to a stop.

"What the hell?" Benexx said.

Benson looked ahead in time to see one of the Atlantian dancers prance right into the back of the suddenly halted float in front of zer.

"The track must have lost power. Probably tripped a surge protector with all these pods bunched together."

"Um, I don't think so," Benexx said. Benson was about to ask what ze meant, but saw zer pointing to the side. He followed zer finger and realized all the lights in the shops and apartments were out.

"The whole block lost power?"

"Looks like it," Benexx said.

The crowds started to react to the unexplained outage, milling about and beginning to push and shove. Benson knew what a crowd that was about to turn ugly looked like and moved quickly to head it off.

"Hey! Eyes on me!" he shouted from the top of the float. Begrudgingly most people did just that. "Good. Now, it's just a little hiccup in the power. I'm sure it'll be fixed in a minute. Refresh your drinks."

Apparently, this sounded like a spectacular idea to many of the assembled humans and Atlantians alike and the crowd settled back down again.

"Dad," Benexx leaned in to whisper. "What's going on?"

"Don't know, Squish." Benson glanced back at the trident. "Let's get a better look." Without a second thought, he started to climb the wooden shaft.

"You can't be serious," Benexx said. "You're fifty years old. Come down from there."

"Fifty-two, and you can't make me," he answered as he reached the crossbar.

"You're going to fall and hurt yourself," Benexx said, reflexively mirroring a dozen years of parental input.

"Nu-uh," Benson's inner five year-old responded with glee.

"Oh lord. Fine, whatever. I'm not visiting you in the hospital."

Benson wrapped one arm around the center tine of the trident and blocked the setting sun from his eyes with the other. Through a wide gap between buildings, he could see all the way to the harbor. No lights shone in any of the windows, or any of the streetlamps for as far as he could see.

Benson tried to connect with his wife, but the request threw up an error message. <Network Unavailable.>

"Unavailable?" Benson muttered. That meant the signal repeaters sprinkled throughout the city were down as well, and that Theresa was outside his plant's own limited range.

"What do you see?" Benexx asked.

"Power to the whole city is down," Benson said, careful to keep his voice loud enough for zer to hear, but quiet enough not to agitate the crowd.

To zer credit, Benexx pitched zer voice lower to match. "What could cause that?"

"Beats me. It's not like we're in the middle of a hurricane. Hold on."

Something impossible in the sky above the city pulled Benson's gaze to it like a harpoon. The thin, arrow-straight, almost one-dimensional black line of the elevator cable... shifted. With rising horror, Benson watched as a sine wave carried down from the infinity of space like a whiplash along the entire length of the beanstalk.

With the speed of a lightning bolt, the wave collided with the anchor station floating in the harbor, rocking the half-million metric ton platform with the violence of an angry parent shaking a petulant child. Waves radiated out from the anchor station and crashed against the shoreline.

Benson's mind recoiled at what he'd just witnessed. For the last fifteen years of his life, the delicate but impossibly strong black thread reaching from the surface up to the Ark had never wavered. It was a landmark, a monument. It didn't just... *change*. Without realizing it, Benson's face went ashen. The sudden shift did not go unnoticed by his adoptive offspring.

"Dad?" Benexx's voice dripped with trepidation. "What's wrong?"

Benson swallowed, hard. "Everything."

That's when the bomb went off.

CHAPTER ELEVEN

Jian's body stiffened like he'd been shocked.

Sweat pooling on his skin and on the verge of hyperventilating, Jian's eyes darted around the cockpit, trying to regain his bearings. The setting was familiar, but slightly off, starting with the fact he wasn't sitting in his shuttle's command chair.

Indeed, he wasn't sitting in his shuttle at all.

"What happened?" he shouted into the cabin.

"Commander," the shuttle's pilot said from the command chair without looking back. "You're awake. That's great. We weren't sure you'd recover before we got you back to the Ark's sick bay."

"WHAT. HAPPENED."

"Well..." the pilot said hesitantly. Jian thought he recognized the voice. Albertson. She was a couple of classes ahead of him and Kirkland in flight school and had already been running her own missions for over a year. "You were involved in a collision," Albertson said finally.

"Yeah, I know," Jian answered. "I was there. How bad was it? I assume since they sent you out to grab us that we didn't cut the elevator ribbon."

"Not for lack of trying," Albertson said. "Your shuttle's port wingtip clipped the beanstalk and sliced through about fifteen percent of it. Another five percent frayed before the spider drones could halt the tear. Two elevator cars had to disengage and freefall back down to the surface, and power to Shambhala had to be cut until repairs are made."

Jian looked around the cockpit for the rest of his crew, minus Madeja, obviously. The last couple of minutes before the impact were a fuzzy rush of images and emotions, but the picture of Polly drilling a hole through Madeja's eye and out the back of her skull kind of stood out.

He searched the faces of those seated around him for Kirkland, Rakunas, anyone, but found none.

"Where's my crew?" he asked sharply.

Albertson looked back over her shoulder. "You don't know?"

Even in the null gee, Jian's stomach sank.

"I'm sorry, Jian, but you were the only survivor."

"That can't be right." Jian rebelled at the thought. "I closed the damned doors. They had helmets."

"They..." Albertson cleared her throat. "When we found them, none of them had gotten their helmets and hoses secured before the impact. They passed away from asphyxiation, unfortunately. Everyone except the tech we found in the cockpit with you. Her injuries were quite a bit more... obvious."

There was something in her tone that set off alarm bells. It was only then that Jian's mind cleared enough to take a full account of the scene. The restraints built into a shuttle's chairs were already restrictive, with five-point crash harnesses securing their occupants with the sort of pressure normally reserved for bondage fetishists. But those restraints didn't extend to the ankles and wrists, both of which Jian found had been securely strapped to the chair frame with cargo tie-downs.

Reflexively, Jian's arms jerked against the straps, twisting and straining for freedom. It was hopeless. The belts were rated for keeping multi-ton containers firmly in place under the stress of high-gee maneuvers.

No combination of one hundred humans could hope to break them.

"Commander Albertson," Jian said breathlessly. "Why are my arms and legs restrained?"

"It's just a precaution, commander, I assure you."

"Then cut them loose!"

"I can't do that just now, Jian," Albertson said delicately. "I have orders to keep you restrained until we get back to the Ark. There are some... concerns the rest of the crew has about the incident, and they'll feel a lot better once they have a chance to ask you about them personally."

"What kind of fucking questions?" Jian shouted. "A lunatic took over my shuttle, killed my crew, and tried to crash us all into the Ark!"

"Yes, that much is certain. The question, I think, is *which* lunatic."

"What?" Jian shouted. "You can't believe I did it! I'm the only reason the *Atlantis* didn't plow into the Ark itself at thirty thousand kph, for God's sake."

"What I believe isn't important, Jian. It's not my call to make. Now, we're almost at turnover. I have to concentrate on flying. So I'll have to ask you to be quiet, or one of my crew will close your visor. Are we clear?"

Jian fumed, but refused to answer, choosing instead to break eye contact and glare at the ceiling.

"All right then," Albertson said. "Try to relax, commander. We're almost home."

Jian kept silent for the rest of the trip, choosing to listen instead. The rest of Albertson's crew wasn't particularly chatty, probably because they were using a private plant link to prevent him from eavesdropping, but occasional cross talk did occur.

What he learned did nothing to help sooth his pain. His crew were all dead, and worse, they hadn't even managed to recover all of their bodies before they had to abandon the *Atlantis*. The impact with the ribbon had sheared off his shuttle's port wing almost at the root, sending it into a hellish six gee flat spin that rendered Jian unconscious and sent the shuttle careening away from the Ark at almost thirty thousand kph. Because Jian had regained control in the last few moments before impact, Flight Control had been able to tap into the *Atlantis*'s flight computers and take her over remotely. But with half of the thrusters they needed to bring its chaotic spin to a heel reduced to pulverized wreckage, it hadn't been an easy task.

By the time Flight stabilized *Atlantis*'s course, fired its rocket motors to slow it into a gradually-expanding spiral orbit, and scrambled Albertson's crew for the rescue attempt, the shuttle was more than fifty thousand kilometers away from the Ark and retreating quickly. Each additional orbit would see the *Atlantis* spiral another two thousand kilometers and change further away from Gaia until it escaped the planet's gravity entirely. Its final orbit within the solar system hadn't been projected yet, but since there wouldn't be a chance to return to it with more fuel for its empty tanks before it passed beyond the safe operational ranges of the other shuttles in the fleet, *Atlantis* had been declared lost.

His shuttle scrapped, entire crew dead, and the elevator ribbon nearly severed wasn't how Jian had pictured his first command playing out. Indeed, it was far, far beyond even his most fervent nightmares.

When Jian spoke again, all of the fight had drained out of his voice. "Can someone please tell me which of my crew's bodies you weren't able to recover?"

The cabin fell deathly silent. No one wanted to answer him, or even make eye contact. Finally, Albertson stepped up.

"It was Rakunas," she said evenly. "I'm sorry."

"Yeah? Sorry are you?"

"*Yeah*. He was my friend, too. We were in the same primary school class."

"What happened?"

Albertson turned back around to face her displays. "He came free of the cargo bay at the moment of impact, before the doors had closed all the way. His body then continued out on its own trajectory."

"And you couldn't swing back to grab him?" Jian asked.

Albertson shook her head. "We're running inside our safety margins on fuel as it is."

"I understand." And he did, even if he didn't like it. The rest of the short trip back to the Ark passed in somber quiet. The deceleration burn dug Jian's restraints into his wrists, even through his skinsuit's thick sleeves. But the burn passed, and soon enough Albertson gingerly maneuvered her shuttle into its cradle in the aviary.

The gantry clamps and umbilicals ran out to secure the shuttle to the Ark's hull as everyone inside breathed a sigh of relief, Jian included, even if he was dreading what came next. Sure enough, as soon as the inner hatch indicator turned green to show a positive seal, the door swung inwards as two men in Ark constable uniforms floated in, stun sticks held prominently in their hands.

"Permission to come aboard, Commander Albertson?" the leader of the unit said.

"You're already aboard, constable," Albertson answered dryly.

"Yes… well, we have orders to take the prisoner, Jian Feng, into custody."

"I wasn't aware Commander Feng had been placed under arrest," Albertson said as the temperature in the cabin dropped.

"But you have him restrained!" the lead constable protested.

"For his own safety. He just lost his boat and entire crew. He's understandably a little distraught." Albertson unbuckled herself from the command chair and expertly floated back to face the interlopers. "So unless I am very mistaken, you are here to escort *Commander* Feng to his next appointment. Yes?"

The constable swallowed hard. "If you say so, ma'am."

"This is *my* boat, and I *do* say so." Albertson pushed off and floated back to Jian's seat, then released the cargo straps pinning his arms and legs.

Grateful for the restored freedom of movement, no matter how short-lived, Jian rubbed some circulation back into his wrists. "Thank you," he said quietly.

"I'm sorry about all of this, Jian," she replied just above a whisper. "I don't know what's going to happen now, but I don't believe you were involved in this mess. Others may not be convinced. Don't let them get to you. Keep your chin up."

Jian nodded as he released his crash web and drifted out of his seat into the cabin.

"Mr Feng," the constable said. Albertson loudly cleared her throat. The constable glanced at her, annoyed, but relented. "Excuse me, *Commander* Feng, if you would accompany us?"

Jian grabbed the backrest of his seat and launched himself towards the open hatch. "Try to keep up, boys. I have places to be."

He floated down the transfer tube and into one of the engineering section's main manufacturing bays. What had been a relatively quiet maintenance bay in his youth had evolved from overhauling or remanufacturing equipment as it wore out during the two-century trip from Earth to Gaia. The pace of work was steady, but manageable. Some days, the crew assigned down here just sat around waiting for something to break.

All that changed when the Ark entered orbit around Gaia eighteen years ago. The mission shifted from simple maintenance of the ship's existing infrastructure, to manufacturing a wide scale, seemingly endless array of components and products for the new colony. Some of them were simple, things like buckets and shovels. Some of them were not, like desalinization pods, quadcopter avionics packages, and this was all on top of their preexisting maintenance duties.

Of course, the Ark's army of 3D printers and assembly robots did a significant share of the work, but they required constant monitoring, feeding, and maintenance themselves. And for all of their considerable versatility, there were still many components too intricate, or too small batch, for the printers and assemblers to tackle efficiently.

As a consequence, the bay was absolutely screaming with activity. To his left, half a dozen new deep space satellites for the Early Warning network sat in the queue waiting for their solar panels. To his right, spidery assembly drones crawled over the long, spindly arms of the next antimatter funnel to come down the line.

Unlike the Helium-3 harvester they'd just freed on Varr, this machine was space borne. Four of the devices were already hard at work plying the Van Allen Belts of Tau Ceti F for antiprotons. At more than six times Gaia's mass, and with a core still molten enough to generate a magnetic field stronger than even Earth's used to be, the next planet out was a perfect harvesting ground for the powerful resource. The funnels used miniaturized fusion generators to project their own powerful magnetic fields as they rode the planet's naturally-occurring field lines. The charged anti-particles were then pulled into magnetic constriction bottles inside their bodies until they were full, then broke orbit and returned to Gaia with their cargo.

Or they would, as soon as any of them had a full load of two grams of antimatter, which would be several months yet. Then the volatile crop would be transferred and stored in a specially-built containment unit orbiting past even the Pathfinder counterweight on the far end of the space elevator ribbon, just in case anything went wrong. A perfect explosive, the antimatter was much too dangerous to store onboard the Ark. But then, that's not where it was needed.

While the Ark's reactors were only too happy guzzling the Helium-3 being mined on Varr, the Alcubierre Drive prototype ship's power and mass requirements meant it needed something with a little more kick than even fusion could provide.

"Commander, this way," the constable said.

Jian shook himself back into the moment. All of those thoughts had raced through his mind in a couple of seconds as he tried to find something, anything else to focus on beside the last few hours. Or the next few, for that matter.

One of the techs noticed the three of them floating by the dock and recognized Jian. The news passed through everyone in the compartment at the speed of thought as his arrival was announced through a shared plant link. As one, every pair of eyes silently turned to face him, inspect him. Pity him. Judge him.

It was... unnerving.

"After you, constable," Jian said, suddenly eager to leave the module. A central shaft ran through all of the Ark's modules, acting as both a load-bearing member taking on the stresses of acceleration and deceleration back when the Ark still moved, and as a transit tube for travel between modules. The only exception was the old Zero Stadium. It was the largest uninterrupted space on the entire ship.

Inside the central shaft, the junior constable motioned for Jian to wait against the wall. The inside of the tube had transfer handle tracks built into the inside surface to speed people up and down the Ark's ten kilometers of living and working space. The constable called three of the handles back to their location and waited, stun stick held loosely, yet conspicuously, in his crossed arms. The other constable took up position behind Jian as the three small handholds zipped down the track and slid to a stop about two meters apart.

It was a simple enough system. You grabbed the handle, set your destination with your plant, and the electromagnetically driven handle would pull you along, accelerating up to as much as sixty kilometers an hour on the express tracks and taking you from one end of the ship to the other in as little as ten minutes. All you had to do was hang on for the ride.

Jian looped the small safety strap over his wrist and gripped the ring. "So, where we going, fellas?"

"End of the line," the lead constable said.

The "line" only led one direction from here. The Command Module. They were taking Jian straight to his father. The handle pulled away, tugging gently at Jian's arm while it accelerated. Very soon, they were whizzing through the spine of the engineering module on the track's electric whine. The wind blew through Jian's hair, reminding him of summer vacations spent on Gaia's surface. The wind was always blowing down there, often even faster than the sixty kph blowing past his face now.

He thought about Shambhala at night, its lights dimmed without power streaming down from the Ark. He thought of the friends he still had down there, like Benexx. Ze was eleven years younger than him and had been little more than a precocious child when they'd first been introduced. Jian resented being forced to play babysitter for the weird little creature at first. But Atlantians matured quickly, and as the years rolled on they became fast friends. He'd not seen Benexx this summer as had become traditional. His studies and training for flight duties had taken precedent over a few weeks of frivolity, but they'd still kept in touch.

He wondered what ze was up to now.

They left the engineering module behind as the tracks carried them into the axle around which the Avalon Module rotated. Two uninterrupted kilometers of white walls and color-coded conduits passed by. There were no windows in the axles of the habitats. The outer surfaces of the shafts were festooned with thousands upon thousands of daylight lamps, casting light down onto the farms and citizens below twelve hours per day. It would be daytime in Avalon now, and night in Shangri-La module.

The constables watched him closely as they made the transition through the old Zero Stadium. They had to stick to the viewing galleries along the inside walls, as the stadium itself was depressurized to make way for the elevator ribbon bisecting the middle of the space like an enormous black sheet.

The interior space was jampacked full of anything that was too large to fit inside the engineering module and its maintenance or construction bays. Three entire lift cars sat parked in their capture gantries, waiting for elevator services to restart, while much smaller ribbon sleds gathered near the southern entrance. Crews of both human techs and repair drones were already assembling to head a few hundred meters down the ribbon to begin patching the gash the *Atlantis* had left.

"Would've save everyone a whole pile of trouble if you could have missed the tether," the junior constable said from ahead of Jian.

"Oh yeah, kid? It was either that or my shuttle punched a hole in the hull, killed everyone in the viewing galleries, crippled the docks, and probably severed the ribbon completely instead of just taking a repairable chunk out of it. So until you're flight certified, maybe don't tell me how to do my goddamned job, OK?"

"Quiet," the senior constable barked. "*Both* of you."

The rest of their transit through the stadium passed by in silence, which was just fine with Jian. He preferred to be left alone with his thoughts during the next few minutes of the trip. They passed through the lock from the old stadium and into the spine of Shangri-La. Or, as most everyone else called it, the Tomb. The place where eighteen years earlier, David Kimura's terrorists blew up all the supports underneath the habitat's artificial lake, ripping a massive hole through all six layers of the module's hull and decompressing the entire space, executing twenty thousand people in their mad play to end humanity. Twenty thousand people, asphyxiated in minutes.

Including Jian's mother.

He'd been eight when it happened. He'd only survived because he'd been in the Zero Stadium getting ready to watch a match with his older cousins when the bombs had gone off. His mother had been resting in their apartment in Shangri-La, near the very top of the Qin Shi Huang building. She'd never had a chance to get out. When they finally recovered her body months later, she'd made it down less than ten flights of steps before succumbing to the vacuum.

There was a reason Jian spent most of his time either in the engineering module or in the docks. Even the act of passing through this cursed place left a frost on the surface of his soul that took time and effort to thaw out again.

Mercifully, the trip through Shangri-La was short, and in minutes they had reached the Command module, passing first through its multiple tiers of laboratories before reaching the outer doors and security checkpoints for the bridge sphere itself, the nerve center of the entire ship. They were quickly cleared to enter, and found the great ship's brain experiencing a seizure. Dozens of crewmembers filled the space, darting back and forth from one display or station to another, conferring, questioning, arguing, shouting, and in at least two cases, crying.

Floating at the exact geometric center of the volume, standing erect despite the microgravity, Captain Chao Feng pointed and waved and barked orders as he strained to keep a lid on the scene and prevent it from descending into chaos.

The crew's reaction wasn't surprising, really. The crash was the biggest crisis the Ark had faced since the explosion in Shangri-La eighteen years earlier. Most of them hadn't been working the bridge back then. Hell, many of them hadn't even graduated primary school.

Then, Jian's father turned around from his perch and looked him dead in the eye. Just as in the engineering bay, everyone stopped what they were doing and faced him in unison. Jian knew some of the older faces personally. He'd grown up with them close at hand. They'd been over to his parents' apartment for dinner. A couple of them had even babysat for him.

His father unbuckled from his command chair and pushed off for the door.

"Constables," he said, as he gently touched down and grabbed a handhold. "Thank you. I will take over from here. You're dismissed."

They saluted crisply, then returned to the lock without a word. Chao never broke eye contact with Jian, even if his expression was unreadable. Finally, Jian flinched and looked away.

"First Officer Supan, I'm going to debrief Commander Feng. Take over."

"Aye, captain," Supan acknowledged.

"Follow me, commander," his father said formally.

Drifting across the outer wall of the bridge sphere, moving hand over hand from one hold to the next, his father guided him towards a lock that led to a set of conference rooms. Jian knew them well. He used to play in them on those rare occasions that his mother couldn't watch him and no sitters were available. He'd spent quite a few bored hours entertaining himself under the tables, pretending they were forts in need of defending from the scourge of girls infecting the ship.

The door hissed close behind them, and Chao launched himself into Jian and wrapped him up in a tight hug.

"I thought you were gone, boy," Chao said as his

fingers dug into Jian's shoulders, his breath coming fast and ragged.

The emotional outburst caught Jian off guard. He was expecting to be chewed out. Accused of failure to prevent the catastrophe. Of bringing shame to all that remained of the family line. He wasn't ready for the emotional outburst from his normally stoic and authoritarian father. It snuck past the defenses Jian had been building up for years. As his father's relieved tears drifted in the air past his face, Jian's walls came tumbling down. He wrapped his arms around his father's shoulders and squeezed harder than he had in years.

"For a minute there, I thought I was too, dad."

The moment passed and Chao untangled himself from his son's arms. "Yes, well…" he started, then stopped again to collect his tears with his fingertips before placing them on his tongue. You didn't just leave saltwater floating around that much sensitive electronic equipment, even single drops of it. Old habits die hard.

Chao squared his uniform. "I have to debrief you. And… I have to administer a BILD scan. It's not going to be pleasant."

The sudden shift in emotional momentum almost gave Jian whiplash. "You, what?"

"I'm not any happier about it than you are, son. Believe me, but–"

"A *BILD* scan?" Jian demanded. "Why not just crack my skull open and go through my brain with a potato peeler?"

"It wasn't my idea, Jian."

"Not your idea? You're the *captain*. Nothing goes on aboard this ship without your consent."

Chao took a deep breath. "There's a fine line between consent and acquiescence. Sometimes, it's almost impossible to tell them apart. I'm not an autocrat or a dictator, Jian, no matter what you think of me. I have to work with, and sometimes around, a lot of other people. And it's been made clear to me that the civilian government in Shambhala would feel better if your debriefing included the scan."

"Well to hell with their feelings. I won't submit to it."

"You'll submit to it, or you'll be confined to house arrest. Son, I don't have any choice here. It was all I could do to get them to allow me to be the one to debrief you."

"*You're* doing the scan?" Jian didn't even try to scrub the betrayal from his tone. "Are you completely mad?"

"You'd rather a stranger do it? Someone without any investment in your wellbeing?"

"Oh, you're invested in my wellbeing now? That's new."

"Don't be cruel, son. I thought I could make it a little easier on you, but if you'd rather someone else perform the scan."

"I'd rather nobody do it in the first place! I saved the damned ship, why am I being treated like a criminal?"

His father crossed his arms. "Because we don't know what happened on your shuttle, Jian. Look, I know you've been through hell, but think about what's happened over the last couple days from the perspective of people who weren't on the *Atlantis* with you. First, we discover a million year-old alien base buried in the moon that, for all we know, was left there by the same people who killed the Earth. Then, you took it upon yourself to... *circumvent* instructions from Flight to gain entry to the base where you make friends with a... what the fuck was that thing anyway?"

"His name is 'Polly.' And where is he, by the way?"

"Oh, Christ. You named it. It's secured in a lab behind eight layers of impact-resistant polymer glass, which is where it's staying. Anyway, as I was saying, then on the way back a single crewmember, for completely unknown reasons, manages to overpower the rest of the shuttle's compliment and gain control with the intent of crashing into the Ark at almost the exact same moment a bomb explodes down the well."

Jian flinched at the news. "What bomb?"

"Didn't anybody tell you? Someone detonated a bomb during the First Contact Day parade in Shambhala, less than a minute after your shuttle hit the tether. Two dozen dead, three times that number wounded."

"It was a coordinated attack?"

"No one has claimed responsibility for either of them yet, but the timing makes it hard to believe they're unrelated. And there's more you should know."

Jian swallowed a clump of dread. "Yes?"

"Benexx is missing. Ze was probably injured in the blast. At first, they thought someone had taken zer to the hospital, but ze never turned up."

"What the hell does that mean?"

"The Bensons think ze's been kidnapped. Maybe for ransom, maybe as part of the larger plan. We just don't know yet."

"We have to help find zer!"

"Zer parents will take care of Benexx. They're certainly motivated enough. You can help them right now by clearing up this distraction."

"This is ridiculous. You have the records from the shuttle's computer and the data from my plant. It's completely unnecessary."

"We don't have the shuttle's records, actually. We couldn't recover everything, and a lot of what we do have is corrupted. I know I don't have to remind you, but you're the sole survivor, Jian. It all looks really strange. People are scared and paranoid. This is the fastest way to dispel everyone's questions. Now, enough. You're doing this, right now. Then we can get to the real work."

"This is bullshit."

"Yes, it is," his father agreed. "But it's also necessary."

Jian relented to the inevitable and steeled himself for what was about to happen. "Let's get it over with, then."

CHAPTER TWELVE

Benson woke up to a familiar face, in a familiar setting.

"We've *really* got to stop meeting like this," Dr Russell said.

"Oh God, not again," Benson groaned. "How long have I been out?"

"About three hours. Which isn't really that long for you."

"How bad is it?"

"Shockingly, not very." Russell glanced at her tablet. "You have a mild concussion, a sprained right wrist, and hairline fractures on two of your ribs. Guessing from the pattern of bruises on your right side, I'd say that's where your elbow dug in when you hit the ground. Well, the balcony on the other side from the explosion, actually. That's where the rescue crew found you. As much as it pains me to admit, it was probably lucky that you decided to act like an idiot and climb that trident. You were further away from the blast than the people at ground level."

"Benexx!" Benson shouted, lucidity coming suddenly. "Where's my daugh... child? Where is ze? Is ze all right?"

Dr Russell put her hand on Benson's shoulder, to comfort and calm as much as restrain. "Calm down. You're still going to be dizzy from the concussion and the pain medication I pumped into you. You need to stay put for a few hours, at least."

"My baby. Where is ze?" Benson said, the rush of panic giving way to tears.

Dr Russell took a deep breath. "That... is an open question. And I'm not the right person to answer it. Theresa asked me to call her as soon as you woke up. She's on her way over. She'll have a better idea than I will."

The panic returned, joined by anger. Benson surged up out of the bed and grabbed Russell's forearm. But as soon as he made contact, an electric shock of pain coursed down his own forearm, leaving his hand numb.

"Ow!"

Russell shook her head. "I just told you your wrist was sprained." She set her tablet down on a small table.

"Is ze alive? Tell me!"

"We think so, Bryan. But we don't know. We just don't know."

"How can you not know?" Benson said, shouting without meaning to.

"Because," Theresa said from the doorway, "we don't know where Benexx is or who took zer. Now stop trying to assault your doctor and calm down, jackass."

They glared at each other with the kind of venom only people who'd spent many years deeply in love could manage.

Russell broke the silence. "I'll just see myself out." The door clicked shut behind her.

Benson closed his eyes and tried and mostly failed to center himself. He opened them on his wife once more. "What's going on?"

"We're still sorting through it. But what we do know for sure is somebody hijacked the shuttle *Atlantis* only a handful of minutes before it returned to the Ark. Whoever it was tried to kamikaze the ship. It looks like somebody regained control at the last second and managed to change course just enough to avoid hitting the Ark itself, but couldn't dodge the elevator ribbon in time."

Benson's eyes grew into dinner plates. "Holy shit! The beanstalk!"

Theresa held up a hand. "It's still intact, Bryan. But barely. Feng told me in confidence that the ribbon was sliced thirty percent of the way through. There's enough material left to keep the system in place, but that's about it. All cargo and passenger shipments up or down the beanstalk have been suspended until they can repair it. They had to cut two of the lift cars loose and let them parachute down to the surface. After dumping their cargo."

"Holy shit…"

"That's not even the worst of it. Electrical shorts along the surface of the tether were causing even more degradation, so all our power coming down the beanstalk from the Ark has been shut down. That's why the lights went out right before the bomb went off."

"The *Atlantis*, Feng's boy was commanding it. Is he…?"

Theresa shook her head, sending little waves through her long raven hair. "He's OK, but he's the only one. The rest of the shuttle crew is dead. Jian has been arrested pending an inquiry."

"Holy shit, Jian's wrapped up in this mess?"

"We have no idea, Bryan. It's too early."

"What happened to Benexx?" Benson said, forcing serenity into his voice.

Theresa moved up and squeezed his good hand. "I don't know, sweetie. The power was down, so we don't have any CCTV footage from the surveillance net. We got some glimpses here and there from vid captures various witnesses recorded with their plants, but a bomb had just gone off. There was a lot of running and out of focus footage. Pavel's sorting through it all, but it's slow going. We know ze was alive after the explosion, the float absorbed most of the shockwave. A couple dozen folks at the epicenter weren't as lucky. We lost a lot of people today, Bryan."

Benson grimaced, but after all he'd experienced, cold recitation of body-counts didn't faze him anymore. That part of him died with twenty-thousand other people in the Shangri-La module long ago.

"And you really think somebody hijacking a shuttle to destroy the Ark and a bomb going off in Shambhala almost simultaneously is a coincidence?" he said.

"I *know* it's not, Bryan. I'm not stupid. But they're still dead. A lot of them," Theresa bit back.

"I'll mourn them after we find Benexx," he said instead.

"Bryan… I don't know how we're going to find zer."

"I do," Benson said with steely resolve.

"Oh really?" his wife said without even trying to contain her annoyance. "Enlighten me, coach. How are you going to find our missing child, when your *wife*, zer *mother*, who happens to have unrestricted access to the entire city's surveillance system in her capacity as the fucking *Chief Constable* is running around trying not to panic over her missing kid while the whole damned city is on fire?"

"I chipped Benexx when ze was six," Benson said flatly.

For the first time in at least ten years of marriage, Theresa was struck dumb. Her mouth moved up and down mechanically a couple of times, but no sounds came out. Finally, she rubbed a hand over her face, taking a moment to compose herself.

"OK," she said finally. "You mean to tell me that you, in your capacity as the *Director of Recreation*, chipped our child without zer consent and knowledge, or, for that matter, *my* consent and knowledge as zer *mother*, just in case someone tried to kidnap zer someday?"

Benson nodded. "Yep. Totally did that. Although, in my defense, I was more worried about zer getting lost during one of zer little wilderness outings with Kexx or Sakiko than a terrorist cell abducting zer."

Theresa breathed hard for several seconds while her eyes bored into him like diamond-tipped drill bits. Just as

Benson feared her gaze would erupt out the back of his skull, she spoke.

"You arrogant, delusional, paranoid..." Her face twisted up, but then relaxed with a sigh. "...beautiful asshole. What's the chip's code?"

The sun had retreated below the horizon to the west by the time Benson, Theresa, Korolev, and recently-deputized Atlantian constable Cha'ku stacked up outside of the reddish adobe building on the skirts of the Native Quarter in a neighborhood even the Atlantians living there would describe as "rough." It was a two-story affair not so different from the traditional Atlantian homes found in the villages overseas, and almost indistinguishable from every other building on the narrow, curving street.

<You sure this is the one?> Theresa asked through their plant link so as not to alert the inhabitants to their presence. They'd already run into resistance from a wannabe street gang that withered as soon as they realized Benson's group hadn't just gotten lost on the way back from getting spiced yulka cakes.

Benson waved the tablet he was using to scan for the subdermal chip embedded in Benexx's thigh. <The signal is strongest right here. I don't know which floor, but ze's definitely inside.>

<OK, I'm calling in for the warrant now.>

Magistrate Okuda was aware of the potential raid and had been standing by waiting to sign off on a search warrant as soon as they'd gotten probable cause. It wasn't a hot pursuit situation because no one had actually seen Benexx being carried into the dwelling, so they couldn't just go stampeding inside. One had to respect the niceties of the legal system, even with murderous, kidnapping, terrorist scum.

Korolev passed the time double-checking his weapon again. Both he and Theresa carried standard law-enforcement side arms only a little bigger than an old-fashioned handgun, except they threw self-contained taser cartridges instead of lead slugs. The little devils had enough capacitor charge to dole out fifty thousand volts for a total of twenty seconds and knock even an adult Atlantian fully on their ass. It was more than enough time to get them in specially-made elbow cuffs that pinned their arms behind their backs. Atlantians were real handfuls in hand-to-hand combat, but their nervous systems were still bioelectric and just as vulnerable to tasers as humans.

And if things got really hairy, Korolev had a military-issue P-120 Personal Defense Weapon slung over his shoulder. Benson knew what the rifle was capable of after the Battle of Black Bridge. Not even the rage boiling over inside of him from the abduction of his child made Benson want to see one of them open-up on another living being. Not again.

<OK, we have a green light.> Theresa held up her hand and started a silent, five-beat countdown with her fingers. Korolev leaned back and whispered something to Cha'ku, who tightened zer grip on zer fighting sticks. The two of them had been teammates on the Mustangs for three seasons already, Korolev playing veteran to Cha'ku's rookie. They'd made a good pair on the field despite playing on opposite sides of the ball, and that trust had transferred over to police work. Cha'ku was old for an Atlantian in Shambhala. Ze'd come over the ocean as an adolescent, already in training as one of Xekallum village's warriors when zer parents decided to emigrate. The fighting sticks were nothing more complex than a pair of sixty-centimeter-long wooden shafts with ninety-degree tapered hooks on their far ends about as long as Benson's thumb. They looked like nothing more than crude clubs to anyone who hadn't seen a skilled warrior use them to beat, trap, and bend an opponent's limbs into a random assortment of cooked spaghetti noodles.

And Cha'ku was *really* good with them. Sometimes,

diplomatically, it just really helped to have an Atlantian around when you needed to straighten some of their own people out on a particular point of etiquette. Like, not blowing up a parade and stealing people's kids, for example.

Theresa's countdown reached her index finger, then collapsed into a fist. Go time.

Benson, unarmed civilian that he technically was, lined up behind his wife and Cha'ku, with Korolev and his heavy artillery taking up the rear. Truth be told, he would have preferred to be at the head of the stack, with Theresa as far behind him as possible. But he'd given up that job years ago, and it wasn't like he could have held her back anyway. Someone had their kid, and mama grizzly was likely to sink her claws into anybody that tried to get in between her and finding Benexx, her husband included.

As was traditional in Atlantian construction, there was no door to kick down. The heat at these latitudes made keeping out the cold unnecessary, and the cool-blooded race hadn't really taken to air conditioning for obvious reasons.

It also meant there was one less thing to go wrong while executing a search warrant.

"Constables! Search warrant!" Theresa shouted as they swarmed into the first floor. Cha'ku shouted the Atlantian translation from the back of the line, even if two-thirds of the words didn't exist in Atlantian. Theresa, Korolev, and Cha'ku cleared the first floor with practiced fluidity.

<Nobody home down here,> Korolev said from a side room. Atlantian sleeping quarters were usually on the ground floor, or even in a basement, closer to the heat of the day still trapped in the ground and walls. It was unusual for the ground floor to be empty at this time of day. That wasn't the only part of the house that stood out. What few trappings of furniture and decorations

the house had lay in tatters among a sea of refuse. Torn clothes, crushed bottles, discarded food containers, and piles of dirt covered the floor. A distinct odor of Atlantian waste permeated the space, one Benson remembered only too well from the mushroom fields in his brief trip into the Dweller caverns. You didn't forget that smell.

<It's a drug house,> Benson said. <They were growing those damned bak'ri mushrooms.>

<Looks like they cleared the operation out before we got here,> Theresa said.

<I don't see any stairs leading to a basement. Are you sure the signal is coming from this house?>

<Yeah, it's even stronger now than it was outside.>

<Hey, what do you guys make of this?> Korolev held up a sheet of paper. Not the plastfilm stuff humans used in the rare occasions they needed hardcopy, but a yellowed, rough-cut sheet made of pressed plant fibers. Dark brown ink, off register and smeared in a couple of spots, covered the page in Atlantian characters. Benson's plant automatically overlaid translated English text in red letters. Some separatist wack-job boilerplate about three spears divided being better weapons than a trident.

<There's some over here in English, too,> Korolev said. <That's weird. There were humans in here too?>

<These labs usually have at least one human involved for the chemistry.> Theresa said.

Benson handed the page back to Korolev. <Bag them, we need to keep searching.>

<Move to the second floor,> Theresa ordered. They high-stepped up the slightly-too-tall stairs built for Atlantian legs. Benson took up the rear position and waited for the constables to clear the floor.

"Bryan, get up here!" Theresa shouted with her real voice. Her tone nearly paralyzed him. There was no relief in it, only more panic. Whatever she'd seen, it wasn't good.

After a moment's hesitation, Benson took the stairs

three at a time, not caring what his knees would think about it in the morning. In his haste, he missed the top step and painfully ground a shin against the hard mudstone lip. He ignored it.

Once he reached the landing, Benson saw a flash of movement in a doorway off to the left and followed it. The room was cramped and unlit, a large closet at best. Korolev had switched on his rifle's spotlight to illuminate the scene. Lying unmoving and curled on zer side, an Atlantian rested on the hard floor, zer body and face completely covered by a blanket seeped-through with blood.

So much blood.

The locator's beeping sped up until it became a steady, uninterrupted tone.

Benson's heart beat so hard it threatened to detonate inside his chest. His knees wobbled and his skin went clammy with cold sweat. Theresa buried her face in his shoulder and screamed, her ragged voice half inconsolable pain, half incoherent, blind, murderous rage. Benson held her tight as their tears began to flow, both to comfort, and to keep her from lashing out. They huddled together, discovering the anguish that only parents who have outlived their own children can share.

"I can't look at zer," Theresa said between gulping breaths. "I can't."

"It's OK, Esa." Benson squeezed his wife's shoulders. "You don't have to."

"Ah, Chief? Coach?" Korolev knelt by the body and held up a corner of the sheet. "You need to look at this."

"We'll ID zer later, Pavel!" Benson barked.

"No," Korolev shook his head. "You won't." With a flutter of fabric, he stripped off the sheet to reveal the body underneath. Benson physically recoiled at the sight of the bruised and lacerated corpse. But beyond the bloodstains and the torn flesh, something else was wrong. Ze was too thick, for one thing. Too well-muscled.

Still clutching Theresa protectively, Benson leaned in and looked deeply into the unfortunate victim's face and dull, lifeless eyes.

"That's not Benexx," Benson said.

"Yeah, no shit," Korolev said. "You think I'd make you look at your own dead kid?"

Benson broke his grip on Theresa. "It's not zer." He fell to his hands and knees to get a better look at the unidentified body. Gently, Benson held out his hand and rested the back of it on the corpse's chest. "Ze's still warm." He grabbed underneath the victim's arm just below the shoulder and squeezed the flesh against the cartilage that made up an Atlantian skeleton, one of the few places on their bodies one could reliably search for–

"Pulse!" Benson shouted. "I've got a pulse, but it's weak as shit. Get Doc Russell, now!"

"Bryan," Theresa said quietly, "what about the chip?"

"Right." Benson activated his tablet's ultrasonic scanning feature and passed it over the victim.

"There's some jagged-looking shrapnel in some of these wounds, probably bomb fragments. Wait..." Benson tossed the tablet aside and ran his fingers along the outside of the poor Atlantian's left thigh. His fingertips found what they were looking for: a hard-plastic RFID chip hardly bigger than a rice grain. Less than two centimeters away, a fresh puncture wound insulted the victim's skin. It had barely had enough time to seal up and scab over. Pinching the chip between his fingers, Benson quickly squeezed it back out the channel it had entered through and held it up in front of the light on the end of Korolev's rifle.

"How the hell did they know to look for that?" Theresa asked.

"No idea," Benson answered. "But I intend to ask them." The chip shattered, drawing a small bead of blood from between his fingertips.

"Personally."

CHAPTER THIRTEEN

Benexx flirted with consciousness.

Briefly, at first, like a hesitant blind date. Awkwardly, like the same. But along with the discomfort came momentary flashes of light and sound that zer mind struggled to interpret. Zer addled awareness tried to stitch the glimpses of lucidity together into something discernable. And failed, for the most part.

Ze slept.

After an unknowable length of time, zer mind came back around and found itself. Wounded, bandaged, and utterly alone, Benexx sat against a dank, damp corner in the dark. The last thing ze clearly remembered was standing on the parade float looking up at zer father hanging off the spindly fake trident like a gorilla hanging from a fishing pole. Then, a flash and a wave of heat, the sensation of tumbling, then nothing. Judging by zer headache and the wrap around zer skull, Benexx guessed ze'd landed badly. Someone had picked zer up, tended to zer wounds, and then dumped zer in this… wherever this was.

"Hello?" ze called into the dark. Zer echo answered. Ze called out again in Atlantian this time with identical results. As a child raised by humans, Benexx didn't have much patience for the dark. The enemies from the oldest stories all concealed themselves within it. But, as a child of Atlantis, ze had an answer for it.

Even after spending the last half-dozen summers

vacationing among zer own kind in G'tel, Benexx still hadn't mastered the subtleties of communicating with zer skinglow. But, alone in the dark, refinement hardly mattered. Ze forced open all of zer bioluminescent chromatophores in one big contraction, throwing out zer body's natural blue-green light like ze hadn't done since the first terrifyingly quiet nights ze'd been left alone in zer own private room as an infant.

The rock surfaces around zer held none of zer old nursery's warmth. No mobiles of shuttles and ulik packs spun gently overhead. No haphazardly, yet colorfully painted depictions of dux'ah herds and football games lined the walls.

Everywhere zer body's light reached was met with cold, damp, gray, unyielding stone. And ze meant everywhere. The cavern was warm and damp, which could mean it was either really close to the surface where the caves closely matched the outside temperature, or much further underground where the heat from Gaia's core started to take hold again. There was no good way to tell until ze escaped the chamber and scouted zer surroundings. Certain types of fungus and bacterial colonies only lived at one depth or the other, but the walls around zer looked as though they'd been scraped bare.

Fungal mats weren't all that was missing from the walls. They were also devoid of any doorways or passages into the rest of the cave system. Benexx's pulse quickened and ze felt a tension grow across zer abdomen. Unsurprisingly in a race that spent entire generations at a time living in caves to hide from asteroid impacts, claustrophobia was basically unheard of among Atlantians. Before the humans had arrived, they didn't even have a word for the concept, it was so foreign. But the simple fact was nobody liked being locked inside a stone room with no exit. That wasn't a phobia, it was just basic survival instinct.

But if there were no doors, it did beg the question of how in Xis's name Benexx had gotten into the chamber in the first place. There had been a way *in,* so it only stood to reason that there had to be a way back *out*.

Benexx's eyes had fully adjusted to the light pouring out of zer body by then. Ze meticulously scanned the walls a second time, looking for imperfections that might be hiding a door, patches of mudstone sealing an opening, trapdoors in the floor, or…

Ze looked up at the ceiling. There it was. A shaft, scarcely wider than zer shoulders, but it reached up deeper into the rock regardless. It had to be the entry point. It was also fifteen meters above zer at the apex of severely sloping baffles of rock. Benexx was a fair climber of trees and buildings, but ze was not experienced with spelunking. But, really, how hard could it be?

Benexx stood, testing zer legs and balance. It was obvious by now that ze'd been kidnapped and dumped down here, wherever *here* was. Zer muscles were stiff, and ze winced more than once as ze probed at the bruises along zer right side. But, while tender, nothing seemed torn or frayed. Not for the first time, ze was grateful ze did not share zer parents' rigid, yet brittle bones.

Ze lined up against a promising strip of wall that appeared to afford zer a few more hand and foot holds than the rest of the chamber. Benexx flexed zer fingers, then interlocked them and pulled, loosening the digits in preparation. Ze pressed zer palms flat against the damp stone. If ze were human, the moisture would make the rock slippery and treacherous. But the thousands of tiny suction cups covering the skin on the inside of zer hands meant zer grip was even stronger than if the rock-face had been bone dry.

Benexx climbed a meter, then another, careful to always maintain three points of contact with the rock, moving only one hand or one foot at a time. Another meter. Two more. The ceiling began to angle inward, testing the strength of zer grip. It held, but zer fingers felt the strain. Ze pressed upwards, until ze finally pressed zer luck. One of the fingers on zer right hand peeled free from the rock without warning while ze was reaching for the next hold with zer left. Benexx scrambled to regain zer hold, but it was useless. Ze clung fast to the rock for a moment, hanging upside down by zer feet, just long enough to orient zerself for the coming fall.

Benexx crashed into the floor like a sack full of pudding. Ze rolled with the impact as best ze could, but misjudged zer direction in the dark and slammed into a stalagmite that had been waiting patiently for tens of thousands of years for the opportunity.

It hurt. Bad.

Ze broke down, then. Benexx didn't cry, exactly. Atlantians had tear ducts, but they weren't triggered by anything except dry eyes. Instead, zer skinglow dimmed without zer conscious control and zer muscles started to pulse gently. It was a leftover of evolution, a way to get blood flowing to zer arms and legs faster through zer heartless circulatory system in preparation to fight or run. But ze couldn't do either. There was no sign of whomever had dumped zer down here to fight, and unless ze wanted to run in place, the stone chamber didn't offer a great deal of space for exercise.

The situation's true gravity hit zer for the first time. Lying on the ground, bruised and alone in the dark, ze let go to the shivers as zer skin went almost completely black. Ze'd believed zerself isolated and lonely in the warmth and comfort of zer parents' home in Shambhala. What an utter fool ze'd been. A child. A spoiled child in need of a reality check. Ze'd give anything to be sitting on the couch in their living room listening to zer father tell zer how lucky ze was.

Benexx could taste the fake leather of the couch on zer fingers. The nylon and other polymers mixed with the musk of years of stale human sweat. Zer parents tried very hard to keep a clean house, but they didn't have taste buds on their fingertips. Still, in that moment, ze couldn't imagine anything tasting sweeter. Benexx looked up at the hole directly overhead. Zer only chance at getting home lay on the other side of it.

Shaken, but rejuvenated, Benexx rose unsteadily to zer feet, resting a hand on the stone cone for balance, and resumed zer path to the exit. Through a force of will, ze calmed the vibrations running through zer muscles and pried open zer chromatophores, letting the bluegreen of zer bioluminescence fill the chamber and guide zer way once more. A couple of small but promising handholds that ze'd overlooked further up the wall stood out this time.

Ignoring the soreness in zer arms, Benexx aggressively tackled the rock wall, digging zer fingers into the craggy face with renewed purpose. Ze could taste the rock, feel the slick layer of bacteria that clung to it, used them to get a better seal with zer suction cups. In no time, ze reached, then passed by the spot ze'd fallen from on the last attempt. The soreness in zer muscles turned to heat, then to fire. The slope of the roof was almost parallel to the floor now. Benexx crept across the surface as quickly as ze dared, moving only one arm or leg at a time until ze'd reestablished three points of grip. The screaming in zer limbs urged zer onward faster, to get it over with. But too fast meant falling, ze'd already learned that much tonight. Or today. Whenever it was. Didn't matter. Peel off one hand, set it into the rock. Peel off the other. Ignore the pain. Just another meter to go.

With a final stretch of zer arm, Benexx laid a finger on the lip of the hole in the ceiling. Ze took a moment to expel zer airsacks and bring in fresh oxygen to fuel zer protesting muscles. Or as close to fresh as ze'd get in this dank cave, in any case. The ninety-degree transition from the ceiling to the inside of the hole was going to be tricky, even with the extreme flexibility zer malleable Atlantian physique afforded.

One more meter, Benexx told zerself. *Just one more.* Ze reached up inside the hole with one hand and explored, careful to find the best little crags and folds in the rock to anchor zer fingers. Once zer fingers were wedged in as far as they would go, ze let go with zer other hand and grabbed the inside surface of the hole as fast as ze could before zer hold gave way.

Ze was committed now. A small quake of fear trembled zer body as Benexx let zer feet come free of the ceiling and swing down into open air. All of zer body weight bore down on the tenuous grip zer eight fingers held on the rock. This was the hard part. Dangling by just zer arms, Benexx had to pull zerself up enough to get a toe on the inside of the hole. For what was certainly the first and perhaps only time in zer life, ze wished ze'd participated in one of zer father's workout programs.

Already nearing the point of exhaustion, Benexx commanded zer arms to pull zer up. They flatly refused. Drawing a deep breath, ze dug deep into whatever reserves ze had left and pulled. The strain was enormous. Zer muscles felt like hot coals knotting up under zer skin. Losing zerself for a moment, Benexx called out in pain, frustration, and anger, sending a primal scream echoing through the cavern and into the unseen spaces beyond. But ze didn't care.

Miraculously, mercifully, Benexx's arms started to move. Quaking with effort, ze willed zerself upward, centimeter by tortuous centimeter. When zer chest touched the cool surface of the rock, ze risked all and threw an arm higher up the face of the short tunnel. It found purchase. Like a pendulum, ze swung zer lower body back and forth until zer legs were almost parallel with the lip of the hole. With one last surge that ze was pretty certain tore one of zer smaller stabilizer muscles in zer right leg, Benexx got a toe on the rock and used it to get a three-point hold once again. With zer foot anchored, ze pushed up and took the weight off zer arms. Zer other foot followed, and in a moment ze was bounding up the last short distance to the top. Benexx pulled in zer color cells and let zer skinglow burn as bright as the billions of symbiotic bacteria in zer dermis would shine, flooding the small tunnel and the space beyond with their light.

Ze was less than an arm's length from the top. Ze had enough in the tank to go that far. Ze was going to make it. Ze was defying whoever'd dumped zer down here and was going to escape the cell they'd intended for zer.

The next floor was within arm's reach. With a surge of excitement, Benexx slapped zer left hand on the next level, only to have a foot come crashing down on zer raw fingers.

An Atlantian face leered over the aperture, dark and smirking with malice. "And where do you think you're flying off to, little injri?"

"Ow!" Benexx cried out. "You're hurting me!"

"That's the general idea." Ze ground zer foot into Benexx's fingers to emphasize the point, then leveled the barrel of a rifle at zer face. "Now, crawl back down into your hole, or I'll drill a hole into your pretty face, bearer."

Benexx froze at the sight of the weapon. Ze had no illusions about what would happen if ze was shot at this range. Ze'd practiced with one with zer father at the range once, and had seen them used against some of the more assertive types of wildlife in and around Shambhala, and of course had seen the footage zer father's plant had captured at the battles of G'tel and the Black Bridge fifteen years ago.

But the gun brought up an even bigger concern, beyond its immediate and lethal threat. How the hell had a kidnapper gotten zer hands on one, especially an Atlantian? They were supposed to be biometrically locked to a specific user, not just floating around for anyone to use.

"You're bluffing," Benexx spat, blocking out the pain in zer fingertips. "You may have stolen that gun from the armory, but there's no way you hacked the safeties."

Zer prison guard smirked in the Atlantian way. "Who said I needed to hack it?" Ze moved the muzzle of the rifle a fraction away from Benexx's face… and fired.

The muzzle flash blinded zer dark-soaked eyes in the same instant the shockwave from the shot slapped into zer ears like a thunderclap. Zer vision bleached in white and zer ears ringing, Benexx lost zer grip under the relentless grinding of zer captor's foot against zer fingers.

With a scream ze couldn't hear, Benexx peeled away from the rock and slipped back into the shadows.

CHAPTER FOURTEEN

Jian sat curled up in the corner of his shower and let the nearly-scalding water batter against his skin until his nerves went numb and the knots in his muscles loosened.

Everything hurt. Tomorrow, it would be worse. Spending several hours tightly strapped into a crash couch in an uncontrolled four gee spin will do that to a body, no matter how fit. Jian watched as the last of his weekly water allocation spiraled down the drain between his feet. It was Tuesday. He didn't care. What were they going to do, shut off his water?

"You can bill me," he muttered to no one.

His plant chimed, alerting him to someone waiting at the door.

<Go away,> he sent.

<Jian, it's your father.>

<Oh. Well in that case, you can go away *and* go fuck yourself.>

The connection dropped, and Jian heard the door to his apartment swing open. Damned command overrides. The bathroom door slid open. Jian didn't ever care enough to object.

"Jesus, son. You look like a raisin. How long have you been in there?"

"There's still hot water, so not long enough."

Chao reached over to the shower's control panel and shut down the flow, then threw open the glass door as the fog rolled across the floor. He threw a towel at Jian.

"Honestly, Jian. If your mother could see you like this, it would break her heart."

"Yeah, well she can't, now can she?"

Chao ignored the barb. "Dry yourself off and get dressed. I'll be waiting for you in the living room."

"Why?"

"Because your captain just ordered you to. Now move, kiddo."

"That's cheating."

"Yeah, well I cheated my way into the position. Five minutes, then I'm dragging you out of here, dressed or not."

His father left the bathroom and shut the door behind him, leaving Jian alone, wet, and naked on the floor. He sat there for a long minute until the steam disappeared up into the exhaust fan and the air chilled his damp skin. He briefly considered turning the water back on, but although he didn't mind telling his father to stuff it, he wasn't so far gone that he felt like committing insubordination against his commanding officer.

Damn them both for being the same person.

Jian stood on sore, wobbly legs and steadied himself against the sink basin. The bare metal felt cool against his thigh. Jian toweled himself dry, then wrapped his body in an embarrassingly luxurious bath robe. It was old, threadbare in several places, but made of genuine wool grown by a centuries-dead sheep. It had been passed down through many generations of his family. Just one of the myriad little perks of being a Feng that had passed beneath his notice as a child. But as an adult, he saw them all too clearly.

He'd grown to resent them, but it *was* a very soft robe.

Jian crossed the hallway into his bedroom and opened his closet. What to wear? Well, he'd been ordered to dress by his captain, so his crew uniform made the most sense. Yeah, keep it formal, keep his father at arm's length. He didn't have any choice about dealing with his CO, but he could send the message loud and clear that "captain" was the only capacity Jian was willing to work with his father in at the moment.

He selected a freshly-cleaned and pressed uniform, and donned it with the sort of careful eye that he hadn't used since graduating Flight School. Jian ran a lint brush over his sleeves and shoulders, fixed his hair, then took one last look. Satisfied that everything was ready for inspection, he walked out into the living room to find his father resting on his chaise lounge.

"All right, captain, what am I dressed for?"

Chao stood up and walked briskly for the door. "Follow me."

Jian rolled his eyes, but did as he was told. His father called an elevator. They waited in silence until the car arrived. The doors closed and Chao selected the ground floor.

"I have… news," Chao said once they were alone in the car. "About Benexx."

Jian's eyebrows inched up in anticipation, but his father's face wasn't encouraging.

"Yes? Tell me."

Chao swallowed and squared his shoulders. "Well, it turns out that paranoid lunatic father of zers had implanted a subdermal locator chip in zer when Benexx was a kid and didn't bother to tell anybody. So as soon as he got out of the hospital, Bryan and Theresa tracked zer chip down to some flop house in the native quarter."

"Except Benexx wasn't there," Jian said, anticipating his father's next sentence.

Chao shook his head. "No. Someone had removed the chip and implanted it into one of the other Atlantian bombing victims. We haven't identified the victim yet. The Bensons found zer abandoned in an upstairs room, presumably left there to die. They got zer to the hospital just in time, but ze hasn't regained consciousness yet.

Regardless, it's obvious now that Benexx isn't just missing, but has definitely been kidnapped, and by well-organized people who know what they're doing."

"If Benson didn't tell anyone about the chip, how did they know to look for it in the first place?"

"Good question. Maybe they're just as paranoid as he is."

"Is that what this is about? Benexx's kidnappers? They have to be linked to technician Madeja somehow."

"We're working that angle up here. We dug through Madeja's web traffic, search history, correspondence, social connections, all of it and found nothing out of the ordinary. Nothing, until we searched her apartment, and..."

"And what? She was storing files offline?"

"About as far offline as you can get. Paper. She had a bunch of rough-cut paper newsletters from some frothing-at-the-mouth separatist lunatic calling themselves the Voiceless."

"A member of the crew? Seriously?"

"No, we don't think so. The paper is Atlantian from Pukal. Whoever's writing this trash, they're probably based dirtside and shipped the leaflets up the beanstalk. We never caught wind of them before because nobody ever thought to screen for paper. I mean, paper!? Who even thinks like that?"

"Can I read them?"

"Later. Right now, we're going to a debriefing about the other unmitigated disaster you stumbled into."

"The facility?"

Chao nodded. "The facility."

They reached the ground floor of Jian's apartment building. It was a quick walk to the nearest spoke lift. In its heyday, it was prime real estate. But now with the Ark supporting one-tenth of the population it had been designed for, there wasn't much competition for living space anymore, even with Shangri-La module's towers reduced to permanent shrines to the victims of Kimura and da Silva's attack.

They entered the lift and headed for the hub a kilometer above their heads. With each passing meter, the apparent gravity acting on Jian's aching joints and muscles lessened, until the lift glided to a stop. Jian had been so distracted by the view that he'd forgotten to put his feet in the hold-down loops and floated up in the zero gee. His father grabbed his ankle and pulled him back down, arresting his momentum before Jian hit his head on the ceiling.

"I need you present, son. Don't offer any more than you have to. Stick to the facts alone."

"I passed the damned BILD scan. Isn't my trial over?"

"Your innocence may have been proven, but your *judgment* is still an open question. So if you care about your flight status, stick to the facts. Honestly, Jian, your mother and I raised you to be more level-headed than this."

"Will you *stop* bringing up mom every five minutes?" Jian shrieked. "I'm having a shitty enough couple of days as it is."

Despite his smaller size and advancing years, Chao's face and arms turned to steel. Before he even knew what was happening, his father had Jian's back pinned up against the inside of the lift car, his elbow pressed against his throat. So, his father had taken the hint from his uniform. This wasn't a parent disciplining a child. It was a captain doling out a little bulkhead counseling.

"I've let your tongue flap because I know just how hard this has been on you." Chao pressed his forearm in just a fraction harder. "That ends now. Disrespect me in the privacy of your quarters all you want. But we're in public now, even if we're behind closed doors. Whether you're smart enough to recognize it or not, I am trying to protect you and your future, Jian. And don't you *dare* presume to lecture me on 'shitty days.' I was already a man when

I watched Shangri-La die. Panicked when I didn't know if you were trapped inside among the damned. Watched your mother, *my wife*, die. And no matter what you think about it, I loved her, even if in a complicated and unconventional way. I watched it all carrying the guilt that it was my fault, at least in part. Guilt I *still* carry. Everyday. I don't need reminders from an insolent child, even if he is *technically* a man." Chao took a deep breath before continuing. "I'm going to release you now. And while we are among the rest of the crew, you are going to show the respect befitting of a commander addressing his captain, yes?"

Jian nodded several times in rapid succession.

"Good." Chao let his forearm drop. "I'm sorry about all this, Jian, really I am, especially the scan. I know how... degrading they can be."

"Yeah?" Jian rubbed his throat. "And how do you know that?"

"Because I've been scanned. By Captain Mahama herself, bless her memory. I hated her for it for months afterward. But in time, I came to recognize that circumstances, and my own actions, had made it not only necessary, but unavoidable."

"And you think that because you forgave your captain, that I'll come around and forgive you?"

"Hope springs eternal." His father keyed the doors to open, then held out a palm. "After you."

Back to the command module they went. Back through Shangri-La again. Neither of them spoke. Neither wanted to. Soon, they settled into chairs in one of the command module's conference rooms. Not the one Jian had been scanned in, thankfully, although the only way he could tell was from the room number on the door. Otherwise, they were identical.

Jian glanced around the table as he strapped himself down to keep from floating out of the chair during the meeting. There were already half a dozen people seated in the room in addition to himself and his father, mostly command staff, and a couple of reps from the various science departments, most notably Dr Kania who headed up the Astrophysics unit.

Usually, the crew didn't bother with the chairs and instead just floated in small alcoves built into the walls while they conducted their business. The only time the chairs were pulled out was as a courtesy to "visiting" dignitaries from Shambhala, who found talking to floating holograms disorienting, even to the point of inducing motion sickness in some with weaker constitutions.

On cue, ghostly forms began appearing in the chairs one after another as the holo-projectors mounted in the ceiling warmed up. In moments, they solidified and four new people "sat" at the table. Of them, Jian only recognized two people: Agrawal, the city's current administrator, and Devorah Feynman, the long-serving curator of Shambhala's museum. The woman had to be pushing ninety by now, but gave no impression of slowing down. Why she'd been invited was a bit of a mystery to Jian, however. She was technically still a crew member, but held no official position and hadn't since her retirement.

The resolution of the holograms hadn't been affected much by the accident. While the ribbon had been shut down to lift car traffic and high-voltage power transfer to the surface for fear of further damage, comparatively low-voltage data transmission had been deemed safe by the engineers.

Chao, acting as the chair and host of the meeting, brought it to order with a bang of a gavel, the end of which was tied to the table to keep it from floating away. Some traditions never died.

"Thanks for coming, everyone. We all know what this meeting is about, so let's just cut right to it, shall we?" A wave of agreeing nods ran around the table. "Good. So, the 'facility' as it's been taken to be called. The question before us is what to do about it. But before we can answer that, first we need to have some idea of what it is in the first place. To that end, I've invited Dr Kania, head of the Ark's Astrophysics Department, and Commander Feng, the only person to have actually explored the facility in person."

"Only surviving person," Jian corrected his father reflexively.

Chao shot him a look, but quickly relented and bowed his head. "Of course you're right. Technician Rakunas's bravery and sacrifice should not go without mention. Or those of the rest of the *Atlantis*'s crew. But, we must continue. Dr Kania has prepared a short briefing of what we've learned with certainty over the last few days." Chao ceded the floor.

"Thank you, Captain Feng," Kania started. "I should start out by saying this briefing will be very brief indeed, as we know almost nothing about the facility with certainty. However, here's what we can tell you."

At the center of the table, an image of Varr's surface surrounding the facility site materialized and started to slowly rotate. "What you're seeing here is a rendered image of the cave-in entrance and grounds near where the facility was discovered, extrapolated from pictures and video feed recovered among the shuttle's data and transmissions. We've already determined the age of the scene is somewhere between a few hundred thousand and a few million years. We're confident, based on the differential in the number of impact craters in the immediate scene and the surrounding area that the facility was built inside an excavated hole, and then reburied."

"Why such a large span in the estimate?" Devorah asked.

"There's a lot of variability in meteorite impact rates. We've managed to date enough craters down on the surface of Gaia and on Varr to know the outer solar system goes through periodic instabilities, probably as a result of some sort of orbital resonance with Tao Ceti F we're still trying to understand. This causes higher than average meteor activity for a couple thousand years at a time. We're not sure exactly how many of these storms have taken place since the facility's construction or how intense they were, hence the wide range of possible dates. But we are very confident that a quarter million years is the least amount of time it could have been there."

"Fair enough," Devorah said.

"I've heard it suggested that an older civilization of Atlantians may have constructed it," Chao said. "Is that likely?"

"I wouldn't bet a bucket of reheated tofu on it," Devorah said. "The sort of civilization that's progressed far enough to develop a heavy lift to orbit capacity and large-scale, space-based construction would leave a footprint on the world that would last for many tens of millions of years. Roads, dams, erosive effects of agricultural clearing, mining sites, the kind of advanced industrial capacity that can build a multi-stage rocket would have to be massive. Yet outside of their road network and villages, we've seen no archeological evidence anywhere on the surface of Gaia that any prior Atlantian society had advanced even as far as the current one has."

"My department's findings concur with Director Feynman," Kania said.

<Director?> Jian thought to his father. <Of what department?>

<Devorah is the informal head of Atlantian Cultural Studies. Now pay attention and stay sharp.>

"Anyway," Devorah resumed. "Combine that with the fact any civilization that could build an underground complex on their own moon would also have the capability to deflect or destroy any incoming asteroids and avoid being knocked back to the stone age in the first place."

"That may be," Chao said, "but it wouldn't necessarily protect them from disease, famine, or war. There are a lot of ways to collapse a civilization. We should know, having tried most of them ourselves at one point or another."

"That is certainly true," Devorah conceded. "But again, there would be some evidence of the previous civilization. Not only that, but we've found no mention of any prior advancement beyond their current level of technology in either the Atlantian oral or written traditions. But they've got a buttload of stories about Cuut getting pissed and shoving a big rock up their asses every few thousand years. Awfully tough to break out of the stone age when the reset button keeps getting hit every couple of eons."

"Why don't we just ask them?" Jian said. The room turned and cast disapproving looks at the disruption. He ignored them. "In fact, why aren't any Atlantians sitting in on this meeting? It's their moon we're talking about, one of their Gods. Shouldn't they be hearing this?"

Devorah's hologram smiled. "You know what? That's a *really* interesting question. One I'd like an answer to myself."

An uncomfortable silence blanketed the room as the nominal leaders of humanity glanced at each other, scrambling for an answer. It was Administrator Agrawal that found her voice first.

"We will be only too happy to brief our Atlantian citizens and allies on what we have discovered, once we have ascertained exactly what it is, and our investigation has arrived at appropriate… recommendations for how best to handle the situation."

"You mean once you've already decided on a course of action," Devorah snapped back. "That's what this is all about, right?"

"We wouldn't presume to act unilaterally without the consent of our allies on their territory."

"There are a lot of ways to extract 'consent'," Jian said.

"Any decision will be arrived at in a completely

transparent manner in accordance with all applicable agreements and treaties," Chao said impatiently. "And I would remind the commander that Dr Kania has the floor."

<Shut. Up.> The message came through Jian's plant on a private channel from his father, just to drive home the point. "Anyway," Chao said aloud, "Dr Kania, please continue."

The good doctor nodded her thanks, then hit a couple of buttons on her tablet. The hologram above the table shifted and dove through the collapsed roof and into the pit before settling on the facility entrance. To the left, footage captured by Rakunas's suit camera looped the fragment of video showing the door sucking Jian inside.

"This is where we go from solid science into pretty heavy speculation. Most of the tech Commander Feng's team encountered during their brief expedition inside the facility appears to be nano-based, far and away more advanced than anything we've developed up to this point. But that's not to say we can't learn from it. Their version of an airlock, for example, is brilliantly simple and eliminates any air loss during transfers. Our own nanotech is up to the task already, it's just a matter of implementing it. Frankly, it's a little embarrassing none of us thought of the application before now. We should have a test rig ready to evaluate for the Alcubierre prototype within a couple of weeks. But, moving on..."

The hologram changed again to the feed from Jian's own camera once they'd entered the facility. Swarms of Polly's brethren poured out of the walls and went about their work, ignoring him and Rakunas entirely. Even still, several of those present visibly recoiled from the hologram as if the robotic alien bugs were in the room with them. No matter how much time passed or how advanced humanity got, there would always be something about critters with more than four legs that screamed *nope!* at an instinctual level.

"What you're seeing here are non-biological, autonomous, drones. They appear to be made of roughly the same nanomaterial as the airlock, just repurposed and imbued with some level of virtual intelligence to manage their tasks."

"'Imbued' is a strange word for a scientist of your stature to use, Dr Kania," Administrator Agrawal's hologram said. "With its mystical connotations and all."

Kania shrugged. "It's a reflection of our ignorance at this point. We don't have the first idea how any of this is being accomplished. All we've learned so far from the sample is the individual nano particles seem to be held together and manipulated through a combination of electromagnetism and exploiting van der Waals' forces. But insofar as how they establish and maintain their neural computing networks, or even where the hell their power is being drawn from, we don't have the first idea."

"Hold on, time out," Agrawal said. "Sample? You have one of these things on board the Ark?"

Kania paused and awkwardly glanced to her captain. Chao gave her a slight nod, giving her permission to proceed.

"Yes," Kania said. "Commander Feng, ah... captured one of them and brought it back to the shuttle. Our recovery team transferred it to one of our labs yesterday afternoon. We've only just begun our initial survey, but expect to learn an immense amount about the material, given enough time. And resources, of course."

Jian smirked at the subtle sales pitch. Kania was pushing sixty. She'd come up through the ranks of scientists working to smooth out all the wrinkles to colonization before the Ark had made orbital insertion around their new home. She was used to having to fight for man hours, materials, lab time, even electricity for her projects. Nothing went to waste on the old Ark, and everyone had to fight for priority among the scarcity. A lot of the old guard still acted that way. Consequently, they also tended to get what they wanted.

"Isn't that dangerous?" one of the other representatives from the surface said, one that Jian didn't recognize.

"We've taken all necessary precautions." Kania flipped the footage hovering above the table over to a feed from inside one of the Ark's clean room labs. "As you can see, the sample is being held under armed guard behind fifteen centimeters of ballistic-rated glass. The joints between the panes have been ultrasonically welded to create a seamless, uninterrupted chamber. It is, for all intents and purposes, impenetrable."

Polly strained against its confines. In one moment, it flowed like water into all the edges and corners of the glass, probing for weaknesses. In the next, it reformed in the exact center and sent tiny spikes out into the middle of the glass panes trying to crack it. In the next, it morphed into a hammer and tried to smash it with brute force. Then, it inspected its progress, or lack thereof. Then, the process repeated. Jian cringed as he watched the little creature struggle.

"Further," Kania continued, "the base of the enclosure is equipped with a high-capacity discharge microwave unit. Within three milliseconds of detecting a containment breach, everything inside it will be flash heated to eight thousand Kelvin, more than hot enough to not just melt, but break the covalent bonds of any known compound and reduce it to a cloud of charged plasma. Our safety protocols are more than adequate."

"I don't mean to be crass," continued the rep, "but how the hell do you know what 'adequate safety protocols' are when you don't even know how the thing moves, thinks, or where its battery is? How can you even begin to guess its capabilities?"

"I have a pretty good idea," Jian interrupted. "I'm the only person to see them in action. They're maintenance and repair drones. He's..." Jian's tongue caught on the word "harmless" as a flash of Polly running a spike through Madeja's eye danced across his brain. "... helpful," he settled on instead.

"Actually, commander," Kania interjected before the rep could retort, "I think this would be a good point for you to take over and explain what you saw in the map room in greater detail." The image flickered from the lab over to the cavernous spherical space he'd nearly lost himself in.

"I'm not sure what you want me to tell," Jian said. "I'm not a trained scientist."

"Perhaps not, but you are a trained pilot. Your observational skills and attention to detail are probably equal to anyone on my staff."

"That's kind of you to say, director, even if I don't know how true it is."

"Just walk us through the scene. Give us your impressions of what you saw, touched, and so on. I'm transferring control of the video feedback to your plant."

An incoming authorization alert flashed in the left side of his field of vision. Jian toggled the icon, and a small virtual control board appeared in its place. He reached out and grabbed the table with his hands as if to steady himself. "OK, here goes. We entered the room thinking it might be a natural cavern that had just been incorporated into the facility, but the perfect spherical shape made it clear it had been excavated intentionally. We soon figured out for what purpose." He resumed the playback to the point he sat down in the awkward chair. Watching himself go back through the same motion from two days earlier was a little disorienting. "The chair pretty obviously hadn't been designed with your average human in mind, but it quickly adjusted to fit my body type."

"Who, or *what*, did it seem designed for?" Administrator Agrawal asked.

"That, I couldn't say," Jian answered. "It was just damned uncomfortable until it finished morphing, even through my vac suit."

"Would an Atlantian fit in it?" Chao asked.

"Maybe? It was a little oversized for me, but it didn't look or feel like any of the Atlantian chairs I've seen or sat in before. But, like I said, it quickly accommodated me, and once it did..." Jian let the footage spool out a little more until the room-sized hologram of Gaia erupted from the walls like a fireworks show, complete with "oohs" and "aaahs" from the assembled audience. "... we got quite a show. If you're having trouble orienting yourself inside this map, realize that it's being viewed from the perspective of someone sitting at the planet's core looking out. That's why everything is mirror-image." Jian waited a beat until he saw a dawning of recognition on enough of their faces before proceeding. "Once I was settled in, then the really weird shi... stuff started to happen."

The image zoomed in on Shambhala, then flipped to an overhead view, just as it had done before. The same inwardly-spiraling symbols appeared, like foreign characters being sucked down a drain.

"What are those supposed to be?" Agrawal asked.

"I assume they're language characters like letters or pictograms, Administrator."

"Obviously, but *whose* characters?"

"We've taken a look at them already," Devorah injected. "They don't share any commonalities with any written Atlantian system we've studied. And it should go without saying that it's not based on any known human language system."

"Well who does that leave?" Agrawal said.

"Hell if I know. Please continue, commander."

"Thank you. If you'll notice, it didn't take long before the program, or whatever is in control over there, realized I was having trouble interpreting the displays and reverted to a, a learning module, or a sort of instruction manual, as far as I can tell."

The spirals disappeared, replaced by individual symbols hovering over important buildings and landmarks in and around Shambhala, testing him. Teasing Jian to decipher their meaning.

"I believe the facility was trying to make itself understood," Jian said. "If I were to use any word to describe it, I'd call it accommodating. Forming itself to our needs and doing everything it could to be user friendly."

"Why the hell would it want to do that?" Agrawal asked. "Why would it want to help aliens exploit it to their own ends?"

"It may not know we're aliens," Kania said quietly.

"Would you care to expand on that, doctor?" Chao said.

"Certainly. This facility has been here for a minimum of a quarter million years and is still functioning. It was obviously built with the long haul in mind. A quarter of a million years ago, there were at least three distinct hominid species wandering around the Earth, none of which came even close to sharing a language or sharing a culture. All of us sitting in this room, excuse me, in this room or on the surface, are an average of twenty centimeters taller than our Earthbound ancestors were during the Renaissance. If I were to open the museum's copy of *War and Peace* in the original Russian, who among us could read Cyrillic without a translation program? Those examples are over the span of just a few centuries. Now imagine the changes we'll go through as a technologically advanced race capable of manipulating our own DNA over the course of the next few hundred millennia? Would we recognize ourselves? Would we be able to talk to ourselves? Preparing for deep time means throwing out *all* of your assumptions about what it means to be human, or whoever they were, in this case."

"Philosophical and existential musings aside, that doesn't really answer the central question," Agrawal said. "Which is, what is the facility's purpose? Who built it?

Why was it built? And what is it still doing here?" She held out three fingers. "We know of only three sentient species. Ourselves, the Atlantians, and whoever threw Nibiru at Earth. We know humans didn't build it. Dr Kania is assuring us that the Atlantians didn't build it. That only leaves one possibility." She held out her index finger. "And if it was built by the enemy, then we must assume that their intentions for it were hostile."

"We hardly need to assume it was the same civilization," Kania said. "Consider this. We now have two confirmed examples of Earthlike planets, Earth and Gaia. And on both, a sentient species has developed independently of one another. Moreover, before the end of Earth, we'd found fossilized Martian stromatolites, simple life in the oceans of both Enceladus and Europa, *and* methane-based, self-replicating molecules hiding inside protocellular membranes on Titan which couldn't possibly have arisen from any sort of panspermia from Earth or Martian contamination. They weren't exactly life yet, but probably would have been with another billion years to cook. Here in the Tau Ceti system, we know primitive plant life covers much of the tropical latitudes of Tau Ceti F."

"What about Proxima B?" Chao asked. "It's earthlike."

"Yes, but its atmosphere is too thin to keep liquid water from boiling off. It was probably thicker in the past, and I wouldn't be surprised at all to find fossilized early life around its equatorial terminus, but we've been a little too busy to go poking around there for the last couple centuries."

"Your point, doctor?" Agrawal said.

"My point is we've found life on multiple planets and moons in the only two solar systems we've explored first hand. And intelligent life on both of the worlds with liquid water, thick atmospheres, and abundant solar energy powering their ecosystems. That's a statistically significant finding. Extrapolate it out to the rest of the galaxy and that means *millions* if not *billions* of civilizations exist, right now. There is no reason to assume this facility had to be built by one of the three we have direct evidence of."

"I hate to quibble, but there's a *very* good reason to assume it was built by the race that destroyed our homeworld. Because if we don't, and they find out we're here, we lose Gaia too."

"We've been closely monitoring the facility for transmissions. No radio or laser emissions. It's dark."

"It's dark to methods of communication we recognize or understand," Agrawal said. "We're talking about a race that manipulates black holes. Who knows what other technology they possess? Did I not read something recently about the crew experimenting with quantum entanglement communications for the Alcubierre project?"

"We're in the early stages," Kania said. "And although it's not my department, I can tell you that the entanglement is very, very sensitive. We've managed to keep paired particles entangled for a matter of minutes before the connection breaks. It's incredibly tenuous, and subject to the smallest of outside influences. A stray cosmic ray, or even a neutrino can render the connection moot. Keeping an entanglement intact over the course of days or months is daunting enough. But hundreds of millennia?" Kania shook her head. "I can't imagine any level of technology being able to automate the process on those kinds of timescales."

"But then why the hell did they put it there?" Agrawal turned to face Jian. "It has a map of the whole planet laid out in there. What do you suppose that's all about?"

"I'd rather not speculate," Jian said, feeling the pressure.

"Indulge us, commander."

Jian shrugged. "Well, they seemed to have detailed and current maps about the Atlantian villages, and especially Shambhala. I'd guess they have some sort of sensor network, either in heavily-stealthed orbital platforms we haven't detected, or more likely buried dirtside somewhere out of sight. It's pretty clear it's an observation post of some kind."

"That proves it, then. Someone is spying on us," Agrawal said.

"Well, I wouldn't say 'spying,' exactly. Studying, maybe. We observed the Atlantians for years before making contact, after all. And our intentions weren't hostile. Besides, why would they leave the door unlocked? If they've been watching us so closely, they know we came from the surface. Why let us in at all? And why try to teach me to use all the buttons and levers?"

"Now it's my turn to speculate?" Agrawal said. "Because it's a honeypot trap, tempting us with a few trinkets of technology, but in the end it's just a way to study us even more closely. Assess our cognitive abilities based on how fast we learn. Determine how much of a threat we are. Hell, for all we know, there are facilities like this sprinkled around inhabited planets throughout the galaxy, waiting for eons until some pond scum finally pulls itself up by its bootstraps and develops a space program. Then whoever left it here knows a new light is shining in the cosmos and it's time to throw a black hole in their general direction. Problem solved."

Agrawal stood up from her chair. "It's my speculation that this facility is the Nibiru race's version of the Early Warning network we're constructing on Varr as we speak. A means of identifying potential threats so they can take action. And we've just let them know they need to come back to finish the job. Our first priority should be destroying the facility as soon as possible before it communicates any more intel on us."

Devorah perked up "And how do you propose we do that, nuke it? The Atlantians will never agree to it. It took the better part of eighteen months to convince them to let us gently mine the surface for Helium-3."

"Sometimes it's better to beg forgiveness than ask permission."

"Didn't you just say, 'We would not presume to take unilateral action'?" Jian said with a sharpened tongue.

"I think what we've heard here changes the equation a bit, don't you?"

"Are you sure your judgment isn't being clouded by the fact your city was just hit by a terrorist attack, Administrator?"

"Are you sure yours isn't from losing your shuttle, commander?"

The muscles in Jian's neck stiffened at the barb, but he saw the trap his father had warned him about. "Touche."

"We're getting off topic." Chao's voice was stern. "We're not here to discuss a course of action, not until we've collected all the facts of the matter. Now, Dr Kania, how likely do you think Administrator Agrawal's scenario is"

Kania shifted uncomfortably against the seat restraints at her shoulders. "It is... possible. The discovery of the Atlantians certainly put a stake through the heart of the old Fermi Paradox, but it left another giant question in its wake. If intelligent life in the cosmos is so common, which we can now say with some degree of confidence that it must be, then why hadn't we heard from anyone or seen any evidence of it?

"Before Gaia, there was a theory called the 'Great Filter,' which posited that somewhere along the development of life, a huge barrier to advancement stopped the vast majority of species from advancing to the point of interstellar travel or communications. Some thought this filter was evolutionary, that life itself was very difficult to get going. Or that the transition from simple, single-cellular life to complex multicellular forms was the stumbling block, or moving from complex life to true intelligence. With two examples of species that have passed these barriers less than thirteen light years apart, we know none of them could be this hypothetical filter, and that it must lay ahead of us in our development."

She looked around. The room's occupants sat in rapt attention.

"Which is where we get to the scary bit. Some suggested that the filter wasn't any natural process or limitation. Some thought that most technologically advanced civilizations reached a point where they could no longer control or contain the power of their tech and invariably destroyed themselves as we nearly did half a dozen times in the twentieth and twenty-first centuries. But others proposed a super-predator civilization that hunted down and destroyed emerging civilizations as soon as it became aware of their existence. The timing of the attack on Earth would… lend credibility to this hypothesis."

"How so?" Chao asked.

"Well, think about it. The Industrial Revolution really ramped up in the early eighteen hundreds. That was probably the first time a distant observer could have figured out we had reached a new level of development, based on the sudden and drastic changes to our atmosphere. A hundred years later and we're sending out our first artificial radio signals. A few decades after that and we're detonating nuclear bombs. Then we're landing on the moon, developing super computers, mapping the human genome, all in rapid succession. Our pace of technological progression became exponential. We only had a brief slowdown in the middle of the twenty-first century while we dealt with converting our global infrastructure away from fossil fuels. It's conceivable this super-predator predicted we were only a few centuries, perhaps even a few decades away from becoming a significant threat, and took action as soon as we turned the corner. It may be a pattern it's seen repeated dozen, hundreds, or thousands of times."

"That sounds reasonable," Chao said, "But it brings up two questions, at least for me. One, Nibiru came in fast for a celestial object, but not nearly so fast as one would expect an advanced race to be able to travel. It was barely doing one and a half percent light speed. The Ark easily outran it. If this was a galaxy-spanning super-predator, why not react to the threat more quickly?"

"I don't know. Perhaps it was a limitation on the black hole technology itself. It was a very massive object, after all, nearly two thirds of a solar mass. Getting anything of that size up to even a single percent of lightspeed is a massive expenditure of energy that would require a Kardashev Type II civilization at the least."

"But doesn't that also mean they must have been right in our back yard, astronomically speaking?" Jian said. "Even assuming they fired Nibiru off right at the first sign of industrialization as you suggested, that's four centuries from launch to impact. At one and a half percent lightspeed, that puts the point of origin within six lightyears of Earth. How the hell could we not have seen them? There's almost nothing inside of six lightyears of Earth, certainly not any planets with Type II civilizations just lying about."

"Again, I can only guess, but maybe they have automated defense nodes sprinkled throughout space, lying in the dark between stars where they're unlikely to be detected, just waiting for a new fire to break out, as it were. Maybe we were just incredibly unlucky and happened to be close to one."

"So Earth was murdered by some long-forgotten alien sprinkler system?" Devorah said. "I don't know if I should be terrified or insulted."

"I think it's possible to be both," Chao said. "But that brings me to my next question. If one of these facilities was watching Earth, why did we never discover it? We had entire cities on Luna by the end, to say nothing of our massive mining efforts."

"That I can answer," Kania said. "Even at the height of human activity on Luna, we never directly explored more than a few percent of its total surface area. Varr's surface area is geometrically smaller than Luna's, and yet we still only stumbled across the facility by pure dumb luck. And that assumes any facility in the Sol system was placed on Earth's moon in the first place. Depending on how long it was intended to stay there, the asteroid belt would be an even better position for it, not only to avoid detection, but to be closer to all of the other potential starting points for new civilizations as the sun warmed with age and pushed the habitable zone deeper into the system. Mars would probably have had another shot at supporting life in a few hundred million years. At least one Jovian moon already had life, as did Titan after a fashion."

"You really think the facility was intended to operate on billion-year timescales?"

"It's a self-repairing station made out of nanotech. I have no idea how to even begin to calculate its expected service cycle. And it's pretty obvious whoever this is thinks in much grander terms than we do."

"Point." Chao rubbed a temple and sighed. "What would you gauge the odds of this hypothesis being true?"

"I don't even know where to start that calculation, captain."

"Who cares?" Agrawal said. "If there's even a one percent risk of tipping off the Nibiru race, we have to treat it as an... absolute..." Agrawal turned to face Devorah, who was busy laughing in her chair. "Something amusing, director?"

"Oh, no. Nothing funny at all, Dick."

"What did you just call me?" Agrawal demanded.

Chao slapped a hand on the table. "Decorum, please." The Ark's captain shook his head in frustration. "We're not just supposed to be adults here, but *leaders*. Is it too much to ask that we pretend to act like it? Just for a few minutes?" The room answered with cowed silence. "Better. Now then, Director Kania, if we pulled one of our remaining propulsive nukes from the inventory, would it have enough yield to do the job?"

Jian bristled at the question. <You can't seriously be considering this,> he shot off through their private link.

<I have to consider all of our options. That's what these discussions are for. Now let me hear her answer.>

Kania referenced her pad for a moment, pulling up specs on the beach-ball-sized nuclear devices that had propelled the Ark to Tau Ceti by the tens of thousands. Like nearly everything aboard, the Ark's engineers had included a little fudge factor of a few percent. Better to cart along a few hundred extra nukes than flip to the ship only to discover they were a few hundred short of what was needed to enter orbit and watch their salvation float out of reach.

"This is just some quick back-of-the-envelope calculations, you understand." Kania clipped her pad back to the table to keep it from floating off. "The individual devices are pretty low-yield when compared to the sorts of strategic nuclear weapons we're used to seeing in old war movies. And we haven't fully mapped the facility to know how extensive the tunnel system is." She paused. "However, their uranium chambers were shaped in such a way to direct the majority of their force in a thirty-seven degree cone pointed directly at the pusher plate, which drastically increases their propulsive force, and conversely, their destructive potential in that direction. Couple that with the fact the facility sits in an entirely contained space that will further concentrate the energy, not to mention the EMP effects... No, I can't imagine anything of use surviving that."

Jian reeled. They were going to blow up the whole thing, he knew it in his bones. But he knew his father, and knew that he was already resigned to the path Kania already seemed to be coming around to, and Agrawal was pushing hard for. He'd have to disrupt it another way.

"I volunteer to command the mission to deliver the device," he blurted out. "Should there be one."

"Are you kidding?" Agrawal said. "You've been fighting the idea from the beginning. Now you want to lead it?"

Jian cleared his throat. "I've lost friends, Administrator. Good ones. I'd like to be the one to finish what we started down there out of respect to their memory, even if I don't entirely agree with it. Duty comes first." Jian liked the sound of it. Almost believed it himself.

"Commander Feng's flight status will be decided later," his father said. "For now, I'd like everyone to ruminate on what we've discussed here before we reconvene to decide on our course."

"And when will that be?" Agrawal said tersely.

"As soon as we can prepare a briefing for our allies, Administrator," Chao said. "I understand that time is critical here, but I'm not willing to throw out fifteen years of cooperation and goodwill just to–"

"Um, captain?" Kania interrupted quietly.

"What?"

"We have a more immediate problem."

Chao's fists clenched before he forced them open again. "Yes? What is that?"

Kania swiped the display above the table back to the lab where Polly was held. Or, more accurately, where Polly *had* been held.

The entire room stared slack-jawed at the empty cage. No one spoke. No one dared to breathe.

Except for Chao Feng.

"Oh for *fuck's sake!*"

CHAPTER FIFTEEN

"Well *that* was exciting," Benson said as the holographic display of the meeting with the Fengs and the rest of the Ark bigwigs suddenly went black. "Thanks for inviting me."

His wife slapped his shoulder. "Only you would make a joke right now, Bryan."

"What? I thought this was going to be a waste of time. It *was*, but at least it wasn't dull."

"Ha!" Devorah laughed. "Good for that little guy. His cage seemed too small anyway. They didn't even give him a little house to hide in or anything."

"Are you *insane*?" Administrator Agrawal said, operating near the capacity of her wits. "It's not a pet, it's a hostile, shapeshifting, alien, artificial intelligence and it's loose on the Ark! We could lose the whole ship, or worse still have it turned against us."

Devorah waved a hand dismissively. "Oh calm down, young Jian seems to be rather fond of it. Maybe it's just scared."

"The possibility of that drone or whatever it is grabbing control of Ark's navigational lasers and burning this city down to its foundations doesn't concern you even a trifling bit?"

"Eh," Devorah shrugged. "I'm eighty-six, I'll probably be cremated in a couple of years one way or another anyway."

Agrawal threw up her hands. "I'm surrounded by crazy people. And you two," she pointed at Benson and

Theresa. "You were invited to sit in on this meeting because it might help the Chief Constable in her investigations, and because the government of Shambhala has learned through long experience that there's really no point trying to keep our Director of Recreation out of secret meetings his wife is attending. I'm sure I don't need to tell you that everything you just heard was confidential and not to be shared publicly."

Benson pushed up from the table. "Share what? I've already forgotten the last forty minutes. My memory isn't what it used to be. Now, if you'll excuse me, I have to pick up a friend at the airport."

Theresa stood up too. "And I have a terrorist attack to solve."

Agrawal looked at her, perplexed. "Don't you mean a kidnapping? I assumed you'd be searching for your child."

"If I can solve who bombed the parade, I solve who took Benexx. Besides, one of my more... aggressive deputies is on zer scent." A look passed between Benson and his wife in that moment. It did not go unnoticed.

Agrawal ran a hand over the brown skin of her taut, tired face. "Mr Benson, I'm sure I don't need to tell you how critical maintaining a peaceful relationship with our neigh–"

"You're awfully sure of a lot of things, Administrator," Benson said with a smirk. "I know what you're worried about, and no, I'm not going to go on a rage-fueled quest for vengeance that leaves the native quarter a smoking ruin. I'm just going to get my kid back. No fuss, no muss."

"And if someone gives you 'fuss'?"

"It will be handled proportionally on an individual basis." His tone was playful, but his tone invited no further conversation. He put a hand over Theresa's shoulder. "Now, if you'll excuse us."

The two of them left the room, leaving Devorah, Agrawal, and a handful of other underlings to stare at each other.

"That man is dumb as a rock," Agrawal finally said.

Devorah chuckled. "Oh, no doubt. But he's also as hard as one, and he's picking up momentum. A smart person knows when they see a boulder rolling downhill there's no point throwing themselves in front of it."

"What does a 'smart person' do in that case?"

"Simple." The persistent scowl weighing down on Devorah's mouth turned up at the corners. "Get out of the way."

Benson jumped out of the transit pod before it came to a full stop. He was late, having wasted time on the meeting in the Beehive, even if it had provided some valuable intel on the rest of the playing field. But Benson didn't care about the rest of the playing field right now. He was laser-focused on his one-on-one matchup.

Someone had kidnapped his kid. Someone had forgotten who he was and *desperately* needed a reminder. He was *Bryan Fucking Benson*. Two-Eighteen PE Zero Championship MVP. Savior of Mankind. Hero of the Battle of the Black Bridge. And while he might be missing a step these days, and his left knee was better as a barometer than a joint, and he had to get up at three o'clock every night to pee, he sure as *hell* had enough gas left in the tank to yank Benexx back from whatever dux'ah-shit-for-brains had come up with this ill-advised, doomed-by-Xis-to-fail, suicidal scheme to mess with his family.

He'd come a trigger pull away from killing a village elder to protect Benexx before he'd even met zer. Now, fifteen years of life and memories and love later, Benson couldn't even guess how far he'd go to get zer back. And a very immature, very angry little voice in the back of his head that hadn't seen the spotlight in many years was eager to find out.

But, with age came patience. After finding the flop house, he'd wasted a day canvassing the neighborhood, interviewing potential witnesses and getting stonewalled in a way he hadn't experienced since the Laraby investigation back before they'd landed. The problem wasn't a language barrier. In the years since First Contact, Benson had learned to speak Atlantian almost as fluently as English, and perhaps even better than Mandarin. Even with the strange and constantly-shifting hybrid slang used by both Atlantian and human teens alike in Shambhala, Benson rarely needed to consult the translation program in his plant anymore. Which was fortunate, considering how glitchy his replacement had proven to be, even more than a decade after it had been reimplanted.

No, the problem wasn't linguistic. It was cultural. Invisible walls that might have been there all along, separating the refugee Atlantians living in the native quarter from their human hosts, had grown so tall in the days since the bombing that neither side could reach over them. Or, at the very least, was unwilling to try.

With age also came humility. Even to Benson, in small measures. Just enough, in his case, to know when to ask for help.

"Kexx!" Benson spotted his old truth-digger friend as ze emerged from the jet way and into the terminal with zer gangly teenaged female human apprentice in tow.

"Benson," Kexx wrapped zer noodly arms around Benson's shoulders. "Your hair is losing its color, my friend."

"Not as fast as your crests. Did someone put you in the wash with their whites?"

Kexx ran a four-fingered hand over the half dozen parallel rows of crests folded flat against zer scalp. In the years before zer transition to elder, they had been a riot of purples, greens, and blues in swirling, almost tie-dyed patterns. But, like the black in Benson's hair, they were fading fast.

"Time is catching up with both of us, it seems."

Benson untangled from the embrace and held his friend's slim shoulders. "I'm *relieved* to see you."

"Of course. We came as soon as we heard about Benexx."

"I see that." Benson looked back at Sakiko, wrapped in traditional Atlantian vestments with only the barest enhancements to ensure her modesty among a human population. She stood aloof and scanned the platform as if she was hunting for something. Which, in truth, she was. "I wasn't expecting you to bring your student as well. Or her... pet." Sitting obediently, if nervously, behind Sakiko was the ulik she'd taken in. Benson couldn't believe the plane's crew had allowed it onboard.

"Chief Kuul insisted," Kexx said. "In fact, ze nearly sent a full hand of G'tel's finest warriors to escort us. It took some time to convince zer that they would only be in our way."

"Hello, Sakiko." Benson smiled warmly at the girl.

"Hello, uncle."

"I see you brought your, um, friend."

Sakiko scratched the creature behind its head crests. "Wouldn't dream of leaving zer behind. Best sense of smell on the continent."

"You do know I was almost eaten by a pack of those things, yes?"

Sakiko just shrugged. He'd not seen her now in two, three years? She'd grown, but still looked like a bag of beanpoles. She was taller than Mei, and her face wasn't nearly as soft or rounded. More angular, although not unattractively so, just more European, doubtless her father's contribution to her genetics. A father she'd never known, due to her mother's... occupation at the time of her conception. She'd been offered the opportunity to run a gene search to identify him, if only to answer if he was still alive or if he'd been one of those lost in Shangri-La module. She'd declined in terms that left no ambiguity in her feelings on the subject.

Benson had always been strangely proud of her for that.

"How's your mother?" Benson asked.

"The ambassador is well. She sends her regards."

A very formal answer. She was here for business, then. That's how Sakiko was coping with her best friend being kidnapped. Good. White hot rage got people in trouble. Got them hurt or even killed. But cold, calculating anger? That he could use.

"Theresa and I are glad you're here. I'm sure Benexx would be relieved to know you're here for zer, too."

"Only one way to make sure ze finds out."

Benson peeled his lips back and exposed his teeth. Only someone who had never been the hunter would mistake it for a smile.

"Then let's stop wasting time standing here flapping our gums. We have work to do. Zer birthday is in three days and I want zer home for cake and ice cream."

The trio walked briskly back towards the transit pod station. "What do you know so far?" Kexx asked.

"Very little. We don't even have much video footage of the attack. All of the CCTV cameras along the parade route went down when the power from the beanstalk was cut and didn't come back on until someone in the Beehive remembered to loop them into the backup power distribution a few minutes later."

"Unlucky timing, there." Kexx ran a hand over zer crests. "Much too unlucky. The attacks were coordinated. You can't throw an attack like this together in a handful of seconds. Who just has a bomb that powerful handy *just in case* the lights go out? They knew when the Ark was going to be hit, down to the minute."

"No doubt. Anyway, all we have are a few blurry seconds of plant footage from a couple of bystanders showing a handful of Atlantians *and* humans pulling Benexx out of the rubble. There's too much dust still in the air to ID any of them, although Theresa is trying to get something out of the plant GPS records to peg the humans at least. But at this point, I don't even know which if any of them are the kidnappers, or if they were legitimately just good Samaritans trying to get zer to safety only to have zer yanked on the way to the hospital."

"Samaritans? A new faction? We could speak to their leaders and perhaps find the individuals who pulled Benexx free," Kexx asked.

"No, it's not new. It's..." Despite being an ambulatory, sentient cuttlefish, Kexx had become such a fixture in Benson's life, it was easy to forget ze hadn't actually grown up among humans. "It's just a turn of phrase, means people doing the right thing for its own sake."

"Ah. I see. Thought you were going cold in the head for a moment."

"Why so little footage?" Sakiko asked. "It was a parade. Surely there were more witnesses."

"It *was* a parade," Benson corrected. "Then it became a terrorist bombing and most of our potential witnesses were busy running the hell away from it."

"Cowards," Sakiko said as they piled into a waiting pod.

"Don't judge them too harshly, Sakiko," Benson said once the door clicked shut. "You weren't born when Shangri-La happened. It left most of us kind of twitchy where bombs are concerned." Benson turned back to Kexx. "Anyway, we tracked Benexx's locator to a, er, residence in the Native Quarter, but someone had gone to the trouble of removing it from zer and sticking it in one of the other victims of the bombing."

"Were they alive?" Kexx asked in an even tone.

"Yes, but I don't think that was the plan. If we'd have been a half hour later, they wouldn't have made it. Doc Russell is looking over them now. Whoever ze is, ze's a tough kid to have pulled through, even for an Atlantian."

"Your people are just wimps. Lose one little limb and you're done working for the day."

Benson smirked. "Ours don't grow back without a lot of help, as you well know."

"Hold on," Sakiko interrupted them. "You had a

tracking chip implanted in Benexx?"

"Yes."

"Did ze know?"

Benson shrugged. "I didn't tell zer mother, so you can bet I never told zer."

"That's insane!"

"Really getting tired of people calling me names for being right. If whoever took Benexx hadn't known to look for zer chip, I would have saved you two the trip. Now, can we move on?"

"Do I have a chip?" Sakiko asked in a panic.

"Oh, yeah. Your mom insisted. It's been inside your left eye since you were three."

Sakiko's face contorted in such a way Benson was certain she was trying to look inside her own eyeball. Kexx laughed, and for the first time since Benexx had gone missing, Benson joined zer, even as Sakiko's face soured.

It felt perverse to find a moment of levity while his child was being held only Xis-knew-where, selfish even. But Benson and Kexx went way back. They'd fought together in the Battle of Black Bridge, and saved each other multiple times along the way. In the aftermath, they'd been important figures in the many months and years of negotiations between the uneasy allies.

Hell, it was only thanks to Kexx that Theresa and Benson had ended up with Benexx in the first place. Ze would've never been in their lives if Kexx hadn't conceived of the adoption as a sort of olive branch between the races.

Benson had older friends, but none better. This weird, color-shifting alien was family. And even though fear and uncertainty still clung to his heart like claws of ice, seeing Kexx sitting there across from him in the transit pod, Benson knew that shit would start getting done.

"May I talk to zer?"

Kexx's voice snapped Benson back into the moment. "Hmm? Sorry."

"The survivor. May I speak with zer?"

"Not yet. Ze is still under heavy sedation. Russell had to remove a couple of big splinters from zer brain cavity and there's still quite a bit of swelling. It may be a few days before ze comes around again, and Xis only knows if ze'll remember anything. Or how much of *zer* is even still there."

Kexx nodded. "This residence, then. We should start there. Take us."

Benson punched the updated stop into the pod's control panel. "By your command."

The pod slowed to a stop only a few blocks away from the flop house. But even still, the walk was not uneventful. A crowd had assembled around one of the large electrical junction boxes that had been set up to provide basic power to this quadrant of the city. They'd been intended to be stopgap measures until more permanent infrastructure could be installed. That had been eight years ago. The native quarter had never stopped growing long enough to take them offline and replace them. Brownouts and other malfunctions were common, exacerbated by illegal but largely-overlooked pirate cables spliced into the mains. For a people who hadn't even heard of either electricity or metal less than a full generation ago, the Atlantians living in Shambhala had proven to be quick studies.

As Benson, Kexx, and Sakiko approached, it became obvious from the crowd's voices and skin patterns that they weren't interested in being passive spectators to whatever was happening. Atlantians averaged about a head taller than humans, so Benson couldn't get a good look at the eye of the storm. But his ears picked out a familiar voice.

<Korolev?> he sent with his plant.

<Coach! What are you doing here?>

<Just passing through on our way to the flop house. I've got Kexx with me.>

<Really? Can you spare yourselves for a second? This

crowd is getting restless.>

<Coming right up.>

"What's going on?" Kexx whispered.

"We're playing peacemakers."

"You, a peacemaker? Cuut be lenient."

"I'll try not to take offense at that."

"Don't try too hard."

Benson glowered back at Kexx even as he gently elbowed his way through the crowd. Once inside the circle, he saw Korolev, two additional constables, and a pair of pale-skinned technicians working on the junction box whose skin tone had very little to do with their level of sun exposure.

Korolev and the other constables sported riot gear and stun batons. Korolev alone had a rifle slung across his shoulders. While it wasn't an immediate threat, it did serve as a potent reminder of what could happen if the crowd decided to take things too far.

"Well, well, well. What's all this, then?" Benson announced to the assembled crowd.

<You're kidding me with that, right?> Korolev sent.

<It's a classic for a reason, Pavel.>

<If you end with, 'Move along, nothing to see here,' I'll stun you myself.>

Benson ignored him and turned to one of the more belligerent looking protestors, one of the rare Atlantian elders living among the sea of children and adolescents. Get zer to calm down and the rest would follow suit.

Probably.

"And here come the rulemans to bust our heads and shock our limbs!" shouted an Atlantian not even a meter from Korolev's face. Zer crests were washed out, but zer muscles remained firm. An elder, but a fresh one. Obviously the leader of this little gathering. "Watch them close, children. Watch their lies become their action."

Benson put up his hands, palms out, showing that he was unarmed. At least for the moment. "No one is stunning anyone, elder. Open hands. No weapons. No fists. We're just talking. Like civilized people."

"Say the thief!"

Benson let the barb pass without comment. "What's the problem here, elder?"

"Not your problem, ruleman."

At that, Kexx bristled. "Do you know who this 'ruleman' is, elder?" ze said with the sort of patient voice one might use with a disruptive toddler.

"Not matter. Just another deadskin trying to take our power. But we say enough!" The elder pumped a fist in the air and flashed a hostile pattern through zer skin. Echoing waves of color and light radiated out through the rest of the crowd, taking their agitation up another notch.

"Whoa, everyone. I'm not a ruleman. I'm just a coach." Benson spotted a young Atlantian he thought he recognized from one of the youth rec leagues.

"You're Tikik, right? You were so good at dodgeball the human kids didn't want to play against you. They forfeited whole games." Benson saw the gamble work as the youth's feet shuffled under the attention. Thank Xis he didn't screw up the kid's face, that would've shot his credibility right in the ass. Benson ignored the elder and instead focused on Tikik. "C'mon kid, you know me. What's going on here? Why is everyone so upset?"

"We're just trying to–" one of the techs interrupted, but Benson silenced him with a finger and a glare.

"Go on, Tikik."

"Elder says they taking away our power. For our lights and water and false fire."

Benson looked over his shoulder at Kexx. "Ovens," ze said. "False fire means ovens."

"Of course." Benson turned back to the techs Korolev was protecting. "Is that true?"

"Well, yeah. Beehive ordered it. We're running on backups and batteries. We can't afford the pirates anymore. Not until we start getting power from the Ark again, and who knows how long that will be."

"But deadskins get to keep their power!" Tikik said to an approving nod from zer elder. Someone was trying to get noticed so they could rub wrists. Hormones set a lot of political policies.

"To keep the city running," the tech said, "the transit pods, the wastewater treatment facility, the desalinization plant. We need them to stay alive."

"No, *you* need them," the elder barked. "Human tongues need tasteless water. Humans need pods because they too lazy. Atlantians just want water pumped and light at night and false fire to cook our food. But that too much to ask if it mean you have to walk."

Benson couldn't help but smirk. But there was genuine anger behind the snark. He looked around at the faces in the crowd, looked beyond to the streets and homes they lived in. There were so many of them already, and they had so little. For a moment, Benson tried to imagine the outcry from the human quarters of Shambhala if they all suddenly had to drag their own water from the river and collect firewood to cook their dinner.

If he was honest, the crowd would probably be a lot bigger and a lot angrier than this one.

"The elder has a point," Benson said, much to the shock of everyone in attendance, the tech and elder included. "I know I could stand to walk more. How about you two? Why don't you take a little walk? It would do you some good."

"But we have a work order. We can't just wander back unfinished."

"Well, let's put it another way." Benson threw an arm around Korolev's shoulder. "I'm going to take a walk with my friend here. He could use the exercise ahead of next week's game. Isn't that right, Pavel?"

"Um..."

"Of course it is. And I'm sure he's going to tell his

constables that they could use a little cardio activity as well, right Pavel?"

"I hate you."

"We kid around. Anyway, we're all going for a walk in that direction." Benson pointed towards the flop house, then pointed back at the heart of Shambhala. "I suggest you take a walk in *that* direction, unless you're really keen on finishing up your work here without these constables hanging around. Cool? Cool." Benson spun around and pointed a finger at the elder. "And *you* are going to make sure they walk out of here without so much as a scratch, right?"

Some of the elder's fire dimmed under Benson's glare. Zer crests fluttered. "We agree," ze said finally.

"Excellent!" Benson threw his hands in the air in celebration. "Glad we could sort that out like elders should. We set a very good example for all of these kids. You honor yourself and your people. Now, if you'll excuse us, I have to find my own kid."

Without another word, Benson dragged Korolev away from the crowd. The other two constables tagged along behind like imprinted ducklings.

"No," Korolev whispered to the closest one. "You two shadow the techs out of here. Keep your distance, but make sure they're safe."

"The elder assured us they would be," Benson chided.

"Trust, but verify," Korolev replied.

Benson snorted, wondering if his favorite Russian descendant recognized the irony of using that particular phrase.

"You handled that well, Benson," Kexx said.

"Yeah well he's not the one that's going to get called into the chief's office for abandoning their post," Korolev said. "Oh, and hello, Kexx. Good to see you."

"Oh, I've got it much worse than you, Pavel. I have to share a bed with the chief. I'll probably be sleeping on the couch after she gets chewed out by Agrawal for letting her husband interfere in official business." Benson paused. "Again."

"Still, it was the right thing to do. Sco'Val owes you a favor now," Kexx said.

"Sco'Val? Is that the elder's name?"

"I've not seen zer in many years, but I believe so."

"Was ze from G'tel originally?"

"Pukal, but I saw zer often enough during harvest."

"That's good to know." Benson filed the information away for later use.

"I don't remember this part of the city looking quite so... unfinished," Kexx said as ze toed over an exposed length of plumbing conduit that hadn't been hooked up to a water source. Benson looked around at the dirty streets, the ramshackle buildings, breathed in the foul air, and saw the Native Quarter, really saw it, for the first time. And he felt ashamed.

"It's been growing too fast, we haven't had the resources to keep pace," he said weakly, knowing it was true but knowing how insufficient the explanation sounded even to his own ears.

Kexx seemed to recognize his discomfort and let the thread drop. They walked in silence for a block, each busy taking note of everything they saw.

"Coach?"

"Yes, Pavel?"

"Where are we going?"

"Shut up, Pavel."

"OK, coach."

The flop house came into view. The crime scene tape still stretched across the front entry, but Benson's eyes caught a darkened silhouette hiding just inside the doorway.

"Look sharp," Benson muttered to Kexx and Korolev. Sakiko took notice of the stiffening of her master's body and put a hand on the hilt of her dagger, which technically she wasn't supposed to be openly carrying in public, but since Benson wasn't a constable anymore and Korolev hadn't raised a fuss, she didn't see any reason to bring up the point.

Benson walked carefully, but purposefully, up to the building's entrance. He kept his hands held open and a few centimeters away from his sides to show whoever was hiding inside that he was unarmed and not an immediate threat. The next few seconds would tell if that was wisdom or foolishness.

"You can come out. We know you're in there."

"Stay inside," the voice said.

Atlantian, Benson thought. *And very familiar.* "OK, that's fine," Benson answered. "But I don't know if you're alone, or armed, or what. So we're going to stay outside for now. OK?"

The shadow shifted forward into a sliver of light. Benson smiled. "Sco'Val, isn't it?"

The elder shot a look at Kexx, but gave an affirmative flicker of light across zer chest.

"How did you beat us here?" Benson asked.

"Shortcut."

"Shortcut?" Korolev said. "It was a straight line coming here."

Benson held up a hand. "Why did you come here, Sco'Val?"

"You help us back there." Sco'Val nodded towards the square. "I help you here. Then, we done, yes?"

"Of course," Benson assured zer. "How can you help me?"

"I know what you look for. It is not here."

Benson's heart raced. "And you know where it is?"

"Might know someone who do."

Benson's jaw clenched. "Take me to them. Now."

"Not now. Before dark. Meet here."

"Fine, but you'd better be here." Benson stuck a finger in Sco'Val's direction. "Don't make me come looking for you."

CHAPTER SIXTEEN

Something thudded heavily against the rock floor and interrupted Benexx's lamentations. On reflex, ze doused zer skinglow until ze was nothing but a shadow, then scurried away from the threat until zer back was pressed firmly against the clammy wall.

"It's not a bag full of sukor bugs, if that's what you're worried about," came a voice from the hole in the ceiling, different from the one who had caught zer trying to escape. "Go on, open it. There's food, and some human medicine for your cuts so they don't weep. But there's not a lot, so use it sparingly."

Benexx brought zer skinglow back up, just a fraction at first. Enough to see, but not so much that ze didn't have enough left in reserve to flash to full brightness and momentarily blind a threat. Down here in the caves, it could buy you a second or two to maneuver into a more favorable fighting position, or escape. Uncle Kexx had taught zer the trick many summers ago on an educational excursion to the Dweller caverns with Sakiko. This cavern did not feel like a Dweller cave. It was too quiet, for one thing. And the smell was, wrong. How ze would kill to have either Kexx or Sakiko here now, or even to have paid more attention to all of the lessons zer uncle had tried to teach.

In the middle of the floor, right under the hole in the ceiling, lay a frayed bag made of course fabric. Cautiously,

Benexx moved towards it. It was woven from yulka stalks stripped and cured with halo tree sap to preserve and strengthen the strands, a common process for making large quantities of cheap, yet durable fabric among the tribes of the road network. But the information didn't help Benexx place zerself. Like the yulka crops themselves, the immigrants from Atlantis to Shambhala had brought the process with them and continued to use it in their new city.

Zer legs tensed for a sudden retreat, Benexx threw open the bag's flap with a flick of zer wrist. But there was no danger. Just as the voice had said, there was food. Dried berries, a handful of seeds, some inexpertly-prepared strips of dux'ah jerky, all sitting in a bed of a spongey red fungus ze didn't recognize but assumed was edible. After what must have been two days since zer last meal, Benexx's stomach roiled in anticipation of the feast. Ze hungrily dumped the food out onto the floor, along with a small plastic container of antiseptic cream, which ze set aside until ze was done shoveling the food into zer mouth.

Benexx ground the tough seeds between zer tooth plates, then spat out the remnants of the outer husk. "So what are you supposed to be, the good cop?"

"I don't know what that means."

"Of course not. What's your name, then?"

"I'm not supposed to tell you."

"Right, how silly of me." Benexx grabbed a piece of jerky and ripped off a chunk. It was gamey and very salty. Even to zer salt-tolerant tongue.

"So what's your job here?"

"I am to help you."

"Yeah? Throw down a rope, then lead me out of this nightmare."

"Except with that," the voice said with patient impassivity.

"Fine. You want to help me? Send down a waterskin

or a bottle or something. *Fresh* water. I'm getting pretty sick of licking condensation off these rocks."

"I will see what I can do."

"You do that," Benexx said through a mouthful of dried berries. Already, ze could feel the stones in zer stomach grinding up the more fibrous parts of the jerky and mashing the seeds. Even the small measure of food in the bundle would go a long way to restoring zer strength. But the cold in the cavern meant digesting it would take time.

Ze finished the last of the jerky and passed the spongy red fungus back and forth between zer hands, tasting the unfamiliar item before committing it to zer mouth. It tasted like dirt with strong hints of ammonia, so just like any farm-grown fungus that had been washed in haste. Ze didn't recognize the species, but considering it had been cultivated, it probably wasn't poisonous, and ze was desperate for every calorie ze could get. So Benexx held zer metaphorical nose and tore off a corner of the square. Its texture left something to be desired, but the taste was mild enough and it went down without a fuss. Ze quickly scarfed down the rest and turned zer attention to the jar of antiseptic salve.

Several of the wounds on zer arms and legs were already itchy and warm to the touch, sure signs of a growing infection. It was entirely possible that zer immune system had never encountered some of the bugs hiding in the scum of this hole and would need all the help it could get. Careful to ration the bitter-tasting balm, Benexx prioritized those lacerations and scrapes that already exhibited signs of infection, and those that had cut deep.

Fortunately, a little bit of the cream seemed to go a long way, so ze switched from triage to preventative medicine and rubbed a little bit onto every wound ze could reach. Which considering how flexible an Atlantian's joints were, was almost all of them. When ze'd finished, there was even a small supply left to reapply to the more serious cuts later.

Benexx's cold mind drifted back to the question of where exactly ze was. Ze turned the jar over in zer fingers, inspecting it. Benexx checked the manufacture date: less than two years ago. It was a formulation specifically tailored for the Atlantian physiology and the sorts of native microbes that like to make a home in their bodies. Human doctors had settled on the mix less than a year after First Contact. Since then many tens of thousands of jars identical to this one had been widely distributed in both Shambhala and throughout the village network in Atlantis. Like the sack, it was far too ubiquitous an object to tell zer anything useful.

Ze opened the bag's flap and tucked the jar inside for safekeeping, then placed it behind one of the squat stalagmites protruding from the floor, safely out of sight. Then, ze moved to another stalagmite and retrieved a little crafts project that ze'd quietly worked on for the last couple of days – at least ze was pretty sure it had been a couple of days.

Benexx moved to the edge of the dim circle of light in the floor cast from the exit above, and waited. For how long, ze couldn't say with any precision, but long enough that ze had to shift several times to keep the muscles in zer legs from cramping. Omnidirectional joints had many advantages, but the ability to comfortably stand unwavering for prolonged periods of time was not among them.

Eventually, Benexx heard footfalls coming from somewhere above and tensed.

"I found a waterskin," the voice called down to zer. "I'm lowering it down now."

Sure enough, a bladder filled nearly to bursting dangled in the opening above and slowly crept down as it was lowered hand over hand. "Honestly, I don't know how you drink this flavorless water. It's revolting."

So, a surface native, from near a coast, Benexx thought.

Dwellers got the majority of their drinking water from underground freshwater springs, and villages further inland got theirs from rainwater that collected at the center of their craters. Ze filed this tidbit away.

"It's an acquired taste," Benexx called back up as the skin reached zer level. Mercifully, ze untied the fastener to the spout and greedily swallowed. The liquid was cool, like the rest of the cavern, but far from the triple-filtered purity ze'd come to expect from the taps in Shambhala. Ze didn't care. After two days without any more than what zer tongue could scrape off bare rock, ze would have drank dux'ah piss.

"That's enough for now," zer cordial captor said. "You'll make yourself sick if you drink too fast."

Benexx ignored zer warning and gripped the waterskin even more tightly, wrapping a hand around the rope and meeting resistance.

"Come now, don't be cold-headed," the voice said. "This rope isn't tied off to anything. You can't possibly climb out with it."

"Wasn't intending to climb out." Benexx smiled, and with a quick, decisive jerk of the rope, ze yanked zer captor off balance and pulled zer screaming down to the floor to land in a crumpled heap.

Benexx wasted no time. Ze grabbed zer still-moaning victim underneath the shoulders, then dragged zer back towards the far wall of zer little prison. The screams had drawn attention, there was no way to avoid it. Benexx hurriedly dropped zer captor in a writhing pile, then grabbed the end of the rope ze'd been holding and coiled it in until ze'd reached the end tied off to the waterskin. Ze made quick work of the knot, then threw the coil of rope into a far corner before doing the same with the waterskin. Rope was always good to have in any survival situation, and if zer captors were as lazy about searching the cavern now as they had been before they'd tossed zer down here, Benexx might just be able to keep it.

Ze knew they'd been careless preparing the cavern, because not long after Benexx had been caught trying to escape, ze'd stumbled across the remains of... something in a far corner. Some unfortunate creature had fallen into the pit and breathed its last breath down here in the dank dark untold years ago. There was very little of the carcass left, having been reduced by bugs and bacteria to little more than a desiccated skeleton. It hadn't been very large, but the long "bones" of the legs were more than adequate for zer needs.

The skeletal systems of creatures native to Gaia weren't like those of zer human parents or friends. Atlantians and all other land dwellers had arisen from an ambitious group of invertebrates, not bony fish, which had never taken off in Gaia's oceans. As such, their bodies weren't supported by rigid calcium and phosphorous rich bones, but flexible filaments more akin to cartilage. But even these filaments hardened as they dried after death. And although they couldn't take an edge for shit, they could be stripped and honed like wood into a crude but effective point, good for a few decisive thrusts into soft tissues. Another trick Uncle Kexx had shown zer. So Benexx had spent the last two days doing exactly that. The "spear" was scarcely longer than a stylus, maybe two handspans from base to tip. But it was enough to reach through the dermis and sever one of the nerve trunks that ran from the base of the neck and down either side of an Atlantian's body if you knew where to poke.

Which Benexx did.

The new resources acquired and hidden, Benexx ran back to the fallen captor and propped zer up, then slid in behind the wounded Atlantian to use zer as a body shield. At least one of zer captors had a rifle, and ze intended to present as small a target to them as possible. They'd be here soon, Benexx could hear their footfalls.

"You... tricked me," zer captor turned hostage said woozily.

"Shut up," ze said reflexively in English.

"I'm hurt."

"You think I give a dux'ah shit?" Benexx pressed the shank to the sweet spot at the base of zer neck and pushed, not hard enough to break the skin, but enough to drive the point home. "Not another word or you'll be hopping on your right foot and bathing with one arm for the next six Varrs. Got it?"

There was no response, which either meant ze'd understood perfectly, or had passed out. Whatever. A rope dropped down through the ceiling. Benexx tensed and moved zer head behind zer hostage's. For a moment, ze felt a little surprised at zerself for not feeling any guilt over using an injured person as a bullet shield, but the feeling passed as soon as the harsh white light from the rifle-mounted torch fell onto the two of them.

Benexx expected shouting, threats, maybe even the deafening crack of gunshots. But there was nothing. Just the sound of feet gently moving over bare rock. A second light source appeared. They were trying to flank zer.

The muscles in zer arms tensed as panic and bile rose in zer throat. "Not another step or your friend gets paralyzed!"

The footsteps stopped. Still silence. Benexx risked peeking one eye out from cover, but all ze could see was the painfully bright lights burning a spot into zer night vision. Benexx ducked zer head back.

"Well?" ze shouted.

"Well, what?" The familiar voice sent a surge of dread like an electric jolt through zer. It was the same guard from the first day. The one who caught zer at the very lip of the exit as ze tried in vain to escape and cast zer back down into the pit. "What is your plan, little bearer?"

Benexx had to admit, ze really didn't have one. Ze'd hoped to pull down zer guard quietly, or at least that everyone else would be too far away to hear, or too far away to reach before ze could escape. Neither had panned out, and now Benexx was completely winging it.

"I'm going to walk out of here, or your friend dies."

"So, you're going to climb up one of our ropes while holding a dagger to Shu'luk's neck. Is that your plan? Because it's not great." The voice radiated calm, confidence, even amusement. Benexx wanted to drive a shank through zer smug mouth and out the back of zer head.

"I'm making it up as I go," ze said instead.

"I can see that," the voice said mockingly.

Benexx heard a foot shuffle against the rough stone of the floor. Ze wasn't sure who was moving. Ze didn't care.

"I *said*, not another step!" Ze pressed the shank into zer hostage's neck, hard. Enough to draw blood and a yelp, but the shuffling continued.

"I'm not joking with you."

"That's for sure. There's nothing funny about how you're wasting our time," said the voice. "You're surrounded. You're under-armed. There's no way you can hope to get past us and climb out of the only exit. And your hostage was willing to blow zerself up for the cause in the parade, so returning zer now would be no less noble. You have no escape, no plan, and no leverage. I'm going to count to a fullhand. If you haven't released Shu'Luk by the time I finish, I'm going to shoot zer in the head and leave you down here alone with zer body."

"Good," Benexx spat. "I could really use the meat."

"One..."

"You're bluffing."

"Two."

Benexx couldn't believe this was happening. Ze'd hoped to extract some small concession out of them, some snippet of information in exchange for zer hostage's safe release. Ze expected to be punished afterwards, beaten, denied food and water, whatever. But ze couldn't believe ze was going to get *nothing* for zer trouble.

"Three."

"You wouldn't return one of your own."

"You city types are soft. Five."

"You skipped 'Four'!"

"You wasted four. Six."

Benexx couldn't see Shu'Luk's face, but ze could see zer skinglow and taste zer sweat. Ze was injured, possibly badly. Ze had a shiv digging into zer skin less than a finger away from paralyzing zer left side, and ze was being threatened with death in less than two seconds from one of zer own people. Ze should be on the verge of panic and incoherence. But the light and patterns of zer skin exuded calm, and zer sweat was clean, free of the taste of stress pheromones that were impossible to suppress.

Zer hostage either didn't believe that ze would get shot or stabbed, or ze honestly didn't care if ze lived or died.

"Seven!"

"All right!" Benexx shoved Shu'Luk's nearly limp body away, dropped the shiv, and put up zer arms, slow stripes of light and black radiating outward from zer core to zer fingertips in the Atlantian signal of submission.

"Thank you for cooperating," the voice said cheerfully, then signaled for their compatriot to move up to retrieve Shu'Luk without taking the muzzle of their rifle away from Benexx's head. Ze could only see their body as a faintly glowing outline against the nearly pitch black shadows of the far wall. But ze recognized the stance. It was practiced and solid, subtly adapted for Atlantian physiology, but held tightly against the shoulder and braced with the other arm. It was the stance of someone who had been well-trained.

So, maybe Benexx had gotten something in exchange after all. But then, as the other captor leaned down to grab Shu'Luk's wrist, Benexx caught a glimpse of the face hiding behind the blinding spotlight.

"Jolk!" Benexx forgot about the guns trained on zer face and exploded at zer former street-harasser's face, shank raised high in an icepick grip, ready to plunge it into Jolk's right eye. Benexx's sudden charge caught Jolk completely off-guard. Confronted by the unexpected threat, Jolk froze like the Italian ice they served in the streets of Shambhala in the summer.

For a flash, Benexx thought zer blow would land. It might be the last thing ze did, but at least ze would get a chance to gouge out one of Jolk's eyes. They never grew back quite right. But as zer arm swung down in a perfect arch, building deadly momentum with each handspan, the other gunman stepped up with even greater speed. In a swirl of movement, the butt of zer rifle connected with Benexx's lower jaw, snapping it shut painfully and sending zer head rolling back at an odd angle. The sudden jolt to zer head disrupted Benexx's sense of balance and caused zer brain to glitch momentarily. Without coordination from zer central brain, the peripheral nodes of Benexx's nervous system fell back under local control. In the fraction of a second zer brain was resetting itself, zer legs individually tried, and failed, to maintain the motion they'd already been committed to.

Benexx returned fully to zer senses in less than a second, but by then, ze was already lying face down on the cool, smoothed stone of the floor.

"Not bad for a bearer. You didn't tell me ze had so much fire in zer blood, Jolk," the apparent leader said.

"I..."

Clutching zer bleeding chin with zer free hand, Benexx came up to one knee. "Made you flinch, Jolk." Ze smiled and held out zer shank as threateningly as ze could in the direction of the leader's spotlight. "And ze saw you do it. Some warrior you've got here, afraid of a bearer with a dry old bone while ze's holding a rifle. You should have zer emptying latrines. That's all ze's good for."

Ze looked away. "Jolk, take Shu'Luk up the ropes. Once you're at the top, cover my climb in case your friend here gets any ideas about stabbing me in the back."

"But–"

"*Now*, Jolk. I'll deal with you later."

Jolk obeyed, dragging Shu'Luk's still-limp body back to the ropes, then pulled zer up onto zer shoulders, slung zer rifle, and started to climb hand over hand out of the cavern, making sounds of great exertion the entire way.

Now alone with their leader, Benexx turned back and noticed they had taken a long step back, giving zer some breathing room in case Benexx decided to charge a second time.

"I already know their names," Benexx said. "I'll figure yours out soon enough. You may as well tell me who *you* are and what *your* plan for kidnapping me is."

"You *do* remember there's a rifle pointed at your head and you've already given up your only leverage, yes?"

"Hard to forget."

"And you're still making demands of me?"

"I was a precocious child."

Zer captor actually laughed at that. "And every bit zer parents' brood, another little truth-digger for the family line. No, young bearer, I'm not going to just give you what you seek."

"Stop calling me 'bearer!' My name is Benexx. But you already knew that."

"It's meant as a title and a sign of respect to your station, young one. Although I wouldn't expect you to understand that, raised as you were."

"I know what sort of *station* bearers are held in back in Atlantis. I'll make my own, thanks."

"As you wish, but I'm still not telling you anything. You'll have to tease it out of the rocks." Ze shined the light down to the ground where Benexx's shank lay. "You know I can't let you keep that."

Benexx shrugged.

"Still defiant, hmm? We'll see how long that lasts after another few days without food or water." The leader reached out a foot and effortlessly grabbed the shank between zer dexterous toes, then transferred it to a pocket in zer skirts before heading to the ropes. "Do you have our guest in your sights, Jolk?"

The other spotlight traced along the floor until it bathed Benexx's body. "I do," Jolk called down from the circle in the ceiling.

The leader grabbed a rope. "I'd stay put if I were you, young one. After what you pulled, I wouldn't be in any sort of hurry to give our friend Jolk an excuse to pull that trigger."

Ze slung the rifle over a shoulder, then ascended the ropes with very little effort. Strong, then, even more confirmation that ze was no ordinary Atlantian.

Benexx watched zer disappear over the lip, watched the ropes retract out of reach, and listened as zer enemies withdrew to tend to their wounded member. Ze took stock of what ze'd learned from the encounter, and started laying the groundwork for zer next move.

CHAPTER SEVENTEEN

The command module entered its seventh hour of lockdown, and not even the high-efficiency particulate filters inside the conference room Jian, his father, and half the department heads were sequestered in could keep up with the creeping funk of sweat and anxiety. Everyone had left their seats long ago to float around the compartment and establish their own little temporary territories while the search for Jian's missing pet continued. Nerves were beginning to fray.

"For God's sake, Kania," Chao Feng said. "Stop drinking juice."

"I'm starving, I need calories and there's nothing to eat."

"There's also nowhere to *piss*. We're in zero gee. Where are you going to go, in the corner?"

Kania was about to object when the hologram at the center of the room flickered into existence with a blinking green connection request icon.

"Accept," Chao said, rubbing a temple.

The connection went through and an image of the inside of the lab with the optimistically named "containment chamber" appeared, guards and technicians swarming throughout the room. Someone whose shoulder stripes marked them as a specialist second class, but whose face marked them as barely out of the crew academy. Jian suspected they'd picked the short straw and had been given the unenvious job of delivering bad news to the old man.

"Yes?" Chao said. "What's the situation? Have you recaptured the drone?"

"Ah… hello, captain. Sir," the youth floundered. Jian felt a pang of sympathy for him.

Chao apparently didn't. "Dammit son, we've been cooped up in here for seven hours. Did you retrieve the drone or not? Out with it!"

The specialist swallowed hard and started to blush under the lashing. Jian nudged his father with an elbow. <Dad, dial it back a notch. The kid's terrified.>

<Ugh,> was the only response. "I'm sorry, specialist…"

"Jurich," he answered.

"Jurich," Chao repeated back to him. "We're all just a little tense in here. Please, proceed with your report."

"Yes, sir. Unfortunately, we have not been able to recapture the alien drone, or even determine what direction it took after leaving the containment unit and exiting the lab."

"I'm still a little fuzzy on exactly how it escaped your impenetrable, foolproof prison," Chao said, shooting a pointed look at Kania.

"We may have an answer for that, actually." The specialist's eyes flicked as he dug through a plant menu in his augmented reality display. A moment later they saw a blown-up image of the outside of the clear ballistic polymer that made up Polly's cage. Jian stared intently at it, trying to figure out what they were supposed to be looking at when he spotted it. It was a small circular distortion in the material about two or three centimeters across, barely a ripple, but Jian could see the slight bending it made in what should have been straight lines and angles in the shelves and cabinets behind it. A red circle appeared around the ripple to mark it for anyone without a pilot's eagle eyes and attention to detail.

"As you can see, there's a small but significant blemish

in the polymer of the cage. After reviewing the security footage of the drone's escape, we've determined that it was able to interact with the material of its cage at a molecular level, allowing it to temporarily unbind the covalent bonds between atoms and move through the material."

"Wait, you mean it just passed right through solid matter like some kind of ghost?" Jian asked.

"Not exactly, more like it was able to cause a localized phase shift in the material, turning it into something akin to a non-neutonian fluid in a localized area. It did so without anything as blunt as melting it with heat. Possibly some sort of manipulation of the strong nuclear force. We really don't know yet at this point. That's why none of the sensors that would have triggered the safeguard system were tripped."

"That's impossible," Kania said.

"Any sufficiently advanced technology will appear like–" Chao started to say, but Kania cut him off.

"Captain, I swear to God if you finish that tired old Clarke quote, I'll shove you out a lock myself. Sir."

Chao grinned. "Noted. But then the question is why didn't it use this little trick as soon as we stuck it in there? Or even when you all had it locked up in a crate back on the shuttle for that matter?"

"I can't answer that, sir," the specialist said.

"I have a guess," Jian said. "I don't think it minded being in the box on the shuttle."

"Why not?"

"Because I'm the one who put it there."

"So?"

Jian shrugged. "I think he trusts me. And as for why he didn't use this trick rightaway in the lab, my guess is he wanted to exhaust all of the more conventional methods available to him before revealing this new capability."

"You believe it's thinking strategically?" Kania said, clearly unsettled.

"Yeah, I do. Polly is a smart little shit."

"Well now *that's* an unsettling thought," Chao said. "Jurich, can the drone use this ability on any material?"

The specialist shrugged. "I couldn't even begin to speculate, sir. We assumed it was a collection of networked nanites, but it's acting more like a collection of networked *molecules*. For all we know, it could turn itself into a gaseous form and pass through the air recycling system undetected."

Chao grunted. "Well then, staying locked in here is a huge waste of time. Lift the lockdown."

"Sir?" Kania said. "We still have a hostile alien force loose on the ship!"

"He's not hostile," Jian bit back, but his father shushed him.

"I haven't forgotten. But our little... guest... can pass through polymer at will. Do you know how much of our internal structure is made of plastics and other composites? It can pretty much go where it wants. So since we can't possibly trap it, I don't see how it helps us to stay locked in this cage while it roams freely. Do you?"

"Well, when you put it like that..."

"And *that* is why they pay me the big bucks," Chao said. "Good meeting, everyone. Let's head to the Koi Pond. Sushi's on me. *After* I hit the head. I'm going first, captain's prerogative."

"How can you eat at a moment like this?" Kania asked.

"With chopsticks." Chao pushed off and floated for the door. He punched a command code into the panel and it slid open. "Well? Who's coming?"

His stomach full of blue gill rolls and more sake than was strictly prudent, Jian flopped down on his couch and breathed out the day's stresses. His head didn't quite stop spinning even once prone, owing in no small measure to his sake intake. He glanced up at his end table and realized he was seeing double as he couldn't get his eyes to resolve the two images of his vase into one.

The door chimed.

"Oh for Cuut's sake. Come!"

The door swung open as his father swept in.

"I'm having deja vu," Jian said, looking up at Chao. "Didn't we just do this like, nine hours ago? Same room and everything?"

"I need to speak with you."

"We just had dinner! Before that we were locked in a room together for eight hours. We couldn't have talked then?"

"Not privately, no."

"You do remember we have computers in our heads we can use to send each other messages, yes? No typing or anything."

"I'm just as eager to be in my flat as you are to have me out of yours, son, but I need you to listen to me right now. Sit up, please."

Begrudgingly, Jian pushed himself up from the couch and was surprised to see only one of his father staring back at him disapprovingly. His eyes flitted over to the vase. Still two of them. A wave of anxiety rolled through his stomach. Jian waved a hand in front of his face.

"Is everything all right, Jian?"

"Yeah, I just," he looked at the vases again. "It's been a while since I've... indulged quite this much."

"Why do you have two of those?" Chao pointed at the vases.

Jian shrugged, suddenly compelled to distract his father from it... er, them. "My Feng Shui girl said they focus the room's chi. Did you really want to talk about my vases?"

"No." Chao sat down on the opposite chair. "Of course not. You did well in the meeting, mostly."

"High praise, there."

"Just..." Chao raised a hand, flexed it a couple times, then lowered it again. "Listen, please. I've made the difficult, but necessary decision to neutralize the installation. Immediately."

"You can't do that," Jian said.

"I assure you, I can."

"You *shouldn't*, then. What about 'consulting with our allies'? When did that go out the lock? It's their moon, dad."

"That went out the lock when your little pet escaped containment and gained basically unlimited access to the nexus of our space-based manufacturing, planetary defense, and power generation efforts. We still have way too many of our eggs in this old basket. You heard Kania during dinner. She believes it's networked with the larger system on Varr, simultaneously being controlled by it and reporting back what it finds. I can't allow that. If we destroy the facility, we probably cut it off, and stop any intelligence leak back to whoever left it there in the first place."

"You're overstepping your authority. Our treaty with the Atlant–"

"Our treaty includes a provision that allows 'Commander, Ark'..." Chao looked at the stars on his left shoulder. "Yep, still me... 'to take necessary action to ensure the safety of the citizens on the surface or in space in the event of insufficient time to gain approval through regular channels.'"

"That provision was written to allow us to shoot down any last second asteroids we spot before they can impact the surface without having to go through the usual religious rituals, not to deliberately place a nuke on the surface of one of their Gods."

Chao just shrugged. "Well, Varr is *technically* a captured asteroid."

"Don't get cute, dad."

"We're past cute. This is about survival, for all of us, the Atlantians included, whether they're savvy enough to really grasp it yet or not."

"Oh yes, humanity charging in on our white horse to protect the poor savages from their ignorance. Because we've been so good at that, historically."

"We're turning over a new leaf down there." Chao inclined his head to indicate Gaia, even though he couldn't really know its position, spinning as they were at several hundred kilometers an hour.

"But it's a complete waste!" Jian's voice ratcheted up. "We're pouring resources and man-hours into the Early Warning network when we have a listening post sitting right in front of us that probably makes anything we're able to build look like a child's telescope. We should be trying to use it to listen and look for the enemy, not blow it up."

"That's just the problem, Jian. It's so advanced, we have no way of knowing whether or not it's looking back at us while we're looking for them."

"But we should at least *try*."

"That's enough, Jian. It's done. The decision is made and I will deal with the fallout. Of which I'm sure there'll be plenty. But these are the sorts of calls a leader has to make. Because they're hard and no one else really wants to take the blame later."

Jian rubbed his eyes. They were starting to hurt. "Why are you telling me this, then?"

"Because I want you to command the shuttle that transports the nuke."

"Ahh, whu…" Jian tried to work his mouth, but his teeth kept getting in the way of his tongue for some reason. "What?" he managed at last.

"I must admit, I was surprised when you volunteered to lead the mission to neutralize the installation. But it was a cunning move. You can't do your reputation any good grounded."

"My reputation?" Jian scoffed. "What does that matter?"

"Our reputations are all that matter, Jian. And right

now, your reputation is in danger of solidifying into the insubordinate hothead who disobeyed orders and got his whole crew killed, lost his command, and nearly severed the elevator ribbon. But there's a competing narrative. The quick-thinking hero who wrestled back control of his boat from a terrorist and saved the Ark with minimal damage and loss of life."

"They're both true," Jian said.

"Yes, but people are only going to *believe* one. It's a rare person who can hold contradictory views of the same thing in their head at the same time. We have to make sure more people believe the latter than the former. We do that by getting you back in the pilot's seat as soon as possible, preferably in a high-profile assignment. There will be questions, I'm sure, and some objections. But nothing I can't smooth over."

"Jesus, dad. I just lost my friends. I almost died myself. I haven't even been to the trauma counselor yet. I've barely gotten any sleep. I'm strung out. My nerves are fried."

"We can get you something to help you sleep."

"That's not the goddamned point!" Jian immediately regretted shouting as a surge of pressure went through his brain. He put a hand on his forehead. Without a word, Chao got up and went to the small kitchenette and poured a glass of water, moistened a hand towel with cold water from the sink, then rolled it up and returned to place it on Jian's head and set the glass on the table next to the mystery vase.

"You're dehydrated. Drink. Sake hangovers can be life-altering."

"Why do you care so much about rehabilitating my reputation?"

Chao rocked back in the chair, almost as if he'd been physically punched. "Because I care about your future, Jian. Don't you know that? I want you to be happy and successful."

"You want somebody to carry on the family legacy, and I'm all that's left."

Chao sighed and raised a hand at the ceiling. "Have I truly been so bad at this that our own son doesn't know I love him?"

"Don't do that," Jian said.

"Do what?"

"Talk to mom like she's still here."

Chao rested a hand on his heart. "She is still *here*. I talk to your mother a lot. You'd be surprised how much she has to say."

"Yeah? And what's she saying now?"

"That the Alcubierre prototype will be ready for space trials in less than a year. That she's going to need a captain."

Jian swallowed hard, a line of sweat breaking out over his forehead. "Are you offering me command of the *Enterprise*?"

"No, I'm... Wait, the what?"

"The *Enterprise*."

"We haven't officially named it yet. We're going to run a vote."

"Oh please, dad. We named this bucket the *Ark*, didn't we? Legends are important. Do you honestly believe mankind's first *literal warp-drive starship* would ever be named anything but *Enterprise*?"

Chao smirked. "I've been quietly hoping for *Yamato*, myself, but you're probably right. But no, I can't offer you the command, I'm trying to make sure you stay in the running to earn it. And that means you being out in front of the public doing big, strapping, brave things."

"Like nuking an alien facility before we have a chance to learn anything about it. Yeah, that sounds sufficiently macho and short-sighted to entertain the plebs."

Chao sighed heavily. "I congratulate you, son. It took me a lot longer to become that cynical. So you won't do it, then?"

"Of course I'll do it. You'll send somebody anyway, and how many chances do you get to set off a nuke?"

"Not many, if you're lucky. Engineering is rigging up a remote detonator and transceiver to one of our remaining bombs now. It'll be a few hours before they're done fabbing it up and testing the system. Then we'll still need to finish prepping one of the shuttles for flight. But we've got to hurry. The window for a return flight closes tomorrow at 2330. So get some sleep, but be cleaned up and in a flight suit for a mission briefing by 0900."

"You mean I get to sleep in? That's the best news I've heard in days." Jian's expression became somber. "Speaking of news, have we heard anything on Benexx?"

"No. I'm sorry. Bryan and Theresa are doing everything they can. But it's not looking good. There's been no ransom demands, no contact from the kidnappers, nothing."

"Shit." A hollow feeling gnawed at Jian's stomach. It felt like impotent hopelessness.

He rolled over on the couch, away from his father. "You're right, I need to sleep."

"Of course. Now, if you'll excuse me, I have to go find your new pet before it tears the ship apart." Without another word, Chao took a thin blanket off the back of the couch and tucked Jian in for the night, then dimmed the lights as he left.

As soon as the door latch clicked shut, Jian threw off the blanket and jumped to his feet. Probably too fast, as his head reminded him a moment later with a crescendo of hammers trying to pound their way out from the inside of his skull. He tried to push it to the back of his mind and turned his attention to the vases. He grabbed up one in each hand and headed for the bathroom, the only place in his flat that didn't fall under a surveillance camera's field of view.

He brought the vanity's lights up to full and inspected the two vases closely. Their surfaces both felt rough to the touch like one would expect unglazed pottery to feel. Their weights weren't perceptibly different. He squeezed them, then clinked them together and listened to the sound. The one in his left hand vibrated gently like a struck bell, as he anticipated.

The one in his right, however…

Jian set the real vase down on the sink, then held the imposter up to the light of his vanity. "OK, Polly. The jig is up. You can drop the disguise."

Nothing happened. Frustrated, Jian shook the vase. "C'mon. I'm serious. I know it's you, so knock it off."

For just a second, the vase trembled. It was such a strange feeling, Jian's hand nearly released it out of startled reflex. The trembling ceased as quickly as it began and the vase just… melted in Jian's hand. The texture and color shifted in an instant from rough pottery to something very much like liquid mercury, only with less than half the density. However, instead of dripping through Jian's fingers, its surface changed again into a more gelatinous form before sprouting legs, torso, head, and a familiar, three-eyed face.

"That was really creepy, Polly."

Polly looked on impassively.

"How the hell did you find my quarters?"

Polly cocked its head.

Jian sighed heavily. "Well, I suppose I should bring you back to Varr with me…" He paused, realizing his stupidity. "Oh right, I'm going there to nuke it." Jian shook his head. What a stupid, stupid waste. The place was swimming with tech breakthroughs that might take decades to reach at their current pace of development. Who knew what capabilities it had lying dormant, waiting to be discovered, perhaps even retasked and used for the Trident's grand purposes?

And why the hell shouldn't they? If it really was left here by their mortal enemy, the very best thing its secrets could be used for would be the defense of all of

Gaia's people. America reached the Moon using captured enemy technology and knowledge. Why should this be any different?

But, as his father had said in no uncertain terms, the decision had been made, and it was final. The wheels were already set in motion and there wasn't anything a lowly shuttle jockey could do, no matter how ambitious his father's future designs for him might be.

Jian slapped himself for his selfishness. Here he was, laying in his comfortable apartment after a delicious meal, ridding a good drunk, pondering his potential future as a starship captain, while one of his oldest friends had been half blown-up, kidnapped, and squirreled away into whatever godsforsaken spider hole zer captors had stuffed zer into. Benexx was all alone, in mortal danger, surrounded by enemies, and here Jian was hungover on his fucking couch.

Jian sat bolt upright and pounded all of the water his father had set out, then slammed the glass back onto the table hard enough that had it been real glass instead of plastic, it would've shattered. He'd lost most of his friends in the last few days, and he would be thrice-damned by Xis, Cuut, and Varr themselves if he let another one slip away. He had a purpose now, a goal. But how could he help Benexx from tens of thousands of kilometers away? The elevator cars were shut down until the ribbon was fixed and they weren't about to take a shuttle out of the rotation just to send one person down to the surface.

And he'd already committed to the Varr mission anyway, which would only take him further away from Gaia as he flew the nuke out to destroy the facility.

The facility, he realized. The giant alien duck blind, pointed straight down at Gaia.

"Jian, you idiot," he mumbled. The plan sprang into his mind fully-formed. He knew exactly what he had to do, and exactly how he was going to do it. If he failed, he'd probably be killed. And even if he succeeded, he'd be kissing his career goodbye, his relationship with his father, and quite possibly his freedom for the next twenty or thirty years.

It wasn't even a contest. Chao wasn't the only one in the family that made snap decisions.

A gentle tapping on his wrist reminded Jian that he wasn't alone. He looked down at Polly and smiled.

"Hey kiddo, can you make yourself into a tablet?"

CHAPTER EIGHTEEN

Sticking closely behind their impromptu guide, Benson thought he'd seen the rough parts of the Native Quarter. He was wrong.

"It no far." Sco'Val ducked zer head under a laundry line as they cruised down the alley at a brisk pace. "Another fullhand bluks," ze said in the common Atlantian mispronunciation of "blocks." Apparently, "bluks" were a type of semi-precious gemstone used in ceremonial beadwork back in Atlantis, and most of the adults who came over as refugees couldn't really pick up the subtle difference in pronunciation anyway.

"Benson," Kexx whispered from behind him, "this place feels like walking through halo trees."

His truth-digger friend referred to the rings of thick, bramble-like trees that surrounded the villages of the road network across the ocean. Vines packed with explosive seed pods waiting to prey on the clumsy or unwary. Looking around, Benson could appreciate the parallels.

"Yeah, I know what you mean."

"I don't understand this forest, Benson."

"It's just like G'tel's halo trees, except instead of seedpods that throw baseballs, they're people with rocks and knives."

"That, I can understand."

"Just don't forget that the rocks here can come from five stories up. Watch your head."

Behind his friend, Sakiko and her brooding pet ulik stalked along the street. Benson wasn't sure which of them looked more menacing.

<You've got a spare mag for that cannon in your pack, right?> he sent to Korolev through their private link.

<Three mags. One in the gun, two in reserve. Standard load out.>

<Isn't that a little overkill for patrol duty?>

Korolev waved an exasperated arm around at their surroundings. <Does it look like overkill?>

Benson's favorite cornerback had a point. The buildings in this part of the quarter hadn't exactly been built to code. The adobe structures had benefitted from human construction techniques, internally reinforced with a lattice of woven branches in place of rebar. It had allowed their mudstone formers to grow them well beyond their traditional three-story height, some of the more ambitious engineers pushing them to six and even seven stories. *Atlantian* stories, which were each at least half a meter taller than comparable human structures to account for the average Atlantian's taller frame.

But they'd been built slapdash, unplanned. Extra floors were added after the fact to give extra space to growing families living in the same home. They looked like stacked sandcastles, and were only marginally more structurally sound. There had been several collapses already. External bracing had been hastily manufactured and slapped in place by human engineers to stabilize the tallest of the structures, but it still felt like a stroll through a forest in a heavy windstorm while you waited for something to come crashing down on your head.

Benson had grown up around *much* taller buildings. Hell, the tallest buildings in Avalon module reached six hundred meters, more than halfway to the central axle a kilometer above ground level. No, what was foreign here was the claustrophobia. Buildings in the Ark's habitat modules were surprisingly well-spaced, considering how many people had packed inside them.

Here in the Quarter, however, the dwellings had not only grown up, but out, until the narrowest alleyways could scarcely accommodate two people abreast. This densest part of the Quarter was a veritable maze of corridors, dead ends, overhangs, and even tunnels carved through the foundations of the buildings themselves. Blind alleys, sunken doorways, and balconies were all potential ambush points for the unwary.

Benson marveled at the complexity of it all even as his paranoia ratcheted up another notch. He could scarcely believe all this had been built in just the last fifteen years, yet there he was, walking smack through the nexus of it all towards God-only-knew what.

<Now that you mention it, no, definitely not overkill.>

<We should call for backup,> Theresa said. <This is only a few blocks away from where Miles and Gallant got jumped two weeks ago.>

<Miles is a rookie and Gallant is a casual racist asshole,> Korolev said. <You can't walk around calling Atlantian kids 'Calamari' in their own neighborhood and not expect to get your head kicked in sooner or later.>

<He's right about that,> Benson said. <Besides, Pavel has a machine gun, Kexx is a breath away from being a venerated elder, Sakiko brought her own personal woodchipper, and I'm a folk hero, remember?>

Theresa sighed audibly. <Who's Chief again? Is it me? Because I could swear it's me.>

<It's totally you, baby.>

<Good, so listen, *coach*. A lot of these street kids have taken to running in gangs, half of them are high on bak'ri, and the other half either can't tell humans apart, or don't bother making distinctions between rulemen of either species. So heads on a swivel, you testosterone-saturated idiots, OK? Things have gotten weird around here.>

<Yes, dear,> Benson said with a smirk. His wife might act annoyed by their bravado, but there was a reason she'd

married a sports legend. Theresa liked her men strong and a touch arrogant. Anyone would need to be to keep up with her, even at fifty. Ahead of them, the alley arrived at a dead end. But instead of stopping or turning around, Sco'Val deftly grabbed a pallet with the adhesive suckers on zer toes, set it aside, and fell through a hole in the street.

"What the fuck?" Benson said aloud before he could catch himself.

Theresa looked at Korolev. "Did you know they had tunnels?"

Korolev shook his head vigorously. "News to me, boss."

"Get your light in there, Pavel, but take it off your rifle. We don't need to shove a muzzle in anyone's face."

"Not yet, at least," Korolev muttered.

Benson fell back to have a quiet word with Kexx. "What do you make of this? A Temple of Xis?"

Kexx shook zer head. "I do not believe so. There has to be a divine archway marking the passage between Xis's womb and the world above. Just a hole in the ground would be very disrespectful. Blasphemous, even."

"Shit, I'd hoped we were walking into a holy place with its lay-off-with-the-fighting policy."

"Sorry to disappoint, my friend."

Benson glanced over at Sakiko, who had been uncharacteristically quiet since they'd exited the tram, but remained as stalwart-looking as ever. "I think your apprentice should stay up here and serve as lookout."

"The hell I will," she said flatly.

Kexx cleared zer throat. "That is not language to speak towards an elder."

"Humans don't have elders. He's just old."

Benson stuffed a finger in her face. "That's right, I'm old, kiddo. And I'm the kind of crafty that only comes with getting old. You're not there yet. And if something goes wrong in that hole, I don't want to have to tell your mother that I couldn't protect you. It would break her heart, and I can't stand the thought of seeing her in that kind of pain. So you and your weird dog go stand at the junction over there, scream your lungs out if a mob suddenly appears to ram itself up our backsides, then run like a scalded dux'ah in the other direction. Understood?"

Sakiko spat at the dirt by her feet. "If a wave of native quarter rats come down that hole, a few seconds of warning isn't going to do you jackshit. You'll need knives with experience fighting in close quarters. When was the last time you fought Atlantians underground? Because I fought a fullhand of raiders in an abandoned Dweller tunnel last month."

Kexx put a firm hand on her shoulder, but Sakiko shrugged it off.

"I apologize for my student," Kexx said sternly.

Benson waved zer off. "It's fine, Kexx. She's worried about Benexx. You think ze's down there, don't you Sakiko?"

"Yes."

"And you're not going to listen to reason, no matter if it comes from your Uncle Bryan or your elder Kexx, are you?"

"No chance."

"Well then, come along, little one." Benson extended a hand toward the hole with Theresa and Korolev probing the darkness below with a flashlight. Sakiko walked up to join them. "And bring your hound. We might want its nose."

"You should not encourage zer rebelliousness, Bryan," Kexx said in a low voice to avoid being overheard.

Benson snorted. "She's almost eighteen, Kexx. Human kids don't need any encouragement to rebel at her age."

"I've noticed." Kexx sounded tired, exasperated even. "It's truly amazing how Xis granted zer all the knowledge it took me a lifetime to acquire with none of the experience. An incredible creature, the human teenager."

"Yeah, well Benexx hasn't been a peach lately either.

Theresa wanted me to talk to you about it, actually. But it can wait. What do you think we're walking into here? Should we be worried?"

"There is always danger underground."

"Well that's reassuring. Did Sakiko really fight off eight raiders in a Dweller tunnel?"

"Ze neglected to mention ze had *some* help, but yes. That thrice-damned ulik of zers didn't hurt matters either."

"I expect not. C'mon, let's see where this goes."

The drop to the floor of the tunnel was almost four meters. There was no ladder; Atlantians were such naturally adept climbers they needed none. The quartet of humans trying to reach the bottom were less well equipped. Of them, Sakiko had the most climbing and spelunking experience, not to mention the youngest and most lithe body. She reached the floor in scarcely more time than their guide had taken. Her pet followed quickly after, splaying out its four limbs in a way that would have dislocated the joints of any Earth quadruped.

"Your turn, Pavel," Benson said. "Show that little spider monkey how it's done."

"Oh no, coach." Korolev patted his rifle. "I have to cover your ingress."

"Fine, whatever." Benson turned to his wife. "Ladies first."

Theresa batted her eyelashes. "You mean you won't be down there to catch me if I fall?"

"Ugh, fine." Benson leaned across the mouth of the tunnel and let his feet dangle over the edge before turning around and supporting his weight on his hands. Which was a mistake. Even in a brace, his sprained wrist stabbed at him painfully.

"What do you see down there, Sakiko?"

"Nothing, uncle."

"You mean there's nothing to see, or you can't see anything?"

Sakiko snorted. "Relax, old man. I can see fine. There's nothing dangerous down here, other than me and Gamera."

"OK, fine. But if I get a spear up my ass as I'm climbing down, I'm going to be *very* disappointed."

"You safe, truth-digger," Sco'Val shouted back. "Under protection."

"Didn't realize I needed protection in my own city," Benson muttered to himself as his left foot found purchase, but he realized the elder had called him "truth-digger," not "ruleman." That was something. The hole was narrow enough that his arms and legs could touch each wall face with relative ease, so Benson sort of chimney climbed down, muscles burning and joints popping the entire way, especially his wrist which was still tender from the bad landing he'd taken after the bombing.

The air at the bottom of the hole was stale, loamy. It had the slightly salty bite of a freshly tilled yulka field. *So, no ventilation down here,* Benson thought. Atlantians could tolerate significantly lower levels of oxygen than humans could, owing to both their cooler metabolism and to their semi-permeable skin acting like one big passive lung. Human kids learned quickly not to bother getting into breath-holding contests with their Atlantian peers. As long as they were down here, Benson would have to keep an eye out for signs of hypoxia, because if any nasty gasses were leaking in from the soil, or a colony of oxygen-scavenging bacteria had been busy, the humans would be the canaries in this particular coal mine.

However, other than the stale air, the tunnel was indeed clear of obvious threats, which Benson could only confirm thanks to the blue-green light radiating from Sco'Val's skin, far more than the Atlantian needed in order to see down here with zer excellent low-light vision. Ze'd cranked up zer bioluminescence as high as it would go so Benson could scan the scene for himself. He recognized it for the courtesy it was and nodded his thanks to the elder.

"C'mon down, love. We're secure."

Theresa made her way down with only a couple of slips. Before long, Korolev and Kexx joined them.

"OK, Sco'Val..." Benson motioned down the tunnel, "...lead the way."

Ze turned and walked briskly, skin still shining bright. Atlantians couldn't beat humans in a flat sprint because of their omnidirectional joints, but the gait granted them by their long limbs made up for it by walking at a pace that forced most people to break into a slow jog to keep up. It quickly became clear that this wasn't just a lone tunnel leading to a hidden chamber, but an entrance to a network, growing bigger with each branching intersection they turned down and level they climbed into. Benson tried to keep track in his head in case they had to make a quick retreat – left, left, right, down a level, right, left – but it wasn't long before he lost the thread entirely. He was about to say something to Kexx when he noticed Sakiko making small marks in the packed clay and dirt in between the wooden supports in the walls with each turn.

"What are you doing?" he whispered.

"Dropping yulka."

"Is that like 'leaving breadcrumbs'?"

"I guess so."

"Roger that."

"Roger who?"

"Nevermind."

Sakiko scoffed. "Ugh. You're so ooold."

"I know. I should really get it looked at."

She shook her head and moved on. Benson smiled. Apart from the angle of her eyelids, Sakiko was the spitting image of her mother. Mei had been a couple years younger than Sakiko was now when Benson first met her in the derelict basement levels of Shangri-La module, and already several months pregnant with her future daughter.

Mei had been demure back then, out of necessity. Being an underage prostitute for an underground Messiah cult didn't encourage asserting much individualism. But she was the first to see through David Kimura's mask, and she was the first to turn on him and sound the alarm, saving what sliver of humanity remained in the process, twice. Once Kimura's influence had been... forcibly removed, Mei came out of her shell and never looked back. The same defiance shone like a beacon in Sakiko.

"What are you staring at?" Sakiko said nervously. Gamera chirped, echoing zer master's sudden change in mood.

Benson smiled warmly, as if looking at his own child. "An old friend's good work. What do you say, kid? Shall we kick over some rocks and see what tries to run away?"

"Works for me."

The walls of the tunnel changed sharply. Instead of packed clay and wooden staves, the surface transitioned into mudstone, the native analogue to concrete. The surfaces were smooth and level, expertly formed by craftsmen who knew their jobs well. After a few paces, ornate organic patterns emerged, sculpted into the mudstone before it set completely.

"Just like our tour of the Dweller caves before Black Bridge, hmm?" Kexx said from behind his shoulder.

"Don't jinx it. As I remember, we did a lot of fighting and running and almost dying the rest of that afternoon."

"Yes, a good day."

"Maybe when I was still in my thirties," Benson lamented. "Now, a good day is lying in the hammock on my roof with a bucket of lagers."

"Maybe tonight, if Xis smiles on our efforts."

"Maybe," Benson agreed. He was not a believer, not in any of the triumvirate of Atlantian Gods, or the endless pantheon of deities mankind had dreamed up over the millennia, but he appreciated his friend's sentiment nonetheless.

Light spilled out into the hallway ahead of them from just around a gentle bend. It didn't have the warm yellow glow of torchlight, or the bluegreen of Atlantian skinglow. It was sterile white light, artificial.

"They ran LEDs down here?" Korolev asked.

"Certainly looks that way."

Kexx leaned in. "Not to Jack shit, but–"

"*Jinx* it, Kexx."

"Oh," Kexx pondered. "Who is Jinx?"

"No, it's… Never mind right now. Not to jinx what?"

"I was just going to say how much these walls look like the entrance to the Dweller's Temple of Xis's Womb."

"Yeah… but you just said it wasn't a temple."

"The main entrance was not, but the tunnels are quite a bit more extensive than just a single temple."

They turned the corner, and déjà vu hit Benson like an unblocked defensive end. The ramp down and the entrance to the chamber didn't merely resemble the temple from the Dweller caverns they'd visited fifteen years ago, it looked like an exact duplicate, down to the millimeter. All that was missing was the patina and worn edges left by centuries of use. They entered the circular chamber itself, ringed with columns and seats, exactly as he remembered.

"Well, that's unsettling," Benson quipped.

"What is, honey?" Theresa asked.

"That looks exactly like the Dweller temple Kexx and I almost got shanked in back before Black Bridge. Like, *exactly*, except brand new and with LEDs instead of torches."

"Like the ancestors themselves returned from Xis's womb to rebuild it," Kexx added emphatically.

"You don't think it was, you know, already here?" Korolev asked.

"No," Sakiko said. "This mudstone is fresh and unstained. Less than ten years."

"Seven years," Sco'Val said. "Ze wanted the Dweller

Temple copied after hearing about the Bearers who ruled from under the ground. We agreed."

"Ze who?" Theresa asked.

"Sco'Val speaks about myself."

As one, they all turned to regard the source of the small, yet firm voice. An Atlantian bearer stood there, hunched over with age and burden, held up by an attendant at each arm, yet somehow standing taller than anyone in the room. Sco'Val fell to zer knees.

"Oh, shit," Kexx mumbled.

"What?" Benson said. "Who is that?"

"It's *zer*, the Bearer with No Name."

That got Benson's attention. The Bearer with No Name, the spiritual parent of every last Atlantian in Shambhala. The figurehead for an entire community.

And someone who went missing a decade ago.

"Are you sure, Kexx? No one's seen zer in ten years."

Kexx regarded Benson with a pained expression.

"The truth-digger is correct," ze said. "I have no name. Many have tried to give me one, but I resist. If I have a name, I could speak only for myself. Without one, I am free to speak for all my people."

Memories came flooding back to the surface of Benson's mind. A missing person, an underground hideout, a forgotten leader.

Still, Benson had enough experience with this sort of thing to know when to show deference. Lord only knew how he'd survived long enough to learn *that* lesson. He leaned down, not prostrate on the ground like Sco'Val, but enough to bring his face level with the frail figure before him, signaling that he considered zer an equal. Ze was old for an Atlantian, wrinkled and dulled by the years. The contrasting bands of color on zer skinglow lacked the sharp definition of youth. Permanent spots where the chromatophores had simply forgotten how to constrict had cropped up like broken pixels on a video display.

Ze had been old for a bearer of fertile age when ze'd

come to Shambhala asking for asylum. Now, ze was ancient. But no one seemed to have the courage to tell zer.

Benson thought of Devorah, the undead museum curator (or cybernetic, depending on who you asked), saw yet another parallel, and smiled.

"Something amuses you, truth-digger?" the bearer asked pointedly. Benson looked back at Kexx, assuming ze'd done something to raise the bearer elder's ire, but Kexx only blanched at him.

"I was speaking to you, Ben son."

Realizing his mistake, Benson's head snapped back. "I'm sorry, bearer. I've just never been called a truth-digger by an Atlantian of your… standing before. I assumed you meant my friend, Kexx."

"You dig through the dirt and filth of lies to find truth as Kexx does, do you not?"

"That was my job, yes. Long ago. My wi… mate, Theresa, holds that job now." Benson held a hand out to his wife, who gave a curt bow in reply.

"We cannot stop being who we were, truth-digger. We can only add to it."

"That is very wise. And I'm sorry, I did not mean to offend you. You just remind me of an old friend."

"How?"

Benson paused, unsure of how to answer, but fairly certain "You remind me of a tiny, ancient, angry Jewish woman who terrorizes school children and council members equally" was the wrong approach.

"Her strength lies in her wisdom and resilience, not in her physical body."

"Oh, you mean *Devorah*," the bearer said.

Benson flinched. "You know her?"

"Oh yes, very well. Ze's crazy."

It was so unexpected, Benson laughed easily for the first time in days. "That she is. And she still won't stop working."

"Ze will work for zer people until ze returns, then ze

will work for zer people before Xis. Who do you work for today, truth-digger?"

"I..." Benson stammered, caught off guard by the question. He looked at the bearer's face, into zer eyes. They were clouded over with many years of seeing too much. Ze was almost certainly blind, but Benson couldn't help but feeling like ze was looking through him like a recently cleaned window.

"I'm supposed to say I'm working for Shambhala, or whatever."

"But?"

"But I'm here for my child. I'm working for Benexx. Everything else can burn behind me, as long as ze's safe."

"You would watch your village fall for one who is not even of your blood?"

The muscles in Benson's neck flared involuntarily. He grabbed Theresa's hand and squeezed. "Benexx is *our* child. *We* named zer in the proper Atlantian ceremony overseen by Chief Tuko zerself. We've raised zer, cared for zer, tucked zer in, taught zer everything we knew, and learned from zer things we never could have known without zer. Blood is irrelevant. We chose our family. Now, can you help me find zer, or are you wasting my time?"

It was the Bearer with No Name's turn to smile. Ze looked up at one of the attendants who helped steady zer. "I would like to sit, please." Benson watched quietly as they maneuvered zer into the largest chair and waited until ze was settled and comfortable.

"Let us talk, truth-digger."

"Let's."

"My eyes are not what they once were, but my ears hear farther and clearer than they ever have."

Benson nodded. "And what have your ears heard in the last few days?"

"Much, but first, we're going to talk about what they're going to hear before I help you."

A pit opened up in Benson's stomach. "I'm not authorized to negotiate on behalf of the city, bearer. I can promise you the moon if you like, but I can't deliver it."

"You are influential among your people, truth-digger. And ours. You, your mate, and your child are powerful symbols across the city. When you talk, all listen."

"You flatter me, bearer. I just don't want you to walk away with… inflated expectations."

"I understand. But we've gone through the… what do you call them? 'Proper canals'?"

"Channels, bearer," Kexx said.

"Channels, thank you. We have gone through the proper channels for years without success. Time for something different."

Benson's jaw tightened. "Is that what the attack at the parade was? *Something different*?"

"We had nothing to do with that despicable act."

"Then who did?" Benson snapped. Theresa put a soothing hand on his shoulder.

"Patience, dear. Let zer speak."

"Your mate is wise, Benson," the Bearer with No Name said.

"And if ze doesn't get to the point soon, bite zer head off," Theresa added.

The bearer's attendants stiffened, but ze waved them off. "I sometimes wonder how humans manage to keep that fire of youth burning for so long."

"It's the hot blood," Theresa said. "We have a hard time cooling off."

"Perhaps so." The bearer adjusted zerself in the chair and smoothed out the scales of zer skirt. "Have you been so deep into our part of the city before, truth-digger?"

"Not this deep, no." Benson shook his head. "Honestly, we didn't even know these tunnels existed."

"Although it does answer how some of the suspects we've pursued managed to disappear into thin air," Korolev added.

Theresa shushed him, but Benson thought it brought up an important point. "My… colleague is right. Have you been harboring criminals down here? Helping them evade the constables?"

"Your constables are one of the things we wish to talk about," the bearer said.

"Go on."

"We want our own truth-diggers and warriors walking and working in our part of the village. Your constables, they see rule-breakers everywhere, not children. You humans poison our children with your drugs, then beat and arrest them for being sick with them."

"We didn't bring bak'ri here, bearer," Benson said defensively.

"No, but your science made it into a weapon against us. You cannot even use it. What other reason would you have for doing it?"

"Well in the beginning it was to isolate the active ingredients and see if they could be used in medicine, but the process got out. The people who purify bak'ri into a drug are criminals, and we come down on them even harder."

"We are veering from the path. Our own truth diggers in our own spaces. Yes or no?"

Benson crossed his arms. "They already are. Theresa has been recruiting and training Atlantian constables as fast as she can. Three of my football players are already walking the beat in their own neighborhoods."

"As bracelets!" the bearer snapped back. Benson didn't get the reference, but Kexx was there to lean in his ear.

"Tokens," Kexx whispered. "Village elders will often wear bracelets made by rivals during trade disputes to ease tensions, but it's sometimes seen as an empty gesture."

Benson nodded his thanks, then addressed the bearer once more. "They are not bracelets, they are trusted and valuable members of the force."

"If they are so trusted, why are there not two fullhands of them in the entire city? And why are none of them leaders? Always following along behind their human master?"

"Honey, maybe you could...?"

"Sure." Theresa stepped up. "There are so few Atlantians on my force because there are so few of you here that are old enough to serve. You know as well as I do that most of your people here were born after you, personally, arrived. They're still adolescents. I want more Atlantians on my force, as soon as I can have them. But the adults and elders who are here are busy working, building, and raising the kids."

"They are busy in the fields, digging water trenches, laying seeds, doing the mindless work of animals or your, your... machines, while human children are taught your magics and sent into the sky."

Theresa opened her mouth to object, but what could she say, really? The bearer's words were true. The fact every effort was being made to move up the day that Atlantian children would be given plants and the ability to compete on an even playing field with their human counterparts didn't change the reality of the situation as it existed in that moment.

"Our children are not taught magic," Theresa said finally. "Everything they learn, your people can learn. *Will* learn," she corrected herself. "We just need more time to build the tools we need to teach you."

"Because we are too stupid without them?"

Theresa put up her hands defensively. "No, bearer, that's not it at all. The truth is we're too stupid to teach you without them. We've been using these tools for hundreds of years. We don't *remember* how to learn or teach without them. This is our failing, not yours."

The self-deprecation seemed to do its work as the bearer's features softened. Ze pointed at zer attendants. "These two will leave with you. You will teach them to be con-staples and send them back here. There will be others."

If the attendants were surprised or distressed by the development, they kept their emotions well hidden. Not even a ripple of color or light passed over their skin.

"Good," Theresa said. "The academy takes three Varrs, and they'll still have to be supervised by one of my human constables."

"Why?" ze asked sharply.

"Because that is their tradition as much as it is ours," Kexx stepped in. "Do we not pass our knowledge from master to apprentice?" Ze put a hand on Sakiko's shoulder. "This is my apprentice, Sakiko. I believe you know zer mother, Mei." The bearer fluttered an acknowledgement. "Sakiko will eventually replace me as G'tel's truth-digger. But not until I am satisfied that ze's ready. I don't think it's unreasonable for our human friends to ask the same."

The bearer was silent for a moment while zer skinglow pulsed in contemplation.

"If they're anything like my other Atlantian constables, we will learn just as much from them as we teach," Theresa added diplomatically, but Benson knew it was true.

"We agree," ze said finally.

"Great!" Benson said, hoping to seal the deal and move on. "Now, about the–"

"Does ze always interrupt like this?" the bearer asked Kexx.

"Not always..." Kexx rubbed zer chin, "...but often."

Benson flushed, but tried to remain on track. "OK, what else do you need to hear?"

"We need to be given greater priority in building, water, and elek... elekt..."

"I believe you mean *electricity*, honored bearer," Kexx said.

"It is so," ze answered. "Elek-tricity. We are forced to sip from your river with reeds while your houses overflow with it."

"Nobody's houses are overflowing with it right now," Benson said. "Our main supply has been cut off by someone who almost succeeded in destroying the Ark, where most of our... river still flows from."

"Yes, I've been told about your city in the sky, although I've never seen it."

"I have, honored bearer," Kexx said again. "I was invited, fifteen years ago. I stood in their sky city. It is as miraculous as the stories. Perhaps more. Our friends are very wise."

"But they just said they are stupid!"

"They can be that, too. Just as we can, no? They know they are not the Gods, and they do not pretend to be, even though they could. That has to mean something."

The bearer's skinglow ebbed subtly and reversed direction, drawing its patterns back towards zer chest instead of radiating outward. "One of my early mates worked as a trader between the villages, truth-digger Kexx. Ze was weary of 'wise' traders who talked too fast to follow. It was too easy to end up on the losing side of a trade when they knew things you did not. Too easy to get cheated."

"Are you saying we're cheating you, bearer?" Benson said, trying to keep his voice from betraying the offense he felt at the accusation.

"This is what I see. I see your El-a-va-tors and shuttles filled with rocks you tell us are valuable going up to your sky city. You tell us you build things up there. Where are they? You take from Xis, but what do you return to Zer? What do you return to Zer people?"

"I thought we were all Xis's people, honored bearer," Kexx said sharply.

"Don't be cold-headed. You know what I meant."

"I know that you came here because our people were going to kill most of your brood, bearer." Kexx squared zer shoulders. "I know that these humans took you in without hesitation and spent Varrs shielding you from our own people. I know that you knew they would because of the example *my friend* set when ze wouldn't stand by silently during a culling. I was *there*, honored bearer, in the temple where *this* human..." Kexx shoved a finger at Benson's face "...pointed a gun at one of *our* elders, to defend *our* children, on the same day ze fought alongside us to protect G'tel against a Dweller attack. After ze defeated a trained warrior with a mere fishing trident. I saw it happen. And I will not stand here today and hear *his* motives questioned!"

In the fifteen years Benson had known Kexx, he'd never known zer to sound or look so aggressive, not even in the middle of a fight. Ze was too professional, too detached and precise for anger. He'd also never once heard zer use a human gender pronoun.

He wasn't the only one to notice.

The bearer took a moment to compose zerself before responding. "You believe in these humans so totally, truth-digger?"

"I believe in this human, his mate, and those he calls friend, as surely as I believe in Xis, Cuut, and Varr. They are far from perfect, but they are exactly what they claim to be. I would wager my life on it. I *have* wagered my life on it."

Kexx's punch landed. The conversation took a pause as if a bell had rung to signal the end of the round. Everyone retreated to their respective corners of the ring to regroup for a few heartbeats. Or, however Atlantians ticked off awkward stretches of silence.

The Bearer with No Name resumed, finally. "Atlantians," ze said with a sigh. "We didn't have a name for ourselves until you humans arrived and taught us just how different two peoples could be. We claimed your name for us, because it was the first one we heard, like hungry infants at their naming ceremony, starving for knowledge. As you named your child, Benson truth-digger, humans named us."

"I think I understand, honored bearer," Benson responded.

"And how well do you think you have cared for your children here?"

"Not well enough," he said without thinking through his answer. "We can, and should, do better by your people in Shambhala. We're all one Trident."

"A trident you held." The bearer slumped back in zer chair, almost shrinking before his eyes. "My ears have heard enough." Ze tugged on the skirt of the attendant to zer left. "Show them. Let them see."

The anonymous attendant fluttered an acknowledgement and they both departed the chamber while the bearer gazed upon zer guests with clouded eyes.

Benson swallowed, hard, then looked over at Sco'Val. He'd forgotten their guide was even in the room for as quiet as ze'd been since making the introductions. He was beginning to suspect the demonstration in the street that he'd disrupted was not so spontaneous as he'd assumed. Had Sco'Val been testing him, scouting out his reaction on behalf of the bearer? If so, he'd obviously passed the audition.

But it didn't answer the question of what he'd been brought down here to see. His hope of a quick and painless reunion with Benexx was fading. Theresa, feeling the same anxiety, laced her fingers in his and squeezed.

"It's going to be OK, baby," he whispered. "We're getting zer back if I have to dig up the whole city with my bare hands."

"I know we will, dear."

Benson drew his wife close and kissed her forehead as she rested her free hand on his chest. The attendants returned, carrying a stretcher between them, a blanket draped over it. For a millisecond, Benson's body went rigid with terror for what was hidden beneath. But as they set it down and he got a better angle, it was obvious the object wasn't a body of any kind.

He leaned down and pulled back the blanket. The object definitely wasn't a body, it was a bomb.

Benson jumped back, so startled he almost tripped over himself. "Jesus fucking Christ." He put a hand over his now racing heart. "A little warning next time!?"

"Pavel," Theresa said. "Get back up into plant range and get an explosives tech down here. Fast. You," she pointed at Sco-Val, "lead him back up to the surface."

"I know the way out," Sakiko said eagerly. "I'll take him back."

Theresa looked to Kexx, who nodded zer approval. "OK, go. Quickly, and don't say anything about this to anyone until we get it disarmed, understood?"

Sakiko saluted and grabbed Korolev by the wrist. "C'mon, this way." The two of them, plus Sakiko's pet, darted out of the temple.

Benson had already gotten over his initial shock and leaned back in to inspect the device. It was a slick piece of work, boasting several kilograms of the sort of demolitions charges the mines further inland were using. Whoever had built it had a steady hand. The wire leads between the blasting caps and detonator were orderly, the soldering was neat without much excess or drippings. It was the deadly work of an experienced craftsman. If it went off down here, it would liquefy everyone and collapse the chamber.

The explosives packaging had been stripped, which was smart because there were no batch numbers to track, but it wouldn't be terribly hard to run inventory checks at the sites to see where the stock had gone missing from. Industrial grade explosives like these were chemically complex and resource-intensive to produce. It was very unlikely anyone cooked them up in their kitchen, not without blowing up their city block in the process.

"Where did you get this?" Benson asked the bearer. "And when?"

"It was found inside the main temple of Cuut, not far from here, the day after the attack on the parade. We think it was meant to go off at the same time, but failed. Failed to kill me."

"You were in the temple when the attack happened?"

The bearer nodded. "I led a ceremony."

"We have a common enemy."

"Perhaps."

"You really should've let us move it."

"We didn't want anyone disturbing it. What if a child found it and started playing?"

Benson sighed. "There are a hundred ways to set one of these off. Pressure switches, accelerometers. You're incredibly lucky it didn't explode the second you picked it up."

"What my husband is trying to say, honored bearer, is in the future, let us know if you find another one of these. We have people who can disable them safely, so no one is put at risk."

Benson looked up at his wife. "What do you think, honey? A third prong in the attack?"

"Probably. They already timed the run on the Ark and the parade bomb. But why didn't it go off?"

"We'll let the bomber boys figure that out. Right now, we need to get everyone out of these tunnels until it's dismantled."

"Agreed."

"We will not abandon our temple," the bearer said with finality.

"I don't mean to be imprudent, bearer," Kexx said. "But if that bomb explodes down here, we'll all be turned into soup. This is temporary, our human friends will be done before the evening cleanse." Kexx turned to Benson. "Right?"

"Er..." Benson checked the time in his plant. Three hours and change until the night's cleansing ritual. "Sure. Absolutely. You won't even know we were here."

The bearer made a grand show of considering this. Finally, ze stood. "I am tired. I will return to my rooms and rest until it's time for the evening cleanse. My attendants will accompany me. *All* of them." Without another word, the undeclared leader of the Atlantians in Shambhala swept out of the temple with a half-dozen lackeys in zer wake.

"Did…" Benson stammered. "Did ze just give us a three-hour window to clean this up?"

"Seriously?" Kexx asked. "Really, my friend, for a detective, you have a strange knack for overlooking the obvious."

"Don't get me started," Theresa added.

Benson looked back down at the deadly device. He'd come down here looking for a clue, a lead, anything that could point him in Benexx's direction. This was a pretty big one. And even though it failed to go off when its builder intended, Benson was determined to make sure it blew up in their face.

CHAPTER NINETEEN

The sound of rope hitting the floor cued Benexx that ze had company incoming. Ze stirred, just as Jolk came down the rope hand-over-hand. Benexx darkened zer skinglow to the point it felt like ze was squeezing zer skin shut, then moved to the shadows behind a stalagmite. Jolk was alone, and armed with a rifle. Ze didn't look to be in a particularly good mood.

Jolk turned on the light mounted to zer gun and swept it around the chamber. Benexx ducked back behind cover.

"There's no point hiding, changfu. Come out!"

Quietly, Benexx climbed onto the top of the stalagmite. From the new vantage point, Benexx caught a strong scent of bak'ri hooch wafting off Jolk on one of zer fingers. So, ze'd been drinking. That was good and bad. The Atlantian moonshine would dull Jolk's senses and reaction time, but ramp up zer aggression.

"Finally fetched my dinner, did you?" ze taunted back, trying to bounce zer voice off a wall to misdirect Jolk for another few seconds. Another trick ze'd learned from Uncle Kexx. It worked, turning zer attention away from zer hiding place at forty-five degrees. Not out of zer peripheral vision, but it would have to do.

"Not exactly," Jolk answered. "But I have an appetite. And you're going to feed it."

"One of us is going to bite something," Benexx called

again, bouncing zer voice from the opposite wall, causing Jolk to spin around the other direction, exposing zer back.

"Did you really think I would let you embarrass me in front of Elder Sula without consequence?" ze shouted.

Sula, Benexx thought. Jolk let the name of zer master slip. What a complete idiot. Ze filed the information away, more determined than ever to get out of here and bring zer mother's resources crashing down on these assholes.

Benexx tensed and closed zer eyes as the light swept right past the stalagmite ze was perched on top of, but Jolk didn't look up to spot zer. The intense light must be screwing with zer night vision.

"I've got something for you, bearer. Something that will remind you of your proper place." Jolk took zer hand away from the rifle's foregrip and held up zer wrist for Benexx to see. Zer hand peeled off the bracelet around zer wrist, exposing a flap of skin. A trio of bright purple fingerlike proboscises wiggled their way out of the flap and waved around in the open air. Benexx's fingertips dug into the rock beneath. So, Jolk had rubbed wrists with an elder and planned to make good on zer threat to fill Benexx's back with zer filthy brood.

I'd rather die, Benexx thought. No, ze *committed.* That was a line ze wasn't going to let them cross. Beat zer, starve zer, isolate zer, and ze would find a way to endure. But not that. Jolk was almost a head taller than zer, and more heavily muscled, and armed, but in that moment, Benexx didn't care. One of them was going to be lying dead on the floor in the next few minutes, and ze'd been pushed to the point that ze didn't give a thrice-damn who.

Jolk spun zer wedge of light around the chamber in frustration. "Show yourself!"

"Gladly," Benexx growled, then leapt through the air and stretched zer arms out for Jolk's neck. Jolk heard and spun around to face zer, the muzzle of the rifle climbing up in slow motion like a Cuut-damned John Woo film.

In the split second before they connected, Benexx released zer death grip on zer skinglow and flared out to zer full brightness, bathing the entire chamber with zer bluegreen light. It had the desired effect.

Jolk flinched from the sudden light, and Benexx hit zer horizontally. Despite zer smaller size, Benexx's momentum was considerable and caught Jolk completely off guard at the shoulders. The impact folded zer over like a napkin and sent them both sprawling onto the unforgiving rock of the floor. Benexx managed to keep a hand around Jolk's neck and squeezed. With zer other arm, Benexx reached down to try and get a grip on the rifle, but Jolk anticipated the move and pulled back. But ze didn't anticipate Benexx lashing out with zer legs.

Benexx was far from an experienced fighter, but ze'd had some training, both against humans and other Atlantians. Zer father had insisted. Rolling around in the dust of this cave, ze was glad he had. Ze'd learned several things sparring with a variety of opponents. One, humans hit *hard*. Their rigid skeletons meant they had the next best thing to built-in clubs for fists, elbows, knees, feet, and heads. Second, that unarmed fights with or between Atlantians almost always ended up on the ground in a grapple, and that Atlantian feet were, for all practical purposes, not functionally different from their hands.

Sure, their toes were a trifle larger, and lacked the chemical receptors of their fingers (thank Xis, otherwise ze'd be constantly walking around tasting whatever ze was stepping in) but they were just as dexterous. If you knew what you were doing, it was like fighting with four arms instead of just two, a distinct advantage in any ground fight.

Benexx made sure to take it to the ground at the first opportunity. Down here, strength, reach, and speed were less important than form, precision, leverage, and flexibility, as Jolk was about to learn the hard way.

Benexx got a foot on the vertical forward grip of the rifle and clamped down for all ze was worth, then wrapped zer other hand around Jolk's throat.

Now, Jolk had to choose. Let go of the gun and pry Benexx's hands free of zer neck, or focus on getting the rifle into position to turn zer head into a soup bowl. It wasn't as straightforward a decision for an Atlantian. A human caught in such a position would have maybe ten seconds of consciousness to work with before oxygen starvation caused them to black out and their body to go limp.

But Jolk's slower metabolism and decentralized nervous system meant ze had a minute or more to try and break Benexx's grip, and even if ze passed out, the peripheral nervous nodes in zer arms and legs would go right on trying to execute the last set of orders they'd gotten from the brain, just in a much less coordinated way.

Jolk stalled for time, trying to bring a foot up to grab the gun, but as flexible as Atlantian joints were, they weren't *that* flexible. Recognizing it was hopeless, Jolk reversed zer leg and used it to try and flip zerself up and over Benexx in a reversal, but Benexx was able to counter the new leverage with zer free leg, at least for the moment. It wouldn't last, though. As hard as ze'd worked and practiced, zer bearer body was simply weaker than Jolk's. Benexx had gotten the drop on zer opponent and placed zerself in the best possible position, but Jolk was stronger, larger, and had better endurance. It was a battle of attrition now, and Benexx's muscles were already burning with pain from the intense exertion. Ze couldn't outlast Jolk. If ze didn't find a way to win in the next ten seconds, ze was as good as dead.

Or worse.

Jolk finally made zer choice and abandoned the rifle, moving zer hands up to grab Benexx's wrists.

To hell with this, Benexx thought. Ze couldn't maneuver

the rifle well enough with one foot to actually train its muzzle on zer foe, but ze could sure as hell use it as a club. With a flick of zer leg, Benexx whipped the stock end of the gun up in a fast arc before bringing it crashing down directly onto Jolk's head with a squishy *thud*.

The unexpected impact caught Jolk full in the face so hard it actually bounced. Dazed, Jolk's grip on Benexx's wrists slacked. Ze pulled an arm free and decided it was time to stop playing nice. With all the strength ze had in zer fingers, Benexx clamped down on the one spot ze knew Jolk had no defense against. The sweet spot on the shoulder, just below the neck, that caused a seizure-inducing neural feedback loop.

It was a low blow, unbecoming of an Atlantian warrior. But, as ze'd been reminded over and over throughout zer life, Benexx wasn't a warrior. Zer was *just a bearer*. The poor, defenseless thing. As Jolk's arm went into spasms, and the look of shock and betrayal spread across zer face, Benexx felt a fleeting moment of pity. Which lasted just long enough for zer to remember what Jolk intended for zer should ze lose.

Benexx sent the butt of the rifle crashing into Jolk's face again, for good measure.

With one arm temporarily paralyzed and zer brain reeling from both oxygen starvation and multiple impacts, Jolk's resistance faded fast. Enough that Benexx was able to get on top and pin zer shoulders down without releasing zer deathgrip on Jolk's neck.

And a deathgrip is exactly what it was. The fact that no one had yet come to intervene meant that nobody else knew Jolk was down here getting zer ass kicked. Ze had probably been assigned a guard shift, and decided to take the opportunity to extract zer revenge.

Benexx had never killed anyone before. Hadn't killed *anything* before, excluding fish ze'd caught. But ze didn't have a choice now. Ze'd committed to killing Jolk the moment ze leapt off the rock. If ze let Jolk go, zer window of escape closed. Even if ze left Jolk unconscious on the floor, ze'd soon wake and sound the alarm that Benexx had slipped away.

And ze had to do it with zer bare hands. Sure, Benexx could just blow Jolk's head off with the rifle, but the sound of a gunshot would echo through the entire cave system and bring everyone else running.

Jolk's mouth gasped for air like a landed fish, while zer skinglow started to fire random static instead of coordinated patterns of stripes and dots. Zer pupils fell out of synch, one constricting to a wavy slit, the other almost fully dilated. Benexx had to look away, but ze didn't slacken zer grip, even as the muscles in zer forearms burned and cramped under the strain.

After an interminably long time, Jolk's writhing ebbed. Benexx stole a look down at zer handiwork, and immediately wished ze hadn't. Jolk's eyes stared off lifelessly in different directions, while zer flesh had taken on the pallid, featureless color of dead skin, save for a handful of individual chromatophores misfiring like broken pixels on an old fashioned digital screen.

Returned to sender.

With effort, Benexx uncurled zer fingers from Jolk's neck and covered zer own mouth to keep from screaming at the horror of it. Regret washed over zer like a wave, and zer first instinct was to start CPR just in case it wasn't too late to revive zer victim.

In the end, zer own survival instinct won out over Benexx's altruism. Ze needed to get moving. Every moment down here was a moment ze should be spending getting further away.

"You chose this," ze whispered to the corpse. Emotion overtook zer, and Benexx allowed zerself a few moments to flicker with grief. Ze felt sick and thought ze might vomit. But ze couldn't afford to lose the scarce calories and nutrients in zer stomach, so ze had to breath deeply until the nausea passed.

It was time to move. Ze grabbed Jolk's body by the feet and dragged it out of the line of sight of the hole in the ceiling, back behind the same rock cropping ze'd hidden behind and left the legs lying in view. Any cursory inspection from above would just show Benexx sleeping behind a rock. They'd have to come all the way down into the chamber to discover the truth. Ze grabbed the small bag of food and other supplies and tossed the strap over a shoulder.

Then, ze retrieved the rifle, spent a moment refamiliarizing zerself with its controls, then checked that it was loaded. It had a full magazine, but the idiot hadn't even cycled a round into the chamber. It had never been a threat during the fight. Benexx just shook zer head and thanked Cuut for sending zer such an unbelievably incompetent enemy for zer test, then pulled the charging handle back and quietly slid a fresh round home. Ze checked that the safety catch was engaged, extinguished the flashlight at the rifle's end, and slung it over zer other shoulder.

Freedom beckoned at the other end of the rope. Benexx was grateful for it, but as ze wrapped zer tired hands around the cord and the extra weight of the pack and rifle settled into zer shoulders, ze knew the climb out presented no small challenge.

Benexx reached up and tried to hoist zerself up the rope, but after less than a meter zer arms already threatened open revolt. Ze needed rest to recuperate from the exertion of the fight, but every minute down here just increased the odds someone would come to check on zer or relieve Jolk. Benexx planted zer feet on the rope, taking a significant fraction of weight off zer arms and cramping hands. Slowly, ze walked up the rope, using zer arms to guide and stabilize zer centimeter after agonizing centimeter.

With a herculean effort, the lip of the hole finally came within reach. Ze released the rope and got a hand on the cool, damp stone, half afraid the whole thing had been a setup and Sula's foot was about to crush zer fingers and send zer tumbling back down to the floor for a second time. But no foot came. Gingerly, cautiously, Benexx pulled zerself up enough to get a peek at the area immediately around the hole. It was just as dark as the chamber had been, no torches or chem lights laying around, and only a very faint green glow of bioluminescence from a handful of fungal colonies.

Ze dialed up a little more skinglow to get a better look at zer surroundings. Much to zer relief, Benexx didn't see another solitary soul. Ze said a thanks to Cuut more out of habit than humility and scrambled zer way onto the floor. Benexx lay there for a while, focused only on moving air in and out of zer chest and soothing zer muscles against the cold rock. Just long enough that they stopped burning beneath zer skin.

After not nearly long enough, Benexx forced zerself to get up and start moving again. Ze paused to give a cursory inspection of the inventory of the area right around the hole. There were some crates off to one side that looked like they'd been used as makeshift chairs, a small pile of food packaging, mushroom stems, that sort of thing. Temporary items for a temporary space. Ze spotted a plastic bottle shoved off to the side as if it had been hastily hidden. It was only a third full of an amber liquid. A quick taste of the lip with zer fingertip confirmed it was bak'ri hooch. Probably the very bottle Jolk had consumed to bolster zer bravery before coming down the rope and ultimately meeting zer fate. If the bottle had been full when ze started, Jolk had been very drunk indeed.

Benexx had no intention of finishing the bottle, but the hooch had uses as a disinfectant much like alcohol, and the bottle itself might come in handy as a water container, so ze tucked it into zer pack. Ze remembered the rope, and after a moment's reflection decided rope was always a useful thing to have in a cave, so ze found the anchor point, worked the knot loose, then coiled it up and threw it over zer shoulder with the pack.

Ze was as equipped and prepared as ze was going to get. Benexx scanned the passage. It was a rough tunnel that curved at an angle in each direction. One end curved up and to the left, passing out of sight after maybe thirty meters, the other curved down and to the right. There wasn't much to choose between them, but Benexx reasoned that, being a cave, the exit would generally follow the direction of "up," so that's the way ze settled on.

Slowly, deliberately, Benexx made zer way down the tunnel. Careful to keep zer footfalls as silent as possible and zer skinglow just bright enough to keep zer from bashing zer head on a rock overhang or from falling into another hole in the floor. During summer trips to G'tel, Uncle Kexx had tried to teach zer how to shift zer patterns to blend in with zer surroundings, a type of built-in, adaptive optical camouflage. But Benexx had never mastered the technique. Honestly, zer attempts to do so had been half-assed. Ze never envisioned a situation where ze'd need the skill, living as ze did in Shambhala.

Ze resolved to make Kexx teach zer again, provided ze survived long enough to see zer uncle once more.

Here and there, chambers and smaller passages branched off from the main trunk of the tunnel. Benexx paused to search each one, both to see if ze could find anything useful, and to make sure no one caught zer from behind as ze moved deeper into the network. Not that ze knew what to do if ze did run across someone. Shooting them would solve the immediate problem, but create an entirely new and bigger one.

Still, if it came to it, ze would stand and fight. Maybe if ze was really lucky, ze'd make a big enough bang that zer parents would hear about it and know how ze'd chosen to go out. They would be proud of that, at least. Provided zer father was even still alive, that is. Benexx pushed the dark thought to the back of zer mind as ze reached the next chamber. None of the tunnels and passages ze'd seen so far appeared to be excavated, or even expanded. They were roughly oval, likely naturally-occurring lava tubes much like the ones that were common beneath Atlantis. Eddy currents in the lava flow created the roughly spherical chambers at random intervals.

Was it possible they'd transported zer entirely across the ocean? It seemed improbable. All transoceanic transport happened either onboard one of Shambhala's small fleet of airliners, or one of their remote cargo drone ships. It seemed impossible that they could've smuggled zer onto one of the planes without security catching on. It was at least conceivable that ze could've been stuffed into a shipping container on one of the drone ships, but an ocean transit aboard one of them took days. The superficial injuries ze'd received from the blast would've healed more by the time ze'd woken up.

Benexx shook off the question. Ze was getting too far ahead of zerself. Where ze was wouldn't matter until ze found the way out of these infernal caverns. One foot in front of the other, ze moved through the caves. Quiet as a ghost in its tomb.

CHAPTER TWENTY

The transfer tube from the engineering module to the shuttle wasn't very long in physical terms, only six or seven meters. But to Jian, in that moment, it might as well have been a kilometer.

Although no one in the maintenance and flight ops divisions knew it yet, the shuttle *Buran* was only minutes away from making an unscheduled departure. Or Jian was only minutes away from getting dragged out of the command chair by his snatch handle and thrown under house arrest until the court-martial finished deliberating which lock to throw him out of.

One of the two.

As he floated down the short airlock, Jian gripped the "tablet" in his right hand even tighter. It took a conscious effort to keep his breathing measured. The sweat beading up on his palms and forehead however, he had no control over.

In relation to the shuttle, Jian was falling headfirst towards the floor. This was because nestled inside their docking cradles, the immense craft faced inward, making it both easier for maintenance crews to tend to them, and to keep the ablative ceramic tile reentry shields facing outwards to space as an extra layer of protection against micrometeorite impacts. So when he reached the "bottom" of the tunnel, he spun around his own vertical axis one hundred and eighty degrees and faced the hatch that led into the command deck from the cargo bay.

Even docked to the Ark, all of the lock doors remained buttoned tight until they were needed. Jian was glad for the precaution, as he wore merely his cloth flight suit, not the vacuum-rated skinsuit that would keep him alive long enough for recovery ops to snatch him back aboard in the case of a violent decompression.

Being outside the Ark's protective shell in just his longjohns made him uneasy, but there were appearances to maintain. He wasn't here to steal the *Buran*, after all. What a crazy suggestion. He was just doing a completely routine pre-flight inspection to make sure everything was shipshape before heading back up the tube to get sealed in and squared away for the actual flight.

The pressure equalized with a small hiss as the light above the hatch turned green. Jian hit the release and the hatch swung inward. For just an instant, Jian could've sworn he felt the tablet in his hand shiver.

"Oh, hello, commander," came a voice from the other end of the flight deck. Jian froze in place as he drifted through the lock. There wasn't supposed to be anyone else aboard. His timeline was too tight to deal with interlopers. If he couldn't come up with something to shake off the tech in the next ninety seconds, he'd have to–

"Sir?"

The question snapped Jian back into the moment. "Hmm? Sorry, what did you say, technician?"

"I just said hello." The young tech gave him a concerned glance. "Are you feeling all right? You look a little pale."

Jian's heart raced. She suspected something. He needed to brush her off fast, or else... He put on an awkward smirk. "It's just nerves. I've never flown with a nuke before."

The tech answered with a knowing nod. "I hear you. I helped wire that thing up, and just between you, me, and the bulkhead, it gives me the creeps."

Jian smiled with genuine relief. "I won't say anything if you won't."

"Thanks for that, sir."

"Is that what you're doing here? Working on the nuke?"

"Yes, I'm just finishing up final network integrity tests. Make sure it actually goes boom when you press the button."

"From many tens of kilometers away in orbit," Jian said. "Preferably."

"Ha, you're brave. I'd be halfway back to the Ark before even thinking about setting it off, signal strength be damned."

"It's that powerful?"

"No, not really. Its yield is only in the five-kiloton range, and most of the yield will be pointed straight down into the rock. Without any atmosphere to transfer the blast energy, you could probably be standing on Varr's surface only six or seven klicks away without getting your suit dusty. I'd just feel better with a three-kilometer-wide ablative shield between me and it, you know?"

Jian nodded. "I do indeed. Hey, I just realized I left my test kit back up the tunnel, and I really need to get started on my preflights. If you're done, could you pop up and grab it for me? I'd really appreciate it."

"Sure thing. I'm just running out the clock down here anyway. Gotta look busy for the boss, you know?"

Jian chuckled. "I do indeed. Thanks, Miss…?"

"Claiborne," she said as they floated past each other. "I'll just be a minute up there, sir."

"No worries, take your time," Jian said. She smiled at him as she moved into the lock. Jian thought he saw a flicker of attraction in her gaze, but it was fleeting. The hatch bolted shut behind her. "You're about to have the rest of the day off."

There was no time to spare, he'd already wasted over a minute with Claiborne that he'd have to make up somewhere in the countdown. Jian kicked off hard for the command chair, pushed down with his arms, and landed squarely in the seat hard enough that he had to grab the armrests to prevent himself from bouncing back out again. Five seconds later and he was not only strapped into his chair, but linked into the *Buran*'s network through his plant. He could see all of the ship's systems sitting in standby. Fully prepped and green for launch.

A launch that wasn't supposed to be coming for another two hours.

The moment Jian started toggling over the shuttle's system icons from Standby to Ready status, someone was going to know something very wrong was happening and try to shut him down. Which was why he waited for twelve, eleven, ten...

Several hours before, Jian had uploaded what on the surface looked like a harmless software update into the Flight Operations Center. But, instead of fixing bugs in the fleet's onboard navigation systems interface with the GPS network, it had a more nefarious purpose. The malware was a rush job that wouldn't have survived any level of scrutiny if Jian hadn't uploaded it by hand directly into the engineering module's network, using his credentials to bypass at least a half-dozen layers of security.

It had cost Jian most of the credits in his savings. By the time it had been routed through a dozen fake accounts, ghost routing numbers, and shady middlemen, the programmer who actually wrote it would end up with less than sixty percent of the total. And after a few days of digital forensic investigation, it would almost certainly mean they would be spending quite a long time in a dirtside jail cell.

Just the cost of doing business on the black market.

...three, two, one. *EXECUTE.*

Throughout the *rest* of the shuttle fleet, the first stage of the three-part worm sprang to life. Avionics and navigation computers booted up, and immediately set about tearing themselves apart. Every file, every program, every byte of data stored in memory was relentlessly purged, until all that remained was the foundational operating systems themselves, which on instructions from the worm, deleted themselves before shutting off the lights.

With that, the Ark's entire shuttle fleet was dead in space. Their computer banks empty, barren, inoperable. No physical damage had occurred, of course, and the data as well as the operating systems were thoroughly backed-up inside the Ark's own memory core. But the process of restoring them to flight-ready status would take hours, perhaps an entire day. By then, the intercept window with Varr before the moon's motion took it out of range for the rest of the orbit would have closed.

For every shuttle except the *Buran*, that is.

Jian furiously flipped the shuttle's system icons over to Ready status as the blood pounded in his ears. Clicks and whirrs sounded through the flight deck as the sleeping bird began to wake and stretch its wings. Warning alarms were doubtlessly blaring across Flight Ops as well as up in the Command Module, but Jian was confident they'd be lost among the alarms for all the *other* shuttles that were doubtlessly flashing angrily across displays and plant interfaces throughout the ship. At least Jian hoped they were.

But in case they weren't, Jian needed to cut the data uplink between the *Buran* and Flight, or else they would take remote control as soon as someone spotted him. That would end his little grand theft shuttle adventure before he'd even gone a kilometer. But first, he needed to release the external clamps which kept the shuttle locked into the cradle.

Normally, the release command came from Flight, not from the command deck of the shuttle, but Jian had planned for that as well. With a flicker of his eyes, he toggled his plant interface to a new screen, only a few hours old. It was the second part of his package from the hacker that had already knocked out the rest of the shuttle fleet. Jian said a little prayer in hopes this patch was just as effective as the first one, then pressed the icon that would open the backdoor into Flight's operating system.

There were supposed to be at least three firewalls preventing him from doing this. Jian had no idea what vulnerability his anonymous hacker had found to exploit, but in less than a second, a new virtual console appeared within the augmented reality environment overlaid on his field of vision by his plant.

For clarity's sake, it exactly matched the physical console sitting less than a hundred meters away in the Flight Ops Center. Jian knew it well, having spent several weeks of his pilot training sitting strapped into a chair learning all of Flight Op's systems so he knew what their capabilities and limitations were while he was out in the black, sometimes separated by light minutes.

So he knew exactly where the *Buran*'s cradle release was. He clicked it, breath frozen in his lungs.

A thundering heartbeat passed, then another. But just as Jian was about to hit the icon again, the shuttle shook with the familiar vibration of clamps popping free. The cabin lights flickered as the umbilicals followed a moment later and the *Buran* switched over to internal power.

Relieved and exhilarated, Jian grabbed the shuttle's controls and opened up the taps on the dorsal thrusters. Instantly, dozens of liters of water flash-boiled into superheated steam and came screaming out of the shuttle's nose, tail, and wingtips at almost a thousand kilometers per hour.

With a mighty heave, the beast pushed away from its lair on pillars of clouds.

Jian didn't wait around to savor the small victory. The moment the *Buran* cleared the cradle gantries, he was already out of his seat and floating for the com station. With practiced familiarity, Jian popped open the panels protecting the sensitive electronics suite that made up the shuttle's communication's system. With little fanfare, Jian tore out the trio of modules that formed the triple redundancy of Flight's data uplink.

All he had left was the shuttle's whisker laser. And only *he* controlled where it was pointed and who it talked to.

System warning alarms flashed across his vision as well as the shuttle's command consoles. Jian disarmed them and settled back into his seat to warm up the *Buran*'s mains. He needed to burn hard and fast for Varr if he was going to hit his window.

As the bank of a half-dozen rocket motors spooled through their start-up sequence, an incoming call icon blinked at the upper left corner of Jian's plant overlay. His father. The plant link was short range without the data links, and couldn't directly interface with the shuttle's systems. Still, Jian wasn't in the mood for a lecture. He dropped the call and returned his attention to the task at hand.

His father's call came through again, except this time he didn't bother with the courtesy of ringing.

<What the hell do you think you're doing?> Chao demanded.

<I'm a little busy right now, dad. Signing off.>

<No, wait!>

Jian almost cut the connection again, but the tone in his father's voice had shifted from authoritarianism to desperation. He couldn't help but feel a pang of sympathy for the old man.

<Be quick.>

<Just answer my question, please,> Chao pleaded. <What are you doing?>

<I'm executing my mission.>

<And what is that, exactly? Because it's clearly deviating from the mission profile you were briefed on.>

<That's an understatement. I'm going to use the facility to find Benexx.>

<No, Jian, I won't allow it!> A paternalistic tone crept back into his voice.

<You can't prevent it, dad. I've pulled the plug on the shuttle's data links. As soon as I'm clear of plant range,

you're not going to hear from me again until this is all over.> Jian took a deep breath. <Actually, it's already over. Because I'm not going to help you break our treaty with Benexx's people just to destroy a *priceless* piece of technology.>

<I don't fucking care about the treaty, son.>

<Obviously.>

<Just... shut up and listen. This isn't about us anymore. If you come back right now, maybe, *MAYBE*, I can cook up something to bury this. A power surge, data corrupted by a solar flare. Something to save your career. But, if you light off your engines, Jian, that's mutiny. And I can't protect you from the consequences anymore.>

Jian grit his teeth and exhaled through his nose, hard. <I'm not asking for your protection, dad. I don't need you to hold my hand, or bribe the other parents to bring their kids to my birthday party anymore. This is my decision, and you are on the wrong side of it. I'd like to think you know you are, but it doesn't matter. I'm hanging up now and burning for Varr.> Jian glanced down at the "tablet" he'd brought aboard, stowed in its own little crash webbing. <Oh, and tell your people they can stop ransacking the ship looking for Polly. He's here with me. I'm taking him home where he'll be safe. Commander Feng, out.>

<Jian, I lov–>

The link dropped before Chao could finish his sentence. Not that he needed to. Jian knew what his father was trying to say. Just, given the circumstances, he had some trouble believing it.

Jian put the thought out of his mind. All the *Buran*'s engines showed green. For a bird that entered her third century decades ago, she was in excellent health. A testament to the skill and dedication of the maintenance crews who even now were probably staring slack-jawed at their displays while Jian stole all of their hard work.

Without a moment's reflection or hesitation, Jian

firewalled the throttles. With only Jian aboard and very little cargo in its hold besides the nuke and a few weeks' worth of food and water rations, the *Buran* took off like a shot from a gun. Jian's body pressed into the back of his chair at six gees, seven, eight, going from eighty kilos to more than five hundred in seconds. As it cleared the parabolic blast shield at the aft end of the Ark, Jian began another countdown.

The Ark was a massive beast of a ship. And like any beast, its teeth were housed inside its head. An array of navigational lasers, each powerful enough at full-output to burn a meter-wide hole through an iron asteroid, studded the front of the ship. For two centuries, they had been used to clear the path ahead of the ship as it barreled through deep space at five percent lightspeed. For the last eighteen years, they'd been busy clearing the space around Gaia of orbit-crossing meteors and other proto-planetary debris.

And as soon as that head spun around to face him, Jian was as good as charcoal. Unless he could blind it. The only drawback to the Ark's immense size was its ponderous rate of movement. It would be eleven minutes from the moment the captain gave the order to burn the *Buran* out of the sky until it was in position to fire. This wasn't normally a problem with asteroids they could see coming from months or even years away, but Jian wasn't a normal problem.

Nor was his solution. After ninety-three seconds on full burn, Jian cut thrust to zero. The elephant sitting on his chest stood and wandered away. He took two deep, gasping breaths to clear the stars from his vision, then unstrapped and headed for the cargo hold.

"Crazy, Jian. This is stone fucking crazy." He snapped his helmet visor closed as he gazed down at the nuke sitting in its transfer cradle. Jian grabbed up the remote detonator and hit the cargo bay door release. Above him, the bifold doors peeled back, exposing the black of space and the milky arm of the galaxy beyond.

Hurriedly, Jian unbuckled the tie-down straps holding the nuke fast to the deck until it floated gently a few centimeters off the plating. Five minutes twenty left. *Too close, much too close,* he thought as he lined up the bomb's front with the Ark behind him. He needed the nuke's destructive blast cone pointed squarely back at the Ark and the hell away from his shuttle. With immense care not to impart any rotational inertia, Jian gave the case a gentle push out of the cargo bay. He watched it go for five, ten, twenty seconds, until he was sure it wasn't going to spin back around on him.

Satisfied, he hit the toggle to close the doors and returned to the fight deck where he strapped back into his chair. An external camera feed confirmed that the package was still floating in the proper orientation. Two minutes ten until his goose was cooked.

Angling the *Buran*'s aft slightly off-bore to keep the package out of his exhaust plume, Jian firewalled the throttles again. He needed to put space between his shuttle and the bomb. The further the better. Fifty seconds.

Jian tried to lift the detonator in his right hand, but it felt like trying to lift a shuttle by himself. Reluctantly, he backed off the throttles, down to five and a half gees. Just enough that the detonator budged. With great effort, he inched it upwards where he could punch the code into its keypad with his other hand. Why they hadn't just linked the damned thing into his plant network was beyond his reckoning. Thirty-five.

The detonator display went green, confirming it was armed and ready to send the signal that would convert several kilos of plutonium into fire and fury.

Six.

Five.

Four.

Three.

Jian pressed the button.

CHAPTER TWENTY-ONE

"Hey, Kexx," Benson wiped at the dust from the tunnels that had accumulated on his forehead once they were alone outside again. "Where did you say Sco'Val came from on the road network?"

"Pukal. Ze was a frequent member of their trade delegation during harvest time."

"Yeah? They make paper in Pukal?"

"Why yes, some of the finest. Their craftsmen have mastered the pressing process, and the wetlands surrounding their village grow ideal plants that fail to take root everywhere else they're planted. No one knows why, but their paper is highly sought after for scrolls and the like. How did you know that?"

"Just a hunch. I–"

High above them to the east, a bright flash in the evening sky shone like the birth of a new star. Everyone froze and looked up at the sight.

"What the fuck was that?" Korolev asked.

"Nuke," Theresa answered. "Had to be. A meteorite would streak through the atmosphere, and nothing else would be powerful enough to be seen from orbit like that."

"That was the Ark," Korolev said, not even trying to hide the fear in his voice.

Benson shared it. For a Gaia-shattering moment, Benson thought someone had finally accomplished what

David Kimura had tried to do almost twenty years earlier. A quake went through his knees at the thought. His head swam, and he thought he might be sick.

A call broke through Benson's plant without ringing. <People of the Trident. My name is Commander Jian Feng.>

Benson looked past the young man's face suddenly floating in his vision and to his wife, who wore a similarly perplexed look.

"Are you seeing this, too?" he asked. Theresa nodded, as did Korolev. It was a mass announcement, then.

Feng's boy continued. <Three days ago, I was leading a routine resupply mission to our Early Warning site on Varr when we discovered an underground facility of unknown origin. I've been ordered by… the *Ark* leadership, to rendezvous with Varr and detonate a nuclear warhead prepared by our engineering team below the moon's surface to destroy the facility. This decision has been made unilaterally, and without consultation from the religious authorities in Atlantis, or the native community in Shambhala.>

Jian's image paused and ran a hand through his raven hair before resuming. <I believe this is an illegal order, which violates if not the letter, then the spirit of the treaty between humans and Atlantians that has kept the peace between our people for the last fifteen years. Which is why I have decided not to execute this mission. The flash many of you just saw in the sky along the elevator ribbon was the nuclear device that had been rigged up to destroy the facility. I instead used it to cover my escape by temporarily blinding the Ark's targeting sensors with its EM pulse and fallout. This will, hopefully, buy me enough time to get clear of the Ark's navigational lasers before they incinerate my shuttle. Don't worry, the Ark herself is undamaged. I have also taken steps to prevent anyone else from completing this mission either, not until Varr's orbit brings it back within the range of our

shuttles in several weeks.

<It is my hope that by the time a new launch window opens, the relevant authorities from all the points of our Trident will be able to deliberate and have their voices heard in a decision that I believe is best made by *all* the people of Gaia. There are those who will say that by taking this action, I am committing mutiny, or even treason. I respectfully reject that perspective. I will not stand idly by while mankind repeats the mistakes of its ancestors and abridges the sovereignty and autonomy of yet another indigenous people, because our own long, often embarrassing history reveals the folly and repeated failure of that arrogance.

<To my friends and... family, I don't ask for your approval, only your consideration. This decision weighs heavily on my conscience, but I know in my heart that it is the right one. One way or another, I'll see you all soon. This is Commander Jian Feng, signing off.>

As Chao's son finished his pirate broadcast, Benson knew in the pit of his stomach that in the coming years, everyone would look back at *this* as the moment all hell broke loose. Theresa and Korolev's faces wore the same exasperated, slack-jawed expression Benson felt as they stood around the entrance to the Atlantians' secret tunnel network.

So, he hadn't hallucinated it. Somehow, that didn't make him feel better.

"Oh, fuck..." Theresa's voice trailed off as her hand covered her mouth.

"Seconded," Korolev said.

"Do you suppose that went up on the local network screens, too?" Benson asked.

"I think we have to assume it did if he managed to rig it into the entire plant network. That's a clever hack job."

"Then word's going to get out among the Atlantians pretty quick." Korolev tightened his grip on his rifle. "We shouldn't stick around here for long."

"What is the matter?" Kexx asked on behalf of zerself and Sakiko, who was also without a plant. "The three of you went blank for a while. Well, more blank than usual."

Benson decided to give zer the condensed version. "Chao Feng's kid just hacked our network and publicly announced he'd been ordered to drop a nuke on Varr without an OK from your people."

"That is... problematic," Kexx added, in what would likely turn out to be the understatement of the decade.

"No shit. He said he's refused the order and stolen the shuttle to keep it from happening until everyone can sit down and talk about it. That flash was the nuke. He blew it up to cover his tracks."

Sakiko laughed. "Of course he did."

"Why do you say that, Sakiko?" Theresa asked.

"I know Jian. He hates his old man. Something like this was bound to happen eventually."

Benson's teeth ground against each other. Here he stood cut off on the surface, smack in the middle of a powder keg of terrorists, restlessly aggrieved natives, and his own missing child, and the Gods decided to throw a match on it in the form of a nuclear-tipped father/son dick-measuring contest in high orbit.

Could this week get *any* better?

"Honey, I think you should activate your reserves," Benson said.

"How many of them?" Theresa said after a moment's composure.

"All of them."

"Yeah, I think you're right."

"Are we sure that's wise?" Kexx broke in. "We've just heard from the Bearer with No Name, and zer biggest concern was too many human constables patrolling the Native Quarter. If you send fullhands more deadski..." Kexx caught zerself before finishing the epitaph. "Forgive me, friends. I don't know where that came from."

Benson slapped zer on the shoulder. "It's fine, cuttlefish. You were about to say that sending even more deadskin constables out in force is just as likely to trigger a riot as prevent one."

"That is the thrust of my spear point, yes."

"Well, I don't know that you're wrong, but what else can we do? Not showing up will be seen as a sign of weakness and will invite a riot just as surely. Unless you have a few dozen trained Atlantians hiding in your, er, pockets?"

Kexx grimaced. "That's just the thing. I could have, but I turned down Kuul's offer to send zer personal fullhands of warriors along with Sakiko and me. Now, I really wish I hadn't."

"So do we all," Korolev broke in. "But let's express our regrets on the move, OK? Less talky, more walky." His posture righted. "Sirs," he said, remembering himself.

Benson shrugged his shoulders. "He's not wrong. Let's de-ass the area with the quickness."

"What about the bomb?" Theresa asked.

"Oh, shit, I forgot."

"You forgot about the *bomb*?" Theresa scolded. "How does a man who's been blown up twice forget about a bomb?"

"It's been a long couple of days, OK honey? Somebody just set off a nuke. I was distracted. How quick before the bomb techs get here?"

Theresa's eyes unfocused for a moment as she consulted her plant. "Fifteen minutes. Maybe more if they start running into resistance."

"We have to wait, then, and secure an egress for them."

"Call up a quadcopter," Korolev said. "Just fly the damned thing out once they've disarmed it instead of trying to walk it out of here under guard. Take it straight to the station house. Put it down right on the roof."

"That's a good idea, Pavel," Theresa said. "I'm calling up the airfield now."

Benson found his eyes tracing along the narrow alleyway, checking the angles, looking for heads peeking around corners, hanging laundry fluttering, drapes being pulled back in windows, anything that would give away impending danger. They'd been down in the tunnels for more than an hour. Benson knew how tight knit neighborhoods like this one could be. Even without plants, he'd bet a real meat dinner that everyone within five blocks knew they were here, that there were only five of them including Kexx, and that there was only one rifle between them.

If there was ever a perfect time and place for a mob to overrun them, it would be then and there. Benson hated himself for thinking about the Atlantians in his city, their city, in such a way, especially with his dear friend Kexx standing not a meter away from him. But things had been evolving in Shambhala for years already. Looking around at the grime, the weeds, and the foundations of buildings already cracking from being built too high and too cheaply, Benson knew they'd failed to manage that evolution. They'd ignored the Native Quarter, told themselves comfortable lies about the Atlantians knowing how to fend for themselves while ignoring the compounding squalor. It was their world, after all. Nevermind that they were an ocean away from everything they'd ever known, and had been asked to live under rules written for humans.

If this news from the Ark brought things to a head, Benson wouldn't even blame them for it. He just wanted to get his weird little family clear before the carnage really got underway.

The bomb techs arrived without incident, either because word about the proposed violation of Varr hadn't penetrated as far and as fast as Benson had feared, or because the Bearer with No Name had made it known that it was in everyone's best interest to grant them safe passage until the bomb was disarmed and removed.

Personally, Benson figured it was even money.

They made short work of the bomb, which was not an assessment against its maker, only the limitations placed on them by available materials.

<Is it safe?> Korolev asked over the plant link. Smart. There was no need to announce the bomb's safe condition before they absolutely had to.

<Yeah, it's inert,> the more senior tech answered.

<That didn't take long.>

<Well the triggering mechanism wasn't very complex, really. I don't want to call it crude, though. The electronics are simple, pretty obviously printed off on any of a few hundred home 3D rigs, but the components are robust and cleverly designed. They're entirely analogue, which makes them basically unhackable. Our usual sweeps with the wifi crackers wouldn't catch them, unless we got lucky and one of the chem sniffers got a hit.>

<Is this what blew up the parade?> Theresa asked.

The tech nodded. <Can't be exactly sure of course, but the yield is right and what little bits of the components we've managed to pick out of the stucco seem to match up. There's a high probability this is a copy of the device that detonated at First Contact Day.>

Benson looked at Theresa and smiled. <Which means DNA, fingerprints, hair samples, and all sorts of other goodies.>

She nodded. <Unless they scrubbed it down to the molecular level, we should be able to get something.>

A sudden rush of air came from overhead as one of the city's electric quadcopters swooped into position just above the residential towers. The cockpit bubble was empty, being flown as it was by remote, both to save weight and to keep a pilot out of danger while it hauled the device. A Rescue & Recovery winch hung from beneath the central fuselage and quickly played out some thirty meters of cable and dangling orange harness straps.

They had the device winched up in a couple of minutes

and ready to lift away. Theresa gave the controller back at the airfield the green light to dust off. Their care package would be waiting on the roof of the Station House under armed guard by the time they got back.

Getting back was the more immediate problem. The quadcopter's arrival and sudden departure had brought out the curious. Within moments the streets filled up with dozens of Atlantian onlookers. Then hundreds. Some of them held improvised clubs, rocks, or even crude cooking knives in their hands.

<We need to go,> Theresa said through their private link. <This isn't looking good.>

<I'm not going to argue the point. We're moving, Pavel. Stay close to the bomb techs. Keep them safe, but most importantly, keep that cannon pointed down. Do not point it at anyone, not even if provoked. Not unless your life or one of theirs depends on it, OK? This is important. These kids have nothing but rocks and knives to fight back with.>

<A knife can still kill, coach.>

<Yeah, but it doesn't look as bad as a constable firing into a crowd of adolescents,> Theresa said.

<Feels just as bad...> Pavel said, but didn't protest further.

They moved out, down the alley, around the corners. At each intersection, Benson had to politely, but firmly, push through Atlantian youths that seemed increasingly intent on crowding their egress. Benson was no linguistic expert, but he could read body language. The crowd was growing hostile, and worse yet, bold. Their skin patterns were beginning to merge, passing subtly from one individual to the next, until the ripples turned into waves that spread out from one youth to the next subconsciously. Benson had seen it before among gangs of Atlantian kids right before they built up the nerve to do something stupid.

<Getting awful tight in here,> Theresa said.

<That's what she said,> Benson snapped off reflexively.

<Oh for fuck's sake. Now, really?>

<Gotta keep things light, dear.>

<Why don't we put Kexx up front? Just a thought.>

<A good thought.> Benson dropped back a step to confer with his friend. "Kexx, they might give you a wider berth. Would you mind?"

"Not at all."

But Kexx leading the caravan did not have the desired effect. Instead, the growing horde became even more restless and aggressive. Voices started taunting Kexx, calling zer a "pet" and "halfskin", a cruel insult aimed at the massive burn scar covering most of zer back that could no longer produce light or shadow, a remnant of the Ark's nav laser that destroyed the Black Bridge at the climax of the battle of the same name.

Sakiko stood at her mentor's side and hurled insults right back at the mob, in their own language. Benson's plant translator had trouble with some of the more… creative ones, but it was obvious the girl had a gift.

An object arching through the air caught Benson's eye. A rock, sailing right toward Theresa's head. Well-worn neural paths, many decades old, took over as the visual information left Benson's eye, was processed through the motor control and spatial recognition portions of his brain, and down the nerve trunk to his right arm. Benson's hand sprang up to intercept the rock with grace and ease, and was immediately reminded that he still had a sprained wrist.

"Ow! Son of a bitch!" Benson's first impulse was to switch hands and hurl the rock at the nearest protestor's stupid head, but his instructions to Korolev extended to him as well and he let the projectile drop harmlessly to the ground.

"Nice catch, honey," Theresa said. "You do remember you have two hands though, yeah?"

"You're welcome." Benson gingerly rubbed his aching

wrist before turning to face the direction the rock came from. "Who threw that? C'mon, don't be shy. Step up and take credit. It was a great throw. You almost hit my mate *in the head*!"

The crowd of faces leaned back perceptibly from the sudden emotional outburst, but held their ground.

"Well? Either let us pass in peace, or let's get down to it." Benson dragged his foot through the dry dirt to make a line, then started loosening up his shoulders. "Step right up and let's sort this out one at a time. I'm not as quick as I used to be, and I'm not running as many kilometers as I did, but I figure I've got a solid five minutes of asskicking in me. Bet I get through eight or nine of you before I get winded. Who's first?" Benson looked around at their now silent faces. He recognized one here and there, kids who only a couple of weeks before had gone through a summer rec program, or even tried out for the Mustangs' roster. They at least had the good sense not to make eye contact.

Just as Benson believed his point had been made and he could lower his guard, something rustled from deep in an alley to his left. As he turned to face the disturbance, the sea of faces parted to reveal a beast of an Atlantian. Benson had noticed zer face a full head and shoulders above the crowd before, but assumed ze'd been standing on a crate.

There was no crate, just the better part of three meters of the biggest sentient being Benson had ever encountered.

"Jesus," Korolev said. "Is ze half-dux'ah?"

"What are you feeding the adolescents here?" Kexx asked incredulously.

The brute looked down at the club in zer hand and dropped it unceremoniously to the ground. Then, ze pulled a well-worn metal kitchen knife from the band of their traditional skirt and sunk it deeply enough into the nearest mudstone wall to make it stick.

Benson swallowed hard and dropped a foot back into a ready stance as the beast lumbered down the alleyway with purpose. Even lanky as ze was, the youth had to weigh a hundred and twenty, maybe a hundred and thirty kilos. He'd get two, maybe three good strikes in before getting wrapped up like a Christmas present and dragged to the ground. He had to get inside the monster Atlantian's reach, get behind zer, maybe try that Vulcan nerve pinch Korolev discovered about ten years ago. At least with one arm out of the fight, the tables would be level. Of course, Benson would have to climb just to get to zer shoulder.

The fighter leaned forward, and the looming walk turned into a charge as ze sprinted the last few meters to where Benson stood. Scratch that, he'd have one shot.

"Oh, shit," Benson muttered as he hauled back with his good left arm and tensed his core muscles in anticipation of the rib-bruising impact.

But it didn't come.

Instead, Theresa slid in between her husband and the stampeding ogre, held up her sidearm, and smartly shot a taser round right at the base of the Atlantian's bulging neck. The 9mm round spun out of the barrel, sunk less than a millimeter into the Atlantian's flesh, then opened like a flower and discharged fifty thousand volts of pulsing current through the target's skin, toppling zer like a tree and sending zer skidding through the dirt to come to rest at Benson's feet, still twitching.

"Esa, what the hell?" Benson barked.

"Ze threw that rock at me."

"No ze–"

Theresa turned to face the equally stunned crowd. "And I've got seventeen more of those bad boys in this magazine. We all saw zer throw that rock at a duly-appointed city constable, namely me. *Didn't we*?"

Judging by the wildly bobbing heads, a consensus quickly coalesced among those assembled that yes, they had in fact seen that person in particular throw the rock. Quite clearly, now that she mentioned it. There was no question that ze had been the one solely responsible for throwing the rock at the crazy human lady presently pointing a stun gun at everyone. There could be no question.

"You're evil," Benson whispered.

"You're welcome."

"I could've handled zer."

"Oh, honey, no. Not even ten years ago and with both your hands healthy."

Benson looked down at the brute, only now recovering from the taser's assault on zer nervous system. She was right, he couldn't have taken this one on in an even fight, not even in his Zero prime. But neither was he going to admit it to anybody.

"So, are we arresting zer or what?" Benson asked loud enough for the gathered to hear.

Theresa's voice remained elevated. "Nah, ze's a good kid. Just got caught up in the moment, right? We *all* got caught up in the moment, but it's over now and we're all going to go back home and cool off, yes?"

Once more, the crowd showed their deference to Theresa's wisdom in a way reserved for respected philosophers and people who have demonstrated a willingness to use firearms in public.

"Outstanding. We'll be going now." She pointed the muzzle of her gun at her prostrate victim. "Somebody help zer up and make sure ze gets home safe."

Several friends of the incapacitated rushed to help. In the end, it took four of them to lift the behemoth back to zer feet.

"When this is all over, remind me to invite zer to tryouts for next season," Benson said.

The rest of their egress from the Native Quarter was uneventful. A handful of spotters shadowed their progress, but kept a respectful distance well outside the effective range of Theresa's stun rounds.

"We got off light," Korolev said. "That could've been a whole lot worse."

"No," Kexx said, "We didn't. Just delayed the inevitable. That was a chaotic rabble, leaderless. I doubt they'd even all heard the news yet. Half of them probably just tagged along with their friends because they were bored, or high. But tonight, at the cleansing pools, or tomorrow at Temple, they'll hear about Jian's mission from their elders, and they'll find focus. By tomorrow night, they'll be organized."

Everyone let that sink in for a moment. Theresa was the first to respond. "But these people grew up here, Kexx. They've spent their entire lives in and around Shambhala. Why are you so sure they'll respond to the news like your people in Atlantis would?"

"Because they're still Atlantians, Theresa. Varr is sacred in ways that not even Cuut and Xis are. Ze fought for us, not over us. Ze represents our final salvation. And even if these adolescents grew up here, their elders did not. The Bearer with No Name did not. And they have not forgotten the old stories, even if they came here to forge new ones alongside your people. I'm afraid you don't understand just how deeply this betrayal will be felt."

"But it didn't happen," Benson said. "Jian denied his father and stopped it from happening."

Kexx's skin fluttered, betraying even zer conflicted feelings. "Let us hope that is enough."

CHAPTER TWENTY-TWO

Benexx stalked around in the dark tunnels and caverns for what seemed like days, although ze had no way to know how much time had actually passed. Zer captors had realized ze'd gone missing and come looking.

They'd swept through in pairs, skin glowing as brightly as they pleased, scouring the tunnels for their missing hostage. At one point, ze could see the dirt between the toes of one of their feet from the rock shelf ze'd scurried under for cover, close enough to reach out and touch. Close enough ze didn't dare to breathe. They moved on, and through the grace of Xis, ze'd managed to outpace, evade, or hide from them each time they'd drawn close since.

So far.

Ze'd given in to sleep at one point, holed up in a tiny alcove halfway up a wall scarcely big enough for zer to curl up in. Thankfully, Atlantians weren't prone to snoring, unlike zer father.

What ze did know was zer waterskin was getting light, as was zer bag of food. If ze didn't find resupply soon, ze'd be going on a crash diet.

A nagging feeling crept into Benexx's mind. Ze couldn't place it at first, but it eventually coalesced into a sort of eerie familiarity. Deja vu, zer mother had called it once. That's when the space and the smell reoriented in zer mind and Benexx realized with sinking dread that ze'd been in this spot before. Ze was still for a long breath, quiet, listening for sounds of pursuit or hidden enemies. But silence was all that filled zer ears. Benexx took a risk and brought zer skinglow up for the first time since escaping the hole ze'd been thrown in, only to confirm zer worst fears. Ze was standing only meters away from where ze'd started.

Benexx's hands balled into twisted fists as ze swallowed a scream that would've been loud enough to bring the ceiling itself crashing down on zer. Ze'd forgotten Uncle Kexx's training. Ze should've been leaving trail markers to avoid doubling back as ze had. Sakiko wouldn't have forgotten. Sakiko had always been the more attentive student.

Benexx gave zerself a ten-count to let the anger and self-recrimination wash over zer, and break against the battlements of zer psyche.

"Shouldn't have taken that left turn at Albuquerque," ze whispered, smirking at zer own joke. Benexx was probably one of only a couple fullhands of people alive who would get it, thanks to zer father's untraditional parenting methods and esoteric sense of humor.

Ze walked over to the hole in the floor that opened to the improvised cell ze'd spent the last few days languishing in. Where ze'd languish still if ze hadn't escaped, except with the added horror of Jolk's wretched spawn beginning to grow in zer back. Benexx spit into the hole and muttered a curse that would've earned a grounding from zer parents as soon as their translators explained what it meant. Actually, ze father would probably know, the amount of time he spent in a locker room.

The plan hadn't changed; ze needed to get as far away from the literal hell-hole as possible. Benexx looked back over zer shoulder. Ze'd passed a few larger chambers in the last couple hours of walking because ze couldn't see the far side of them and didn't want to risk being caught out in the open. But now, it seemed likely one of them was hiding the way out.

Frustrated but determined, Benexx set off in the direction of the nearest chamber, although it was still a considerable distance. The cave network was absolutely massive, and what had at first looked like a straightforward system of ancient lava tubes had grown into a dizzying labyrinth of tunnels melted through the rock by long-gone magma, as well as limestone caverns eroded by rain. The first set of human geologists to set foot in the place would doubtlessly be overjoyed at the discovery, but Benexx had well and truly run out of patience.

Retreading ground ze'd already covered once before, Benexx quickened zer pace through the dark, still alert, but at the same time more confident that ze could avoid any surprises. The vastness of the place worked to zer advantage in one respect. No part of the caves ze'd seen so far indicated any sort of long-term settlement, not now or even in the distant past. They were virgin territory, lacking the worn footpaths, fungus farms, and other refinements of a Dweller city. It would take a small army of people to thoroughly patrol the place, and ze was fairly sure ze was dealing with a terrorist cell. Religious zealots, separatists, whatever they were, they probably only numbered a fullhand or two. Which explained why ze'd only run into three search parties since escaping.

Ze reached the junction to the first chamber in half the time it had taken to leave it behind, despite taking care on the return journey to leave zer little trail markers. Ze'd just have to hope they were subtle enough not to be noticed by zer pursuers. The cavern beyond was huge, and deep. Dots and irregular patches of soft blue light emitted from colonies of bacteria and fungus coated the walls, giving the space shape and volume. Something about it seemed odd to Benexx's eye until ze realized part of the floor was mirroring the wall next to it.

Water! ze thought with relief and excitement. It was

then ze recognized the smell of the pool on the air, however slight. Even perfectly still, clean water had a smell. It was subtle, and easy to overlook in the mingled layers of odors in the stale air. Still, as thirsty as ze'd become, Benexx couldn't believe ze'd missed it on the first pass.

Ze let the rifle hang from its sling and held up zer hands to get a sense of what else might be hiding in the chamber. The moist air in the caves held odor well, and the sluggish airflow meant it could linger for many hours before fading. There was the usual muddy scent of the bacteria and fungus sticking to the walls, the rusty smell of the rocks themselves, a pinch of salt, a whisper of ammonia and hydrogen sulfide, not nearly enough to worry about, and… and…

Benexx's hands snapped shut from the shock of the smell. It was subtle, even more subtle that the water had been, but it was there, and it was familiar. So familiar, it couldn't be mistaken for anything else.

Human sweat.

But what were humans doing down here? Other hostages? They must be. Zer captors must be holding their prisoners in widely separated cells to keep them from comparing notes, organizing, or otherwise increasing their odds of escape. It was probably the first smart thing they'd done, considering how inept their efforts at holding zer had been.

Benexx caught zerself starting to gloat. In truth, the only reason ze'd escaped wasn't because there was anything wrong with the cage they'd assigned zer to; it was because Jolk was a petty, vindictive little bully who tried to take advantage of zer and lost. If Jolk had even a little more discipline, ze'd still be floundering at the bottom of that hole, or worse, dead. Both zer mother and Uncle Kexx had hammered home the dangers of overconfidence and underestimating one's opponent.

Zer father, well, he had a different philosophy about

these things. His overconfidence had its own gravity. It pulled people along for the ride without him having to do anything.

Propelled by the chance of seeing a friendly face for the first time since zer nightmare had started, Benexx entered the cavern, zer mission of escape morphing into a rescue attempt. Hostages meant guards, although ze didn't detect any fresh Atlantian pheromones on the air. It was only then ze became aware of zer own smell, and just how powerful it had become after days in captivity. Any Atlantian should be able to smell zer from a hundred paces, and even a human could pick zer up from across a decent-sized room. Ze'd need to fix that. Fortunately, the solution was only meters away.

Ze clung fast to the wall and moved with great care to remain as silent as possible until ze reached the edge of the pool. Its surface was as calm and still as glass, and every bit as clear. Even in the weak bioluminescent light of the cave, ze could see straight down to the bottom of the pond as if there was nothing there at all. It was almost disorienting. The water was so pristine that Benexx felt badly about polluting it. But it only took a moment for zer thirst to win out. Out of habit, ze touched a finger to the water to check its freshness. Too fresh, as ze suspected, fresh enough for humans to drink unfiltered. Like all Atlantians, ze preferred water with a little brine to it. But, in a pinch, fresh would have to do. Ze uncorked the waterskin and gently lowered its mouth into the water, careful not to make any bubbles as it filled or send any telltale ripples across the surface to the other side of the cave beyond what ze'd already cleared as safe.

Once it was halfway full, Benexx lifted the skin and drank from it greedily. Ze didn't remember ever being so thirsty. Ze could feel the cool, tasteless water rejuvenating zer body and mind. Ze could think clearly again about something other than zer next drink. Then came the really dangerous part. Ze looked at the strap holding the rifle to zer shoulder. It was probably designed to be safely submerged underwater, but ze wasn't sure, not really. Ze'd only ever fired one once at the range by the cliffs overlooking the ocean by Shambhala and hadn't bothered to learn much more about it than its basic operation and safety protocols. Ze'd fired a nice group, but that was at paper, not people.

It wasn't worth risking zer only effective weapon, even on the off-chance water would make it inoperable. So ze stripped it off and set it down gently on the shore. Then, one foot at a time, ze slowly eased zerself into the pool, sinking lower with each passing moment until the waterline reached zer neck. The pool was deceptively deep. What ze'd thought was probably no deeper than zer waist instead kept going many meters past zer wriggling toes. It was also *cold*. About a meter and a half below the surface, a thermal plane dropped the temperature at least seven or eight degrees below the layer at the surface. It was bracing, invigorating even, and floating in the crystal-clear pond was the first little luxury ze'd felt since waking up on the floor of the strange cave days before. Still, ze couldn't afford to hang around, losing body heat and growing cold-headed.

Benexx dipped zer head below the surface, fully submerged, and quickly ran zer hands and feet over every square centimeter of zer flesh that ze could reach, which being Atlantian, was most all of them. Zer suckers scrubbed away at days of accumulated dirt, bodily oils, dead skin, and assorted filth. The first proper cleansing ze'd had since the night before the parade.

Then, Benexx allowed zerself a moment's indulgence and kicked off for the bottom of the pool, leaving a cloud of detritus behind zer in the pure water. Eventually, it would settle out and be nothing more than the newest layer of sediment. It took zer three long strokes of zer arms and legs to reach the bottom before Benexx reached out a finger and touched the silt, just as ze, Sakiko, and

Jian had done in the crater lake southwest of G'tel three summers ago.

Despite the cold, floating in the water, unconstrained by gravity and liberated to move about in three dimensions, Benexx felt zer first moment of genuine freedom since waking up in this awful place. Atlantians had never really left the water behind as humans had. It showed whenever the friends swam together. Benexx always reached the bottom first, if the other two managed to reach it at all. Sakiko was the stronger swimmer at the surface, but under the water Jian had a confidence and fluidity that came from his youth aboard the Ark, playing in the old Zero Stadium and hanging around his parents in the micro-grav of the command module. He never got disoriented, but he could still only hold his breath like a human.

Cautious not to disturb the silt, Benexx pointed zerself for the surface and fluttered up through the water column, slowing to a crawl just before the crown of zer head breached the surface. Ze grabbed the craggy lip of the pond and pulled zer body out of the water with the same muscle-burning delicacy ze used slipping into it.

Light and movement from the other side of the cave caught the corner of zer eye instantly. Fear froze Benexx's limbs in place like a statue, too afraid even to turn zer head to inspect the threat.

Instead, as the water drained out of zer ears, Benexx listened. When no excited shouts of "There ze is!" followed after a fullhand of beats, ze forced zer body out of its paralysis and turned around to face the disturbance. At the far side of the cave, someone approached, skinglow bright and either a hand torch or a rifle with a mounted light in their arms. Atlantian, then. Whether it was the elder, Sula, or another conspirator ze hadn't identified yet, Benexx couldn't tell from such distance.

Their gait was quick and purposeful, but their light was being held in a cone straight ahead as they made their way down the path, no sweeping side to side as one would if they were searching for someone. The light shone perpendicular to where ze stood by the pool, leaving zer in shadows, for the most part. Anyone standing behind that light would've had their night vision ruined after seconds, unable to differentiate reflections of the soft bioluminescence of the chamber from the true dark of everything else. A guard, maybe? Heading to whatever cell the human prisoner or prisoners were being kept in for a change of watch? Probably.

With the realization ze hadn't been spotted, but still could be if ze wasn't careful or if the walker was lucky, Benexx reached down and gently grabbed the pack, waterskin, rifle, and moved them out of line of sight. Then ze backed against the wall and made zer best imitation of a rock. Ze even experimented with matching zer skinglow to the surroundings as Uncle Kexx had tried to drill into zer.

Just then, the presumed guard stopped short and turned zer light onto an entryway to a side chamber about halfway down the length of the cave face, then walked through and disappeared. A brighter light, harsh and artificial, sparked to life and cast itself from the passage and against the far wall, well away from where Benexx hid. Voices emanated from the hole in the wall. One alert, the other sounding slow and groggy. The human hostage, probably, although ze couldn't make out what either was saying. They were too quiet, muffled, and distorted by echoes.

The conversation continued, with the groggy one coming up to speed. Probably they'd just been woken up and needed a minute to come to full consciousness. Benexx certainly did in the morning. Then two figures emerged from the mouth of the passage and began walking back the way the guard had come initially. One was definitely the Atlantian Benexx had watched enter only a few minutes before, while the other was definitely human.

This was zer chance to free the prisoner. If ze moved

fast and silently, ze could take the guard by surprise before they left the cavern, maybe even get right up behind and bury the muzzle of zer rifle in the back of their skull before firing, taking them out cleanly while hiding some of the report of the shot at the same time. Then, ze could hand the guard's weapon off to the human and... and...

Benexx realized something was wrong as the two strolled away, side by side. The guard's rifle was still pointed ahead to light the way, not at their prisoner. And their conversation, while still difficult to make out, sounded calm, almost convivial. A few days seemed an awfully short time for that level of Stockholm syndrome to set in. The truth hit zer like a hammer fall. The human wasn't a prisoner like zer; they were *working with* the conspirators. They were part of the same group, as ridiculous as that sounded.

But, at the same time, it explained a great deal. Like, where had Sofa and Jolk's guns come from? How did whoever had kidnapped zer and presumably attacked the parade gotten their hands on remotely-detonated bombs?

The answer was walking away from Benexx at a leisurely pace. Ze had half a mind to go through with zer plan to execute the guard. But instead of handing the human a gun, ze'd tweak the plan just a little bit and hand them a bullet instead. In the knee. Then start asking them questions every bit as uncomfortable as their freshly shredded joint.

Benexx surprised zerself. Ze'd never taken a life before escaping from Jolk, and that had been a brutal, personal affair. It had frightened and disgusted zer. Now here ze was, not but a day or so later, chomping at the bit to do it again. Hardly bearer-like impulses. But what ze was most surprised and disturbed by was just how undisturbed ze was by the prospect. What did that say about zer soul, Benexx fretted.

Besides, the risk of discovery was just too great. Ze might just as easily blow the approach and wind up gunned down and bleeding out on the footpath. So, ze waited. Ze waited until both of them had exited the enormous chamber. Waited longer until ze couldn't hear the sound of the human's shoes against the rocky path. Then waited longer still.

When ze was absolutely sure they were well and truly gone, Benexx crept around the pool and across to the far wall, then made zer way down it, clutching the stock of zer rifle all the way. White light still spilled out into the cavern from the passageway branching to the right. Wearily, Benexx put zer back against the wall and listened for signs of life. Sensing none, ze crept close enough to stick a hand in the entrance and sniff for the presence of another person, but detected only stale pheromones and sweat from a single human body.

Benexx breathed deeply, trying to calm zer racing bloodways. Ze raised the stock of the rifle up to zer shoulder and steeled zerself for a fight, should it come to that. With a silent prayer to Xis, ze rolled from cover and swept into the passage, the muzzle of zer gun clawing for a target almost of its own volition.

But it became quickly apparent to zer just how ill-advised setting off any kind of spark in this particular chamber would be. All around zer, naked mining explosives laid in the open air, sitting on make-shift work benches among tangles of wires, blasting caps, electronics, and hand tools. It was a bomb factory, probably the point of origin of the very bomb that almost killed zer back in Shambhala during the parade.

Benexx's first instinct was to run away. But it wasn't long until zer fear fueled an even more intense and primal emotion. Ze wanted to make a big bang on zer way out. These were the tools to do it. Zer mouth curled into a smile devoid of mirth or compassion.

"Now we're talking," ze said, the first words ze'd spoken aloud since escaping the cell these bastards had thrown zer in.

CHAPTER TWENTY-THREE

A jolt ran through Jian's body at the piercing sound of the proximity alarm. His muscles stiff even in the micrograv of the *Buran*'s flight deck, Jian cast about in confused near-panic trying to identify the screeching wail.

It took a full three seconds before his sleep-paralyzed brain rebooted fully and he realized the alarm was nothing more than the alert he'd set for himself once the shuttle was a thousand klicks out from its turnover point for insertion into Varr orbit. He checked his plant's clock. Sure enough, he'd been dead asleep for almost thirteen hours. Apparently, he really wasn't built to stay awake for the better part of two days after all.

In his defense, it had been an unusually stressful couple of days. There was stealing a shuttle with a nuclear bomb in the trunk, committing treason and mutiny against his own father, detonating said nuclear bomb, and then two straight hours strapped into his command chair while his stolen shuttle bucked and jerked like a dux'ah trying to throw a novice rider to keep his former colleagues from scoring a lucky hit. Even with their sensors temporarily blinded by the electromagnetic pulse of his nuke and the expanding cloud of radioactive fallout behind him, they could still map his trajectory towards Varr and take potshots.

Lasers being what they were, Jian didn't know if the Ark had tried to turn him into a debris cloud or not, because there wasn't anything around him to reflect their light. It wasn't like *Star Trek* phaser beams that glowed helpfully to let you know they'd gone by. He liked to believe that Captain Chao had stayed the order to fricassee his only son, but there was no way to be sure.

Jian realized something was missing. His head swiveled around in his seat searching for his little compatriot. "Polly?" he called. "Polly? We have to secure for burn." Jian didn't know how much English the little AI actually understood, but he suspected it was more than he let on. Wasn't that always the problem with ancient, self-assembling, nanite intelligences?

A metallic clicking from above his head betrayed Polly's existence. Jian looked up to see the little insectoid automaton peering down at him from the side of the flight deck's air exchanger.

"There you are." Jian reached up and held out his hand. Polly pushed off and gently grabbed Jian's fingers with his pincers, then crawled down the fabric of his flightsuit's forearm. Jian reached down and opened the flap on a spacious pouch pocket on his suit's leg. "Better get stowed away, little buddy. I'm about to hit the brakes something fierce."

An invisible line in space rapidly approached. On one side of the line there was a safe and orderly insertion into Varr orbit. On the other side there was overshooting his window and burning so much fuel to compensate that he wouldn't have enough left for the burn back to the Ark. Not that he was super-eager to return, but even jail would beat a race between asphyxiation or dehydration ending him onboard this shuttle.

The mains had been cold since the daring escape from the shuttle's cradle on the Ark's outer hull. Ideally, Jian should've woken up an hour before to run them through a proper pre-flight checklist, but that wasn't in the cards. Which was OK with him; most of the pre-flight was supercilious bullshit anyway.

Only around a dozen items on the checklist were actually necessary to get the engines lit, the rest were meant to double-check the maintenance monkeys to make sure they'd dotted all of their i's and crossed their t's. Jian went through the important parts of the list and felt the turbo pumps spooling up, ready to dump thousands of liters of raw hydrogen and oxygen into the bells the moment he throttled up.

But first, he had to flip the ship ass over teakettle. Jian looked up at the flight clock, seconds ticking away as the invisible line in space drew closer. He'd never done any of this alone, not in something as big as a shuttle, not even in simulations. He'd always had a backup in his copilot double-checking his numbers, making sure he remembered to flip all the right switches, disengage the right safeties. Most of the time, that person had been Kirkland. Xis, he missed her sharp tongue now.

Jian nudged down the nose and warmed up the aft ventral thruster packs. Gently, slowly, not wanting to expel too much reactant mass. He was going to need as much of it as he could get for terminal maneuvers on the surface. There was no gliding in for a gentle landing on an airless moon.

The *Buran* slowly crept into position while Jian watched the artificial horizon with laser focus. With three degrees left, he hit the thruster packs again, and the giant bird slowed to a stop exactly one hundred and eighty degrees along the z axis away, relative to its starting point. Then, Jian goosed the throttles, more tentatively than he had during the escape, letting the engines warm up and take the heat and pressure in stride instead of all at once and risking a flameout or worse. Soon though, they were up to one hundred percent, Jian was pressed into his chair like he was being squeezed in a vice, and the imaginary line in space passed by without comment or notice.

The shuttle's bottom settled onto Varr's dusty regolith an hour later. This time, Jian managed to set down in an LZ on the nearer side of the fissure that had nearly swallowed technician Madeja. Knowing what he did now about the little traitor's plans, he wished he'd let her fall. It certainly would've saved everyone a module's full of trouble to have just let her tumble down the crevasse to die of a suit tear or a shattered visor. She was dead either way, and a lot of good people would still be alive in her place.

Jian locked down the shuttle's command console in preparation to leave. He was confident none of the shuttles he sabotaged back on the Ark could've made their launch window. There was one on the surface on Gaia, but it was too far out of range even with a full tank of fuel to both escape the planet's gravity well and still catch up with the rapidly receding moon. They could stop at the Ark itself and tank up, of course, but by the time they'd finished, the launch window would be closed.

However, there remained a remote chance that part or all of the team working on the Early Warning radio telescope on Varr's far side could come calling. It would be a long hike and it would require some substantial modifications to boost their little rock hopper's range, but they were technicians and mechanics, after all. Jian didn't want to risk it.

With the shuttle secure, Jian moved on to the suit prep station at the back of the flight deck. He spent the next half hour struggling to fit himself into one of the extended expeditionary suits. Technically, they were designed for a single person to be able to don in an emergency by themselves. In practice, they were an enormous pain in the ass to wriggle into without someone to help you. It was one of the reasons even their flight suits had a limited vac rating. Jian hadn't put on one of the rigs by himself in years, and his rustiness showed. Polly looked on curiously, yet unhelpfully throughout the entire process.

Panting, Jian finally pulled down the visor of his

helmet and ran the suit through an integrity check. Green board, he was ready to go to work. The expeditionary suits had enough air for the better part of a day without any replenishment. Jian expected he'd need considerably more time than that. His plan was dependent on the facility to provide the heat and air, just as it had begun to do during his first visit. He'd been hesitant to take his helmet off back then for all the reasons Rakunas had listed at the time, but he didn't want to have to constantly cycle back to the *Buran* to recharge the suit. Instead, he slung a duffle over his shoulder filled with twenty liters of water, five days of food rations including a few extra apple cobblers, and a sleeping roll.

Jian was going camping. It seemed appropriate, considering the last time he'd camped was alongside the very friend he was here to locate. Polly took a position on his shoulder pad and settled in for whatever adventure awaited. Once the airlock cycled, Jian climbed down the short ramp to the surface and was met with a shock.

There, on the starboard underside of the wing, something had gouged out a three-meter long and almost meter wide section of ablative heat tiles. He moved to inspect the damage, perplexed as to why the shuttle itself hadn't registered the impact. The edges of the furrow were charred into ivory-white flakes. At the center, opaque rivulets of melted ceramic glass had formed. That explained it. Nothing had struck the wing. Nothing except photons.

"Son of a *bitch*," Jian muttered. Well, that answered the question of whether his father had shot at him with the Ark's nav lasers. From the looks of it, the laser had only caught the *Buran* with a glancing blow, probably making contact for no more than a few hundredths of a second before the shuttle's evasive maneuvers took it out of contact again. A direct hit would've sheared the wing completely off.

The tiles were shot, and even some of the wing's

internal structural members had been exposed. The shuttle wouldn't be making any trips down to Shambhala until the entire section was replaced. That complicated matters. There was only one way for him to get to the surface now in one piece, and he *really* dreaded the prospect, but it would have to wait.

Jian shuffled his feet until he was clear of the shuttle's wing, then took long, arching hops in the three percent gravity. The Helium-3 harvester had moved on long ago, but he could still see the hole where the ceiling leading to the facility had caved in.

It wasn't nearly as far of a trip as the last time. For all her bravado, Kirkland had always been the cautious, by-the-book sort. She'd suggested the further LZ the first time around because it was as far away from the cave-in and fissure as she could reasonably get before everyone started complaining about the schlep.

In fact, Jian's LZ was so much closer to the cave-in that he misjudged the distance of his last hop. With only a few meters to spare, he recognized that he was about to overshoot his landing spot at the lip of the crater and was instead about to add the rest of the sinkhole's depth to his current fall.

His arms pinwheeling impotently against inertia, Jian tried and failed to alter his course. The expedition suits actually had a limited micro-grav thruster capacity in their extremities... which was a fact Jian managed to forget in the moment of panic as he tumbled helplessly over the edge of the cave-in. His flailing managed only to spin his feet out from underneath him as the floor rose up to meet him in slow motion. Varr's gravity was so weak, and his rate of acceleration under it so lethargic, Jian had time to calm himself and prepare for the inevitable impact. It wouldn't be fast enough to be lethal, but neither would it be pleasant. The biggest danger would be a suit puncture against one of the jagged rocks in the pile at the middle of the cavern he was about to collide with. The pads on the outsides of his forearms and shins were even more reinforced against tears than the rest of the suit, so he stuck them out and balled up his fists to try and protect the delicate finger joints of his gloves.

Polly, for his part, had the good sense to move from Jian's shoulder onto the life support pack on the back of his suit. Jian saw where he was going to "land," and it wasn't encouraging. A big slab of rock sitting on top of the pile at about forty-five degrees, its jagged edge pointed at him like the teeth of some long-extinct leviathan. Jian struck it unevenly, first with his left forearm, then his right, causing him to bounce off it and tumble down onto the rest of the pile. A sharp pain ran up his left arm, but he had no time to think about that before he landed again, first on his helmet, then his right shoulder, before finally coming to rest on his right side.

Inside his visor, a suit integrity alarm blared. A three-dimensional outline of his suit appeared in his plant's field of view with a blinking red area showing where the sensor net woven into the fabric of the suit itself detected the tear, just below his right shoulder blade. The tear wasn't very large, only point zero eight cubic meters per second. But without the rope ladder he'd planned on anchoring to the roof of the cave-in, he had no way to climb back out of the hole to return to the *Buran* to stitch it up.

Swallowing hard, Jian reached into a pouch on his thigh and pulled out an emergency patch to seal the rupture and stripped the plastic backing off it to expose the adhesive. But with the bulky material of his suit, he could only reach his hand around far enough to get a corner of the patch in place.

"Fuck, fuck, fuck!" Jian strained against the hard plastic shell of the suit's chest plate, trying to find the extra few centimeters of reach he needed to seal the tear as his air slowly leaked out into the vacuum. He tried to reach around with his other arm, but the shoulder joint limited his range of motion just enough to prevent it.

Jian forced himself to measure his breathing. Passing out from hyperventilating wouldn't do him a lick of good.

Think, think! Jian admonished himself. He cranked up the brightness and width angle of his suit's built-in lights to get a better look at the walls of the cavern. In the super-low gravity, his vertical jump was super-human, but still shy of the lip of the hole above. But maybe if there were a ledge or other protrusion he could grab onto and push off from again.

Nothing. The walls were almost completely smooth, having been excavated or melted out in the first place. Maybe he could roll his back against one of the rocks enough… to…

Jian felt something skittering up his leg even through the material of the suit, like being poked with a dozen chopsticks. A very old, seldom-used corner of his brain reviled at the sensation. But before he slapped away the monster, Jian's internal IFF kicked in and he realized it was just Polly. The little AI bug continued up the back of his leg, past his waist, and came to a stop just below where he'd been trying to affix the patch.

The chopsticks started hammering below his shoulder blade in rapid succession like a sewing machine, moving up and around in a rectangular pattern. Inside his plant display, the leak rate slowed, then trailed off until it reached zero. The suit was still registering the tear, but he wasn't losing any more atmosphere.

Polly appeared on his right forearm, gazing at him expectantly with his three glowing green eyes.

"You sealed the patch?" Jian said incredulously, knowing full well that the automaton couldn't hear him through the vacuum. Regardless, Polly winked at him.

Jian put his left hand over his heart and bowed, as his father would. "Thank you."

Polly crossed his left front pincer over his… chest… and mimicked Jian's bow. Full of surprises, the creepy little insect was.

"Well then," Jian bent over and retrieved his duffle, "shall we go to work?"

Less than five minutes later, Jian emerged on the other side of the gooey airlock. The corridor leading deeper into the facility's interior was drastically changed from his last visit only a few days ago. Instead of the ramshackle mess of dents, ice incursions, and millennia of accumulated dust, the tunnel was immaculate, as if it had just been commissioned that morning.

Jian consulted his plant recording of the prior visit and found a section of wall he remembered being breached by an enormous dagger of water ice frozen hard as granite. The ice wedge was gone entirely, replaced by a nearly flawless section of tunnel wall. Jian leered at the section, and after considerable inspection he was just barely able to perceive the seams where the breech had been closed off and welded shut again.

"Your friends have been busy," Jian said in the general direction of Polly, who'd wandered off further down the tunnel of his own volition. Jian followed after his diminutive companion, wondering where the rest of the drones, or whatever the best word to describe them might be, had gone. Perhaps they'd completed their repair work and had simply returned to hibernation until they were called upon again.

Curious, Jian pulled up a menu in his plant's suit interface. The life support pack had a small suite of sensors that monitored atmospheric conditions. Being a space suit, these conditions usually registered a series of big fat goose eggs. But now, just as Jian had hoped, the atmosphere in the corridor sat at a breathable seventy-eight percent nitrogen, nineteen percent oxygen, two percent carbon dioxide, and another point of trace gasses. A little out of balance by Earth measure, but exactly on the nose by Gaia standards. Not only was it breathable, it sat at an ambient temperature of eighteen degrees Celsius. The exact average temperature across the surface of Gaia.

Someone or something had taken great pains to make the facility accommodating for a native of Gaia. Jian wasn't of Gaia, exactly, but he'd spent most of his life there, and figured that was good enough. With no poisonous gasses in the air or other chemical hazards his suit's sensor suite could detect, Jian's only real concern was airborne microbes, which, given the circumstances and his desolate surroundings, seemed like a fairly remote risk.

"No time like the present," Jian said as he amped himself up to crack the seals on his helmet. Hesitantly, he reached for the two paddles on either side that would release the visor. They had to be pushed down and pressed in simultaneously to prevent them from being unlocked accidentally. The locks clicked, and with a small hiss of pressure equalization, Jian slid the visor up and into the crow of the helmet, still holding his breath.

Just as his lungs started to burn for fresh oxygen, Jian exhaled fully, then took a shallow breath and held it for a second, his hands in place above his head to snap his visor shut again at the first signs of trouble. The air was surprisingly fresh on Jian's tongue. He'd expected it to be stale and musty like a cave. Instead, it had the crisp, slightly metallic taste of mechanically processed air. Which it was, of course. Jian rather strongly doubted there was an aeroponics farm deeper down supplying the oxygen. More likely it had been freed up from the ice of Varr itself through electrolysis.

He stood there for a full minute, breathing deeply and monitoring himself for dizziness, tingling in his extremities, stars in his vision, or any other signs of trouble with the air, but none materialized.

"OK then." Jian adjusted the strap of his duffle, shuffle-hopped his way down the tunnel, and took the fork to the right leading to the map room. Just as it had before, as soon as Jian sat down in the chair at the center of the spherical chamber, the walls came to life with a dance of light and color. Gaia stretched out all around him from its strange perspective from inside the globe, quickly joined by the spiraling symbols hovering over areas of interest on Atlantis and Shambhala.

Jian leaned over to retrieve a bottle of water to sooth his parched throat. The air in the facility was crisp, but bone dry. He'd have to keep an eye on his hydration as long as he was down here.

By the time he looked up again, the display had changed. The spiraling symbols had once again unrolled, slowed, and enlarged, exactly as it had been when Jian left. It was as if the room recognized its latest student and restarted the lesson. Not that it helped much; the iconography was just as indecipherable to Jian's eyes as it had been the first time, and he didn't have months to learn a new language from scratch. There had to be a way to speed things up, or at least pick up the basics.

Jian opened a menu on his plant and enabled his translation software, set its parameters for both audio and visual feed access, then opened a clean file for "New Language." The translation matrix was good at cataloging symbols, pattern-recognition, and detecting syntax, but without either two way conversations to work from, and limited only to the processing power and data files held in his own unit, Jian didn't expect it would be able to expedite things a great deal.

There was really nothing for it, Jian realized. He reached down into his pack again, retrieved an apple cobbler and a fork, and settled in for the lesson.

CHAPTER TWENTY-FOUR

It took the rest of that day and a good portion of the next to fully disassemble the bomb, run all of its components, and scrub them for fingerprints, skin cells, strands of hair, blood, sweat, dried saliva, anything.

It was clean. Almost impossibly so. Theresa quipped at one point that it was clean enough to pass planetary protection protocols. And while that was an exaggeration, Benson sympathized with the frustration behind the sentiment. It reminded him of the Laraby case, actually, with his ridiculously clean love nest which, of all places, should have had an ample amount of DNA samples to collect. Somebody in the Ark's underworld had figured out how to thoroughly sterilize large volumes and spread that little trick around.

However, while the exact identity of the bombmaker still eluded them, they hadn't completely dead-ended. Theresa had put out an order for an explosives inventory check on the walk back to the station house. The results came back the following evening. One of the seven mining operations on the continent had filed a reorder request after reporting receiving only twenty kilograms of an expected two-hundred kilogram resupply. Just one problem; two hundred kilos had been tracked coming down from the Ark, signed for coming off the elevator car, and scanned onto the delivery drone.

Someone had tricked the receiving end software out

of a decimal point and made off with one hundred and eighty kilos of high explosives and used it to kill dozens of people and kidnap Benexx. Benson was going to find out who. Theresa had to stay behind to handle the back end of the investigation, as well as keep an eye on the increasingly restless Native Quarter, but she'd given her blessing to let Korolev come along on his little field trip.

Benson's only concern with the expedition was neither of them would be very convincing playing the "good cop" during the questioning. Korolev was almost as ruthlessly protective of his, er, *niece* as zer parents were.

Kexx and Sakiko offered to tag along as well, despite the fact Kexx was even more uneasy about flying than Benson was.

They took a pod down to the airfield to commandeer one of the quadcopters for the trip. Which ended up taking quite a bit of cajoling from Benson before the air master would approve the battery charge expenditure for "non-essential business." Benson had to keep himself from throttling the man at that statement, but electricity rationing had begun to hit everyone pretty hard while the Ark raced to repair the beanstalk and restore the flow of power.

With the weight of the four of them and their gear, the little quadcopter only managed around a hundred minutes of flight time. And that was provided they weren't in a huge hurry. But it was more than enough endurance to give them a round trip to any of the satellite farms, mines, or quarries that defined the outer reaches of human infrastructure on the continent. For now, at least.

"How you doing back there, partner?" Benson glanced over his shoulder at Kexx. "You're looking a little pale."

"I'm looking forward to standing on the ground with great anticipation," Kexx answered.

"C'mon. It's not every day you get to enjoy an injri's eye view."

"It's not any day *I* enjoy that view."

Benson laughed. "I know what you mean, buddy. Believe me. We're only twenty minutes out. Just close your eyes and imagine you're swimming in the ocean."

"There's so many wildcat homesteads," Sakiko said as she peered out the bulbous canopy glass. The quadcopter's rotors sat above the cockpit at a slight dihedral, both for stability, and to afford its passengers as unobstructed a view as possible.

"Just north of four hundred at last count," Korolev replied. "About eleven hundred people in total. A new one pops up almost every week."

"Humans, or…"

"Mostly humans. The Atlantians I think define themselves as village builders. They grew up being told they were better than the nomads because they were building roads and civilization, while our people were cooped up in that fishbowl being fed stories about taming a wild frontier, getting their own patch of land to settle instead of living in an apartment tower with a thousand other people." Korolev shrugged. "Honestly, I'm surprised there aren't more of them."

"That sound about right to you, Kexx?" Benson asked.

"A little generalized, but yes. My people are very proud of what we've built, and we know the benefits of working together."

"The biggest cities started out as a single home," Korolev said. "These wildcat plots will add a home for the kids when they grow up. Then they'll put down real roads so they don't have to hack through the forest to bring in their crops. Then they'll start building stores so they can trade with each other instead of going all the way into the city. We're looking at Shambhala's future suburbs."

"Yes indeed," Benson concurred.

Two more of the little prefabs streaked by underneath. Everyone who had come down from the Ark was entitled to a house, but it was only free inside the city limits of Shambhala. The wildcatters had to either pay up to transport the 3D construction printers out here, or build their own shelter. From Benson's quick and dirty survey, the ratio ran about four to one in favor of prefabs. And some enterprising dissident could be hiding Benexx in any one of them.

"It must be difficult to patrol such a large area," Kexx mused.

"Not really, there's almost nothing to patrol," Korolev said. "These people pretty well keep to themselves. That's why they're out here in the first place. And when things do crop up, they tend to hash out conflicts among themselves. We only get sent out here a couple times a month. Usually on anonymous tips."

"Tips for what?" Kexx asked.

"Drugs, mostly. Somebody cooks up amphetamines in the barn and their neighbor's kid gets hooked on them. Or, you know, the barn blows up. Hard to do if you're just storing yulka beans."

"I don't know. Yulka beans made me explode once," Benson said.

"Yeah, I was there," Korolev said.

Almost every homestead had a small field where they grew crops, or kept a handful of animals. Most were either right on the river, or within easy walking distance of the ready water source. The city's large fields were further inland, irrigated using diversionary channels and grids of belowground pipes. A few of the wildcatters further from the river had dug their own diversionary channels off the mains, which was technically illegal, but obviously wasn't high on the enforcement priority list. Honestly, the leadership back in Shambhala was probably happy for anyone who willingly left the city taking pressure off the city's growing pains.

"What did Theresa want us to talk about?" Kexx asked, probably trying to distract zerself from the flight.

"Hmm?" Benson said.

"Back in the tunnel you said Theresa wanted us to talk about something."

"Oh, right. Well, it'll seem a little petty at this point, but before the attacks and Benexx going missing, we were having a lot of trouble connecting like we used to. Ze's been irritable, combative, and short-tempered. Especially with me."

"Combative with you? How unprecedented, my friend."

"Fine, even more combative than the baseline average. We expect it out of hormone-poisoned human teenagers–"

"Still sitting in the cabin," Sakiko said.

"–but we're kinda in uncharted territory with Benexx," Benson continued, ignoring her.

Kexx chuckled. It wasn't even a human affectation ze'd picked up. From the very beginning, laughter was the one thing the two races hadn't needed translated for each other, a fact that had probably saved an awful lot of misunderstandings and violence over the ensuing years. "Cuut endowed our adolescents with all the tools they would need to break the bonds of family and get thrown out of the hut, too. They just do it a couple of years earlier. When the community finds their behavior completely intolerable, they're put through the Rite of Hulukam."

"What's that?"

"We kick them out of the village and don't let them back in until it looks like they're about to starve. Usually takes a Var or so. The elders say it's to help the youth find their spiritual center, but really it's to get them to stop being such self-centered little dux'ah shits. Bearers like Benexx aren't usually as bad as the rest, but they're hardly immune."

"That's certainly one solution," Benson said. "Not sure I can sell Theresa on it, though. Right now, all I want it to get zer back."

"We will," Kexx said. "If we have to shake down Xis zerself for clues, we will."

Benson turned his attention forward. The mining site was coming up on the horizon. While it wasn't the environmentally destructive open-pit or stripmining operation so popular among consortiums on old Earth, its footprint was still significant enough to spot from several klicks out. Benson opened his plant to get a feel for the site. Mostly automated, like the rest. A little over two dozen people on scene to play shepherd to the mining equipment. Most of them human techs, but a handful of Atlantian laborers and an elder to consecrate everything and make sure Xis was properly attended to under their traditions. It was zer body they were plundering, after all.

There wasn't anything particularly interesting about the mine itself. Of those operating on the continent, it was mid-sized, extracting necessary but unsexy ores of iron, copper, and aluminum, with only traces of tungsten for variety. The most prestigious mining assignments were all in Atlantis, where a fluke of geology and the Atlantians' peculiarly sensible social priorities meant they'd only recently turned to excavation after running out of gold nuggets in dry riverbeds to pick up by hand.

"We should probably give them a ring. Let them know we're incoming in fifteen minutes or so."

"Roger that," Korolev said, then closed his eyes to bring up his plant's com directory. "Hmm. That's weird."

"What is?" Benson asked.

"Well, the camp's nav beacon is showing up strong enough, but I can't get anybody on coms."

"They're not answering?"

"No, there's no connection at all, like their local network is down."

Benson opened his own directory and tried to connect with identical results. "That *is* weird. Down for maintenance or updates?"

"I suppose it could be..."

"You been out here yet, Pavel?"

"Yeah, couple years ago. Not long after the site got up and running."

"What was the call for?"

"Some domestic bullshit between two of the workers. Took me and another constable to physically separate them."

"Who was at fault?"

Korolev snorted. "No telling. They were both nuts, fed off each other. Just a really ill-advised pairing, you know?"

Benson nodded. "Been in a couple of those. Sex was usually amazing. Never worth it in the end, though."

"Ew," Sakiko wrinkled her nose. "Child onboard, remember?"

"Child? You're eighteen in what, three months?"

"Four. And I won't want to hear about your sexual history then, either."

Benson smiled and returned to Korolev. "What was your impression of the site foreman?"

"Ms Lind? Hardnose. No nonsense. She was one of the first wildcats out this far. Built a house all by herself at night while surveying the area for the mine during the day. Good lady, doesn't have a lot of patience for stupidity. She had those two I mentioned earlier transferred out of her mine to opposite sides of the planet by the end of the week."

"So not somebody you'd expect to let a terrorist cell operate with impunity under her supervision?"

"Yeah, no."

"Roger that."

The quadcopter slowed to a hover over the mining site's modest landing field, then spooled down its electric motors to come in for a silky smooth landing. Benson was still not a fan of flying, and he'd been intensely apprehensive about being taxied around in the little autonomous eggs for quite a few years after landing. But the autopilot had never failed, and had even seen him safely through a couple of the nasty seasonal squalls that Gaia's coasts kicked up without warning.

Still, his stomach thanked him as soon as the soles of his feet settled into dirt again. Korolev hopped out on the other side and grabbed his gear off one of the rear seats. A quick weapon check later and he was squared away.

"The operations shack is on the far side of the compound, over there." Korolev pointed to the northeast, but all Benson could see were lavender trees. "Lind will either be in there or down in the mine itself."

"I don't see it."

"It's up on the ridge overlooking the mine, just behind the treeline for shade. Follow me."

They walked up a well-worn dirt path in silence. Benson noticed Korolev's rifle had migrated from his shoulder and down into a low-ready position. Not out of fear of any of the mine's workers, but out of caution for the half dozen different critters out here who still regarded humans and Atlantians alike as a viable source of protein. This far from Shambhala, true wilderness was never more than a football field away, and fifteen years of experience hadn't been enough to fundamentally rewire millions of years of instinct among the local carnivores.

They weren't the only troublesome creatures that called the forest home. "Ow!" Benson called out as he slapped something on the back of his neck. It went *crunch*, then fell away. Benson wiped the greenish goo onto his pants. "What the hell was that?"

Kexx nudged the dead bug with a toe. "Don't know, never seen one before. Nasty piece of work, though. Oh, and you're bleeding."

Benson touched a finger to the burning spot on his neck. Sure enough, it came back with a dot of crimson. "Dammit! Why do they always find me?"

"It's not because you're made of sugar and spice, that's for sure," Korolev said. "The operations shed is just around the bend up here."

The shed was a modest prefabricated affair. It was a standard, four-room administrative design, probably airlifted by shuttle and dropped in place already fully assembled and ready to go to work. The small com array on the roof looked intact enough, leaving the mystery of their radio silence open for the moment. But it wasn't the only kind of silence that caught Benson's attention.

"Pavel," Benson said.

"Yeah, coach?"

"This is a mine, yes?"

"Last time I was here, yes."

"Then why isn't there any noise?"

Korolev stopped dead and swiveled his head around, as if taking in the scene for the first time. "Holy shit, you're right. It's dead quiet. There should be drills, mine carts, skid loaders."

"Maybe everyone's on break?" Sakiko said, her hand suddenly gripping the handle of her dagger instead of resting on top of it.

Korolev shook his head. "This place is almost entirely automated. The machines work around the clock unless one of them breaks something important. The people are just here to troubleshoot."

Benson grabbed his sidearm and double-checked to make sure a round was chambered. Its little stun rounds wouldn't do much against a determined carnivore, but they had just dropped a notch on his threat spectrum.

"The first one of you wise asses to say, 'It's quiet. Too quiet,' is getting a stunner in the neck."

"That's fair," Korolev answered.

They reached the door of the ops shack. Benson stepped forward and gave it a big knock to announce their arrival, but as soon as he did the door swung inward from the contact. Benson jumped back half a step, first thinking someone had pulled the door open from the inside. Korolev's rifle went from low ready to shouldered in an instant.

"Hello? I'm Bryan Benson. I'm here with Constable Korolev and representatives from Atlantis."

Silence.

"We're looking for Foreman Lind. We just have a few questions for her. Hello?" Benson looked back at Korolev and Kexx and made a palms up shrug. "Stack up?"

"Roger," Korolev answered. "I've got the big broom, I'll go first."

"Broom?" Kexx asked.

Korolev patted his rifle. "Yeah, it can really clean out a room."

"I see." Kexx turned to zer young apprentice. "Sakiko, you will go behind Benson. I will be our tail."

Sakiko, uncharacteristically, nodded and obeyed without comment. The four of them took places along the outside wall of the ops shack. Once everyone was in position, Korolev held up three fingers for their countdown. Two. One. His arm dropped back down to his rifle as Korolev surged for the door and kicked it the rest of the way open enough to swing it back into the wall, proving no one hid behind it and sweeping his half of the room. Benson hadn't run any room-clearing exercises in more than fifteen years, and they'd never featured firearms back then, only stun sticks. But as soon as he started moving, it all came flooding back. He entered the building right on Korolev's heels, sidearm out and his eyes sighted in along the front post, looking for anything in his half of the room that scanned as dangerous.

"Clear left," Korolev called.

"Clear right," Benson answered.

They repeated the process twice more for the small breakroom/kitchen, and the conference room. The final room was a small unisex bathroom that required only a cursory peek from the door to prove it was unoccupied.

"Is it just the two doors in and out of here?" Benson asked.

"Yeah," Korolev said.

"Will you go watch the front door for me? Sakiko, can you watch the back?"

"I guess."

"Thanks. If anyone, or anything tries to come in, do not engage them. Just shout your head off and fall back here."

Sakiko made her way to the back door without complaint.

Benson looked at Kexx. "She's awfully quiet. What's wrong with her?"

"Ze's nervous. Ze doesn't like to show it, but I can tell. This place has zer spooked."

"She's got plenty of company, there." Benson looked around the office/reception area. "Do a walkthrough with me, will you?"

"This is a human building, what am I looking for?"

"Same thing as always, old friend. Whatever I'm not looking for."

The building had power, so it wasn't a disruption in the solar grid or batteries that had brought down the network. Benson went to the desk and tried to access the computer terminal, but it was locked out.

<Hey, Pavel. I need a constable's override on this terminal,> he sent.

A few seconds later, the login page disappeared, replaced by the system's interface.

<Done, chief.>

<Thanks.> Benson skimmed for the last few days of entries and correspondence, only to find that there were none. Everything stopped on the morning of the First Contact Day parade, aside from a couple of pieces of mine equipment sending automatically generated error messages which had apparently gone unread. A few system messages sat queued up, waiting for the local net to recover so they could upload to central routing.

"Well that's ominous as hell..." The mine's machinery had apparently gone into automatic shutdown two days ago when one of the ore haulers had a breakdown along the main tunnel, blocking traffic and preventing operations from going forward. That explained the silence.

Benson opened the network interface and ran a diagnostic to try and find the connectivity issue, but it threw an error code he'd never seen before. Changing directions, he dug back into the archived data and read a few of the most recent entries from Foreman Lind. It all seemed pretty normal. A tech calling in sick, griping up the logistical chain about delays in repair parts for one of her mining drone rigs. Exactly the sort of day-to-day minutiae one would expect to crop up running an industrial operation. On a hunch, Benson copied the last two months' worth of entries and saved them to his plant to review later anyway.

Out of habit, Benson flicked open Lind's calendar, just for a peek. It was much the same as her messages and log entries. Work rotations, preventative maintenance schedules, production quota projections. Lind had an eye for detail and obviously ran a tight ship. So then where the hell was she? Benson's stomach churned with the same slightly nauseous feeling he had during the Laraby investigation, after he'd gone missing but before Benson had recovered the body floating a few klicks away from the Ark. His fear was this mystery wasn't going to end any happier.

But at the same time, he was certain now that he was on the right track to finding Benexx. And there wasn't a damned thing in Heaven or Gaia that was going to shake him loose of the scent now.

An item on the calendar jumped out at him. He'd overlooked it scrolling past, but an unfamiliar word leapt out at him a moment later. He scrolled back to read the day's notes. It was dated two weeks before the parade.

Wednesday, 14th: Atlantians have asked off for Chumincha holiday (sp?). Push back breaking ground on Tunnel 3a until 16th when the elder returns to perform necessary blessings for Xis.

Benson scratched his chin. He'd been working with and living around Atlantians for fifteen years now. He was lucky to call several of their number close friends. In all that time, he'd never heard of any holiday called Chumincha, Chimichanga, or any close approximation of it. And he didn't remember so much as a peep coming from any of his players two weeks ago, or from anyone in the Native Quarter, for that matter.

"Hey, Kexx," Benson called out. "C'mere a minute."

Kexx's oblong head appeared through the doorway from the breakroom. "Yes? Did you find something?"

"Not sure if I did. Is there an Atlantian holiday called…" Benson referred back to the calendar, "Chumincha? Chumin'cha? Anything like that?"

"Er…" Kexx stumbled. "I don't think so. What time of year?"

"Two weeks ago."

Kexx shook zer head in the exaggerated way ze always did when imitating human gestures. "No, definitely not."

"Not even a Dweller thing?"

"No," Kexx said with finality. "I can't speak for the customs of the nomadic clans, but I've spent enough time among the Dwellers by now to know their sacred days."

"Yeah, that's what I thought. The nomads still haven't sent any of their elders, have they?"

Kexx's skinglow fluttered the Atlantian equivalent of a shrug. "Not officially. Some have probably filtered through as refugees, of course. But nothing openly. They still don't even have an ambassador in G'tel, much less Shambhala. Messages are passed through traders, runners when the need is urgent."

"Yeah, figured that's what you were going to say."

Benson sighed and laced his fingers under his chin.

"What are you thinking, old friend?" Kexx asked.

"I'm thinking that someone made up a fake holiday and tricked Foreman Lind into giving them a little convenient time off to build bombs and organize an attack. I don't suppose you know the elder who's stationed here to consecrate the dig, do you?"

"Sadly, no. I can tell you who's been posted at the active mines in Atlantis, but there's too much going on over here to keep track of."

"That's OK, we can look zer up later. Right now, I really think we need to get down to the mine and have a look around."

Kexx swept an arm towards the door. "After you, partner."

Benson pulled everyone out of the shed and grabbed his hand torch out of his pack. He turned to Korolev. "How do we get down to the mine entrance?"

His friend pointed towards the other trail leading away from the shed and their quadcopter. "Down that way. It's not far."

Around the back of the hill, the main mine tunnel came into view. Several yellow-painted, dirt-streaked pieces of equipment sat idly just outside the mouth of the tunnel, waiting for the blockage to be cleared so they could resume their pre-programmed work. One of the loaders overflowed with blasted rock that had yet to be dumped into the processor. The ore in this mine was so rich that Benson could see coppery flecks with his naked eye. Compared to Earth, Gaia's crust was light in heavy metals. The Tau Ceti system was more than a billion years older than Sol had been, and came from an earlier generation of stars that were metal poor by comparison.

But unlike Earth after millennia of mining, Gaia's crust was virgin, and even the lower quality ore was drastically richer than the rocks with traces of one percent or less by weight that remained on Earth after nearly its entire surface had been picked over.

At this early stage, the mines were still following rich veins of ore concentrated over millions of years of geologic activity. The ugly, destructive open-pit mines of the past weren't necessary. At least not yet.

The tunnel was a good four meters wide, more than enough for all of them to walk abreast, but still just barely enough clearance for the machines. It was also black as charcoal. The machines all used lidar and GPS to get around, and people were seldom in the mine, so there had been no sense in lighting the tunnels. Benson really wished they had anyway. The cone of light from his hand torch was adequate, however. And it was accompanied by the light on Korolev's rifle, as well as Kexx's skinglow, on the front of zer body, at least.

The tunnel was moist and smelled of rust, rock powder, industrial lubricants, and the sharp ozone taste of discharging capacitors. It also didn't bother sporting any shockcreate or internal reinforcement bracing that a tunnel built for passenger travel would feature. Stray rocks coming loose from the ceiling didn't pose much threat to industrial machinery. They did pose a pretty big threat to the four unprotected heads and their squishy brains walking through the cavern at the moment. Benson regretted not searching the shed for safety helmets.

"Everybody keep an eye on the ceiling. If you see any rocks that look shady, call them out and move around them."

"On it, coach," Korolev said, pointing the light and muzzle of his rifle at the roof of the tunnel.

"Just don't shoot them, Pavel. That won't help."

"Yeah, yeah."

The procession moved cautiously down the perfectly circular hole carved through rock that had lain undisturbed for hundreds of millions of years, pausing only to avoid any portions of ceiling that appeared prone to collapse.

No one spoke, their eyes were too busy chasing shadows. The tunnel was not a straight shot downward into Gaia. Instead, it meandered like a river, following the rich vein of ore through the rock.

"Losing my plant signal, coach," Korolev said.

Benson glanced up at the signal strength indicator in his peripheral vision. It flashed red, then went to a solid crimson "X" with his next step. "Yeah, same here. Too much rock above us."

"Poor babies," Sakiko taunted. "Stuck with just the senses Xis gave you."

Benson glanced back at Kexx. "You don't beat her enough."

"Now, now, Benson. Let's not skip directly to child abuse. There are other remedies we might try."

"Loader's ahead." Korolev's voice held an edge that put an end to their banter. The blocky yellow loader was little more than an oversized rock cart, but it took up almost the entire tunnel's width. It was difficult to discern the front from the back of the automated vehicle, as it lacked a cab or seat for a driver. Indeed, it was probably designed to work equally well in either direction. The loader's hopper reached almost all the way to the ground, leaving only a few centimeters of clearance.

"Don't suppose you can shimmy under there, could you Sakiko?" Benson asked.

The teen squatted down to get a better look at the gap. "That's a no. I could probably go over the top, though."

"Here, take my light." Benson handed her the hand torch. "And don't be stupid. If you see anything dangerous, turn your butt right around."

Sakiko nodded understanding and tucked the light into one of her traditional Atlantian wristbands, giving her light while keeping her hands free, then hopped lithely onto the face of the loader. She scampered up like a cat climbing a tree, then disappeared over the lip of the hopper.

"It's empty," she called out. "Must have been on its way back to refill when it broke down."

There was the sound of feet shuffling, a little grunting, and the bouncing of the hand torch's light against the ceiling.

"I'm on the other side," Sakiko shouted back. Benson couldn't see any part of her through the loader. Anxiety washed over him. He'd sent her because she was the smallest, and the most agile. Sakiko was so near to adulthood that for just a moment Benson saw her as another member of the team, instead of his dear friend Mei's priceless little girl.

Because of that mental slip, his favorite niece was alone in the dark and cutoff from immediate help. The command to abort and withdraw was on Benson's lips when Sakiko's shriek filled the tunnel like a flood.

CHAPTER TWENTY-FIVE

With extreme caution, Benexx laid out the materials ze'd absconded with from the bomb factory onto the floor at zer feet. Six bricks of explosives, each weighing two kilos; three blasting caps; a couple of small wire coils; small radio receivers with built-in battery packs; and even a remote detonator.

At least ze was pretty sure that's what everything was. It wasn't the first time Benexx had envied zer parents' plants. Ze could've been running an app to track zer movements and automatically map out the portions of the cave complex ze'd already covered. Ze'd be able to look at the components in front of zer and get a detailed breakdown of each item individually, as well as instructions on their use to foolproof the process. With all that memory and information on demand, ze'd hardly have to learn anything at all.

Instead, Benexx and every other Atlantian was mired with the devastating handicap of having to absorb and retrieve knowledge the old-fashioned way. It put them at a distinct disadvantage to their human peers in ways most of them couldn't even fathom.

But ze could. Ze saw it in real time while ze struggled to pick up and retain new information that they could download in a blink and retain with perfect clarity indefinitely. Zer parents were very good about encouraging zer, reassuring zer that ze was a fast learner and smart. But that just made it all the more frustrating.

Still, ze'd adapted. Zer tablet was never far from zer side and functioned as a sort of external plant much of the time. Ze'd developed quite a knack for tinkering with software, finding backdoors and work-arounds in user interfaces. Ze had a talent with electronics, and what was a bomb but a short-lived circuit board?

Which was why Benexx was like, ninety percent sure ze had everything ze needed to make an extremely crude, but still effective bomb that ze would even have the luxury of triggering without having to commit suicide. Ze had zero experience with explosives, but if the corny action movies ze'd watched with zer dad growing up were anything to go by, there was enough boom here to do some Van Damage.

Ze had to be sure. Which was why Benexx busied zerself rigging up the system, minus the blasting cap and explosives. Those, at least, ze was sure of based on the copious warning labels alone. Ze could've carried more of everything out of the bomb builder's alcove, but ze'd been cautious, nicking only as much as ze realistically thought could go missing without triggering an inventory check. Still, ze'd been sure to get far, far away from where ze'd stolen them before stopping in a secluded chamber to test the components.

Benexx measured out two lengths of wire, then bit them off between zer teeth plates and carefully stripped the insulation off the last few centimeters of each end, exposing the bare copper. These ze threaded into the small ports in the receiver marked (+) and (-). The receiver had a variable channel dial on its side marked 0–9. There was a corresponding dial on the remote detonator. Benexx sucked air through zer plates. If there were any other bombs rigged up within the range of the remote, there was a one in ten chance zer little test would set them off. Of course, if one of the bombs did go off and kill or maim one or more of zer kidnappers, Benexx wouldn't feel particularly torn up about it. Ze just didn't want to risk alerting them to zer new capability before ze was ready. Still, it would mean they kept bombs with primed blasting caps in place and receivers powered up. Anyone with such Godsawful safety protocols deserved to be minced.

A ten percent chance was already low, but Benexx figured ze could improve zer odds even further. Zer haul from the factory also included a pair of pressed yulka cakes. Ze munched eagerly on one while tackling the problem. After a moment's consideration, ze set both receiver and remote to channel two. The numbers three, five, and seven were considered lucky by various sects of humanity, while Atlantians had a particular affinity for three, four, and eight. Of the remaining numbers, poor old boring channel two seemed the safest bet.

Now ze just had to hope the bombmaker didn't think just like ze did.

Small green LEDs signaled a strong connection between receiver and remote. Ze'd have to cover those up with… something. In zer free hand, ze picked up the exposed wire ends and held them only a few millimeters apart. Out of excuses, Benexx took a deep breath, said a little prayer to whichever god or gods might lend zer an ear, and pulled the detonator's trigger.

A tiny blue arc of electricity jumped across the gap between the leads and connected the circuit with a quiet *buzz*. If the blasting cap had been plugged into them, zer hand would've been blown off.

Instead, the little electric arc light cast its shadow across a smile that curled up menacingly at the corner. The rifle ze'd taken from Jolk was purely a weapon of last resort. The moment ze fired it, everyone in the caves would come running with rifles of their own. Benexx would like to think ze'd die bravely and drag a few of them along on zer return to Xis, but ultimately, that's the only way it would end.

But this... this was different. This bomb was an *offensive* weapon. Ze now had the capability to pick where to strike, when, and do so without revealing zerself. Ze could hurt them, badly. Use it as a diversion. Use it as a booby trap. Use it to cut off a path of pursuit. This gave zer options. This changed zer from a fleeing dux'ah to a stalking ulik, if only a singleton "pack." Benexx hastily disassembled the test rig and shoved everything back into zer bag. Sula and zer conspirators had tried their best to blow Benexx up, might still have succeeded in blowing up zer father.

It was time to repay their kindness.

CHAPTER TWENTY-SIX

The alien iconography blinked above the projected surface of Gaia, taunting Jian incessantly. He checked his plant's chrono. He'd been down in the pit for eleven and a half hours already. His eyes felt like they'd been plucked out of his skull, lightly marinated in lemon juice, dipped in sand, and stuffed back into their sockets.

Jian grabbed a water bottle and squirted a short stream onto his face to wash away the sweat and give his eyes some moisture. Then he dug into one of the pockets on the arm of his flight suit and retrieved a pair of pills from a small cylinder. One red, one yellow. The red was a reasonably strong painkiller he hoped would blunt the coming headache he felt developing behind his right eye. The yellow was a strong stimulant, a nozey-dozey as the other pilots called them. They were supposed to keep a pilot alert during long-duration flights, but they often found other uses for them.

He'd wiggled out of the cumbersome and hot expeditionary suit hours ago. It sat crumpled behind the map room's chair like a discarded layer of skin. He'd need to don the suit again before returning to the shuttle to resupply in another day or two, but in the meantime Jian lounged in the relatively unencumbered comfort of his flight suit. Although even that was starting to itch.

He rubbed his eyes until streaks of light wandered across his field of vision. It felt like flight training all over again. Sleepless nights spent cramming for exams, flying high on strong tea and stronger drugs just to keep awake. Except this study guide was written in a language Jian couldn't even read, he had no idea what was on the final test, and if he didn't pass, his friend would probably die. No pressure.

Jian stood with a groan and stretched. His legs threatened to fall asleep if he didn't get up and work some blood into them every hour or so. Slowly, he paced back and forth on the catwalk bisecting the map room, careful to stay away from the edges. Whoever built the facility hadn't seen the point of handrails, either because they didn't have hands, or because they figured anyone dumb enough to fall off the edge of a catwalk deserved their fate.

Behind him, the now-familiar-but-still-kinda-creepy scratching of Polly's insectoid legs against the deck followed as he paced. Like a loyal pet, his little autonomous friend hadn't left his side since they'd exited the *Buran*. Polly seemed worried about him. Of course, it was just as likely Jian's brain was anthropomorphizing the little bionic bug, but that's how it felt whenever he glanced over at his trio of peering green eyes.

The expedition hadn't been completely fruitless. Jian had figured out how to manipulate the map of Gaia, zoom in on items of interest, and select them to get more detailed information. Of course, that information still popped up in a language he couldn't read, but at this point he was willing to embrace the small victories. The level of detail the projection had available was insane. Jian had spotted one of the drone cargo ships plying trade between Atlantis and Shambhala by the wake it left on the ocean. The display's resolution was enough to read the registry number off the side of the drone's hull. Data spooled out next to the ship's image. He'd tagged those characters in his plant's translation matrix as probable speed and bearing data and gave it something to chew on for a while, hoping it could pick up on new patterns.

He'd made a couple of dozen similar assumptions as he jumped from one point of interest on the map to the next, trying to give his plant enough connections to make a breakthrough. But there was a big risk in doing so. When he looked at the data streaming next to say, Shambhala, he was assuming the ancient alien intelligence that programed its user interfaces found the same sorts of things interesting about the city as he did. For all he knew, the beings that built the facility couldn't care less about population figures, resource consumption, or construction rates and instead focused on the total weight of potassium contained in the city's inhabitants or the number of windows in its buildings.

Aware of the monkey wrench cultural assumptions could throw into the translation process, Jian tried to be as general in the connections he made for the program as possible. But he had to balance that caution against being too nebulous and giving the matrix connections so broad as to render them effectively useless.

Frustration gripped Jian. He wasn't used to having so little control over a situation. He was a pilot; maintaining control was kind of central to his profession. This sitting passively on his hands, waiting for something, anything to happen... it wasn't exactly his speed.

Jian glanced back at Polly scurrying along behind him and stopped, then held out his forearm, inviting Polly to climb up to his perch. The tiny creature complied eagerly and soon clung fast to the fabric of Jian's flight suit.

"We're going to be here forever, aren't we?"

Polly held up his manipulators.

Jian sighed heavily, then looked at his feet. The situation was rapidly approaching hopeless. Jian could spend months down here in the bone-dry chill of the map room trying to learn this dead language without making enough progress to matter. Benexx would be long dead by then, and his whole insubordinate expedition would count for nothing. He'd have wasted his career on a crazy plan that any sane person would have known was doomed from the… start…

Polly had held up his claws in a "no idea" gesture. Like he understood what Jian had asked. Or at the very least like he'd known he was being asked a question but didn't understand it. Either way, holding up his claws was a human gesture. It was something Polly had learned from Jian.

Jian had taught it to him.

Jian smacked his own forehead with an open palm. "Fucking duh," he said aloud. He'd approached this entirely backwards. He was trying to learn the alien super-intelligence's language, when he should have been trying to teach it *his* language. If the nerds back on the Ark were right, that's what it had been built for in the first place. To act as a bridge between the past and the present, adapting to whatever cultural and linguistic drift had occurred over the eons.

He sprinted back to the chair and plopped into position, as awake as he'd felt since entering the chamber. Jian zoomed in to the projection of Shambhala and selected it. The now familiar, yet still unreadable text began to spiral inward next to the city. Jian cleared his throat.

"Shambhala," he spoke clearly and loudly, careful to enunciate each syllable.

The text next to the city froze in place, then disappeared entirely. In its place, a pulsing white oval circle appeared. Something was listening to him.

"Shambhala," Jian repeated.

A curved, flowing character appeared in the air, followed by another, and another. Three characters, three syllables in "Shambhala." They were syllabograms, not unlike Chinese or corresponding Japanese characters, Jian was sure of it.

Jian tagged them in his plant's translation matrix and assigned the correlation a ninety-nine percent certainty.

Then he moved to Shambhala's harbor and selected the beanstalk leading up to the Ark.

"Space Elevator."

Five characters appeared, the first separated from the other four by a tiny curving slash mark that Jian recognized from the other texts. It was ubiquitous, like a period, or a comma. It was used to separate the symbols, he guessed. To delineate a pause, a start of a new word. A press of the space bar was his assumption. He moved on to other icons, repeating the process and tagging the results.

Then, Jian decided to push the envelope. He held two clenched fists in the air.

"Zero," he announced, then extended a finger. "One." He extended another finger. "Two." He repeated the process. "Three, four, five, six, seven, eight, nine, ten."

When he ran out of fingers, Jian put his hands down and waited. The projection flashed, processing what it had just seen. Then, a new character appeared in blue, harder edged than the ones it had been using to catalogue Jian's map labels. Then another crimson symbol followed in line behind it, this one attended by a bright green dot below it. And another, this one with two bright green dots, another with three dots. The pattern continued until thirteen characters hovered in front of him, zero all the way through the ancient program's base-twelve numerical system.

Jian's chest flooded with satisfaction.

"Now we're talking."

CHAPTER TWENTY-SEVEN

"Sakiko!" Kexx shouted, but Benson was already moving, clawing his way up the back of the loader in a desperate bid to reach the girl in time. Kexx moved even faster, barely slowing down as ze transitioned from flat ground to scrambling over the yellow beast. Atlantians weren't worth a cup of hot spit in a sprint, but bloody hell, could they climb.

For not the first time, Benson cursed at Mei for refusing to let Sakiko get a plant when she was an infant, but Mei had been steadfast. He reached the top of the loader's hopper and started to pull himself over the lip, but as soon as he did, his ample shoulders became wedged between the metal wall and the rock ceiling of the tunnel. For a fleeting moment, Benson felt the raw, claustrophobia that comes with being immobilized. But then, supple, flexible hands grabbed the collar of his jacket and heaved him into the dirty interior of the hopper. Most of the strength of youth remained in Elder Kexx's limbs.

Together, they ran to the other side of the hopper. Kexx's skinglow pumped out as much light as it could, casting the tunnel beyond in its otherworldly bluegreen hue. Sakiko stood there, alone, pale-faced, feet frozen to the ground, with Benson's hand torch laying in the dirt, shining its white cone at...

"Oh no." Benson sucked air through his teeth. "Korolev, get up here pronto."

Kexx crawled zer way down and took Sakiko's small frame in zer arms. "It's all right, little one," ze said as ze turned the girl away from the ruined body on the ground in front of the loader. "It's done. You've just been startled, there's no shame in that." Ze bent down and flipped Benson's hand torch back up to him.

"Thanks."

Korolev joined him at Benson's side a moment later. Benson pointed the light down at the corpse with its matted mop of auburn hair.

"Damn," Korolev said. "What a mess."

"Foreman Lind?" Benson asked.

"Yeah."

"Are you sure?"

"Wish I wasn't, coach."

"That explains the shutdown," Benson said. "Loader's lidar registered an obstruction in its path, probably assumed it was a small cave-in or something, then shut down, sent out the error code, and waited for someone to come and clean it up."

"Which means," Kexx continued his train of thought, "that there wasn't anyone left to come find Lind. Either because they all defected to the terrorists, or..."

"Or their bodies are deeper in the mine." With some effort, Benson squeezed his way out of the hopper and paced out the murder scene. Korolev followed.

"Hey, Pavel. Our rear is pretty well secured by the loader, but we're exposed from deeper in the tunnel. Do me a favor and go down a couple dozen meters, point the business end of that death machine down the mine, and try to look really irritated."

"Won't be a stretch, coach."

"Good boy." Benson inspected the ground with his hand torch to avoid contaminating the scene more than necessary. Tracks covered much of the ground, both human shoe soles and the splayed "X" of Atlantian footprints.

"Hey, Pavel. Watch your step. There's tracks all over here."

While the natives living in Shambhala had taken to shirts and pants, they'd rejected shoes wholesale. They simply received too much feedback from their feet, from tastes, to vibrations, to some weird bioelectrical sensation that Benson still didn't understand but Kexx and Benexx insisted was real.

Benexx.

Ze was down here, Benson would swear to it. But that's exactly why he needed to slow down, move cautiously, and do things by the book. He knew damn well that rushing in powered by blind rage was a good way to get everyone he cared about killed, even if the adrenaline and testosterone flooding his arteries didn't have much mind to listen at the moment.

Benson quashed the bloody little fantasy that had started playing out in his head and returned to the present. Foreman Lind's body was a mess of slash wounds and limbs sitting at impossible angles. Her clothes were soaked through with blood that had coagulated and dried days before. It was mostly devoid of insect analogues in the chilly cavern, which was a small mercy. About a half meter from her outstretched right hand laid a small rock pick. Benson didn't have to get any closer to recognize the dried Atlantian blood staining the pointy end of the improvised weapon. But he knew there was a lot more story to tell in the footprints around him than what he could see.

"Hey, truth-digger," Benson beckoned at Kexx. "C'mere a minute for a consult."

Kexx obliged, pulling zer faltering apprentice along in zer wake with a steady hand. Benson had never seen headstrong Sakiko in such a hesitant state. The sight of Lind's body had clearly shaken the young woman to her core. Had she never seen a dead body before, Benson wondered? No, that wasn't it. She'd never seen a dead *human* body before.

"All right, Sakiko," Kexx said warmly. "Don't look at the body, I will handle that for now. Look at everything around the body. The tracks, the drag furrows, the... blood. Use your tracking skills and tell me what you see. Can you do that?"

"Yes..." she said timidly, then swallowed and centered herself. "Yes, elder." Without another word, Sakiko reached for Benson's hand torch once more. Benson placed it in her outstretched palm without comment or complaint. With great deliberation, Sakiko paced out the scene from where Lind's body lay, moving backwards through the timeline of the encounter, mindful not to step on any of the footprints laid down by either victim or her attackers, reconstructing the attack in her mind's eye before speaking.

"OK," Sakiko said. "There were five of them. Four Atlantians and one human, not counting the victim." She shined the light down at her feet. "They walked back up from deeper in the cave and stood in a rough semi-circle right here. The fore... ah, woman came to a stop right there and met them face to face." Sakiko took a step back and pivoted to the outside of the semi-circle of attackers she'd already outlined. "They were standing still for a little while, talking probably? The one human shuffled his feet nervously while they confronted each other."

"Hold on," Benson interrupted. "How do you know it was a 'he,' and how do you know they were fidgeting?"

Sakiko pointed her borrowed light at shallow divots in the dusty rock. "Because those boot prints are twenty-six or twenty-seven centimeters which borders on absurd for a human female, deep enough to mark whoever wore them at seventy-five kilos, and wiggled around in place enough to be the scared kid dancing stiffly in a corner at prom, OK?"

Benson looked at the smudges in the dirt and saw exactly none of what Sakiko had just described hidden within. Lost, he looked up at Kexx, who only shrugged.

"She's really quite good at tracking," her mentor said, zer skinglow fluttering at the shoulders with pride.

"I'll take your word for it, old friend. Sakiko, forgive my interruption and please, continue."

Sakiko looked back down at the dirt and resumed the retelling. "The Atlantian in the middle moved first, I think. The other prints fall a little short and lay on top of zers. The victim wasn't expecting the attack and took three big, uneven steps backwards. She was unbalanced, trying to find her footing. She was cut with a blade here," Sakiko pointed at an impossibly small drop of blood that had dried into a tiny bowl of sand grains. "And here. But she didn't turn to run. No, wait. She'd already been flanked. She decided to fight back, right here." She pointed at a spot where even Benson could see Lind had dug in her heel, transferring her weight from retreat to a forward lunge.

"She attacked three, no, four times. She got a solid hit on one of them. Not the one who started it, the one to zer left. Their blood streaks the ground for almost two meters as they dragged themselves out of the fight."

"Did they survive?" Benson asked.

"Not sure. There's not nearly enough blood to ensure a kill. That's all I can tell you from this. Anyway, she kept fighting, but they had her on three sides. The wounds piled up. One of the hits lamed her right leg, there. She's dragging her foot for the rest of the fight until she finally falls down. There was no death stroke. I think she just bled out."

"Is that your opinion as well, Kexx?" Benson asked.

"To the last step. As I said, my apprentice is very good with tracks." Kexx put zer hands on Sakiko's shoulders. "You breathed life into the way this woman chose to return so it may be known, Sakiko. Well done. I am proud of you."

"Thank you, elder." Sakiko knelt down to Lind's head

and gently stroked the dead woman's hair.

"Sweetie, are you all right?" Benson asked, but Sakiko just kept stroking.

"She wasn't expecting a fight. People she knew and trusted turned on her and killed her. But she didn't take it laying down. She fought back, made sure at least one of them wouldn't forget her."

A terrible question flashed across Benson's mind. "You didn't... know her. Did you?"

Sakiko looked back up at him and wiped away a tear. "No, I didn't. Wish I had now, though. She sounds like my kind of lady."

"Mine too," Benson said. "Kexx is right, we know what kind of lady she was, thanks to you. Now, how about we go find Benexx and kick some heads in, yeah?"

Sakiko's face darkened. "That sounds lovely."

"I thought it might." Benson stood and turned back towards the loader, then raised his voice so everyone could hear. "We should report in with the station house about Foreman Lind's death before we push deeper. Can we reverse this loader out of here? I'd prefer to have an open backfield if things go south and we have to exit the mine in a hurry."

"I'll give it a try," Korolev said. Benson stood by impassively while the constable negotiated the loader's programing with his plant. A series of clicks and electric whines signaled his success. The mechanical mule stirred to life. Electric motors in each wheel turned as it sprang into motion. Unloaded, it moved surprisingly fast back up and out of the tunnel. Benson didn't feel great about leaving Lind's body behind and exposed. It felt disrespectful.

"Hey, Sakiko. Could you run back up to the administration building, grab a tablecloth or a sheet or something to cover her up?"

"Of course."

Sakiko took off at a run, while Benson and Kexx

followed behind at a more leisurely pace. Korolev took up the rear, walking backwards with his rifle muzzle still aimed warily down the mine.

"She's good, Kexx. You're teaching her well," Benson said.

"We teach each other. Just as you and I once did. But yes, she is very good. I'll be leaving G'tel in good hands when I retire."

"And how long will that be?"

Kexx smirked. "Not just yet. I have a few more summers to contribute."

"Then what? Settle down with some spry young thing, recruit a bearer, and crank out a brood?"

"I don't think so. There are more than enough little ones running around Atlantis as it is now that the culls have ceased. We're going through our own growing pains. I don't feel any particularly strong drive to add to them."

"Pity, you'd make a great parent."

Kexx nodded towards Sakiko's retreating form. "Sometimes, it feels like I already am."

Benson put an arm around Kexx's shoulder. "Amen, my friend. What a strange and wonderful world we've built."

"Lot of building yet to do."

The "loss of signal" message at the corner of Benson's vision disappeared, replaced by a weak, but stable connection. Seventeen messages appeared in his plant's queue, all marked urgent, all from Theresa. Benson was still in the process of opening the most recent one when a call request came in from his wife. He accepted.

<Hello, wife. What's–>

<Bryan, where the hell have you been? I've been trying to raise you and Pavel for half an hour!>

<We were underground, out of signal range. Esa, we found the foreman out here. It wasn't pretty.>

<Forget it. Get in the quadcopter and get back here on the double.>

<What? No, you're not listening. The foreman is dead. Her own workers killed her. This is the cell that bombed us and took Benexx. I'm sure of it.>

<It. Has. To. Wait. Bryan. I need you here, right now.>

Benson couldn't believe what he was hearing, but he trusted his wife. If she said finding their child had to wait, it must be important.

<Esa, what the hell is going on?>

<The Atlantians are rioting, Bryan. Shambhala is burning. I need all-hands-on-deck, or we're going to lose the city.>

CHAPTER TWENTY-EIGHT

After spending the last two days running or hiding from zer dogged captors, Benexx assumed it would be a simple matter to pick up one of their patrols and tail them back to wherever their central staging area was so ze could bury them all.

That assumption had proven rampantly optimistic.

After playing around with the remote detonator for a while, Benexx discovered it had several handy settings in addition to its direct trigger pull, including scheduled detonation or delay "fuse." It also had an internal clock synched up to Shambhala Standard Time. Ze hadn't had any accurate gauge of the passage of time since waking up in the cell they'd dropped zer in days before.

Benexx could hardly believe how much of a relief it was to just be able to look down and check if five minutes had passed, or five hours. Indeed, ze'd learned that it had only been five days since the attack at the parade. If anyone had cared to ask, ze'd have sworn it must've been a moon, maybe longer.

It also meant that zer birthday was yesterday. Ze was fifteen now, and by Atlantian reckoning, an adult. All things considered, ze'd have preferred to stay a child for a little longer. Ze'd done too much growing up in the last few days.

Thanks to the clock, Benexx knew with confidence that ze'd been stumbling around looking for zer quarry for the better part of seven hours now without so much as a flicker of skinglow in the distance. No one had come looking for zer in that whole time, no patrols, no guards at doors or intersections. No hushed voices or footfalls. And the only scents they'd left were stale and weak, hours old at the least. It was as if they'd pulled up stakes and left, abandoning the search for their hostage entirely. But neither was ze any closer to finding the exit to the infernal labyrinth.

"Typical," Benexx whispered to no one in particular. Ze'd stalked around to each spot ze'd had to hide from patrols before and waited for at least an hour before moving on to the next one. Ze couldn't seem to shake them when ze was on the lamb. Now that ze *wanted* to find one, nobody was home. They were being quite inconsiderate of zer schedule. "I'll have nothing good to say in my review of this resort."

Benexx's head rolled back before ze could catch it and banged against the hard rock wall ze leaned against. Ze rubbed at it and swore under zer breath. Ze didn't know how long ze'd been awake, but it felt like days. Ze'd stolen a few fitful naps here and there, but so much time spent not only awake, but struggling to maintain sharp focus while zer body hovered barely above operating temperature was taking its toll. Zer body would come along to collect sooner rather than later. Ze rubbed zer eyes until warm glowing blobs appeared, then faded away just as quickly as they'd come.

That was, all but one of them.

Benexx's hand moved to rub it away, but before it did, zer eyes refocused and the bluegreen smudge resolved into the glowing outline of an Atlantian's body. It was real, and it was walking almost straight towards zer.

Fear returned like a crashing wave, fear of being recaptured, of being beaten or worse, of being thrown back into zer cell, or of ending up dead on the cold floor like Jolk. But the heat of zer rage quickly cut through the icy wave of fear and boiled it off. Benexx brought the muzzle of the rifle to bear on the newcomer, but did not turn on either the torchlight or the holographic sight, either of which would give away zer hiding spot. It was purely defensive. If ze had indeed been spotted, ze would shoot them, preferably in a non-lethal spot, run as fast as ze could in the opposite direction, and pray they stopped to help their injured member, buying zer enough time to hide and start the process over.

It would be a hard shot to make without the aid of the computer calculated reticule, but with each approaching step it became just a little easier, even as the danger of discovery ratcheted higher. Benexx's grip on the rifle's trigger tightened to take up the fraction of a millimeter of slack, then exhaled in anticipation of the shot, just as zer mother had taught zer.

The Atlantian sauntered towards zer until they were so close Benexx recognized their face. It was Sula zerself. Benexx had to fight back a sudden impulse to just shoot zer through the head in cold blood.

Hold, Benexx admonished zerself. *Hold fire.*

Sula held zer own rifle, but it hung on zer shoulder by the strap instead of in a ready position. Ze didn't spot zer missing hostage hiding in a hollow, and didn't notice the muzzle of Benexx's stolen rifle lined up with zer center mass. Sula just kept walking, an angry grimace glued to zer countenance like wallpaper. Ze didn't lock eyes with Benexx. Didn't look zer way at all. Instead, Benexx's tormentor paced right past zer without so much as a glance and continued down the corridor without wavering.

Benexx waited five seconds, ten, then finally pulled fresh air into zer sacks just as they started to burn and let the slack out of zer rifle's trigger. Sula had overlooked zer entirely, the plan was still viable. Ze uncurled from the little cubby hole ze'd been hiding inside, gingerly shouldered the pack with the bomb, detonator, and what remained of zer food, then set off in pursuit.

Sula wasn't difficult to follow. Zer skinglow was bright enough to light up a good-sized room. Ze noisily stalked through the corridors like a newborn dux'ah crashing through halo trees. Either ze hoped to flush Benexx out of hiding, or ze simply didn't care about all the attention ze was drawing to zerself.

But then again, why should ze care? Sula obviously hadn't yet appreciated that zer role had changed from predator to stalked prey. Benexx desperately hoped to keep it that way until zer trap was sprung. Ze still hadn't seen, smelled, or heard even a hint of an exit. For all ze knew, they'd sealed off the way out after they'd brought zer down here. It wasn't unheard of among Dwellers. In the old tales, Dweller caves were shut off from the ash and poisonous air of the surface after an asteroid impact for years at a time. Maybe Sula had simply pulled back zer patrols figuring Benexx was too well hidden and intended to starve out zer wayward hostage.

The hunger pains in zer stomach told zer that it probably would've worked in another couple of days. Benexx had come to accept that ze might never leave this place. Might end up buried under thousands of tons of cold rock, left to be discovered only by some far future archeologist. A mystery, a footnote in history. All ze wanted now was to live long enough to make sure ze wasn't the only artifact of interest they discovered.

Sula took a hard right and disappeared into a small side tunnel Benexx had overlooked completely during zer blind meandering through the cave since escaping. Benexx hustled as quickly as ze dared so ze wouldn't lose the tail. Trading a bit of silence for speed, Benexx caught up and put zer back against the wall just to the side of the new passage. Ze could still hear Sula moving through the tunnel, but it was no longer the regular cadence of a walk. Instead, Sula grunted with apparent effort.

Benexx's bloodways chilled at the sound, afraid of

what it meant lay ahead. Sure enough, as ze craned zer head around the corner to get a look, ze spotted a rope hanging from a large hole in the roof of the passage. Sula had moved up to a new level. If Benexx followed, ze'd have to sling zer rifle and climb with zer hands, weighed down by zer gun, waterskin, and the bomb in zer pack. Slow and defenseless, in other words. The rope was a perfect ambush point. If Sula had gotten so much as a whiff of Benexx on the air, ze could be waiting at the top of the rope with zer rifle leveled at the hole in the floor and there would be no way for Benexx to know until the trap was already sprung.

The apprehension that had already taken root in zer chest grew so fast it nearly burst. Ze wanted to spin around one eighty and run in the other direction.

And yet...

Ze put a hand on the rope, but stopped. Any wiggle at the top would give away the fact someone was dangling from the other end of it. Instead, Benexx slung zer rifle and grabbed two handfuls of wall. Unlike the half-hemisphere of the cave ze'd been caged in, this climb was more or less straight up and offered plenty of handholds. It still wasn't an easy climb, especially without making any noise, but it was manageable.

Halfway up, maybe about four meters, Benexx felt the rifle sling begin to work its way off zer shoulder. One of zer hands shot over to grab it before it slipped off, but then the other immediately peeled free from its hold. The weight of the pack hanging from zer shoulder dragged zer back that much faster. Falling backwards with only zer feet still stuck to the wall, Benexx's arms spun like wind turbine blades, flailing for a hold, any hold.

Zer hand brushed against something floating in space and reflexively clamped down, halting zer fall. It was the rope, but ze didn't have time to worry about it as the rifle fell off zer arm and spun towards the floor. In one smooth, desperate motion, Benexx grabbed the rope with both hands, then released zer grip on the wall and kicked a foot out at the tumbling gun.

Ze curled a single toe around the nylon sling. The slack went out and the rifle's weight snapped the sling taunt, nearly ripping it free of zer grip and sending it clattering down to the floor for everyone within a hundred meters to hear like the ringing of a bell. But zer grip held, barely, and ze got the rest of zer toes around the sling a moment later.

Hanging from the rope, one foot clinging to the wall, and zer gun dangling from the other, Benexx let out a long, relieved breath. Ze rehung the rifle *across* zer chest this time, then pushed off from the rope and clung tight against the wall and looked up, expecting to see the muzzle of Sula's gun appear at the opening above at any second.

It didn't, and the anxious knots in Benexx's limbs slowly unwound as the undulations of the rope settled. Tentatively, ze resumed the climb. After the near disaster, ze was motivated to get the hell out of the chute and back onto level ground where ze at least had a chance to retreat or hide. Hanging by zer fingers in this chute, ze felt painfully exposed.

Keeping focused on the rock instead of the hole at the top, Benexx made the rest of the climb without incident. Ze paused just below the rim and listened intently for a ragged breath, a shifted foot, a safety catch being clicked off, any signal that ze was about to lift zerself into a trap.

There was nothing outside the retreating sound of faint footsteps. Sula's, Benexx assumed.

Ze reached up a hand at a time and grabbed the lip of the hole and pulled zerself up onto the new level. The air was different up here somehow. More… fertile, somehow? Yes, it smelled like the beds of turned dirt and fungus crops ze'd tasted touring the Dweller caverns with Kexx and Sakiko three summers ago. They were growing mushrooms down here, which meant the caves had been occupied for months, at the very least. Maybe zer assumptions had been wrong and they'd smuggled zer to Atlantis after all. Stowed away in the belly of a transport plane maybe? That would explain why there hadn't been enough time for zer wounds to heal more.

Benexx shook zer head. It still didn't matter where ze was as long as ze remained underground. Ze was wasting time, and the distance between zer and Sula grew by the second.

Keeping a sharp eye out for any hint of skinglow, artificial human light source, or even strange scents, Benexx came to zer feet and started in the direction of Sula's diminishing echoes as quickly as ze judged prudent. The path under zer toes was worn smooth, well-traveled by many feet over many months. That wasn't the only difference. In addition to smells of underground agriculture, ze picked up hints of Atlantian pheromones, human sweat, smoke from cooking fires, and the sharp undercurrent of mingled bodily wastes. Nor was it just smells. The air itself carried more heat, Benexx felt it. Just on zer skin for now, but it wouldn't be long before zer blood carried the warmth deeper into zer core.

This level of the caves was different than the ones ze'd explored. It felt... lived in. Which only made sense, the more ze thought about it. You wouldn't put a bomb factory next to your living room, after all. You'd want to keep it isolated, on the far end of the village where the damage would be minimized if anything went wrong. The same logic applied to zer jail cell. Apparently, the old human real estate axiom of location, location, location was a universal constant.

Benexx caught just the briefest glimmer of skinglow, maybe no more than an elbow, as Sula again rounded a corner. But there was more. The bend in the corridor glowed, not with the bluegreen of Atlantian bioluminescence, but the amber of fire. There were whispered voices on the air as well. This was the place, finally. Instead of running in gun blazing, Benexx put zer back to the wall and did zer best to be just another hole in the cave. Zer blood raced as ze reached the door, partly out of fear, partly out of excitement, and partly because it was in a race to draw heat into zer muscles, organs, and brain(s).

Ze reached the doorway, which, for once, actually deserved the name. Its edges had fresh tool-marks. Someone had worked the natural opening wider with hammer and chisel. Benexx snuck a hand into the doorway to grab a scentshot. Dux'ah fat torches, jerky, spices, stewed fungus. Dinner time. Zer hollowed-out stomach churned with hunger, but ze ignored it. There was just enough smell of pheromones and sweat to know the crowd sitting down for the evening meal was a mix of Atlantians and humans, but ze couldn't get any read on how many. Uncle Kexx would have. Zer sense of taste and smell bordered on clairvoyance.

Once more, Benexx stuck zer head around the corner for a lightning quick, one-eyed scan of the chamber beyond. What ze saw filled zer with an odd mix of dread and elation. There were somewhere between a dozen and two fullhands of conspirators sitting on the floor around a pair of large cooking fires, too many to count in the brief glance ze took, and more than even zer most liberal guess had been of their strength of numbers.

Which *would* have been atrocious news if ze'd been forced to fight zer way through all of them, but, since ze was delegating the work of taking them out over to zer new best friend, the fact they were all so helpfully clustered together in one place was simply wonderful.

Benexx set zer rifle down gingerly on the floor of the cave and unslung the pack from zer shoulder. The bomb had grown increasingly heavy the longer ze carried it. Ze'd be glad to be rid of the extra weight dragging zer down, in more ways than one. While the succulent and savory smells of a hearty meal wafted through the doorway, Benexx busied zerself prepping the device that would ensure it was zer tormentors' last supper.

There was a spike in conversations between courses, which Benexx exploited to run a system check in the hallway. A new scent emigrated from the room beyond: yulka cakes drenched in dipoora pollen sauce. It was a treat for children, one ze'd had more than zer fill of over the summer. But right then, the smell made zer mouth water.

Benexx shook off the thought. Ze needed to decide where to place the bomb for maximum effectiveness. Ze wasn't a demolitions expert by any means, but ze had a basic understanding of the physics involved. The tunnel out here would channel and redirect most of the blast energy away from zer targets. Leaving it inside the doorway was better, but ideally it would go smack in the middle of the dining room where the surrounding walls would contain and amplify the explosion and turn everyone inside into a finely-strained jelly.

That was the ideal placement, and a happy little daydream played out in Benexx's head where ze walked confidently into the very center of the room, smiling at all of the faces stunned into silence, set down the bomb, stole a cake from out of Sula's gawking mouth, sauntered out of the room, set off the explosion without looking back, then ate the cake.

Yippe kai-yah, motherfucker.

Benexx shook zer head again, trying to clear the cobwebs from zer mind and regain focus. The combination of hunger and a sudden surge of warmth after days of running below zer optimum body temp threw all sorts of interesting physiological error codes as zer metabolism ramped back up only to find it had almost nothing left to burn.

Optimal placement was out, but if ze was sneaky Benexx thought ze could at least get the bomb down the short passage and rested against the inner wall, which was almost as good, and had the added bonus of not vaporizing zer as ze hid in the tunnel. Probably.

Benexx cradled the bomb in zer arm and went completely prone. Ze concentrated on matching the hue and patterns of zer skin to the rock of the entryway. The effort resulted in a subpar facsimile that would almost certainly have earned zer uncle's disapproval, but it was better than nothing at all.

While zer captors and conspirators ate their cakes, Benexx inched toward both zer vengeance, and only chance of salvation. Like a skip-rock fish stalking through the tidal pools of the New Amazon river delta, Benexx crawled towards zer prey.

The cake course finished, and everyone spoke up appreciatively towards the cook, even the humans. Benexx rolled zer eyes, but took advantage of the sudden uptick of noise and distraction and brought zerself to within arm's reach of zer target.

The cook presented the next course; dux'ah fat gravy over falafel, a nod to their human guests. Benexx loved the falafel that street vendors in Shambhala sold, on warm summer nights, after football games. Ze'd never wanted one of the spicy balls of deep-fried chickpea paste so badly in zer life.

Neither, as it happened, had zer stomach, which registered its desperation with a long, low, and loud *guuuuurgle*.

Everyone stopped. Time itself stopped. After an interminably long moment, every head in the chamber, some still bearing an open mouth full of half-chewed food, turned as one to the doorway where Benexx lay. No one spoke, either from shock or simple rejection of the absurdity of the scene.

"Um," Benexx finally ventured. "Hello."

Sula, sitting near the middle of the room between the two cooking fires, stood and struck a finger in Benexx's direction.

"GET ZER!"

That was all the incentive Benexx needed to reverse zer course out of the room.

Stupid, stupid, stupid, ze admonished zerself as the first poorly-aimed rifle rounds splashed and ricocheted against the stone hallway above zer head. Benexx scrambled backwards like a pond-skimmer as tiny flechettes of stone and twisted metallic-polymers exploded from bullet impact craters on the walls around zer, tearing at zer skin like a swarm of biting insect analogues, leaving superficial-yet-stinging flesh wounds in their wake.

In zer haste to escape, Benexx almost left the makeshift bomb behind in the hallway, but grabbed it at the last instant with a foot. Keeping low and against the opposite wall to the incoming fire, ze made zer way back to zer rifle and pack in the outer corridor. Once ze had everything in hand, Benexx headed in the opposite direction from where ze'd come at a dead sprint. Ze dug out the detonator from the pack and discarded the rest. Whatever food, medicine, or water ze had left was just dead weight now.

The first of zer tormentors spilled out of the doorway as if they'd been shoved, but Benexx was ready for them. Wheeling backwards, ze held up zer stolen rifle, spotlight and sights turned up to full illumination because why-the-hell-not at this point, centered the computer-assisted reticule on zer enemy's chest, and pulled a trigger in anger for the first time in zer life.

A quick one-two-three burst erupted from the rifle with a deafening cadence, filling the tunnel with the echoing sounds of its thunderclaps. The first two rounds missed their target by less than a finger-length, but the third struck home into the right side of the first Atlantian to present themselves. The recipient rocked back from the sudden transfer of kinetic force, but quickly came to their feet and returned fire. Lacking hearts to stop, Atlantians were devilishly difficult to kill with single shots unless landed directly in the head, a fact that was both beneficial and detrimental to Benexx's chances in the short-term.

The tiny bullets sliced through the air faster than sound itself, some barely missing Benexx's head. Ze turned and ran down the hallway, deafened by the gunfire, muzzle flashes seared into zer vision. Ze pointed the rifle back down the tunnel and blindly sprayed a long burst as ze retreated, hoping only to convince zer pursuers to get back under cover and put an extra bit of distance between them.

Sprinting through the dark, Benexx was suddenly struck in the left leg with a white-hot pain just above the knee. Ze let out a shocked yelp of surprise as much as agony as zer leg gave out and sent zer crashing to the floor in a heap. The rifle skittered away from zer grip and came to rest against the far wall, its cone of light pointed back down the hallway, while the bomb remained in zer other hand.

Ze'd been shot. The bullet passed cleanly through the meat of zer leg without hitting the cartilage or expanding very much, not that it hurt any less. It felt like ze'd been run through with an electrified spear. Benexx scrambled back to zer feet, heavily favoring zer left, and moved to grab the gun, only to be driven back again by a barrage of incoming fire aimed at the light. The shooter thought ze still held it. In an instant, Benexx decided to use the diversion to maximum effect.

Ze planted the bomb on the opposite side of the passage even as another burst of fire tore into the rock face, then hopped away as quickly as ze could, dragging a hobbled left leg behind zer. Even over the ringing in zer ears, Benexx heard shouting break out behind zer, goading zer forward. Digging through the pack, zer fingers urgently felt for the detonator until they wrapped around the familiar pistol grip and pulled it free.

Then Benexx's retreat came to a screeching halt. A rock wall blocked the passage ahead. Zer head spun, clamoring to spot an opening in the rock, a hole in the ceiling or floor, anything that ze could use to continue onward.

Nothing. It was a dead end.

The sounds of feet slapping on stone and shouted commands filled zer ears as despair flooded zer mind. There was no way out, and ze hadn't covered nearly enough ground to have gotten clear of the blast radius.

A voice accustomed to being heeded barked at zer to turn around. A weakened, exhausted part of Benexx's brain obeyed without resistance. Sula stood there, several steps ahead of a half dozen of zer compatriots, three of which held their own rifles.

"Nowhere left to run now, little bearer. You are proving to be more trouble than you're worth. Your value to us as a hostage does have limits, you know, no matter who your parents are or how famous you think you are. I have half a mind to order you shot right here and dump you in a hole next to Jolk. You two deserve each other."

A ray of red hot fury shot through the stifling blanket of hopelessness that had descended over zer soul. Dying down here alone was bad enough, but the thought of zer body spending eternity trapped next to Jolk's filth?

Benexx held up the detonator where everyone could see it. The temperature in the cave seemed to drop twenty degrees in less than a second. Sula's skin went blank with the shock and realization that ze wasn't in control of the situation after all.

"What is that?" ze asked.

Benexx pointed to the pale-faced human bombmaker standing to Sula's right. "Ask him, he knows."

Sula conferred with the man, who nodded confirmation.

"I see," ze said quietly, then cleared zer throat. "And what is your detonator connected to?"

"Oh, just a little bomb I scratched together from a few kilos of your stolen explosives. It's about twenty meters behind you, around the bend. You all ran right past it."

"That puts you in the blast zone as much as any of us."

"Sure does."

Sula smiled warmly. The forced, unnatural sight of it turned Benexx's stomach. "Come now, young bearer. You don't want to die here, alone."

"I'm not alone," Benexx taunted. "You're all right here with me."

"Stop this foolishness!" Sula snapped. "I am not an unforgiving host. You are scared, and cold-headed. You're confused. I'm sure you're starving by now. If you set down that remote, I promise you a fine meal. We will share food from our table, an equal share, in recognition of the… unexpected bravery you have displayed."

"I'm not hungry," ze lied.

"I salute your boldness, but if you think you're going to negotiate your way out of this tunnel–"

"I'm not interested in negotiating anything with you," Benexx interrupted.

"Then what *are* you interested in?"

Benexx savored the terror on Sula's face, ze even managed a smirk.

"This." Ze pulled the trigger, and the world went white with light and noise.

CHAPTER TWENTY-NINE

Icons filled the map room like a swarm of colorful, two-dimensional insects. Jian's head had been spinning for the last hour, trying to make sense of layer after layer of the raw data. For the first full day he'd spent on this rogue mission, his greatest concern was not being able to glean enough information from the facility's sensor nets.

But then he'd made the language breakthrough. The facility's AI systems were devilishly clever and picked up on Jian's linguistic inputs incredibly fast. Now, the data came so fast and furiously, it was like trying to stay seated, on a barstool, on top of a geyser.

The scope, breadth, and resolution of the available data was simply mindboggling. Jian scarcely knew where to begin looking. At least twenty different filters stacked one on top of the other, bristling with information. Jian could look up the barometric pressure, wind speed direction, temperature, humidity, and particulate density at any given altitude above Shambhala. A cargo jet making the trip between Shambhala and G'tel cropped up as an anomalous atmospheric disturbance. Jian tagged it, marked the anomaly as an "airplane," and moved on.

Moving to the water, he could sound off on ocean currents, acidity, salinity, oxygen levels, plankton blooms, even crop fish migration patterns. But there was a big difference between tracking schools of hundreds of millions of fish, and identifying and pinpointing a single individual Atlantian. Staring at the flood of information in front of him, Jian was certain the facility possessed the resolution and sensitivity necessary to find Benexx. And he was just as certain he had no idea how to begin to ask it to.

Instead, Jian had spent the last couple of hours clearing the board of things he figured weren't of use. The layer monitoring ozone thickness and opacity to solar radiation probably wasn't going to be of any help finding Benexx, so down it came. The layer tracking planetwide precipitation and lightning activity was similarly fascinating but useless, so he swept it away. Not that meteorologists and agricultural planners down in Shambhala wouldn't absolutely salivate at the chance to tap into the feed, but for Jian right then, it was a distraction.

Next layer. Trails of dots of various sizes and crimson fading to light yellow reached across the map of Gaia like rivers, but they weren't rivers. Many of them extended straight through the oceans. Volcanic activity? No, more than that. Something from primary school planetology popped out of Jian's longterm memory. These were tectonic plate outlines. There were too many dots to be active volcanoes, of which Gaia's five-plus-billion year-old crust held few.

"Earthquakes," Jian said to the room at large. Yes, it made sense. This layer represented seismic activity. A small knot of dots near Shambhala caught Jian's attention, all tiny and yellow. Jian wasn't sure, but he guessed the size of the dot was proportional to the intensity of the seismic event. The color coding, though... duration? Time elapsed since the event?

He zoomed in on the map until Shambhala and its surrounding area of influence took up most of the wall. There were seven clusters of hits surrounding Shambhala out to about thirty-five kilometers, if Jian was judging the scale properly, as well as a single mystery dot in the heart of Shambhala itself. But there were no volcanoes so close to the city, and the clusters were a long way from the nearest faultline. Jian pulled up a map of the area from his plant memory for reference and immediately resolved the mystery. The clusters overlapped precisely with the various mining operations humans had set up on the continent.

The facility's sensors, whatever and wherever the hell they were, were sensitive enough to pick up the seismic signature of excavation explosions. Which also answered the question of the dot pinned in the center of Shambhala. The facility had recorded the terrorist attack on the First Contact Day parade that had set off the series of events that brought Jian here.

The mystery solved, Jian moved a hand to dismiss the layer as he had a half dozen others, but something nagged at him. Uncertain of where the feeling was coming from or why, but also unwilling to ignore it, Jian left the seismic layer in place and moved on to the next. It was… a soil erosion rate map? Yeah, no. Jian canned it as super-useful for someone, worthless to him. Next layer. Freshwater evaporation and atmospheric uptake rates? Seriously? Gods, these people were thorough. Canned, next layer. Er, something about the northern ice cap. Closed.

Jian kept up the pace, unceremoniously retaining or dropping layer after layer as quickly as he could ascertain whatever dataset they represented and determine its utility to his current dilemma. An alert chimed, signaling a sudden change in the map, at least as judged by whatever programing oversaw the facility's projection. It wasn't the first alert that had popped up since he'd been down here. The last one had been for a nascent hurricane developing deep at sea that might give Atlantis some trouble in ten days or so if the prevailing winds held their current bearings. Not pertinent to Jian's search.

Still…

Jian toggled the alert icon and the map zoomed to the area of interest just a little too fast, overwhelming Jian's sense of scale and speed, leaving him, a pilot with hundreds of hours both in simulators and in real cockpits, feeling just a touch of vertigo. The map display was just that good.

Jian averted his eyes until the map settled and instead looked down at Polly, who had been unobtrusively watching him the entire time. Jian reached out a hand and scratched the strange little insect under his, um, chin. The affection was met with an appreciative trill.

Jian's eyes returned to the plot in front of him, and were surprised to see Shambhala in the frame, albeit to the south. The alert had originated to the north, a handful of klicks outside of what his internal map said should be the furthest reach of human settlements or activity. There were scouting camps that far out, of course, surveying for the next wave of development. But they usually stuck closer to the river. The alert came from the seismic layer. A new small, yet bright red dot had appeared. A quick comparison confirmed that it was in the same size range as the events in the various mines, except the closest mine was kilometers away. There was no reason for an excavation charge to be going off in the middle of the wilderness.

Jian considered the plot for a long moment. Long enough to notice the color of the dot shift subtly away from pure red into a reddish orange. So, the color scale was a measure of time after all. This event had just happened, and he'd been alerted to it in real time. But what the hell was it? And why was it in a remote part of undeveloped forest?

The answer struck Jian like the bombblast the dot represented. The dot in the center of Shambhala and this dot were the same thing: a terrorist's bomb going off. Except the detonation in Shambhala had been a deliberate attack.

This wasn't. Something had gone wrong and a device had gone off prematurely, or while it was being assembled. Whatever, the reason didn't matter. What mattered was Jian had just discovered the location of the terrorists' camp, or their bomb factory at the very least. It wasn't as good as finding Benexx, but it was damned good. Jian thrust a triumphant finger at the alert icon and danced in his chair.

"Got you, motherfuckers! I've fucking got you!"

Jian's jubilation lasted right up until he realized that for his discovery to mean anything, he had to share it with someone.

"Right!" He jumped out of the chair at the center of the map room and scrambled towards the pile of his expeditionary suit. Polly, ever the eager accomplice, trotted along behind him and stood watch while Jian wriggled into the suit as quickly as he could. Even running on caffeine and adrenaline, it took Jian almost twenty minutes to don the Godforsaken thing, and another ten to run all the suit integrity tests for what was going to be not even a ten-minute walk back to the *Buran* before the suit's software safety protocols would even let the O2 start flowing.

For not the first time, Jian cursed the overly-cautious eggheads who'd been in charge of designing these suits, more concerned with covering their own asses than building a system that could be put into use in the shortest time possible. If your shuttle was coming apart around you, the last thing you were worried about was triple-checking the solid waste recapture system.

After an interminable period of time, the assholes who'd programed Jian's suit finally gave their disembodied approval as his board went green and the oxygen started to flow. Jian closed the face of his visor as he leaned back into the black nanite muck of the facility's airlock like a scuba-diver plunging backwards into a Lovecraftian ocean.

Moments later, he and Polly emerged back in the caved-in chamber that had first revealed the facility's entrance to Jian's expedition not even a full week ago. Those five days felt like a lifetime. So much had changed. So much lost. And in Jian's case, willingly sacrificed. For his friends, both dead and living. At least he hoped ze was still living.

His most immediate concern, however, was getting the hell out of this hole. One of the ropes they'd tied off to the broken harvester and used to extricate themselves the last time sat coiled and forgotten in a corner of the cavern. The hole back up to the surface still looked too far to jump, even in the weak gravity, but Jian didn't figure he had anything to lose in the attempt.

To give himself the best chance, Jian scrambled up to the tallest point of the rubble pile left over from the cave-in; a hulking monolith of rock that looked like it had been strategically placed there by Kubrick's production team. The same one that had almost killed him on the way down here the second time. Jian wasn't sure if that was a metaphor for anything. He hadn't been the best student of literature.

Jian looked up at the hole in the roof and visualized landing just past the lip. Ninety percent of achieving anything was simply believing it was possible. At least that had been the bullshit he'd been fed growing up. In the zero gee he'd grown up with onboard the Ark, the leap would have been assured success. At the bottom of Gaia's gravity well, he wouldn't be able to clear a full meter of vertical. But here in the three percent gee of Varr's gravity, he had no idea what to expect.

A leap of faith, then. Not like it would be his first. Jian swallowed hard and crouched down for the attempt, pumping his leg muscles like he would in the gym before a particularly heavy lift. Then he leapt for all he was worth. In such low gravity, it felt more like pushing off from a wall in the Ark. The sensation of his momentum slowing was so slight as to almost be imperceptible to his inner ears. But his eyes could spot the loss even as he ascended through the cavern to superhuman heights. As the lip approached, he slowed to a crawl, until he came to a relative stop three short meters shy of the top. He seemingly hovered there for a long moment, like a famous coyote just after stepping away from the cliff, before he started to fall back to the floor. Jian reached out and tried to get a handhold, but the ice was too smooth and offered nothing to grip.

Jian had quite a bit of time to dwell on falling short as he slowly fell back to the floor. After coming so close, he was sorely tempted to make another attempt. Maybe if he stacked a couple of extra meters of rocks to launch from. No, there wasn't enough gravity to keep them stable.

Jian's gaze settled lazily on the coil of rope they'd carelessly dropped at the conclusion of the last mission. It was useless, of course. With no one to throw it up to, and nothing to anchor it to… unless he tied it off to something heavy that could, no, that was stupid. Anything he tied it to would need to be at least as massive as Jian himself for him to have any chance to pull himself up, and if he couldn't leap his body weight out of this hole, he sure as shit wasn't throwing his bodyweight out.

If only he had a grappling hook, or some bit of equipment or debris that could be modified to fit the task. Polly seemed to sense his frustration and appeared on top of the rock next to Jian's face. He turned his little three-eyed head quizzically, like a kitten. A jet black, six-legged kitten with ice picks for feet. Jian understood why everyone else had taken an immediate dislike and distrust to the drone. Its bodyplan tripped way too many instinctual prejudices against insects, spiders, and swarms of glossy black things in general. The fact was Polly looked like what a kid might draw if you asked them to draw a scary spider monster, and he…

Jian craned his own head. "You look like a grappling hook."

Polly looked on curiously, unable to hear Jian's words through the vacuum, but attentive nonetheless. Jian thought through the idea. Polly was tiny, but in this gravity, Jian's effective weight, even with the suit, was low, probably no more than six kilos or so. Another kilo for the weight of the rope… yes, it was feasible. Now he just needed to get Polly to understand what he wanted.

Jian bounced over to the coiled rope and dug through it until he found an end, then waved at Polly to join him. The drone scurried across the floor in a hurry until he sat perched on Jian's knee.

"OK, little bugger. Let's see how clever you really are." Jian began the demonstration of the plan with exaggerated hand gestures, pointing at Polly, then imitating his limbs with fingers bent into hooks. Then he placed the rope in his palm and pretended to crawl up the wall with it before leveling off at the top and clamping down. Then Jian pointed at himself and made a rope-climbing motion with his hands. The demonstration concluded, Jian leaned back against the ice wall and waited.

Polly looked at him, then at the end of rope, then at the wall. His survey complete, he looked back at Jian and winked a green eye, then reached out and grabbed the end of the rope and sort of… absorbed it. The rope sank into Polly's abdomen like it was being swallowed by tar. As soon as the process was complete, Polly jumped off Jian's leg and sprinted up the icy wall like a scalded cat, the rope undulating behind him like a tail.

Jian shook his head in disbelief. "Really clever, is the answer."

Ten minutes later, they were both safely back inside the *Buran*. But Jian faced a new problem. The com equipment he needed to spread word of his discovery doubled as a backdoor Flight on the Ark could use to steal c c control of the shuttle and drag him back to his father and his judgment.

His only chance was the coms whisker laser which

couldn't be hacked or intercepted by anyone but the intended target, in this case, a receiving station in Shambhala. From there, he could log into the local web and connect with anyone through the plant network.

There was one problem; the whisker laser on the *Buran* was designed for use at distances of geo-synch and below. Varr's position relative to the surface of Gaia was currently an order of magnitude greater than that.

Jian checked the clock. Gaia's rotation had brought the Shambhala receiver into range three hours ago. That meant he had another two and a half hours to find enough power to increase the laser's output tenfold, without blowing it up, before the relative angle between his emitter and the city became too obtuse to maintain a connection.

No pressure.

Jian lambasted himself for not thinking this phase of the mission through earlier. He'd had a day and a half during the trip over here to make and test the necessary modifications. Why the hell hadn't he?

Because you didn't actually believe you'd get this far, an angry, judgmental part of his psyche answered. *You came out here to run away, not to save anyone. That was just your excuse.*

"Fuck off," Jian said to, well, himself. He'd never felt so alone, so isolated. It was starting to play tricks on his consciousness. He floated over to the com station and pulled up the whisker laser interface on the physical panel. He could do it all through his plant, of course, but he wanted tactile contact. Jian enjoyed punching the buttons himself.

The com laser emitter was stowed away in the shuttle's cargo bay. The sensitive optics needed protection from the intense heat and pressures of atmospheric reentry. With the omnidirectional UHF radio being the shuttle's main communication's system, the whisker laser was a redundancy, and afterthought. Using it meant depressurizing the cargo compartment, opening the first leaf of outer doors, and extending the emitter on the shuttle's multi-axis boom.

The cycle took seven painful minutes to complete. Time Jian spent shutting down non-critical systems to free up power for the connection attempt.

[WHISKER COM SYSTEM ONLINE.]

"Oh thank Cuut," Jian announced to the heavens. Before he got really crazy, Jian decided to run the laser at normal power, on the outside chance the engineers who'd built it had wildly understated its true capabilities. Wouldn't be the first time they'd held a little somethin' somethin' in reserve for a rainy day.

[CONNECTION FAILURE. INSUFFICIENT SIGNAL STRENGTH.]

Well, that answered that.

Jian moved over to one of the fuse and bus panels and consulted a series of wiring diagrams to make sure he wasn't about to turn off his air supply. He rerouted power from the navigation system – which wasn't doing anything of use at the moment – the collision avoidance radar, the cargo bay heaters, and the UHF radio system he'd already sabotaged and dumped it all into the whisker laser, quadrupling its output. An act that in and of itself required Jian to spend another twenty minutes overriding half a dozen safety protocols.

[CONNECTION FAILURE. INSUFFICIENT SIGNAL STRENGTH.]

"Shit..." Jian took a deep breath. There was more power to cut, of course, but then the question was how many more attempts the laser could take before it threw in the towel?

One way to find out. Jian went back to the fuse box and shut down the cryo tank fans, the thruster banks, Navigation lights, put the main computer itself into standby, then killed main cabin life support. It would take the flight deck a couple of hours to cool off to the point he'd have to worry about hypothermia, and with only him breathing the air, he'd freeze long before he ran out of O2 anyway. Worse came to worst, he could always crawl back into his long-endurance suit.

[CONNECTION FAILURE. INSUFFICIENT SIGNAL STRENGTH.]

"Damnit!" Jian punched the console in white hot anger and immediately regretted it. Something in his hand gave way with a *POP*. The metacarpal behind his right pinky finger looked like someone had tried to pitch a tent.

Jian inhaled sharply and cursed his stupidity. The break was clean, and he'd managed not to make a compound fracture out of it, but in a few minutes, it would hurt like hell, and he didn't look forward to setting his own bone.

There was one more thing to try, he knew. But it would mean physically rewiring a few components, a task that would be all the more difficult with only his off hand to work with.

The *Buran* didn't have internal power generation. No miniaturized fusion plant recharged its batteries, nor did it sport a passive solar array. In atmo, her oxygen-breathing turbine and ramjet engines bled off some of their output to power the electrical systems. But out here in space, all of her electrical came from fuel cells which tapped into the same internal reserves of liquid hydrogen and liquid oxygen reserves that fed her rockets.

These fuel cells used a chemical reaction between the atoms of hydrogen and oxygen to create electricity, extracting power from the fuel in a somewhat slower, more subdued way than when the two elements met in a combustion chamber. Either way, the end result was consumable energy and pure water. Still, available stores of hydrogen and O2 put a hard cap on the amount of electricity the shuttle could produce and still have enough fuel left in the tanks to go anywhere useful.

Jian intended to use all of that spare fuel to charge up the shuttle's bank of quick-discharge capacitors for a single, high energy burst transmission that would last until the laser burned itself out.

It took almost ninety minutes to make the necessary modifications to the *Buran*'s electric grid, and another twenty-five for the fuel-cells to convert three full days of fuel into electricity and pack it into the capacitor bank. Then another twelve minutes to convince the shuttle's safety systems to accept the whole insane, jerry-rigged system without complaint.

With sweat pouring from his forehead in spite of the growing chill of the flight deck, and his right hand throbbing with pain, Jian pressed the icon to power up the whisker laser once more and held his breath.

[CONNECTION ESTABLISHED.]

CHAPTER THIRTY

Benson's quadcopter passed low over a warzone.

"Ho. Lee. Shit," Korolev whispered.

"Cuut be merciful," Kexx said solemnly.

"I'll need one of those rifles," Sakiko added with all sincerity.

The scene below them was appropriately apocalyptic. The Native Quarter was quiet, eerily hollow. But it only took a glance to understand why. The Atlantians had emptied their ghetto and moved on the rest of the city in force. A wave of native youths crashed against Shambhala's defenders and scattered them like leaves in a strong autumn wind. The Glades were already lost. Benson spotted his home of the last eighteen years as they flew by. It had not been spared.

The muscles in Benson's jaw clenched involuntarily. "I just trimmed those topiaries," he said, trying to force some levity onto the grim situation, but it didn't take. Smoke columns billowed up into the sky from a dozen or more structural fires, which was no mean trick. Humanity had spent the last two centuries and change living onboard a starship. Fire consumed irreplaceable resources, burned through precious oxygen, poisoned the air, and clogged the environmental filters. In space, it was the greatest threat they faced outside of catastrophic meteor collisions. Out of necessity, they'd gotten very good at fire-resistant materials and fire-suppression systems. You *really* needed to want a building to burn to get it to stay lit.

Public transit was already offline after someone had torn up a length of track, electrocuting themselves in the process. Benson had ordered Korolev to divert the quadcopter from the airfield and land it right on the roof of the station house.

They'd had to dodge a thunderstorm on the way back from the mine that ate up almost fifteen minutes of flight time. Their drone's batteries were being drawn down to the dregs. A shutdown warning sounded through the cabin, alerting everyone that the quadcopter would perform a forced landing in fifteen seconds.

"We're not going to make the station," Korolev said.

"Override the shutdown," Benson said.

"Are you serious?"

"They build spare capacity into everything. We'll make it."

"And if we're short?"

"We'll autorotate down."

Korolev blew out a long breath and worked the controls. The alarm chime and countdown disappeared. "No offense, coach, but I'm going to take her a little lower. Just in case."

"Oh, no, please do. I insist."

Korolev set the copter's altitude to ten meters, which was still a hell of a long way to fall if it came to that. The two- and three-story rooftops of Shambhala's residential district swept by underneath them at disturbingly close proximity. The nest of com antennas perched on the station house's roof came into view. Another two hundred meters. They were going to make it.

Right up until the propellers stopped spinning.

The quadcopter died around them, first the even whine of the electric flight motors, then the augmented reality overlay and heads up display in the canopy. Benson's stomach lurched as the quad abruptly lost airspeed and altitude.

"Brace! Brace! Brace!" Korolev shouted frantically just as the bottom of their fuselage clipped the first rooftop and compressed the spines of everyone aboard into their fight chairs. Everyone except maybe Kexx, who didn't technically have a spine, but–

The forward arms of the quadcopter crashed headlong into the second story of a café. The motors snapped off at the roots among the clinking of a thousand shards of shattered window glass. The copter held there for a long moment, until gravity won out and dragged the back of it towards Gaia's embrace as it slid down the building's faux-brick exterior, ripping off chunks of veneer as it fell.

The rear motors hit the sidewalk first, shattering the propellers and fraying the carbon composite of the structural members that held them. What remained of the quad fell backwards and came to rest upside down next to a gelato cart abandoned by its owner.

Korolev hung from his seat's five-point harness. "Spare capacity, huh, coach?"

"Shut up, Pavel." Benson craned his head back to the rest of the passenger compartment. "Everyone OK back there?"

"I am intact," Kexx said.

"Still need that rifle," Sakiko answered.

"When you're older," Benson said, then braced his good hand against the top, now bottom, of the canopy and hit the release on his crash web. The anchors of the five-point harness came loose with a metallic click and sent Benson falling towards the roof, floor. He tried to open the starboard side door, but it wouldn't give, not even with a shoulder check of encouragement. The portside door was more accommodating.

"I'm never flying again," Benson said.

<Bryan!> Theresa's voice burst through his plant link without a connection request. <Bryan, we saw your quad go down. Did you just crash?>

<A bit.>

<A bit!? How do you crash *a bit*? You either crash or don't crash.>

<We had a bit of a crash, yes, but we're all fine. How are you?>

<Me? Oh, I'm great. Surrounded by rioting aliens and getting sick of my lunatic husband trying to find new and innovative ways to kill himself. But other than that…>

<We're about a hundred meters from the station house. We're going to go get in our crowd control kits and head your way.>

<On the double, Bryan. Half these kids are high on bak'ri and feeling no pain. We're already losing ground. Falling back to the Museum. Rendezvous on the boulevard in ten.>

<10-4.> Benson stuck his head back inside the downed quadrotor's cabin. "C'mon kids, time to get out of bed. Mommy's pissed."

Bumped and bruised, but none the worse for wear, they recovered what little equipment they'd brought along from the quad's storage compartment and pushed hard for the station house where Benson and Korolev could get into the rest of their riot gear. There might even be spares lying around for Sakiko. Kexx, well, ze was already pretty damned hard to kill. Ze'd manage.

The normally bustling street that divided the Glades from the Museum District was bare, and eerily silent. The sounds of chanted slogans, crackling of fires, and smashing of windows filtered through the alleys from several blocks away. Remote enough not to present an immediate threat, but ominous all the same. Benson led his mismatched little quartet down the center of the avenue. They were exposed, walking in plain sight, but the wide lanes gave them plenty of visibility and time to respond to any surprises that might pop out from around a corner.

Assuming the rioters hadn't gotten their hands on any rifles.

Benson crossed mental fingers and pressed on. Fortunately, they arrived at the doors of the station house without any amateur snipers throwing potshots downrange at them. The equipment lockers inside had been thoroughly picked through, but Korolev's personal gear was still there, and he managed to scrounge up some older, mismatched pieces for Benson and Sakiko.

They emerged a handful of minutes later donning well-worn and somewhat ill-fitting helmets, chest protectors, shoulder pads, forearm guards, groin and thigh coverings, knee pads, and shin guards. It wasn't ballistic rated, but it would do the job against blunt objects like clubs, thrown rocks, and most edged weapons. There were gaps in the armor all over the place, especially the joints, but it would have to do.

Benson had grabbed a hard plastic tonfa, as well as a clear acrylic shield that already carried the scratches of several past engagements. Sakiko still wanted a rifle, but Korolev put the kibosh on that idea real quick. And since he was the only one with the access codes to the weapons locker, it was his call.

"It's itchy," Sakiko complained as they marched towards the Museum.

"Yeah, well we usually wear shirts and pants under the armor, kiddo," Benson said. "It's going to be ugly when we get there. Stay close to Kexx and me." Benson expected a fight, or a biting retort, but the gravity of the situation had apparently worked its way into even the teenager's brain. She'd been somewhat more somber since they'd discovered Foreman Lind's body. Sometimes growing up took years. Sometimes, it happened in an afternoon.

<Esa,> Benson linked up with his wife's plant. <We're two minutes out. What's it look like over there?>

<Like the little Dutch boy who put his finger in a dike to hold back the ocean. Get here quick.>

Benson started to jog despite the extra weight of the

gear. He'd never given into the temptation to let his workout routine slide, even as the battle grew increasingly difficult as the years piled on. Now, he was really glad he'd been so hard on himself. The rest of the quartet followed suit. The sounds of unrest grew in intensity as the Museum itself came into sight until they drowned out all other noise.

"They're really worked up," Korolev said. "I can barely hear myself think!"

"Lucky you don't do much of it, then," Benson shouted back. "Switch to the squad link. Kexx, Sakiko, just stay close and keep an eye out for hand signals. You might not be able to hear anything over this racket. And stay sharp. Theresa says half these kids are high as kites."

"Lovely," Kexx said.

The Museum campus sat at the very end of the long central avenue that bisected the district. Theresa's forces had set up a perimeter spanning from one side of the avenue to the other with a string of safety barriers and constables wearing the same sort of riot gear Benson and Korolev were wearing, plastic shields, and a variety of less-than-lethal weapons ranging from batons, to tonfas, to stun sticks. A couple of the constables even held the shock shields they used in the jail for extracting noncompliant inmates from their cells. Benson spotted a dozen PDW rifles identical to the one Korolev carried, but they were shoulder slung and being kept out of the confrontation. For now.

But the safety barriers were flimsy affairs, meant more as visual warnings around construction sites than proper barricades. The line of constables worked to hold their ground, but a constant barrage of rocks and debris rained down on them, thrown from deeper in the crowd with the unnerving accuracy Atlantians possessed. The defenders had to split their attention between incoming missiles overhead, and the pulsing mass of bodies on just the other side of their inadequate blockade.

In the crowd's wake, desolation ruled. Every window and door along the boulevard was smashed or splintered. Awnings had been ripped off their frames. Recycling cans were either tipped over with their contents strewn about the street, thrown through storefront windows, or set ablaze. Benches were torn free of their foundations, and several of them had been passed overhead to the very front of the crowd where they were being used as makeshift shields, battering rams, or counter barriers. Street lamps had been pulled down or had their LED bulbs smashed. All of the bushes, trees, and landscaping had been uprooted, slashed, and torn up by thousands of grasping toes. It would take months to repair the damage, and set their manufacturing queue back just as long.

The throngs of rioters flowed and convulsed like a violent sea. Most of them had taken off their shirts and let their skinglow run wild with waves of harsh patterns and light. But these Atlantians had mostly grown up in Shambhala. They lacked the fine control over their skin of their kin across the ocean. Whereas a large gathering of warriors, or a village assembled in ritual prayer looked like a single, coherent, interconnected organism. But this mob, they looked like static loudly blaring from a broken video display.

But as they approached the line, the rioters' chants became clear enough. The translation matrix in his plant lagged trying to sort out the different voices from the din, but Benson didn't need it. "Defilers of Varr," they shouted, over and over, as if in a trance. The rhythm of it all was almost… hypnotic.

Benson found the hedonistic crowd's newfound piety more than a little convenient, but then riots were seldom about their cause célèbre, not really. It was a spark, an ignition source for a preexisting, highly-combustible mix of social grievances, economic stagnation, and emotional despair. Couple those fuel sources with thousands of listless, frustrated, drugged-up youths, and you had the perfect fire triangle of social upheaval.

The ingredients had been present for years, but the humans of Shambhala had let them fester in the dark, so obsessed they were with keeping their eyes fixed on a brighter future they refused to look down and see the suffering around them. Now, they were paying the price for that neglectful hubris. All Benson and his allies could do was work to contain the damage.

A bench came crashing down on one of the barriers, splintering it into a hundred white and orange plastic shards. Emboldened by the breach in the line, the mob surged forward and pressed against the defenders. The center of the line bulged and threatened to break entirely.

<We're here, Esa,> Benson sent. <Where do you need us?>

<Reinforce the middle! Quick!>

<Roger.> Benson grabbed Korolev by the shoulder and opened the squad link. <Patch up the middle. Don't point that cannon at anyone unless they start throwing spears or something really serious.>

<Understood.>

Benson turned to Kexx and Sakiko. "We're going up the center. Stay on my ass and back me up!" he shouted over the surging crowd.

The four of them joined the rest of the thin blue line separating civilization from chaos. Theresa had called in her reserves, which included many of the Mustang's bench of players, including several brave Atlantians standing up to defend the city from their own kin. Benson finally spotted the outline of his wife, standing right in the thick of the action because of course she was. He pushed towards her position at the breech in the middle of the line.

<Hello, dear. Sorry I'm–> Benson's sentence stopped dead when Theresa turned around to look at him. Half of the clear plastic face guard attached to her helmet had cracked and fallen away. An angry purple bruise and a

stream of blood dripped from her left cheekbone.

<You're hurt,> he said flatly.

<I'm fine.>

<Who did it?> he said as vengeance rose in his throat, but Theresa slapped him down.

<Bryan, I need you here, doing your job as a reserve deputy. *Not* settling scores. Clear?>

<Yes ma'am,> he said sheepishly, and advanced to fill in a gap in their coverage. Even in his fifties, Benson was not a small man. He presented a large, tempting target, especially for adolescents with a chip on their shoulders. A lot of people would like a chance to earn the title of the one who beat the Zero hero.

A fist-sized chunk of masonry came flying in at an oblique angle, but Benson got his shield up in time and it skipped harmlessly off the acrylic, leaving another new scratch to mark its course.

"Gunna have to do better than that!" Benson shouted in challenge to the mob.

It answered with a bigger rock that left a crack in his shield.

<Maybe don't antagonize them, honey. They're plenty angry already,> Theresa said.

<I see that now.> Benson changed tactics. "Hey Sco'Val! Has the Bearer figured out you planted that bomb in the Temple yet?"

"You lie!" Sco'Val shouted, loud enough to be heard over the din.

"I saw how you looked at it, Sco'Val. You also knew where the drug house was. And now you're inciting a riot along with all these kids you gave the bak'ri to. You're under arrest as soon as I get my hands around your skinny little neck."

"Do your worst, defiler!" Sco'Val physically shoved several hesitant rioters towards the line. They pressed in with renewed vigor, bowed the barricades inward and put the defenders behind them on their back feet.

<Bryan, why do you *never listen*?> Theresa demanded.

<I was trying to get the crowd to turn on zer!>

<How's that working out?>

<Not brilliantly.>

Driven by bak'ri courage, a squirrely little Atlantian managed to squirt between the legs of two of the defenders on the line, causing one of them to turn their back on the rest of the crowd to try and tackle zer. It was a rookie mistake, a reflex Benson had to train out of his linemen as they learned to trust their linebackers and secondary to pick up anyone who gets by.

The crowd sensed the break in the line and pressed, shoving the turned man to his knees while five, then ten, then twenty rioters flowed over him like hydraulic fluid spraying from a hole in a hose. Nearby constables and deputies moved to contain the spill, but that left the line thin in other places, emboldening the crowd up and down the barriers to press their newfound advantage. Rioters broke through in two more places, and suddenly Theresa's constables were being flanked.

Benson knew a breakdown in protection when he saw one. They were being blitzed, and there just weren't enough linemen to hold back the flood.

<Forget it,> he said to Theresa. <We're boned.>

<We have to protect the Museum!>

<Fall back to the steps. Block the entrances. It's less ground to defend. Leave the barriers here, they're useless.>

Begrudgingly, Theresa agreed. She didn't like giving ground in a fight. It ran counter to her nature. But she sent out the order to withdraw and regroup anyway, because she liked losing even less.

They retreated… *tactically repositioned* themselves halfway up the steps to the Museum's main entrance. The higher ground meant the rioters had to climb up to meet them, and gave Theresa a much better field of view over the situation from which to direct her constables.

Distinct advantages in a battle when your opponents didn't possess firearms.

But as good as their position was, the mob's advantage in sheer numbers rendered any small tactical advantage moot. Their backs were against the wall now, literally. By abandoning the avenue, they'd also allowed the riots to engulf them on three sides. The crush of Atlantian youths, chanting and hurling debris, closed in on the few dozen defenders like a rising tide. A defender went down. Linqvist, an absolute brute of a man who had played for the Mustangs as both a Zero goalie and later a football center. He'd been hit in the head, hard, but his plant data remained intact. He was conscious, but concussed, out of the fight. Kexx and Sakiko ran over to where he had slumped, dragged him up the steps to the rear by the handle on the back of his riot gear. Kexx ordered Sakiko to remain with him, then returned to zer position on the line.

<That does it,> Theresa barked into the com link. <Break out your sidearms and stun rounds. I want that front line pushed back, now!>

<We cross that line, there's no going back, chief,> Korolev said apprehensively.

<If we don't cross it, we'll have to go to live rounds soon!>

As if her plea had been heard, a thundering voice from on high blanketed the plaza like a sonic boom.

"Play. Time's. Over. Kids."

Everyone froze in place, collectively caught with their hands in the cookie jar, afraid to turn around to face their parent's wrath.

<What the hell was that?> Benson said into the link.

<It came from the Museum's public address system,> Korolev shot back.

Behind their deteriorating defensive line, the double doors of the Museum's main entrance cracked loudly, then swung inward on creaking, ominous hinges. Behind them, clad in resplendent crimson samurai armor, a black-lacquered katana scabbard tied around her waist, stood Devorah. A tiny, furious vision in red.

Everyone, from the knot of constables, to the very back row of rioters, looked up to see what the diminutive woman would do next. Once she felt she held the crowd's attention, Devorah stepped out and strode slowly, but purposefully down the stairs, her knees creaking nearly as much as the doors she'd just exited.

"You lot want to fight? Fine, knock yourselves out," her voice boomed. She'd tied her plant into the Museum's outdoor speakers and cranked the dial to eleven. "Rip down lights, tear up trees. Break windows. Have fun. But this!" She lifted an arm, shaking in equal measure from fresh rage and the weight of years, and pointed back at the entrance to the Museum. "This is the history of MY people. It is the collected work of a thousand generations of MY elders. And it's the history of YOUR people, too. We have artifacts from Atlantis in there that go back to before the Shrinking. And it's the history of what our Trident has already built together, here and across the sea."

Devorah pushed her way through the line of constables, down to the foot of the steps of the Museum, her true home. Incredibly, the mob moved back, hollowing out a hemisphere of space around her.

"So have your little temper-tantrum out here, but before any one of you steps a wiggly toe inside my house..." She put a hand on the katana's leather wrapped handle, and the sound of ringing metal echoed through the scene. "...you'll have to fight me, personally."

Devorah held the glimmering katana high in the air in a ready position as the last amber light of the day glinted off its centuries-old polished steel. "C'mon. I'm basically mummified already. Even the weakest among you could finish me off easily. Who wants to have a go?"

Devorah pointed the tip of her naked blade at one of the tallest Atlantians at the front of the column, who looked suspiciously like the one Theresa had to tase to keep zer from turning Benson into reddish pudding. "You, Hul'gik. I remember you from our summer program six years ago. You always had some smart comment for me. How about it?" Hul'gik was a full meter taller than Devorah, but under her sudden withering glare, ze seemed to shrink down to half zer size. "No? How about you, Jimale?" She pointed at another face she recognized a few rows back. "You were one of my fall interns two years ago. Did I cheat you out of lunch breaks or something?"

"Elder, I, um..." Jimale answered weakly.

"Nobody? You mean I got all dressed up for nothing? I had to have this armor fitted. Look, I've got another archeological expedition with G'tel to organize. So if you're not going to have a proper riot, stop embarrassing yourselves and go the hell home!"

Cowed and humiliated, the crowd mulled about and shuffled their feet, but it was obvious Devorah's chastisement had broken the spell of their bloodlust. Benson shook his head in disbelief.

As the back layers of the crowd began to peel away like an onion, Devorah turned around and walked back up the stairs, but paused on the third step. "And you're all coming back here in the morning to help clean up the mess you left on my lawn!"

No one objected. No one said much of anything. Devorah turned around and started back up the steps again.

Benson jogged over and knelt down to hug the old woman. "Devorah, that was amazing. You really pulled us out of the fire with that bluff."

"What? Them? They're good kids, they just need a firm hand sometimes. Here, hold this." Devorah handed the katana over to Benson. "It's getting heavy and I need a damn nap." The gathered officers watched as she returned to the Museum and the doors creaked shut behind her.

Benson just chuckled. "Crazy old bat. I'd hate to play her in poker." He ran a thumb over the edge of the curved blade, and immediately regretted it.

"Ow!" Benson yelped as blood surged out from the slice on his thumb pad.

"What?" Theresa said.

"I cut myself on this damned sword."

"Why the hell did you touch the edge?"

"I thought it was a prop!"

"That's the Honjo Masamune katana. You really think Devorah would tolerate a prop in her collection?"

A chill gripped Benson's heart as he regarded the still impossibly sharp weapon. "She wasn't bluffing."

"No." Theresa said.

"She was really ready to fight them all by herself."

"Yeah, if it came to that."

"... She's nuts."

"Duh, we all knew that, Bryan."

Benson pinched his thumb against his forefinger to stop the bleeding and held the katana away from himself at a more respectful distance. "Then why'd she give it to me?"

"Probably because she knew you'd hurt yourself," Korolev added.

Benson was about to respond when a plant connection request popped up in his field of vision. A 'weak signal' alert hovered next to the tag for–

"Jian Feng?" Benson said aloud.

"What was that, dear?" Theresa asked.

"I'm getting a call request from Jian Feng."

"That little idiot? His stunt is what caused all this!"

"Yes, I remember," Benson said.

"What could he possibly want?"

Benson shrugged. "One way to find out." He accepted the call. The image was grainy, about as compressed and low-def as he'd ever seen. The feed dragged and halted frequently, and was occasionally overwhelmed with static.

<Hello?> Benson said after several seconds.

<Mr Benson!> Jian said three and a half seconds later, and Benson understood why the feed was so weak. The time delay imposed by lightspeed put Jian at more than four hundred thousand kilometers away.

<Yes, Jian. It's me. What can I do for you?>

Three and a half seconds later. <Actually, I've discovered information critical to your investigation.>

<Ah, that's pretty incredible. In the original sense of the word. Last I heard, you were on your way to Varr in a stolen shuttle.>

<Yes, that's true.>

<And you discovered something about my case here on Gaia on your way out there?>

<Yes, I did. You really need to listen to–>

Another feed broke in from Captain Chao Feng. He hadn't bothered with a connection request.

<What the hell is going on here?> Chao demanded.

Jian's face blanched. <Dad? How did you find this link?>

<We have administrative access to the entire network, you arrogant little shit. How do you think?>

<Guys,> Benson said.

<What are you two conspiring about here?> Chao demanded.

<We're not *conspiring*, I'm trying to tell Mr. Benson something important that I just discovered down here that he needs to>

<Oh no, you've *tried* more than enough. Shambhala's burning right now because of your little broadcast, Jian. Millions of dollars of damage, tens of thousands of man hours! Not to mention you *blew up a nuke!*>

<Guys. Can we maybe do this some other time? I'm right in the middle of cleaning up after a riot at the moment and could–>

<Because of what *you* were trying to do in secret, dad. That's on your head,> Jian bit back. <I don't have time for

this. I'm running this whisker laser at about eight times its design output and burning up an hour of standby fuel cell power every minute, so if you'll excuse us...>

<For fuck's sake. Will one of you please listen to what I'm saying?> Benson said.

<So that's how you got onto the local network,> Chao ignored him. <Very clever, but I'm cutting you off now. You're in more than enough trouble as it is.>

<Guys!> Benson snapped. Both Chao and Jian paused, as if they'd forgotten he was there. <Good, now, I'm sure you two have a lot to work out in your father/son relationship at the moment, but I assure you, there are better and more appropriate places for that counseling session than *inside my goddamn head*. So, if there's nothing else–>

<It's about Benexx!> Jian interrupted.

<What? What did you say?>

<The people who took Benexx, I know where their base is.>

<How can you possibly know thaaoooh my God what the fuck is on your shoulder?!>

Some... thing crawled up Jian's arm and glared back at the camera with a triangle of green glowing eyes. It looked like something pulled up in a dredge net from the coldest depth of the blackest ocean.

<Him? That's Polly, he's mostly harmless.>

<Mostly?>

<Hardly, we tore up half the ship looking for that little *móguǐ*. But we're losing the thread,> Chao Feng said. <My son believes he's found a research or surveillance station of some kind. But until we know who built it, their motivations, and what their intentions for us and the rest of the Trident are, we cannot trust any information that comes from it, much less entertain the idea of using it as actionable intelligence.>

Jian rolled his eyes clear back to the base of his skull. <Fuck that. This place has taken no action against me

or anyone else who's set foot inside it. It's even made me a nice little work station with heat, light, oxygen and everything. And Polly's been nothing but helpful. We can trust this intel.>

<That's it, I'm locking this channel.>

<No, Chao, wait!> Benson pleaded. <It's my kid, Chao. Not the codes to the ship's computer, my kid. Nothing is on the line except zer and whoever comes along with me to get zer back.>

Chao's face contorted, his expressions of consternation and sympathy exaggerated by the microgravity.

<Chao, please. It's my kid. Please.>

Chao sighed and rubbed at the furrows in his forehead. <It's never fuckin' easy with you, is it, Bryan? Fine, but from here on out, we're so far off the record you couldn't even see it with that big honking Early Warning telescope on the other side of Varr. Understood?>

<Yes,> Benson said.

<Yes, sir,> Jian said, the "sir" tacked on as a sign of both respect and contrition.

<One of the two of you is going to be the death of me,> Chao said.

<Who's the odds-on favorite?> Benson asked.

<It's even money. Commander Feng, please tell Mr Benson what you think you've learned.>

Jian squared himself up in his seat. <There's an uncharted network of caves a few klicks northwest of one of our mining operations on the continent. Less than an hour ago, there was a seismic event that almost exactly matched the profile of the explosion at the First Contact Day parade. I believe something went wrong and one of their bombs went off prematurely, probably during construction.>

It wasn't much, Benson had to admit, but it was something, and it was something he could move on immediately.

<Send me the coordinates,> Benson said coolly, trying

to keep the sharp edge of vengeance out of his voice.

<I have an approximation. The software up here doesn't use our lat/long grid system, but it should be accurate enough to put you within a couple hundred meters, so long as my scale conversions were right.>

<It'll do.>

Jian uploaded his best guess numbers and whatever other intel he'd gathered about the area. The moment Benson finished saving the file, Jian's screen went dark, replaced by a "Loss of Signal" alert.

<Jian? Jian! What happened?>

<Looks like his whisker laser burned out,> Chao said. <At those power levels, it's damned lucky it lasted as long as it did. He was exceeding its design range by an order of magnitude.>

<Damned lucky for us. Not so lucky for whoever I find in this cave.>

<Don't go off all half-cocked and get yourself killed.>

<Chao, I'm touched. Was that genuine concern I just heard?>

<Life would be boring without you, and I don't want to deal with your grieving widow.>

<Thank you, Chao. Genuinely. And thank your boy for me when you see him at the court-martial. I owe you, big time.>

<Oh, neither of us will live long enough for you to pay me back on this one. Go get Benexx. Bring zer home safe. Ark Actual, out.>

Chao dropped the call, leaving Benson alone in his own head once more. A heartbeat later, he snapped out of it and returned to the world around him and the interrogative glare of his wife.

"Well?" Theresa demanded.

"Chao's boy has a lead on the terrorist's camp. We're going there."

"Now?"

"Now," Benson said, then turned back to scan through

the sea of former rioters as they tried to get out of each other's way and return to their homes in the Native Quarter. "Hey!" Benson shouted at the familiar-looking brute. "Hey, you, Hul'gik isn't it?"

"What do you want, ruleman?"

"You still feel like picking a fight?"

Theresa grabbed his arm. "Bryan, what the hell do you think you're doing?"

"Networking."

The enormous Atlantian rumbled to a stop at Benson's feet, zer toes almost touching his. Benson had to crane his head up almost as far back as it would go just to stop seeing chest.

"Yes, I still want to fight," ze grumbled.

"Excellent. Follow me. We're going on a field trip."

CHAPTER THIRTY-ONE

For the second time in as many weeks, Benexx had been caught in an explosion. Granted, ze'd detonated the second one, but it still had to be well outside the typical rate of incident for an average person.

Even more improbable, ze was still alive to consider the absurdity of the situation.

Benexx's ears rang like church bells, zer chest felt like Dorothy had parked her house on top of zer, and zer head felt like it had been split open with a stone ax. Ze hacked a long, wet, violent cough and came up with a mix of phlegm and blood. Just the act of breathing was painful. So, ze had internal damage to zer air sacks from the overpressure. Wonderful.

But, ze was alive, and that counted for something. The detonator was still clutched in zer hand, but it was dead. Either its batteries had drained, or it had been even more sensitive to the blast wave than ze had been. Regardless, Benexx was back to not knowing what time it was or how long ze'd been unconscious. Ze tossed the detonator aside contemptuously and brought zer skinglow up a little to get a better sense of just how fubared zer situation was. Turns out, it could have been worse.

The chamber around zer had been redecorated with grizzly bits of shredded flesh and frayed cartilage. To zer left, an Atlantian's arm, severed midway down from the elbow, twitched, its fingers still moving, mindlessly following the echo of the last instructions they received.

Nor was it the only trophy of zer work. The bomb had perhaps been a little more energetic than ze'd anticipated. So energetic, it triggered a massive cave-in. The craggy rocks piled up from the floor all the way to the ceiling, cutting the dead-end of the tunnel off from the rest of the cave system.

The stones ranged in size from pebbles to multi-ton boulders. Several bodies, or pieces of bodies, protruded from the spaces between the rocks, mashed into a morbid sort of mortar. Benexx's stomach turned at the sight and ze had to look away.

Ze was bleeding internally, cut off from escape, using up whatever air remained in the chamber with each breath, and ze'd just blown up everyone who had any idea where ze was. So, zer return was in sight. Benexx's spirits imploded. It now came down to a simple question of whether zer airsacks would fill with blood before the air inside them ran out of oxygen.

Something stirred in the rocks and snapped up zer attention. With a mix of amazement and horror, Benexx watched as an arm dug its way out of the rubble. A dirty, blood-streaked face lifted to look at zer. Sula's face, Benexx realized in shock. It was like something out of an old horror movie, the enemy ze thought dead crawling zer way back out of the grave for one last, defining attack.

Benexx kicked with zer good leg backwards until zer back was pressed against the wall, but it quickly became obvious Sula didn't have revenge in mind.

"Help," a noticeably diminished voice pleaded weakly. "Please."

Benexx sat, unmoved.

"Please." Sula stretched zer free hand towards Benexx in desperation. "I can't breathe."

"No?" Another round of wet coughs racked zer chest. "I'm not doing so well on that account either."

"Ple..." Sula tried to shout, but ran out of air before ze even finished the word.

Benexx growled low to zerself, then used zer hands to get upright. The gunshot wound through zer leg kept zer from putting any weight on it, so ze hopped to the pile of rubble and cleared the smaller rocks away from Sula's body. But a large one pressed down on zer right side, pinning Sula to the floor and preventing zer from drawing any but the shallowest of breaths. Benexx grabbed it with both hands and strained to roll it out of the way until the muscles of zer back felt like they were about to snap.

"I can't move it by myself," ze said between ragged breaths. "You have to push."

Weakly, Sula's free arm reached up and added what strength it had to offer. Between them, the rock shifted. Only a fraction, but it moved.

"Harder," Benexx commanded through clenched teeth plates. "Rock it back and forth."

Their momentum built with each cycle, until the stone finally reached its tipping point and rolled away. Sula opened zer mouth and pulled in a gasping breath.

"Why?" ze asked once zer inhalations slowed to a more normal pace.

"Why what?"

"Why do you help me now, when you tried to kill me?"

Benexx worried at one of the wounds on zer face. "Just squeamish, I guess. Blowing you up while you were pointing guns at me was one thing. Watching you die slow and helpless, maybe I'm not that cold just yet."

"It's not in your nature."

Benexx snorted, then spat out bloody phlegm. "And how would you know what's in my nature?"

"Because, you're not a warrior. You're a bea–"

"If you finish saying 'bearer,' I swear to Cuut I'll use whatever strength I have left to bash your head in with a rock. Probably should anyway. You're burning up my air."

"I thought you just said you're not a killer."

"There's a lot of bits and chunks of your friends lying around here that say I am. It's just situational is all. So if I were you, I wouldn't cause another situation." Benexx resumed the work of clearing debris from Sula's body until ze reached just below the trapped elder's waist. Ze gasped at the sight.

"What is it?" Sula asked.

"It's..." Benexx cleared zer throat. "Your legs are crushed under a big-ass rock. Badly. I can't possibly move it. It'll probably be easier to cut them off and grow a new pair."

Sula actually laughed at the suggestion. "I doubt either of us have that kind of time left."

"I suppose not."

"Although that does explain why I can't feel them."

"Sorry."

"No, you're not."

"No, I'm not." Benexx sat back down and stretched out zer injured leg. They sat in silence for a long span. It was so deathly quiet in the chamber. Between breaths, Benexx could hear the blood moving through zer body. It was... unnerving. Ze decided to break the eerie quiet.

"Why?"

"Why what?" Sula responded, matching Benexx's own tone and cadence from minutes ago in a mocking sort of way.

"This. All of this. Why the attack on the parade? Why kidnap me? Why set up a bomb factory down here in, wherever the hell here is? What were you trying to accomplish?"

"To prevent you."

"Prevent me?" Benexx repeated. "Well you'd have to go back in time for that, and I don't think even the humans have the first idea how to actually pull that off."

"Prevent more like you, then."

"Why? What's wrong with me?"

Sula sighed. "You have to ask? Look around you. Bearers–"

Benexx grabbed a rock. "Careful."

"Go on, prove my point. Bearers bring life, not take it. It is not the way of things. But you have been poisoned by the humans. Their disrespect for our ways have perverted you into an abomination."

Benexx gripped the rock even harder. "If my parents had respected 'our ways,' an elder would have sliced my head off fifteen years ago while I was a naked, defenseless infant, because I was too small, or too fat, or too quiet, or too noisy."

"That would have been wise."

"Excuse me if I disagree. The humans I know have shown me nothing but love and compassion. You say I'm unnatural? Good. Maybe bearers everywhere should fight back against the old ways that have imprisoned them. Maybe you think it's not in our nature because you've never allowed us to be anything else but living fish tanks. Did you ever ask any of the bearers who carried your broods what they wanted out of life? Did the question even occur to you?"

"Such questions are dangerous."

"For *who*?" Benexx barked. "In Shambhala, we get to ask our own questions, and come up with our own answers. And not just bearers, either. Youths who would have been condemned to either field work or soldiering have been able to decide how to live their own lives. They've become artists, musicians, athletes."

"And struck with poverty, overcrowded buildings, forced to adapt to human customs, adopting human vices, exploited, pinned under the toes of their new masters. The Bearer with No Name should never have brought them here. The Trident is a false idol, a broken promise. We should either return to our own shores, or drive the humans back up to their sky city entirely. We were not meant to live like this."

"But you have humans helping you, freely. I've seen them. They built your bombs."

"There are humans who share our goals for their own reasons. We work together now so we may come apart later."

Benexx just shook zer head. "Racists working together to destroy each other. Can't you hear how idiotic that sounds? We have bigger problems to face. Whoever destroyed Earth."

"Oh spare me the myths of your parents. Only Cuut Zerself could end a world, and if the humans really did escape Cuut's wrath, Ze would reward us for finishing the harvest."

"Would have, if your little insurrection hadn't been beaten by a lowly bearer. That must just burn you up inside, being beaten by someone who was never meant to be a warrior. How much of a failure does that make you?"

A vibration emanated from the rubble pile, low at first, but it built into a grinding sound, followed by… voices? Shouting? Someone on the other side was still alive.

Sula managed a weak smile. "Perhaps not such a failure after all, young bearer. Some of my allies survived and will be here soon. You did very well to get this far, but it's over now. I've changed my mind about you in one respect, however."

"Oh yeah?" Benexx sneered. "How's that?"

"You are definitely not worth the trouble. Your body will just have to suit our purposes."

Benexx raged. After everything, ze was almost at peace with dying in here along with the last of the monsters who'd taken zer from zer family, zer city, and zer life. But this? Taken alive once more, wounded, without a weapon, all of the last few days of fighting for naught?

No, not like that.

"Maybe it will, but you won't be alive to see it." Benexx lifted the rock high over zer head. Just as ze was about to bring it crashing down on Sula's impassive face, a ray of light broke through the wall of rubble and fell right in zer eyes.

"Benexx?" a bright, familiar voice yelled through the new hole in the pile. Sakiko's voice.

Benexx's arms went weak at the sound of zer best friend's unexpected arrival. Ze almost dropped the rock on zer own head, but instead, it fell harmlessly... onto Sula's face.

"Acha!" Sula shouted.

OK, not harmlessly, but Benexx didn't care as she climbed numbly up the rocks.

"Kiko?" ze asked unsteadily.

"It's Benexx!" Sakiko shouted. "Ze's alive. Looks like total shit, but ze's alive!"

"Thanks..."

"Scoot over," a new, yet very old voice said. With the light shining in zer eyes ruining zer night vision, ze couldn't make out anything but outlines, but the voice, and then the smell, were unmistakable.

"Daddy?" Benexx's voice quivered.

"Yes, little Squish, it's me. Mom's here, too. We're going to get you out of there."

A wave of relief crashed into Benexx and beat at zer emotions until they all hung limp like boned fish.

"I thought you were dead," ze said to zer father's voice.

"We thought the same about you, kiddo. But we're not." His hand reached through the hole and grasped at air until Benexx laced zer rubbery fingers with his knobby ones and squeezed. "It's all right, sweetheart. You're safe. It's all over."

With that, Benexx let zerself relax, truly relax for the first time in days. By the time they finished loading zer into the medical evac quadcopter, ze was fast asleep.

EPILOGUE

Five tense weeks passed while the city, indeed the world, knit its wounds. It was a messy process with a lot of moving parts, and it was a long way from over, but the cooler heads in both Shambhala and G'tel seemed to be winning out.

No, not the "cooler heads" in G'tel, Benson corrected himself. That phrase had an entirely different meaning among his Atlantian friends.

And family.

Doc Russell had discharged Benexx last week, feeling it would be better for zer to finish recuperating at home. Of course, "home" was a little sparse at the moment, their house having been looted during the riots. Temporary plastic tarps covered the windows to keep the weather out until replacement plexiglass could be poured and cut, but they were pretty far down the priority list and regular service up and down the beanstalk had only been restored a few days ago.

Benexx was healing quickly, as was typical of zer race. Absurdly difficult to kill, those folks. But the gunshot wound to zer leg went all the way through and pulped quite a bit of muscle tissue as it did. Ze still needed help getting around, and would for a while yet, but ze'd passed zer rite of Hulukam by any measure.

Besides, Benexx's injuries were trivial compared to the carnage ze'd single-handedly inflicted on zer kidnappers.

Elder Sula was one of the few survivors of Benexx's rampage, and it hadn't come cheaply. Ze was currently cuffed to a bed and under guard in a secured room at the hospital regrowing zer legs and half of zer internal organs. Ze'd sung like a canary in exchange for medical treatment. Of course, ze would've gotten medical treatment anyway, but somehow ze hadn't known that, and Theresa hadn't gone out of her way to correct the terrorist's misunderstanding of Shambhala law.

Sula's testimony had confirmed Benson's suspicions about Sco'Val. Ze'd been caught in a stolen canoe about twenty klicks west of Shambhala furiously paddling towards Atlantis, apparently unaware of exactly what "twenty-seven-hundred kilometers" actually meant. The rest of their coconspirators, Atlantian and human alike, were unmasked in short order and rounded up. The trials would come soon, but not until Benexx was well enough to attend as the prosecution's star witness.

In the aftermath, and with considerable prodding from Devorah, the Bearer with No Name emerged from zer self-imposed hermitage to become the public face of the Atlantian expat community in Shambhala once more, beginning the morning after the riots when ze appeared unannounced on the steps of the Museum to sweep up the mess zer children had left the day before.

There was an immense amount of work to do, but maybe that work had already started. Instead of shattering the Trident as they'd hoped, the bombings and the attack on the beanstalk had only sharpened its tips.

Theresa descended the stairs from the second-floor bedrooms. Fortunately, the ransacking of their furniture and possessions had been mostly limited to the ground floor. However, the looters had made off with the luxurious silk bedsheets that had miraculously materialized in their linen closet after the conclusion of the Laraby investigation eighteen years ago. Theresa had made noises about catching and shooting whoever had done it before they ever reached the station house.

Benson was sure she'd been joking. Well, ninety percent sure.

"How is ze?" he asked.

"Asleep," Theresa answered. "Or that's what ze wants us to think. Ze's probably going to get on a link with Jian again."

"Heh, little sneak."

"I wonder where ze got that from."

"I don't know what you mean. The only thing I sneak these days is a beer or two."

"Or three." Theresa reached down and patted her husband on his slowly expanding belly.

"Whatever, I can still kick ass. For a little while at least. Then I need a nap."

Strictly speaking, they weren't supposed to let Benexx talk to Jian, because Jian wasn't supposed to be talking to *anybody*. At least no one in Shambhala or onboard the Ark. The ballsy ass kid made one last smart play when Varr's orbit brought it back into shuttle range ten days ago. Then again, he'd had almost a month of sitting around with his thumb up his ass to come up with it. Instead of burning for the Ark where he awaited certain arrest and court martial for his exploits, he'd parked his damaged shuttle in low Gaia orbit and suited up in one of the shuttle's emergency, one-time use reentry suits.

Calling the coffin-sized ablative aerogel sled a "suit" was being generous. It had winglets just big enough to keep it aerodynamically stable and pointed head down, a parachute pack, minimal thruster capacity for orientation in vacuum, and that was about it. Jian's jump was the first and only time someone had actually used one of the batshit contraptions since the days of Earth, and even then, the only people brave or suicidal enough to jump out of a perfectly good spacecraft wearing one had been military spec-war operators doing orbital combat insertions, and later civilian thrill-seekers with more money than sense.

But instead of landing in Shambhala, Jian had timed his drop to put him in Atlantis, where he made his way to the gates of G'tel and requested political asylum. A status Chief Kuul was only too happy to grant. Partly as a way to poke back at Shambhala for taking in the Bearer with No Name years before, but mostly because Jian was already being venerated by the population as the human who risked everything to defend Varr from defilement. He was a hero to them, while being a wanted criminal on the other side of the ocean.

As was so often the case, both sides were spot on. Who knew which version of the truth would win out in the end? The details would be left to diplomats and historians.

"Should we stop zer?" Theresa asked as she flopped down on the borrowed couch next to Benson.

"Nah, let zer think ze's getting away with something. We have plausible deniability anyway."

"That's not what I meant, Bryan." Benson made a "go on" gesture with his hand. "I mean, Benexx already had a crush on Jian. Now after he saved zer from those zealots, it's approaching hero-worship levels."

"We saved zer," Benson corrected.

"Using intel he threw away his career to get. That's going to take even a base of flirty infatuation through the stratosphere."

"Wait, how do you know ze had a crush on him? They've been friends for years."

Theresa stared at him with a pained expression. "Oh, honey, you're so oblivious. How did you ever get laid before I came along?"

"I don't know. It always just fell into my lap."

The door chimed. The longtime lovers looked at each other with surprise.

"Are we expecting anyone?" Benson asked.

"At this hour?"

Benson got up, ignoring the twinge in his right knee. Usually, he'd just query the door's security camera to see who'd come calling, but the looters had rather thoroughly smashed it on their way into the house and it hadn't been replaced yet.

Theresa followed close behind, holding a sidearm discreetly behind her back. Benson had no idea where she kept the damned thing hidden, but it never seemed to be more than an arm's reach away.

They stacked up by the door, Benson's body providing cover for Theresa and her weapon. Probably overkill, but there had been sporadic fighting in the days after the riots, and times were still tense. It paid to be overly cautious.

Theresa tapped his shoulder, signaling she was in position and ready. Benson reached out and keyed the door, which swung inward to reveal…

"Chao!" Theresa said as she stepped out from behind her husband and hugged the Ark's longtime captain. "You're sweating like you've run a marathon."

"Hello, Tess," Chao Feng said coyly. "So good to see you. Gravity is a harsh mistress."

"Well don't just stand there. Come in, come in."

"Chao," Benson said, with considerably more surprise than his wife had shown. "What are you doing… ahem, I mean, what brings you to town?"

"I had to come down the beanstalk for some rah-rah powwow with Administrator Agrawal. Thank Gods that's over."

"OK, and now you're in our house…"

"Ignore him, Chao. Can I get you anything? Tea? A beer?"

"No, thank you. I just ate, maybe too much. We don't get a lot of native food upwell and I may have overindulged. I am exhausted, though. May I sit?"

"Been neglecting your full-gee conditioning, huh?" Benson said.

"I haven't had a great deal of free time lately."

"Yeah, I can appreciate that."

Chao groaned as he sank into the living room sofa as if a dux'ah was sitting on his chest. "Listen, I'll cut right to the quick. I haven't talked to my son since the riots."

"So call him?"

"I can't. You know I can't. I can only talk to him off the record. *Way* off."

"And?" Benson said, waiting for the other shoe to drop.

"And I know Benexx is upstairs talking to him right now."

"How the hell do you… Wait." Benson pointed a finger at him. "You're eavesdropping on our home network!"

"No," Chao objected. "OK, yes. Obviously. But it's off the books. All of Jian's accounts and network permissions have been blacked out and he's not supposed to be talking to anybody over here. But between him and your kid's tinkering, they get around it. Ze's a clever little shit. I've… turned a blind eye. I just want to talk to him. That's the only reason I'm here. Please, Bryan, it's my kid."

"Where have I heard that before?"

Theresa elbowed him in the side. "Of course you can talk to Jian." She held out a hand towards the stairs. "Right this way."

Benson started to follow them upstairs, but Theresa put a hand on his chest and pointed for the living room. "Nope, you're sitting this one out, big fella."

"But it's my house!"

"And you can have the whole bottom half of it to yourself for the next few minutes. Shoo."

Benson flushed, but after almost two decades of marriage, knew how to pick his battles. He turned around on a heel and proceeded to flop down on the couch lengthwise. The movie selection Theresa had made for the night was still stuck on the summary. Some insufferable-looking mid twenty-first century rom-com.

Benson wrinkled his nose at the selection and instead

lipped through his plant's entertainment menu until he ound something he wanted to watch. *The Hunt for Red)ctober*. Now that sounded more like it.

He toggled the playback icon, but no sooner had Sean Connery's beard come fully into frame, an emergency :all broke through and replaced the title screen with that oft, pallid face of a young floater lieutenant hovering ımong the buzz and chaos of the Ark's bridge.

"Mr Benson!" the lieutenant yelped.

"Got it in one, kid."

"I'm sorry?"

Benson rubbed a temple. "Yes, this is Mr Benson. What do you want? It's late and you just bust in on Tom Clancy."

"Who?"

"Jesus Christ… Why did you call me, miss?"

"Oh, yes. Of course. I apologize for interrupting, out we can't raise Captain Feng on his plant link, and Shambhala's security feeds put him at your door just before we lost his signal."

Benson grumbled as he got up from the couch again and shuffled over to the base of the stairs. "Chao! Call for you!"

"Are you serious?" Chao's irritated voice came back down from the door to Benexx's bedroom.

"Wish I wasn't. They said they can't reach your plant."

"Because I turned it off!"

"You can do that?"

"*I* can." A little furious tromping down the stairwell later and Chao struck parade ground rest on the floor of Benson's living room. The young, mortified lieutenant tried to match her commanding officer's rigid stance, which, given the fact she was floating in micrograv, ended up looking ridiculous.

"What is it, Lieutenant Pershing?" Chao finally said after returning her salute.

"I'm sorry to bother you, sir. But we've had a report

come in from the Early Warning network site on Varr."

Benson's ears perked up at that. The crown jewel of the Early Warning network had only gone operational two days ago. If they'd already spotted something, it could only mean... Benson's heart froze in his chest. Their mad, desperate escape from Earth hadn't gone unnoticed after all. Somewhere along the line over the last two and a half centuries, the Ark and her exodus had been spotted. Maybe in the first mad dash away from Earth riding on a trail of nuclear explosions, maybe when they'd slowed back down for insertion into Gaia's orbit, or maybe at any point in the last eighteen years whenever they'd let their radio emissions signature grow too bold for the sake of convenience and expediency.

Whatever the reason, humanity's adoptive home was on the chopping block. A quick glance over at Chao's face told Benson that he hadn't been the only one to reach the same conclusion.

"They've found us," Chao said, his voice even, expertly concealing the panic and terror Benson knew he must be feeling, the same emotions that were on the verge of overwhelming his own psyche.

"No, sir. That's just it. We're not under attack. It's not another Nibiru."

"Well then? What the hell is it?"

The lieutenant took a moment to compose herself, as though she couldn't believe what she was about to say herself. "It's a radio signal. A message sent in the clear, totally unencrypted."

"From who, lieutenant?!" Chao demanded, his voice and composure on the verge of cracking.

"Earth, sir. Home." Lieutenant Pershing swallowed hard. "It's a distress signal, sir. And it's only thirteen years old."

Benson looked around the room, first to Chao Feng, then to his wife, both of whom stood slack-jawed in existential shock.

He swallowed hard. "That's not supposed to be there."

ACKNOWLEDGMENTS

This book was started on January 1, 2016, and its final version turned in March 28, 2017. Over the course of those fifteen months, the world shifted. Dark and malicious forces grabbed hold of the most powerful country on Earth, and shook the European Union to its very foundations.

Self-evident truths I had grown up with – the US is a democracy, western civilization is pluralistic, fascism and nationalism are dying ideologies – have been overturned. In their place, a growing sense of chaos and a world on fire have supplanted what turned out to be only comforting platitudes. We find ourselves fighting the same demons that our great-grandparents faced down more than seventy years ago.

But oh, what a fight.

In the last fifteen months, I've seen people of every color, orientation, and walk of life organize and push back in the most incredible and inspiring ways. Always energetic, often outrageous, and occasionally violent, a new sleeper has awakened. Historic and unprecedented numbers of people, united across the world, have stood up to say in one voice, "We will not go backwards."

I want to acknowledge all of you. Everyone who has marched in protest, mailed letters, posted memes, wrote jokes, called their reps, drove to town halls, and even those who threw a punch, all to push back against hate and intolerance, xenophobia and misogyny. You are doing the heavy-lifting of building the future we sci-fi authors dare to dream about.

I doubt the work will be done by the time this modest little book goes on sale. But I know you will continue to carry the fight, and I'll be proud to stand alongside any and all of you in the trenches.

Good hunting.

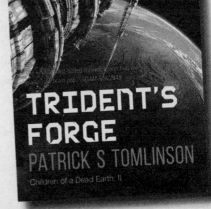

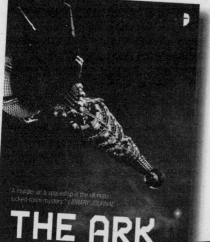